THE
GUEST
ROOM

Also by Chris Bohjalian

NOVELS

Close Your Eyes, Hold Hands

The Light in the Ruins

The Sandcastle Girls

The Night Strangers

Secrets of Eden

Skeletons at the Feast

The Double Bind

Before You Know Kindness

The Buffalo Soldier

Trans-Sister Radio

The Law of Similars

Midwives

Water Witches

Past the Bleachers

Hangman

A Killing in the Real World

ESSAY COLLECTIONS

Idyll Banter

THE
GUEST
ROOM

A NOVEL

CHRIS BOHJALIAN

Doubleday Canada

Doubleday Canada and colophon are registered trademarks of
Penguin Random House Canada Limited

Library and Archives Canada Cataloguing in Publication

Bohjalian, Chris, 1960-, author
The guest room / Chris Bohjalian.

Issued in print and electronic formats.
ISBN 978-0-385-68195-7 (bound).--ISBN 978-0-385-68196-4 (epub)

I. Title.

PS3552.O345G83 2016   813'.54   C2015-901986-9
                                              C2015-901987-7

Book design by Maria Carella
Title page photograph by Helmuth Boeger/Moment Open/
Getty Images
Cover image: © EricVega/Getty Images

Printed and bound in the USA

Published in Canada by Doubleday Canada,
a division of Penguin Random House Canada Limited

www.penguinrandomhouse.ca

10 9 8 7 6 5 4 3 2 1

Penguin
Random House
DOUBLEDAY CANADA

For Victoria.

For Grace.

For the girl in the lobby who was paying the bellman at three a.m.

I don't think I'd love you so deeply if you
had nothing to complain of and nothing to regret.

BORIS PASTERNAK, *Doctor Zhivago*

THE
GUEST
ROOM

Part One

Chapter One

Richard Chapman presumed there would be a stripper at his brother Philip's bachelor party. Perhaps if he had actually thought about it, he might even have expected two. Sure, in sitcoms the stripper always arrived alone, but he knew that in real life strippers often came in pairs. How else could there be a little pretend (or not pretend) girl-on-girl action on the living room carpet? Besides, he worked in mergers and acquisitions, he understood the exigencies of commerce as well as anyone: two strippers meant you could have two gentlemen squirming at once. You could have two girls hovering just above two sets of thighs—or if the girls saw the right combination of neediness and dollar signs in the men's eyes, not hovering but in fact descending upon each of the men's laps. Richard wasn't especially wild about the idea of an exotic dancer in his family's living room: there was a place for everything in his mind, even the acrobatically tensed sinews of a stripper. But that place wasn't his home. He didn't want to be a prig, however; he didn't want to be the guy who put a damper on his younger brother's bachelor party. And so he told himself the entertainment would be some girl from Sarah Lawrence or Fordham or NYU with a silly, mellifluous made-up name making a little money for tuition. He didn't completely believe this, but in some backward universe sort of way, he felt a little less reprehensible—a little less soiled—if he was getting turned on by a twenty-one-year-old sociology major with a flat stomach and a Brazilian who understood intellectually the cultural politics of stripping and viewed herself as a feminist capitalist.

Richard's wife, of course, was not present that evening. Kristin had made sure that she and her daughter were at her mother's apartment in Manhattan. The three of them, three generations of females, one with white hair and one with wheaten and one—the youngest—with hair that was blond and silken and fell to her shoulders, ate dinner at an Italian restaurant the granddaughter liked. It was near Carnegie Hall and had great plaster sculptures of body parts on the walls. Noses. Breasts. An eye. The three of them had theater tickets for a Broadway matinee the following afternoon, Saturday. They weren't planning to return home until Sunday.

There were supposed to be no videos of the bachelor party. One of the women's Russian bodyguards told the men to keep their phones in their pants. He said if he saw a phone, he'd break it. He said he'd break the fingers that had been touching the phone, too. (He was smiling when he spoke, but no one doubted his earnestness.)

So there were mostly just stories of what seems to have occurred. How it went from stripping to fucking. How it all went wrong. There is only what the gentlemen, including Richard Chapman, told the police. The talent's versions? The talent was gone. And those bodyguards? They were dead.

...

The house, a regal Tudor in what was inadvertently a development of regal Tudors, sat on three-quarters of an acre partway up a wooded hill just off of Pondfield Road. The driveway was steep. One morning Richard had started his pewter gray Audi to drive to the train station for his morning commute to the investment bank in lower Manhattan, but realized he had forgotten his iPad. So he climbed from the car—failing first to reset the parking brake—and then watched, at once horrified and enrapt, as the vehicle rolled backward down the incline, first in slow motion but then with the gathering steam of an avalanche as it rumbles its way down a mountain, rolling into the thin road that led to Pondfield, crossing that main Bronxville thoroughfare, and then slamming into a small copse of maples largely denuded of leaves because it was the last week in October. Miraculously, as if the near accident had been elaborately staged by a film crew, the Audi passed cleanly between a garbage truck plodding up Pondfield Road and a Subaru station wagon with one of the schoolteachers who worked with Kristin racing down it. No one was hurt. The car incurred nearly eight thousand dollars in damage, but this was an Audi: it was far from totaled. Arguably, Richard's ego was in worse shape—but, like the Audi, eminently repairable.

The house was almost equidistant from the Bronxville train station, where Richard would catch the train, and Siwanoy Country Club, where he would occasionally play golf on the weekends. His favorite room in the house was a mahogany-paneled library, where he had replaced one wall of built-in bookshelves with a home theater, and where all alone he would watch his beloved New York Giants or he and Kristin would watch whatever sitcoms he had Tivo-ed that week or some combination of mother and father and daughter would watch as a family whatever movie nine-year-old Melissa had selected. Sometimes those movie nights were a testimony to how quickly and how easily the ear cells were mashed into ineffectual chum by loud noise: Melissa only needed the volume set at five or six; her parents, veterans of Nirvana concerts in their teens and then Pearl Jam and Alice in Chains concerts in their twenties, needed it set at jet engine. Sometimes it seemed to Richard that Disney only made movies where everyone whispered.

This room also held Richard's and Kristin's vinyl—and the couple had long rows of albums they had alphabetized like librarians—and the stereo that they both cared for like an antique car.

But Richard also loved the bedroom that he and Kristin shared, especially the bed, which was the perfect height to make love to his wife standing up—that is, he would be standing up, she would be lying on the mattress, her ankles gripped like dumbbells in his hands. He took pride in his daughter's bedroom and the wallpaper—a jungle of lions and tigers (no bears)—that he had meticulously hung himself, as well as the crisp white armoire and dresser where his fourth grader kept an ever-burgeoning wardrobe. These days, as Melissa had grown more fashion conscious, the room always looked a little ransacked: her sweaters and skirts and tights overflowed from the drawers of the dresser and the doors of the armoire. They cascaded onto the floor like the soap bubbles that once flooded the kitchen from the dishwasher the time that Richard had put dishwashing liquid instead of dishwasher gel into the machine.

But the girl's bedroom was no longer awash in Barbies and Barbie doll furniture. And Barbie doll outfits. And the Barbie doll shoes, which Richard had observed should be listed with the TSA as weapons a passenger could not bring aboard a plane in a carry-on. He had stepped on them one time too many in the dark in his bare feet, his sole seemingly impaled by one of the diminutive plastic stilettos, when he was checking the girl's room before he went to bed: making sure that the heat was just right or the window was open (or closed) or she was properly tucked in beneath the covers. But by nine she had long outgrown the dolls. The anorexic amazons had been replaced by plump American Girl dolls with names like Molly (not Miley) and Felicity and Samantha, and even those dolls sat most of the time in a corner of the bedroom, a film of dust atop their demure bonnets and caps. The Barbie collection, a massive assortment of lifeguards, physicians, and pet groomers, had been boxed away in a snap-tight, plastic Tucker Tote the size of a small summer camp trunk and sat now in a corner of her bedroom.

The Tucker Tote was clear, except for the lid, which was blue. One of these days, Richard planned to cart the dolls up the stairs that fell from the second-floor hallway ceiling into the attic.

As for the rest of the house, Richard was largely oblivious. He spent too little time in the kitchen to have formed any serious opinions, and he assumed all appliances were more or less equal. Like a sleepwalker he would pour himself coffee there in the morning, and he would bring the dishes there from the dining room after dinner—occasionally, but only rarely, breaking a plate or allowing a knife to slide off the china and deposit mustard sauce on the hardwood dining room floor. But the kitchen was not the nerve center of the house the way it was in so many suburban homes. Kristin never graded papers at the kitchen table there. Richard never examined company profiles or crunched numbers there.

The same was true of his feelings toward the mudroom and the powder room and the pantry, with its glass cabinet doors dating back to the 1930s.

And so while he knew that the men at the bachelor party would be wandering throughout the kitchen and the dining room and the pantry, he really didn't care. They would be nowhere near the sanctum sanctorum of bedrooms upstairs. Mostly, he guessed, they would be reveling amid the bricks and mortar and magnificent exposed wooden beams in the family's living room or the smaller den beside it. In those rooms, the paint was the colors of hyacinth and squash and brass and antiquarian brown, and the wallpaper was a series of meticulous renderings of garden flowers. (He had hung that, too. He was, he knew, clumsy; but he was also strangely gifted when it came to select home improvements. He was a virtuoso paperhanger, and it gave him ineffable pleasure to paper those rooms that mattered to his wife and his daughter. Only the front hallway had the home's original wallpaper.) The house was a mannered world of very conventional domesticity. And if there was a stripper there? If Philip's friend at the hotel did indeed dial one up? Not a big deal. When she left, when the furniture was moved back into place and the dishwasher had been filled with the men's glasses, the house once more would be a domiciliary keep for his wife and his daughter and himself.

...

The autumn rain drummed against the slate roof, but the men were oblivious, the lower clouds soup and the higher ones columns of unseasonal, crepitating thunderheads. A few of the men, including Richard, were vaguely aware that somewhere in the room an ancient Madonna song was on the Bose speaker dock, but most had stopped listening to the strippers' playlist back on Nelly, because that was when the two girls had started grinding against each other.

Brandon Fisher was sitting beside Richard on the living room couch and leaned forward, murmuring, "Where do you think these girls are from? They're not American." A few minutes ago, Brandon had had one of the girls straddling his lap, her breasts pressed hard against his face; she hadn't seemed to mind when he slipped his fingers underneath the front of her thong. She had even pretended she liked it. And, much to Richard's surprise, their bodyguards didn't seem to care: when he'd seen what Brandon was doing, he'd expected their muscle—two large, terrifying Russian dudes, both with shaved heads—to swoop in and break the guy's hand. But they hadn't. Brandon had simply given the girl a fifty, which she, in turn, had discreetly slipped into the jacket pocket of one of her handlers. He'd licked his fingers and wolfishly raised his eyebrows. Some of the men had howled.

As soon as the girls had arrived, Richard had moved the coffee table into the kitchen. He had moved the coffee table and the wine rack and a side table with a luminescent glass bowl hand-blown by a Vermont artisan into the kitchen. He wanted to be sure that the girls had room to strip and do whatever else his brother's best friends were paying them to do in his living room—because, it was clear to him now, these were not mere strippers. They were something more. Way more. He glanced once again at Brandon's hand.

This was not at all what he had expected and he felt a little . . . unclean. But he also couldn't imagine being anyplace else right now and not getting to see this—though he was still unsure precisely what *this* was and where it was all going to end. He reminded himself that he was drunk and told himself he should be grateful to get to see a live sex show in his living room. But then he had a pang of concern for the Oriental carpet. Did he really want the sex stains of strange women and his brother's friends forever marking the antique rug?

"Russia? The Ukraine? I don't know," he answered Brandon finally. "I mean, the guys who brought them here have Russian accents."

One of the girls was blond, her hair cut into a bob. The other's hair was creosote black and cascaded in waterfalls down her neck and onto her shoulders. She was still in her thong, but the blonde—whose hands were cupping the other girl's ass, her fingers splayed, with such apparent force that the breath had caught in his throat—was absolutely naked but for the glitter that sparkled in the light from the wrought-iron floor lamp.

"Maybe the Middle East," Brandon suggested.

"Not the blonde."

"Hair's dyed," he said.

"I'm thinking Eastern Europe. Maybe Germany? Or, I don't know, Estonia."

Abruptly his younger brother, Philip, cuffed him good-naturedly on the shoulder, causing him to spill some of his beer on his lap. "Dude!" Philip told him, his voice happily, boyishly, boisterously hammered. "Seriously? You have two chicks about to go down on each other six feet away from you, and you're trying to figure out where the fuck they're from?" He laughed, tousled Richard's hair, and then added, "You have been married way too fucking long, my older brother! Way too fucking long!"

...

Philip was thirty-five and a month that autumn night, and he was going to marry a woman five years younger than he was, which meant that she was a full decade younger than Richard and Kristin. A decade is a long time. Think history. It's the difference between—for example—1953 and 1963. Or 1992 and 2002. Philip's fiancée, a lovely young woman named Nicole, was a graphic artist who owned a studio with a skylight in Fort Greene, though she spent most nights at Philip's larger apartment near the promenade in Brooklyn Heights. Philip had a Master of Management in Hospitality from Cornell and ran the reception desk at a trendy boutique hotel in Chelsea. You had to look like a runway model from Prague—tall and blond, with cheekbones only a god could sculpt—to stand behind the black marble podiums and check someone in. He said he was an (and he always said the word with an irony that actually bespoke considerable pride) hotelier.

...

Kristin stood in a navy blue sleep shirt in the window of the guest bedroom in her mother's apartment on Eighty-ninth Street and gazed south at the lights of midtown Manhattan. The cotton felt damp against her shoulders and the small of her back; only moments ago she had emerged from the shower. The apartment was on the fourteenth floor.

She hoped the party was going well and Richard was having fun. She and Richard had decided, in the end, that there was probably going to be a stripper—they knew Philip would want one and they knew his friends would want to oblige—but she figured any woman who took off her clothes in a Bronxville living room was pretty harmless. Good Lord, when she thought back on the way that she and Richard had partied when they'd been in their twenties—when they'd been dating—a bunch of guys nearing middle age drinking beer and watching a stripper in a living room seemed downright innocuous. It might not be politically correct, but it was benign. And Richard worked so hard and had so few friends. There were the guys he played golf with every so often. There were the women and men at the bank. But the reality was that her husband was one of those men who spent hours at the office or traveling, and played almost exclusively with her and with their daughter. She worried sometimes that he was, beneath that clumsy, lovable facade, a little lonely. A little wistful. A little sad. She wondered if he might make a new friend at the party. She rather hoped so.

She decided to text him to see how the party was going, unsure whether he would text back in five minutes, or ten, or not until morning. She had no idea if the stripper was there yet—for all she knew, the woman had already come and gone—and for the first time her mind wandered to what sorts of things a stripper did in a living room in Westchester for a bunch of guys, some married, some not, in their thirties and forties. She guessed lap dances, though she wasn't honestly sure what a lap dance really was. She'd never been to a strip club. She had asked Richard—an intellectual question, not one tinged in the slightest with judgment—whether he thought the woman would be fully naked in their house or still clad in some sort of stripper thong.

"Is there such a thing as a stripper thong?" he had asked in return, kidding, but also curious himself in a puerile sort of way. "I kind of think a thong is a thong."

"Is a thong," she added, recalling the Gertrude Stein remark about a rose. But then she had thought more about it, the idea of exotic dancewear, and reflexively raised an eyebrow. "You know what I mean," she added.

"Thong," he answered, but she could tell he didn't believe that. Or maybe he was just hoping he was mistaken. She couldn't decide from his tone. Heaven knows he liked the look of a woman in a thong; he'd certainly bought her plenty of them over the years. But, of course, she viewed them largely as sex toys. Foreplay. Datewear. Sure, the girls in the high school insisted on wearing them all day long, but they didn't know any better. They were still willing to sacrifice comfort for fashion. Because, of course, there was no more disagreeable panty in the world than a thong. As Richard himself had once joked, "Victoria's real secret is that she's into some seriously uncomfortable underwear."

In the bed behind her in her mother's apartment, a queen with a mahogany headboard with Georgian corners, Melissa was watching an old episode of *Seinfeld* on her grandmother's laptop. Kristin climbed back into bed beside her and started a crossword puzzle from the booklet on the nightstand. Not quite fifteen minutes later her phone vibrated, and she saw that Richard had texted back.

"Bacchanalian," he had written. "Not proud. But I am hoping everyone leaves by midnight or twelve-thirty. I expect to call cabs for at least two of Philip's pals."

She smiled. It sounded like he was having fun. She was impressed that every word was spelled right, though she guessed the phone might have corrected *bacchanalian* for him. She shut it off for the night.

A few minutes later, while her daughter was still awake and contentedly watching a sitcom that had been off the air for nearly two decades, Kristin fell asleep first. She would be awakened by the old-fashioned telephone landline in the apartment just before three in the morning.

...

Kristin knew firsthand that even now—perhaps especially now—well into a digital world of tweets and texts and tones that are personalized, the staccato, reverberating ring of an old-fashioned telephone is jarring. It is particularly jarring in the small, shadowy hours of the night. As three a.m. nears, the odds that good news awaits at the other end grow slim. Not incalculably slim: babies are born after midnight and parents learn that the child they have been praying to adopt has landed. Soldiers call home because this is the one moment when, nine or ten time zones to the east (or west), they have a moment to speak. But Kristin knew the odds are far higher that a call to a landline—to any line—at three in the morning is the ring tone of calamity. Life-changing calamity. That call is the raven. It was how she had learned that her father had died.

Nevertheless, there was no telephone in Kristin's mother's guest room. And so although she heard the ring through her and her daughter's half-open bedroom door, it was her mother who shook herself awake and reached awkwardly across the mattress—across the side on which her husband had slept until the moment when (quite literally) he died—and fumbled for the phone. Lifting it from its cradle and resting it against her ear. Not yet sitting up. Not yet. Kristin's mother was sixty-eight, vibrant and lovely, a widow of three years who was never at a loss for a lunch date or a companion to join her for a movie or the Met or whatever drama was playing at the Barrow Street Theatre. She had a personal trainer named Sting—no connection to the musician—a third her age with whom she worked out twice a week at the gym in her building. She was known to walk to the Nederlander or the Eugene O'Neill before a show and then, afterward, take two subways home to her apartment on the Upper East Side. She allowed her white hair to fall unapologetically to her shoulders. She wore blouses unbuttoned to reveal a hint of collarbone.

And so even though it was her mother who was struggling up through the roiling currents of sleep and trying to make sense of what her son-in-law was saying, Kristin grew alert. She opened her eyes, listened to Melissa's gentle breathing, even inhaled the vaguely fruity—strawberry, she thought—aroma of the child's shampoo. And she waited. She watched the moonlight through the blinds. Somehow she knew that any moment she would hear the creak of her mother's bedroom door and the way her mother shuffled like a little girl in her slippers along the corridor. She would hear her mother's voice whispering through her own partially open door. She would hear the verbal balancing act: urgency mixed like gin amid the tonic of consideration. She would not want to awaken her granddaughter.

Outside, fourteen floors below her, Kristin heard what she guessed was a garbage truck, the engine growling as the vehicle started to accelerate after the traffic light had turned green. Farther away she heard a siren, unsure whether it was an ambulance or a police car.

Then, just as she expected, she heard the sound of the bedroom door down the hall. Her mother was coming for her, each step a harbinger. A tremor. A seismic shift wrought by the smallest of steps.

Alexandra

I was so happy to see New York City. I was so excited. In the crowds, the skyscrapers, and even in the men I saw my freedom. This was my future.

They brought three of us from Moscow: Sonja, Crystal, and me. The rules were clear and the money was clear. I knew they might change the rules because they had done that before, but you always hope. I mean, I do. This time, you hope, the deal won't change. This time, you tell yourself, there won't be any surprises.

Maybe that was naive. They always changed the rules. They always kept you on your back.

That's just an expression I learned. Often I was not on my back. But you don't need to hear gymnastics. No one does.

Anyway, this time I believed them. I really did. It might be two years, they were telling me, and it might be three. But either way, by the time I was twenty-two I would be on my own. And I would be in America. New York City. The center of the universe, yes?

I knew New York City from movies. Sonja and Crystal did, too. Watching movies was one of the ways we'd kill time during the day when we were back in Moscow. Muscovites (a word that makes people who live there sound like cave people, which they are not) loved films that made fun of communism. Or showed the West winning the Cold War (which was before my time). Or celebrated getting rich really quick (which was my time completely). Many of those movies were set in Manhattan. I remember how Sonja and I watched these DVDs of old movies like *North by Northwest*, *Three Days of the Condor*, and *Wall Street*. We learned about the Staten Island Ferry from this movie called *Working Girl*, which had nothing to do with what we did, but the title, if we had known that expression back then, would have made us think it did. We figured out a little bit about the differences between New York City and L.A. from *Manhattan* and *Annie Hall*.

Sometimes the movies were in English with Russian subtitles, and those helped Sonja and the other girls learn English as much as my teaching. And we always watched *The Bachelor* in English. We got the U.S. version on one station and the U.K. version on another. We watched hours and hours of both. The Bachelor always had clean fingernails. He seemed gentle. He didn't have scars. His women always had straight, white teeth, and they applied their makeup perfectly. Their gowns were gorgeous. So were their earrings and their necklaces and their bathing suits. We all loved the moment with the rose. Our men never gave us flowers. Why would they?

For a while we'd lived in a cottage as glamorous as some of the places where the girls who were hoping to seduce the Bachelor were staying, but unlike them we were never allowed to leave. We had one hour of sunlight.

So, it was like I knew New York City before I got there. All three of us did. We knew some of the buildings so well from our movies and hotel room TVs that when we saw the real things, they looked shabby. You know, disappointing. I'm not kidding you or trying to put on airs. The Empire State Building is as big as you would expect when you stand below it for the first time, but on the sidewalk there is all this garbage, and the men look nothing like the Bachelor. There are fast-food restaurants that stink of French fries and grease. Across the street and a block away is a strip club. (Sonja would remember it, and it would be one of the clubs where we would work for a few days.) The first time I saw the Plaza Hotel from the Central Park—a building I knew better by then from movies than I did the opera house in Yerevan, which I had seen with my own eyes as little girl—I stepped in horseshit. And the Times Square? There is nothing like it in Yerevan or Moscow, but the movies had prepared me for the amazing light show made of ads for flat-screen TVs, Xbox games, and fancy bras. What the movies had not prepared me for was that a five-foot-tall thing called a Sesame Street Elmo would try and hit on me there and be flattened by Pavel. This poor little man in his furry red costume never saw Pavel's fist coming.

After they showed us the city, I thought a lot about two important structures on two smaller islands. To the south, there was the Statue of Liberty. I think I had expected more when we stood at the Battery Park and looked at her out there in the harbor with her torch. I joked to Sonja that Mother Armenia, who stands on a hill in Yerevan and looks out across the city, would have kicked her ass. And then to the north was the jail. The Rikers Island. They showed us that, too. They made it really clear that just as they could kill us—a reminder you would think we never needed, but I guess poor Crystal did—they could simply drop us into that jail. They called it "cesspool." That was how they described it. They told us how different an American jailhouse was from the townhouse where we were going to live and how different it was from a Moscow hotel or the cottage. They made big deal about how pampered our life was compared to the life of a prisoner in a cinderblock cell—and how safe, in their opinion, our world really was.

The truth is, I usually felt safer with the men who paid for me than I did with any of our daddies or the White Russian or the guys who "protected" us like Pavel. Even my housemothers could scare me.

...

It was on my twenty-first night in America that everything went to hell. I mean that: to hell. First, Sonja and I learned that Crystal was dead. They'd killed her—our Russian daddies, that is. And then Sonja finally lost her mind. I saw it coming that night—her going totally crazy—but I thought she was going to make it through the party for the bachelor. Nope. I don't know, maybe we had both lost our minds years ago. Probably. But this was the night when Sonja went wild. She went wild and stabbed Pavel, because he and Kirill were the muscle who had shot baby Crystal and disposed of her tiny body God alone knew where.

Here's a memory that surprises me: I saw a bunch of Barbie dolls in this little girl's bedroom that night at the house where they had taken us. They were in a big plastic trunk. The dolls had reminded me of my own collection of Barbies when I'd been a kid, and I still think of that other girl's Barbies sometimes. There was a rubber on the trunk's lid. It was a few minutes after the best man had decided not to fuck me (there was a first), and then we went downstairs. The Barbies were maybe the last thing I would notice before I would see Sonja, naked but for a thong, on the back of that bastard named Pavel. Her legs were wrapped around his belly, and her left arm was hugging his chest. Her right arm was like a piston with a carving knife in it, and she was plunging the knife over and over into his neck.

That's also an image you never forget. Later I would see that his blood was on her arms and in her hair. I would see his blood everywhere.

Somehow, until that moment I had kept it together that night at the party. I was scared not to. I did my job. They had told us what they had done to Crystal, and then put us in the car and driven us out to Westchester to work a private party. (The party was for a bachelor, but the man getting married was nothing like the bachelors we had seen on TV. Oh, he was handsome. He had nice eyes and he was always laughing—at least until he saw Pavel getting killed. But he was not the type who was ever going to get down on one knee and give a girl a rose. I have been around enough men that I can tell pretty quick. Maybe his brother the best man was. But he was twice my age. And the other men at the party? Most were the kinds of dudes who only had girls like us when they paid.) I did whatever they wanted—I even smiled and played along as if it was just another night and another party—because I knew Pavel and Kirill were watching.

But Sonja? She was just biding her time a lot of the evening. She was pretty sure they were going to kill her, too—after the party.

She told me that later. But by then we were gone. By then we were running for our lives.

Chapter Two

"Kristin?"

"I'm awake," she said, just loud enough for her mother to hear. Already her mind was cataloging the possible reasons why someone would call like this in the small hours of the night. She took comfort in the presence of Melissa beside her, but the geographic distance that separated her from her husband—How far apart were they really? Fifteen miles? Sixteen?—was sufficient to inject into her veins a creeping dread against which she was helpless. She climbed out from under the covers, trying to keep the sheets snug for her daughter, and swung her bare feet onto the floor. Her mother was silhouetted in the doorway, her face half in shadow. The small chandelier in the corridor was off, but her mother must have switched on the lamp by her own bed. She looked disturbingly skeletal in the half-light.

"It's Richard," her mother whispered, as Kristin passed her, walking instinctively toward her mother's bedroom.

"That's what I suspected," she murmured. "Is everything okay?"

"I don't know."

Kristin blinked against the glare as her eyes adjusted slowly to the brightness—it felt positively solar to her at this hour of the night—walked around the bed in which her mother had been sleeping, and picked up the phone off the nightstand. It was pink. It was so old, it was attached to the cradle by an undulant, matching pink cord. Kristin was, as she was always when she held the receiver in her hands, struck by its weight. Its heft. It made a cell phone seem so insubstantial.

"Richard?" she asked. It was, according to the digital clock by the bed, 2:58 in the morning.

"I'm sorry to wake you," he said. She saw that her mother was watching her. She was standing with her arms folded across her chest, her worried face oily with the skin cream in which she slept. Her white hair was usually impeccable in Kristin's mind. It wasn't now; it was—like she presumed her own hair was—wild with sleep. "But something happened," he went on, his voice hoisted high onto the ledge between quavering and devastated. He was, she realized, still a little drunk. "Something horrible. We never saw it coming. We never saw it—"

She cut him off: "Are you okay, sweetie?"

"Yes, I'm okay. We all are."

"Okay, then," she said, relieved because he was safe and no one was hurt. Something must have happened at the house; something was broken; something was wrecked. That's all. And he was still drunk and saw it as worse than it was. Much worse. But he was safe and so the sun would rise. "If you're all okay, that's all that matters. If something happened to—"

This time he interrupted her. "I mean I'm okay and Philip's okay. All the guys at the party are fine. More or less, anyway. But the girls—"

"Girls, as in strippers? You mean there was more than one?"

"Yes. And they weren't strippers. Maybe they were. I don't know. But things got wild and some of the guys were . . ."

"Some of the guys were what?"

"It got crazy. I don't know how it started. But some of the guys were having sex with them."

"You can't be serious. They were having sex in our house? What the hell happened? Sweetie, where are you?" A part of her understood that she had just rifled three questions at him, and so she took a breath to try and calm herself.

"Look, the point isn't that some of the guys were having sex," he said. "As bad as that was. As wrong as that was. The point—"

"Were you?" she interrupted. Something in his tone had caused her to flinch—something in the way he had said *wrong*—and when she uncoiled, she had asked the question reflexively.

"Was I what?"

This time, the question caught in her throat. "Were you having sex with them?" Her tone was more incredulity and fear than anger and accusation. *Please,* she thought, *just say no. Tell me I'm being a crazy person.*

"No. I didn't. Not really . . ."

"Not really? What do you mean, *not really?*"

"The issue," he said, not answering the question, "is that the girls . . ."

At some point, she had sat down on her mother's bed. She wanted to shoo her mother from the room, but her whole body was collapsing in upon itself. Her husband had just fucked some stripper in their house. Perhaps in their living room. She was sure of it, and she felt her stomach lurch as if she were on an airplane trying to navigate wing-rattling turbulence. "The girls what?" she asked, her tone numb, her voice almost unrecognizable to herself. It was like when you listened to a recording of your own words: the sounds and the intonation were never what you expected. She glanced up at her mother, who had heard every word that she'd said. Her mother looked stricken.

"The girls killed the guys—the guys who brought them. They killed them. There were two of them—two guys—and now they're dead. Both of them, Kris. The girls used a carving knife we keep in the cutting block in the kitchen to kill one of them. Then they took his gun and shot the other one. And now these two big Russian dudes are both dead."

For a moment she said nothing, her mind trying and failing to process the oneiric horror of what he was sharing. People had died in her home. Men—including her husband—had been fucking strippers in her home. Somehow these travesties were connected, the umbilicus a bachelor party for a man, her brother-in-law Philip, who she didn't especially like. Among the riot of emotions she was experiencing, she understood that fury—rage at Richard's juvenile younger brother—was bubbling to the surface, subsuming even the despair and sadness and embarrassment that her husband had had sex with a stripper.

"Where are you?" she asked finally. There were so many things to ask. There were just so many things she didn't know.

"I'm at the police station. We all are."

"Oh, God. In Bronxville?"

"Yes. They're taking our statements. We're telling them what happened."

"And the girls?" The word *girls* reverberated in her mind; suddenly it seemed like the wrong word. But, of course, that was the word for a stripper. When you passed places like the Hustler Club on the West Side Highway, the signs never boasted "Hundreds of Women." They advertised "Hundreds of Girls."

"They're gone. They disappeared. They killed these two big assholes—handlers, bodyguards, thugs; I don't know what you call them—took their wallets and wads of cash, and then drove away in the car they came in. But they're gone."

In the bedroom doorway, behind her mother, she saw her daughter. She was wiping the sleep from her eyes. She was wearing her Snoopy pajamas: pink-and-white-plaid flannel bottoms and the iconic dog surfing on the top. The word in the cartoon balloon was *Cowabunga.* She was asking her grandmother what was going on, what was happening, who had called.

This child, Kristin thought to herself, her husband saying something more on the other end of the line but the words merely white noise, was a girl. A girl doesn't fuck other people's husbands at a bachelor party and then take a knife to her bodyguards. A girl . . .

A girl was nine.

But the thought was lost to the relentless stream of images—a whitewater cascade that was swamping her and which she was helpless to resist—of her husband atop some stripper on the couch, her ankles upon his shoulders; of her brother-in-law beneath some stripper on the living room floor; of two other men, her mind conjuring for them black T-shirts and tight jeans, the sorts of biceps you only see in the gym, bleeding to death. But bleeding to death . . . where? She saw them dead in the kitchen, imagining their corpses on the Italian tile simply because her husband had said the girls had grabbed one of the very knives that she had used for years to prepare dinner for him and their daughter. *Kitchen.* That was the word that some part of her mind was comprehending from Richard's brief chronicle. But the truth was, the two men could have been killed anywhere: The living room. The dining room. The den.

"Kris?" her husband was saying. "Kris? Are you still there?"

"Uh-huh, I am," she said. Then she asked, "One of my knives?" Four words. One question. It was all she could muster.

"Yes," he said. "One of our knives. The girl with the blond hair. Yeah, I think that's right. It's all this horrible blur. It all happened so fast."

"Okay . . ."

"And there's more."

"How? Seriously, Richard, how could there possibly be more?" she asked, and he started telling her about the condition of the house and the blood on a painting, but the news had grown too cumbersome, too unwieldy for her to assimilate. There was too much and it was too awful. It was too awful for him. For her. For them. She looked across the room at her mother and her daughter. She realized that she was shaking.

. . .

It wasn't clear to Kristin where the memory came from or what it meant: she was sitting alone on the front steps of her family's colonial in Stamford, Connecticut, the shingles a beige cedar, and she was in the fourth grade. Her daughter's age now. It was late on a summer afternoon, a weekday, and her mother was in the kitchen unpacking groceries and then starting to prepare dinner. A storm was nearing from the west, the gray clouds racing across the sky like they were part of a theater backdrop. But it hadn't started raining yet and the air was electric and alive. She had been with her mother at the supermarket, and her mother had bought her packs of *Back to the Future* trading cards and a *Back to the Future* lunchbox. She had loved that film. Had the same crush as many a nine-year-old girl on Michael J. Fox. She had sorted the cards as soon as she and her mother had gotten home, prioritizing the ones with Marty McFly and Lorraine Baines over the ones with the flying DeLorean. Now, decades later, she associated that moment not merely with happiness, but with security. She had felt so safe on that stoop. Her older brother would be home soon enough from wherever he was hanging out that August afternoon, as would their father from work. And inside the house, through the front hallway and past the powder room—that was indeed the euphemism her mother had used for the downstairs bathroom—the sounds of her mother folding brown paper grocery bags and stacking cans in the pantry were replaced by the thwack of the heavy wooden cutting board and then the rapid-fire *crack-crack-crack* as she started to dice an onion. Kristin recognized the smell of barbecue sauce.

The memory waned as Kristin understood the connection— and why her mind had excavated that distant moment now. She thought instead of her own knives: the knives with which, over the years, she had chopped carrots and cubed beef and sliced lamb. She saw the cleaver that she had never used and the bread knife with its serrated edge that she seemed to reach for daily. She saw the nakiri knife that was instrumental when she made salads. She saw the black wooden handles with the three steel rivets. Her knives were handcrafted in Japan. They had been a wedding present for Richard and her.

She stared at her legs, naked from mid-thigh. She wondered

now which knife the strippers had used to kill one of the men who had brought them to the house.

"Kristin?" She looked up from her mother's bed in her mother's apartment. She had sat there after hanging up the phone, stunned and unmoving, her mind finding solace in recollections far from the carnage that perhaps even now was her living room. She was a marble sculpture: Devastated Woman in Sleep Shirt.

"Kristin?"

She rolled her eyes in the direction of her mother. She tried to rise from her paralysis, to focus on what to do next. It was taking work. She had told Richard that she would catch the first train to Bronxville in the morning. She would have driven home that very moment, but her mother hadn't owned a car in two years; she had sold the Volvo wagon after her husband had died. Her mother drove so infrequently now that she lived in Manhattan that it had seemed ludicrous to spend so much money every month on a parking space in the nearby garage. So the plan, which was still evolving in Kristin's mind, was this: she would get dressed. That was the start. She might as well get dressed now. She would catch a train in a few hours to Westchester. Melissa would spend the weekend here with her grandmother and go to the matinee today as planned. Her grandmother would take her. Kristin would drive her car from the Bronxville train station to her house, because Richard had said he expected he would be home by then. Home from the . . . police station by then.

Kristin feared that she was reaching like a drowning woman for normalcy and it was only a matter of time before she failed and went under: two people had been killed in her home after her husband and her brother-in-law and his friends had been watching a couple of strippers.

No: they had been fucking a couple of whores.

She sighed. She was trying to climb up from a deep slough of hopelessness and despair, but there were no convenient vines or tree roots near this quicksand. Whores. In her home. With her husband. People had been murdered in the house where she and Richard were building their life together, where they were raising their daughter. These were the bricks and mortar behind which they felt safest, were happiest.

"Mommy?"

Both her mother and her daughter wanted her. Or, perhaps, wanted only to be reassured that she had not become stone before their eyes. She ran her hands through her hair and then patted the side of the mattress beside her. "Come here, my adorable little one," she said to her daughter. "Sit down beside me."

"Kristin, what's going on? Is Richard okay? He didn't sound like himself on the phone," her mother was saying.

"Richard's fine," she answered. "Daddy's fine," she added, turning her full attention now on Melissa. She tried to recall what she had said at her end of the conversation with her husband and, thus, what her mother and her daughter might have heard. Had she said "sex"? Had she said "strippers"? She had. She had indeed.

Melissa sat beside her on the bed. She was trembling, as Kristin herself had been only a few moments ago, and so she put her arm around the child's shoulders and pulled her against her. "Everything's okay, my little one," she murmured. She knew she was going to have to offer a G-rated version of what had occurred, sanitizing it as much as she could for her daughter. She could fill in the blanks—God, the blanks—for her mother after she had gotten dressed and (she hoped) Melissa had fallen back to sleep. "But there was an accident at the house. At Uncle Philip's bach—at Uncle Philip's party."

"His bachelor party," her daughter said. Of course Melissa knew it was a bachelor party. She was going to be in her uncle's wedding in two weeks. She was the flower girl.

"Yes."

"What kind of accident?"

"Two of the men who were there . . . died. There were some people at the party who weren't invited—who weren't supposed to be there. And there seems to have been a . . . a fight." Kristin could feel her mother watching her, listening intently so she could parse the truth from this carefully dumbed-down circumlocution.

"A fight or an accident?" Melissa asked.

"Oh, I am not quite sure myself," she lied. "But here is what is important: Daddy is fine. And Uncle Philip is fine."

"So it was their friends who got killed? Were they grown-ups I knew?"

"Nope. See? It's all going to be okay," she said, and she tried to believe that short sentence herself. But she couldn't. She just couldn't. And so she held her daughter close and rocked her gently. She tried to immerse herself in the movement, to quiet the roiling despair in her soul. In a minute or two, she would walk the girl back to the guest bedroom and tuck her into bed. Pull the sheets and the blanket up to her shoulders. She would kiss her once on her forehead and once on both cheeks—as she always did when she said good night. As Richard did when it was his turn to read to their daughter and kiss her good night. Then Kristin would get dressed by the light from the corridor. She would brush her hair in her mother's bedroom and perhaps even put on some makeup. She would have some coffee and share with her mother the truth. The shameless and appalling and loathsome truth.

Then she would take a cab to Grand Central and go home.

Alexandra

My mother was a secretary at a brandy factory in Yerevan, and her boss was the president himself. My grandmother—my mother's mother—was a nurse. The three of us had lived together since my father had died years and years ago. I was toddler. He'd died in an accident at the hydroelectric plant where he worked. Electrocuted— one of six men who died that morning, but the only one who died quickly. The other five would drown, which people tell me is a much worse way to die. I think that's probably true from the time a guard at the cottage held my head under the water in the bathtub. Nearly drowning us was one of the ways they would discipline us. There are no bruises. There are no scars. The merchandise still looks good. There is even a word for this: *noyade*. It means execution by drowning. Comes from French Revolution. I looked it up.

My mother's boss was one of those crazy-savvy, post-Soviet players. He went from communist to capitalist like very exotic chameleon. His name was Vasily. Super smooth. He knew all the angles and how to play them. He was a Russian oligarch who came to Armenia from Volgograd and bought a brandy factory on the outskirts of the city for nothing. It might have been a scandal, but it was just one more factory bought by just one more oligarch.

When my mother died, he was there for me. In the long run, of course, this would be earthquake-level bad. Life-changing bad.

But those first days and then first weeks after my mother died? I felt safe. I felt like princess. I felt that in the end—no matter what— everything would be okay.

...

I grew up speaking Armenian and Russian, but I started learning English in school when I was seven. By the time I was fifteen, I was fluent. This increased my value in Vasily's eyes: I was exotically beautiful, still slender, still slight. With some TV time I'd be able to speak like courtesan after fucking American bankers when they were in Moscow for business. That was the plan.

My teachers, Inga and Catherine, really used the word *courtesan*. I think they preferred it to whore.

...

In the years before I was born, my mother told me, Yerevan only had electricity for a few hours a day. Never all day. After the earthquake and the collapse of the Soviet Union, Armenians shut down the nuclear plant on the earthquake fault line. This was a good decision if you didn't want two Chernobyls in one decade, but it was bad if you are trying to build democracy. Blackouts made people miss the Soviet Union. My parents' neighbors said they wished that they lived in villages instead of the city, because the villagers at least had cow shit they could burn to stay warm.

Some people said that peasants in the countryside also ate better than we did, but I don't remember being hungry.

And by the time I was born in 1996, the electricity was back. I could play with my toys all I wanted after dark.

...

Yerevan was a great city, even after the earthquake and the end of the Soviet Union. As little girl, I thought it had to be one of the most beautiful places in the world. The buildings were made of volcanic rock. The opera house was like palace. There were statues and sculptures in our neighborhood wherever we turned.

And it was in Yerevan where I took ballet. Like lots of little girls, I danced all the time. Unlike lots of little girls, I was very good. I was going to be next Victoria Ananyan—next "Velvet Bird." My dance teacher seemed to think so. I danced every moment when I was not studying or playing, and then I stopped playing and danced even more. I was at the studio six days a week.

Someday, I thought, I was going to lead a glamorous life in Russia and then in America. But first I was going to dance *Swan Lake* and *Gayane* at the Spendarian Opera House. First I was going to train with the Moscow State Academy.

But I so loved the idea of going to America. I had met Americans before in Yerevan. By the time I was ten, they were coming all the time. And not just teenagers or young maniacs who believed they were going to rebuild the country. Everyday tourists. I would see them on the Northern Avenue and the Cascades and the Republic Square. They would watch the fountains dance in the square near the government offices for hours. They would have their pictures taken by the opera house or beside the statues of Komitas, Khachaturian, and Saroyan. They were from Los Angeles, which I always associated with the movies. They were from New York City, which would be attacked by terrorists when I was five, but by the time I was ten was simply that city with all the skyscrapers and a harbor with the Statue of Liberty. They were from Massachusetts, which I associated with red socks and only later would learn was the name of their baseball team. But all of these Americans were glamorous. They were like rich Armenians who would visit from Lebanon and Syria and Dubai. Maybe they were even more glamorous.

So, Vasily. A couple years after my abduction, an older girl would tell me that he had probably killed my mother. Or, to be exact, he had had her killed. Vasily wasn't the type to kill someone himself. He had henchmen. He had bodyguards. They would do the Russian businessman's dirty work.

I remember correcting this girl. I told her that my mother had died in hospital. I told her how it had not been pretty at the end. Not pretty at all. My grandmother and I were there. My mother died of cancer.

But this girl said that maybe Vasily had poisoned her. Injected cancer into her blood.

This was how naive and how crazy we were that she could believe such thing.

She said I should go to the police to have my mother's death investigated. But by then I was in Moscow—and I wasn't dancing. Or, at least, I wasn't dancing ballet. Occasionally I was dancing naked for (mostly) sweaty men, which usually didn't even involve a stage and a pole. It involved hotel room ottomans and couches and the laps of the men, and then the bedrooms where I would do whatever they wanted. So who in Moscow was I going to tell? What could people in Moscow do? Answer? No one and nothing. They could and would do nothing. Besides, who would have wanted to help me? Why should someone else get involved? What was the point of rescuing a useless orphan whore?

At the time, that was how I thought.

Anyway, Vasily did not have my mother killed. It was only lung cancer that made it so she couldn't breathe and was always in agony.

But Vasily certainly swooped in when she died.

And then I was fucked—and that is an American pun, of course, but it was also my life.

...

Why did that older girl think Vasily had had my mother murdered? She overheard Vasily talking to a bodyguard about us when he was visiting Moscow. My mother had seen through his story that he wanted to make me superb dancer. Really he just wanted to make me superb prostitute—which he did.

Of course, I am not sure that my mother would have wanted me even to become a ballerina. She was clingy with me—not just protective, but needy. Many people noticed. They would tell me that it was because of the earthquake, followed by her husband's death. She wanted me safe in Yerevan with her, not going away to dance in Russia or Europe or America. I would attend university near our apartment and become a doctor. A pediatrician. I would help Armenia. That was the plan. At least that was her plan. Her mother was a nurse, so why should her daughter not become a doctor?

My grandmother disagreed. She had no objections to me becoming a dancer. I think she had decided that being a doctor (or nurse) was overrated. As Americans say, she was "all in" at the idea of me becoming a ballerina. I tried to bob between the two of them, but one wave or the other would knock me down and give me snootful. My mother would tell me I was a good writer. She had a friend who said that maybe I could become a poet if I wanted to be an artist so bad. Maybe I could become a doctor and a poet. When you're twelve years old, the future seems to have no limits.

But this was all just talk for me. I would tape my toes and I would rub my feet and I would stretch and toss my shoes—especially my toe shoes, which made me so proud—into my dance bag, and off I would go to studio. Some days, I would practically skip down the sidewalk. That was how happy dance made me when I was a girl.

. . .

Yerevan had plenty of orphanages, but I didn't need one after my mother died. After all, I was already living with my grandmother. All that was different was that suddenly I had a whole bedroom to myself. I was no longer sharing one with my mother. And now I was as sad as my grandmother had been for weeks. When you're a teenager, it's hard to believe your mother really is dying. I guess the teenage brain doesn't get it that the chemotherapy is going to fail or the radiation is only postponing things. The teenage brain doesn't accept what's coming. I only saw the little steps forward, not the bigger steps back. My mother was never in remission. The doctors never said she was cancer-free. And yet I viewed her hospital stays and the ways she got sicker only as phases. I saw setbacks, sure. But I believed in the end she would get better. She had to, yes? How could a girl lose her father when she was toddler and her mother when she was teenager? I would join my grandmother in church when my mother was hospitalized, and the reverent fathers were very kind. Looking back, they probably thought my teenage quiet was my understanding of how sick my mother was. It was actually the opposite: total teenage denial.

During the last two weeks of my mother's life, I would sit beside her hospital bed and try and hold her hand. By then I was holding all bones. I would go there for few minutes right after school and before dance, and then I would go again right after dance. It was amazing how quickly she deteriorated those last days. We could still talk when she went into hospital for the last time, even if her sentences were short and often racked by a hacking cough. But by the end, I would just hold her hand. We didn't speak. When she slipped first into morphine cloud—when she finally stopped coughing and her body was no longer spasming in agony—and then into death, I was so stunned.

In the days that followed the burial, Grandmother and I were lonely, even though we had each other. But she had lost a child and I had lost a parent. My grandmother had obviously seen lots of people die, but it's different when it's your daughter. It's different when you have to witness your granddaughter watching her own mother die.

We were both very quiet those days. There really was very little to say.

. . .

Those weeks, we also had Vasily. Or, at least, we had Vasily's people. He would show up at our apartment or at hospital—always foreshadowed by his cologne—and he would hug us. He would tell us very funny stories and laugh at his own jokes like crazy person. And his laugh was so big, so contagious, that sometimes we would laugh, too.

At least a little.

Chapter Three

Richard stood in his driveway, his arms folded across his chest, and gazed at the police cars and the mobile crime scene van. The sun wouldn't rise for another hour and he was cold. He hadn't bothered to get a jacket when they had all left for the police station a while back. His younger brother was on his way back to Brooklyn by now; all of the guests were straggling home.

He couldn't bring himself to go inside. Not yet. He needed a moment. But he was curious as to what awaited him, and so he went to a window, crunching the pine nuggets beneath his shoes and pushing aside branches from the dwarf hydrangea. From there he peered into the living room. He presumed the corpses were long gone, and, indeed, he didn't see the bodyguard who had been killed there. His blood, however, was everywhere. The couch, upholstered with a beige brocade patterned with dark blue shadows of flowers, looked as if it had been sitting on a slaughterhouse kill floor. In the sepulchral, hungover darkness of his mind, Richard saw a cow on a stalled conveyor belt bleeding out above it and wondered briefly where he had ever seen such a thing. Then he remembered. PBS. A documentary. He recalled the thug at the moment of his death and why so much of the blood had wound up on the couch: the man, a Russian with an almost comically bad Boris Badenov accent, had been leaning over its back, reaching for something that had fallen onto one of the cushions. A cigarette lighter, Richard thought—the first of two glimmering flashes, one silver and the other steel. They'd been getting ready to leave, Richard presumed, the four of them. The bodyguards and the girls. He'd just brought . . . Alexandra . . . downstairs. And then the blond one—so tiny, so very, very small, her weight gossamer when she had been straddling him on the couch, pressing her breasts into his face, her nipples erect—had appeared out of nowhere, a raptor, throwing herself onto the Russian's back and plunging a knife deep into the right side of his neck. The fellow had reared up like a horse and tried throwing her off of him, but already he was gagging, his eyes wide. Richard had watched (they all had watched, studies in suburban male impotence) as his blood had sprayed like the paint on one of those pinwheel paint machines for little kids at community carnivals, soaking primarily the couch but also splattering the spines of the novels on the white built-in bookshelves on the nearby wall and—when the bodyguard lashed out one last time before collapsing onto the rug—the Hudson River School landscape by a minor but still immensely talented painter from the nineteenth century. A wannabe Bierstadt. The girl had reached into the dead man's jacket, grabbing his wallet, his pistol from his holster—dear God, Richard recalled thinking, the guy was actually wearing a holster with a gun—and the wads of twenties and fifties and (yes) hundreds she and her partner had earned. Then she looked at the rest of the men briefly (in hindsight, Richard couldn't decide whether that glance was dismissive or regretful) and rushed into the front hallway. Her arms were tattooed with the pimp's blood. There was some on her neck and her cheek. It was like she was a five-year-old who had been finger-painting. A moment later, all of the men at the party, stupefied by the way the hooker had gone banshee, some afraid that they would be next, had heard the gunshots—two pops, a few seconds between them, the noises not deafening but still horrifying because it was the middle of the night and because everyone knew what the sounds were. What they meant. It was then that Richard saw the girl (like her partner, so petite) with the black hair, a gun in one hand and a key ring in the other. He had no idea if it was the same gun the blonde had taken from the dude she had just stabbed, or a second weapon. She, too, surveyed the room before climbing back into her clothes—some of them, anyway, because through the window Richard could see the white blouse in which she'd arrived, draped on one of the living room chairs—and disappearing with the blonde into the night. None of the men thought to stop them. Richard guessed that all of them were, like him, utterly dazed. And, without question, terrified. It was only when they heard the car's engine roar to life in the driveway that any of them stopped cowering. Because, in fact, they had been cowering. They had.

It was his brother, Philip, who spoke first, murmuring, "What the fuck. Seriously, what the fuck just happened?"

But he knew. They all did.

Had it only been forty minutes earlier that Philip had been leaning over that very couch, leering as the girls were on their knees, making out with each other on those very cushions? The girls were both wearing sports jackets they had commandeered from the guys—one, Richard thought, was his brother's—and at the time he had found this only annoying. Not erotic. It wasn't merely that he imagined the poor guys were now going to have jackets that would reek of eau de stripper when they went home; it was that he couldn't see as much of the girls as he wanted. Their bodies. Their hips, their breasts, that part of a woman's collarbone he found so erotically interesting.

Soon, of course, he would see all of that—at least he would see all that he desired of the one with the black hair. She said her name was Alexandra, but obviously she had made that up. At least that was what he assumed. Philip's pal at the hotel, Spencer Doherty, had paid for Philip to fuck one and the party's host and best man, Richard, to fuck the other. (At the party, Spencer had asked the other guests to pony up a hundred or two hundred each to help cover the cost, and most of the men had agreed.) But for a price, the rest of the guests could have a little private time with either of the girls. Or both. Boris Badenov had made that clear. So had the dancers. But private time wasn't an issue for Philip. The groom was so drunk by then that he hadn't even bothered to adjourn to one of his older brother's bedrooms upstairs: he'd taken the blonde on the living room floor while everyone around him had egged him on. Richard had listened as he had led the other girl upstairs to the guest room. (He sure as hell wasn't about to bring her to his and Kristin's bedroom or Melissa's bedroom or even the room with the home theater and their records and two very comfortable couches.) He'd started talking to her on the stairs, if only to drown out the sounds of the men as they raucously cheered his brother, and the woman as she cried out like a porn star.

"Where are you from?" he'd asked her, and she had leaned her head on his shoulder as if they were lovers on a date, and talked about Armenia and Russia, and how in another life she could show him the most beautiful sculptures and parks in Yerevan and Moscow.

"There is a Botero cat at the base of the Cascades in Yerevan," she had said.

"A Botero," he'd asked, "is that a kind of cat? A breed like a Siamese or an Abyssinian?"

She looked up and smiled. "No, silly. Botero is a sculptor. He's from Colombia. It's a plump—plump like big pillow—black cat. A very big sculpture. But the cat has a king's face. Royal."

"Regal?"

"I guess."

"And the Cascades are a waterfall in the city?"

"Cascades are steps in the city. Levels. And there are sculptures on every level," she explained, as she started to unbutton his shirt. He let her. He stretched out his arms to allow her to pull off the sleeves. "I like a man's chest," she said. She kissed his sternum.

"How many levels?"

She looked up at him. "The Cascades?"

He nodded.

"It's been so long. I wish I knew. I wish I could remember. Seven? Maybe eight?"

"You grew up near them?" He thought she sounded wistful.

"Close, yes. Parts of the city are so beautiful. The opera house? Nothing like it. At least for me." She undid his belt and pulled down his zipper. He let her do this, too. He had never been with a woman this hypnotically sexy; he knew he never would be again. He tried to memorize every detail of her smile and her breasts and even her fingers, as his underwear and his pants slid down to his ankles and he stepped out of them. She started to kneel to pull off his socks, but he stopped her and stepped out of them, too, so—like her—he was naked.

"How long have you lived here?" he asked. "In America?"

"Shhhhhh," she whispered, and her dark eyes seemed to sparkle. "Shhhhhh." She stepped backward toward the bed, pulling him with her by holding both of his hands.

...

In the end, they hadn't had sex in the guest room. For a long moment he had stood above her as she sat on the bed, her feet—so small, the arches petite and erotically incurvate, he remembered, the nail polish on her toes an unexpectedly childlike pink—dangling a few inches off the floor. He'd gazed down when he felt her hand reach out to him. He saw the nail polish on her fingers matched the color on her toes.

But instead he ran his own hands along the skin of her thighs and felt the goose bumps. Her skin was smooth and tight, but all he could sense was the reality that the poor thing was cold. And instantly he had taken a step back.

As drunk as he was, there was still some small part of his temporal lobe that recalled he was married. That recalled he was a father.

As drunk as he was, he realized that this had all gone too far. Too ridiculously far. What in the name of God was he doing about to fuck a stripper—no, she wasn't a stripper; she was a prostitute, a call girl, an escort, a whore—at a bachelor party? This was crazy.

Moreover this slight young thing on the bed had to be a whole lot closer to his daughter's age than to his. She was remarkably beautiful and she was his for the moment if he wanted her, but she was somewhere between eighteen (*please,* he thought to himself, *please, please be at least eighteen*) and maybe twenty-two or twenty-three. Maybe. But probably not.

The realization made him shudder with self-loathing.

"No," he said simply, the syllable as much a small cry as it was an actual word. "No."

The girl leaned forward on the bed and he thought she understood. She didn't. Instead, she looked up with a smile—gloriously feigned wantonness—and raised an eyebrow knowingly. She leaned toward him, opening her mouth. Gently he pushed her away, two fingers on each of her temples. "Thank you," he said, the words awkward and obvious and pathetic, "but no." Already he feared that he had forever forfeited much of the self-esteem that came with the titles of husband and father. Were not those lap dances downstairs—those mind-blowing, frictive, erotically aerobic balletics—sufficiently incriminating? Of course they were. And this? Worse. Obviously worse. He was heaving inside with regret, regret at what he had already done and regret at what he was giving up. "I'm married."

She shrugged. "I figured."

"No. I meant . . ." and his voice trailed off. After a moment he began again: "I didn't know this was going in . . . in this direction," he said simply.

She seemed to think about what he had said, and he wondered if she didn't speak enough English to understand the meaning of *this direction.* But before he had even started to elaborate, she asked, "Would you like to just talk?" She patted the mattress beside her, encouraging him to sit down.

"Maybe downstairs we can talk," he mumbled. "I mean . . . we should return to the party."

"You're a sweet man," she said, and weak-kneed he gave in and sat down beside her. He wrapped his arm around her, hoping to warm her. And there they did talk. He asked about her family and was saddened by the reality that she had none. He told her that his wife was a schoolteacher, and how the two of them loved to watch their daughter dance. How two years ago their daughter had been obsessed with Brownie badges. With Barbies, which already she had outgrown.

"Oh, I loved Barbies, too."

"Even in Armenia?"

"Even in Armenia. I had lots of them."

"Really? How?"

"It's long story how I got them. How I got so many."

"Tell me."

But she hadn't, because it was clear the party downstairs was growing especially feral, and he feared he had better return. They both felt the alarm from the internal clocks they'd set when they had started upstairs going off. She hopped off the bed first, leaned into him, her hands on his thighs, and kissed him on the cheek. "Your wife is lucky girl."

He saw the goose bumps had returned to her thighs. "Can I get you a blanket? You could wear it like a shawl, maybe. You're still cold."

"Not really. I'm fine."

And then she watched him get dressed, serene and unashamed by her own nakedness. She talked about what a lovely (she used that very word) man he was, and how kind he seemed. She said she liked the tone of his voice and his stories. She said she liked his smile. When he was done, she rose on her toes as if she were a ballerina and kissed him on the lips, though it was oddly chaste and Richard imagined it was the way a woman might kiss a former lover when she was saying good-bye for the last time. It was perfect in its own way, and Richard thought to himself with optative sadness that *this* was why men fell in love with strippers and escorts: it wasn't the licentiousness, the dissembling, their craven willingness to do whatever you wanted. It was the way they would, out of the blue, surprise you with the psychic ability to know what you needed. He reached into the back pocket of his pants for his wallet, uncharacteristically bloated with bills, and pulled out the fifties and hundreds he had withdrawn from the bank that day for . . . for whatever . . . and gave her all that was left. Nine hundred dollars, he thought. She thanked him and joked that she really had no place to put it.

"When you get dressed, you will," he said.

As they were walking down the stairs, her arm hooked in his as if they were promenading along some nineteenth-century boardwalk, she said, "You can tell everyone we fucked. They'll think we did anyway."

He stopped on the landing and looked at her. How had he managed to miss the fact that her eyes were a velvet brown and the most impeccably shaped almonds he'd ever seen? Her nose was the tiniest ski jump. He decided that she had the most genuinely heart-shaped face in the world, a face that was angelic despite what she did for a living, and he told himself he would believe this even when he was sober. He tried to ameliorate his guilt by reminding himself that, in the end, he had resisted her. He had resisted this naked young thing beside him now on the landing on the stairs of his home, despite the way she had happily yielded herself to him.

He shook his head. Happily? She was a hooker, he told himself, trying (and failing) to be dismissive. She was getting paid to make him feel this way. He had just given her nearly a grand on top of whatever Spencer had spent to line this up. But, the truth was, he was under her spell. She was smart, that was clear. She was kind; that was clear, too. He flashed back to the moment in the living room when she had followed the blonde onto his lap, and she had been grinding her crotch against him. She had brought her face close to his, her lips resting within a millimeter of his; he would have kissed her then, but he still assumed there was a line he was not to cross or the bodyguards would whisk her off of him. He remembered how he had kept his hands on the cushions of the couch, afraid even to run his fingers along the tow-colored down of her arms.

How much had he given her then? A fifty? A hundred? He honestly couldn't recall.

He realized now that she was saying something to him, and he tried to swim up to the surface from the swamplike morass of alcohol and desire and (in the end) self-loathing that were muffling the sounds all around him. She was reiterating that he could say whatever he wanted about what had occurred in the guest room upstairs.

They'll think we did anyway. For a split second he thought he was going to vomit.

. . .

As Richard was walking through his front door, one of the police investigators was making a production of properly swabbing the blood on the tile in the front hallway, while another was methodically dusting for fingerprints and daubing for DNA. They had powder blue surgical booties over their shoes. He saw a third investigator dropping one of the spent shell casings into a clear plastic evidence bag. The fellow had found it—one of two—near the coat rack. "Probably from a Makarov," he'd mumbled when he'd seen that Richard was watching him. "Nine millimeter."

Now he wandered into his living room. The family cat, a five-year-old torty they'd gotten from the shelter as a kitten and christened Cassandra, was sitting atop the breakfront, surveying the activity. She seemed relieved he wasn't another stranger. One of the investigators, a decorous, skull-faced little fellow with receding yellow hair, saw Richard and put down his scissors. He was about to snip a small piece of the bloodstained fabric from one of the arm covers that went with the couch, as well as a piece of the fabric from the back.

"Who are you?" he asked Richard, his tone quizzical.

"I live here. I'm Richard Chapman." He started to extend his hand, but the technician wanted no part of it.

"How did you get in?"

"The front door," Richard told him, measuring his tone.

"Okay, then," the technician said, and he picked up the scissors. "Fine. Let's just allow people to traipse all over the crime scene. What the hell do I know? Must be a new policy. I assume you don't mind that I'm gathering evidence," he said sarcastically, and gave him a pair of booties to wear.

"No, of course not," Richard told him. How could he possibly mind? Besides, at this point he really didn't care about the couch. Good Lord, they were going to have reupholster the whole damn thing. No: they were going to have to get rid of the whole damn thing. They were going to have to buy a new one. Richard told him again that it was fine to cut apart the fabric. They could shred it for all he cared.

The detective who seemed to be supervising the crime scene saw he was talking to the technician and came over to him.

"Not quite the party you were planning," she said to him, her tone more sympathetic than judgmental. She was tall and scholarly looking, her afro cut short, her eyes masked by a pair of tortoise-shell eyeglasses. She was dressed, he decided, like a bank teller. Not a detective. But then, he really wasn't sure how detectives dressed. All he knew about detectives was what he saw on cop dramas on TV. But she was wearing dark slacks, a turtleneck, and a navy blue cardigan sweater. Other than him, she was the only person in the house whose hands weren't hidden beneath a pair of thin rubber gloves the color of a condom. He noticed that her fingers were long and slender. A pianist's hands.

"No, it wasn't," he agreed. He gazed at the debris in the room. She could have sounded considerably more disapproving. She *should* have sounded more disapproving. The room looked ruined: beer bottles, some overturned, littered the floor, their contents dribbling onto the Oriental carpet and the long, solid planks of dark maple. There were broken wineglasses, three that he could see, one shattered and two with the stems merely snapped off from the goblets. It was like they had been beheaded. He saw the bottles, some empty and some merely half empty, of red wine and white wine and vodka and tequila and scotch crowded onto the credenza: smokestacks, he thought, an industrial wasteland. There was a plastic jug of orange juice because Chuck Alcott had been drinking screwdrivers. One of the side tables was so ringed with the marks from glasses and beer cans that it would need to be refinished. Or, perhaps, burned. He should just take an ax to it. Throw the pieces into the fireplace that winter.

"May I ask your name?" he asked the woman.

"Of course. I'm Patricia Bryant."

"I'm Richard."

"I know." Then: "Can I help you with something?"

"No. Probably not."

"Then I think you need to leave."

"I live here."

She nodded ever so slightly. "No one told you, did they? They should have. I'm sorry, but this is a crime scene. You can't be here. I can show you the search warrant if you want. I have no idea how you even got inside: someone should have stopped you."

He wanted to argue, but he knew it would be fruitless. So he calmed himself and asked, "Can I get a few things—for my family? A few shirts, maybe?"

"No. Again, I'm sorry. This is an open investigation. I'm sure you have friends you can stay with. It will just be for a few days."

"My wife is on her way back here from the city."

"I suggest you stop her." Then she gave him a friendly, almost conspiratorial smile. "I mean, you're probably in enough trouble with her as it is."

He looked at his watch. Kristin wouldn't leave her mother's for at least another half hour. He dreaded the call.

Patricia motioned at the bookcases and the spines of the novels that were ruined, the streaks and spots of blood creating a vibrant chiaroscuro against the paler cover designs. "My team can take some of those dust jackets off your hands."

"God, take the books, too. Please."

"Okay."

Almost as one, the two of them glanced at the painting, the wannabe Bierstadt, which had also been sprayed with the body-guard's blood. A great swash went across the trees and the Wedg-wood sky and the small cliff that slid gracefully into the smoky blue of the Hudson. An idea came to him and he said, "When I was at the police station, someone gave me a card for a cleaning service. Any suggestions for someone who restores paintings?"

"Professionally? No. But my cousin teaches in the art history department at NYU. She'll know someone."

"Think it's salvageable?"

"My cousin would know. I don't. But maybe."

"Thanks."

He glanced down at the rug where earlier that evening his brother—his engaged brother—had had sex with the blond whore. Sonja? Yes, that was what she had said her name was. He couldn't decide if he should tell the detective that they should look for traces of the woman's skin or hair there. They would find his brother's DNA; God, they would find his fucking semen. But it's not like his brother was a suspect in the two murders. When they had been at the police station, the principal thing the detectives there had wanted to know was the name of the escort service that Philip's pal, Spencer, had used in Manhattan. Spencer was, in fact, the only one they had really grilled about anything.

Nevertheless, his brother was going to have an awful lot to explain to his fiancée, Nicole. (Of course, Nicole's own brother was not innocent either. Eric had been among the men who, separately, had disappeared into some dark corner of the house with the blonde for God knew what sort of carnal satisfactions.) He wondered if their engagement would survive this. He wondered if his own marriage would survive this. He told himself it would because Kristin's heart was forgiving and big, and they had over a decade and a half together—because, pure and simple, they loved each other—but he had screwed up. All the men had. And, when he thought about the reactions of grown women such as Kristin and Nicole, his mind couldn't help but wander to Melissa's response. How in the world was he ever going to explain this to his nine-year-old daughter? He and Kristin had sometimes joked about how politicians described their sexual misconduct to their children. If you were Bill Clinton, how did you justify Monica Lewinsky to Chelsea? What did you say about the cigar and the beret and the little blue dress? If you were Anthony Weiner, how in the world did you explain to your daughter your apparently insatiable need to text pictures of your junk to strange women?

"You're welcome," Patricia said. Then: "What do you do for a living? Someone said banker."

"Investment banker, yes. Franklin McCoy."

"And your brother?"

"Hotelier."

She raised an eyebrow good-naturedly at the pretentiousness of the word.

"He's a manager at the Cravat. The rooms executive."

"Hip place in Chelsea?"

"That's the one."

She folded her arms across her chest and sighed. "You seem like a nice enough guy," she began. "I'm sure you never expected this level of madness in your living room."

"Nope. Never did."

"It really is—pardon my French—a shitstorm. Can I ask you something?"

"Of course."

"You ever hang with girls like this before?"

Girls like this. He tried to decide what the detective meant. He couldn't, so he said simply, "No."

"Don't go to strip clubs after work?"

"I don't."

"Good for you."

"Thank you. I guess."

"Lots of men do."

He nodded. He knew his brother did.

"And—not judging, just asking—no escort service under some secret code in your phone?"

"Again, no."

She glanced at the spot on the floor where a few hours ago a buffed Russian pimp had bled out. "Where were you when the first dude was stabbed?"

He pointed at the nailhead chest—a polished mahogany—where Kristin often placed a vase with flowers. Resting atop it now were yet more open liquor bottles, dirty glasses, and a bowl of old guacamole that looked like baby poop. Someone had extinguished a cigarette in it. Spencer, he guessed. When he looked a little more closely, he saw there were actually a couple of cigarette butts in it.

"What did you do when you saw the girl had a knife?"

"It happened so fast, there really was nothing to do. One second she was stabbing him, and the next she was in the hallway."

"She. The blond one?"

"Yes."

"Then what."

"As I told your associates at the police station, we heard the gunshots."

"Two?"

"That's right. Seriously, I've answered all these questions."

"I appreciate that. We all do," she said. "Thank you."

"You're welcome."

"You're doing me personally a solid by answering a few more. Making my life a little easier." She smiled. "So one of the girls stabbed the first pimp, and the other girl shot the second one."

"I don't know that for sure. The blonde left the living room and was with her . . . friend . . . in the hallway when we heard the shots. So it could have been either girl, I guess. But I think it was the blonde."

"Why?"

"She seemed a little more . . . wild."

"Uh-huh."

"I mean, I guess it could have been either."

"Gotcha. Now I'm not a prosecutor, Mr. Chapman, but two people were murdered in your house. You and your friends and your brother were engaging in sex with girls who—"

Reflexively he cut her off. "I didn't."

"I was told you went upstairs with one."

"But we didn't have sex."

"Fine. But this"—and she waved her arm across the carnage as if she were a game show host—"will be all over the Internet. In the newspapers. On TV. Franklin McCoy? It seems to me you have a reputation to protect. And based on whose bodies are in the morgue right now and the statements of some of your guests, there is a chance that the little eye candy you had dancing around your living room were not prostitutes. They were underage sex slaves. Big difference."

He wasn't sure whether it was the word *underage* or the term *sex slaves* that caused his legs to buckle, but suddenly he had collapsed onto the faux antique divan. It was supposed to look French. Think a king named Louis and some roman numerals. It was from the Ethan Allen showroom in Hartsdale. He remembered the day when he and Kristin had bought it. It was a Sunday, maybe a week after they had moved out to Bronxville. Melissa had been a toddler on a play date. He and Kristin had had a lovely, intimate brunch, their world alive with promise. He closed his eyes, and the day came back to him, even the sun on his face when he'd climbed into the car and they'd started back to their new home. They were young, and he felt impossibly rich for a guy in his early thirties. He would soon be a managing director. Someday, if he stayed on this track, he would be a managing director and head of mergers and acquisitions. He felt—and this was a word too saccharine in his opinion to figure with any regularity in his mind—blessed.

When he finally opened his eyes and looked up, Patricia was handing him a glass of water.

"I thought we might lose you there for a minute," she said.

He took a sip. "They were in their twenties," he told her adamantly, though he honestly wasn't sure. The one in his bedroom? Alexandra? She might have been sixteen or seventeen. It was possible. She was just so . . . so tiny. He thought of the goose bumps on her thighs. The pink nail polish. "Maybe early twenties," he added. "But they weren't children."

"Well, we'll find out when we catch them."

He knew the basics of their getaway: the girls had taken the black Escalade that belonged to one of the Russians and driven to the Bronxville train station. There they had dumped the vehicle and—at least this was what everyone seemed to believe—gotten on the last train going into Manhattan. Whether they had gotten off at Grand Central or 125th Street or any of the stops after Bronxville right now was anyone's guess, but everyone seemed to presume they had gone all the way to Forty-second Street. And from there? At the moment, they had disappeared. They could have hopped a subway in Grand Central in any direction or taken a cab to any borough—even one of the airports, where, if they had the right sort of help, they might be boarding an airplane right now. They were believed to have two handguns, since both of the dead Russians' holsters were empty, and thus considered very dangerous. Kristin's carving knife was gone, too, though it was hard to conceal something that large, and so one of the officers at the police station had suggested that the girls had probably thrown it away at some point during their getaway.

"This might be a naive question," he asked Patricia now.

"Go ahead."

"If they were sex slaves . . . and we didn't know that . . . are we in legal trouble?"

"Question for a lawyer. But what you didn't know doesn't matter to the law."

"And we didn't pay for sex. We paid for what I guess is called 'exotic dancing.' At least that's what I think we did."

"So the sex was just because you guys are so irresistible?"

"I'm just saying, it wasn't prostitution—or it wasn't supposed to be."

"Again: answer's above my pay grade."

"Can I ask one more thing?"

"Given how impressively unhelpful I have been, I can't see why you would want to. But, please, go ahead."

"If the Russians were holding the girls as . . ."

"Sex slaves," she said, finishing the sentence for him. "Two words. Only hard to say them if you might have one in your house—or as a daughter."

"Sex slaves. I get it. If the girls were prisoners like that, hadn't they the right to kill their captors?"

"You really think that's how the judicial system works? Smart investment banker like you?"

He ran one of his hands through his hair. "Got it."

"Life's not an Xbox game."

"No," he agreed. "It's not."

"Besides: those two girls are a lot better off if we find them first."

"First?"

"Before their—and please hear the sarcasm in my voice—managers. Bosses. I don't know who those two dudes on ice are. Their wallets are gone. I'm sure the IDs in those wallets would have been false anyway. Completely made up."

"Couldn't you figure out who they are by their DNA?"

"You've watched too many cop dramas on TV. CODIS only helps if we have their DNA on file. Unless they have criminal records, there's no reason to believe we would."

"Same with the two girls?"

"That's right. Which is too bad for them. Because those two

corpses the M.E. will autopsy in the morning? They weren't working alone. And even if they were pretty low on the food chain,
there are still going to be some seriously pissed-off people out there
who want those girls back: either they'll want to put them back to
work because they are just so incredibly lucrative or they'll want
to kill them. And if I were a betting woman, I would bet the latter. They'll want to make sure their other girls don't think for one
second they can get away with this sort of . . . disobedience. Let's
face it: as lucrative as those girls might have been, they're still just a
commodity. They're just not all that hard to replace."

He finished the last of his water and stood up. He took a step
and stumbled, nearly falling into the credenza. He held up his hands
for Patricia. "Not drunk," he said. "At least not . . . anymore."

"Just clumsy?"

"I am clumsy. I really am. You would not believe the ridiculous
things I've done in my life," he said, recalling the Audi as it rolled
backward down his driveway. "But just now? That was just me
being . . ."

"Shaken?"

"Yeah. Shaken." He knew he had to call Kristin and tell her
to remain at her mother's. Tell her that he'd join her there. He had
to tell her that she couldn't come home. And in a few hours—he
would wait until eight-thirty as a courtesy, but not a second
later—he would call his lawyer, Bill O'Connell. The very idea
that he needed Bill for something like this caused his stomach once
more to lurch, and he made a mental note to try and recall every
single thing he had said at the police station. God, how drunk had
he been that he hadn't called Bill right away?

"One more thing," the detective said.

"Yes?"

She tilted her head toward the top of the breakfront. "You will
need to take your cat with you."

He glanced up at Cassandra. Sure enough, she was still watching them.

"Okay. Sure. Of course."

"But take nothing else. The rest of your life? Has to stay right here."

He saw the world was starting to lighten outside the eastern window, a thin, quavering band of bleached sky. He realized he was dreading the sunrise: it would illuminate just how much his world had changed since yesterday—and how damaged was the little bark that carried his soul, how far it was from the shore, and how menacing were the waves in between. No one, he knew, was ever going to look at him quite the same way again.

Alexandra

The day after my mother died, Vasily appeared at our apartment, this time with bouquets of flowers. And jars of honey for my grandmother. And traditional pomegranate wine. And less traditional but more modern Armenian red wine. And a necklace for me. And a Bible. And, surrounding him like marble columns and carrying all these presents, two hulking Russian dudes in black suits and shaved heads. You know the look. Gangster. Vasily called them his security. I had seen these guys or guys like them around him before. Vasily owned that brandy factory in Yerevan and another one in Volgograd. He was very big deal. Or at least he thought he was very big deal. Looking back, why would a brandy factory executive need security? I thought it was just vanity. I thought he just wanted to feel like even bigger shot than he was. Nope. It was because of his other businesses—mostly businesses involving girls like me—that he wanted thugs all around him. You probably don't need bashers if all you do is make brandy.

My grandmother and I were both in shock those days. Those weeks. Those months. Neither of us was at our best or thinking straight. Maybe if my mother had not just died, we would have seen through Vasily's bullshit.

He claimed that he knew people in the Moscow Ballet. He said they were *important* people. He told my grandmother this in a hushed voice, as if the truth was so great it could only be spoken in whispers. He added that he would tell my dance teacher this, too.

But maybe I would never have seen through his lies. Remember, I was a kid who loved ballerinas. It was just a few years earlier I had been playing with dolls.

...

My dance teacher was named Seta Nazarian and she had the most beautiful curly hair. Her eyes always were smiling. Her heart was big. But she was tough on her dancers, and I think she missed how orderly the world was when it was communist. Sometimes I worry she would have been in difficult position if she and Vasily had ever spoken. Looking back, I'm honestly not sure she believed I was so good it would have been worth a trip to Moscow for me to audition. Maybe she would have thought so. But maybe not. Would she have guessed what Vasily had in mind and protected me? Again, I'll never know. But I don't think she would have figured it out. She probably would have decided I was long shot for the company. But I was a good student and a good dancer. I really was the best in her class. I think she would have liked what it said about her if I had wound up in the ballet in Moscow. The old communist inside her would have been proud. So I had to try. I think she would have let me.

But we'll never know. Maybe I'm just kidding myself.

Vasily said the plan was for me to train for the audition with a special coach he knew in Moscow. I would train for three months before the audition. He promised my grandmother that I would go to school, too. All the girls and boys in the company did. The dancers, he said, were all very good students. Most made it into the company, but the few (and he said it was very small number) who did not become dancers came home with very good educations. He said this was a detail that he knew would have been important to my mother, but he looked at me like this was not something I needed to worry about. His eyes said I would be a dancer for sure. It was late in the afternoon and the sun was setting and the big room that was the only room other than the kitchen and our two bedrooms was getting dark. I remember thinking that moment how much I missed my mother. I had been living alone with Grandmother since my mother had gone to hospital for the last time. My grandmother was sixty-two and had seemed to age many years in the last months of my mother's life. It wasn't just that her hair now was the gray of cigarette ash. Her eyes were red because she seemed to begin and end her day with tears, and she seemed always to have a cold. She seemed always to have sores on her arms. I worried that I was a burden, since obviously nurses do not make oligarch kinds of money. Besides, it was almost time for her to retire.

So, going with Vasily and his marble column bodyguards to Russia to become a ballet dancer was no-brainer. It really was. I went.

...

When I was twelve, I sold my Barbies on a folding table on a street in Yerevan. I was too old for them. I sold them to tourists for lots of money, which probably sounds crazy since tourists come from places where you can buy all the Barbies you want. But if I sold them to younger girls or their mothers or fathers in my neighborhood, I wouldn't have made very much money. Those people didn't have very much money. It wouldn't have been worth it. The tourists from California and New Jersey bought my Barbies because my mother and I dressed them up in traditional Armenian clothes we made ourselves. For instance, for one doll we sewed an ankle length red wedding dress with a gold lace apron. For others, we embroidered beautiful white lace scarves and shawls. We cut out elegant blue velvet vests and trimmed tiny strips of leather into tiny belts.

I was allowed to keep all the money I made because we didn't need it for food or the rent. Both my mother and my grandmother were working. We weren't rich, but two jobs is two jobs. We did okay. I bought my mother some earrings and a necklace from a vernissage vendor as gifts to thank her for helping me make all those clothes and because I loved her. I bought my grandmother a new dress. For me, I bought blue jeans and a handbag and new leotards. I bought new ballet slippers.

And while I had a big collection, I was never the most loony of Russian or Armenian Barbie doll lovers. There were far worse. I read about one girl in the Ukraine who, when she was a young woman, dieted and worked out and dieted some more, and then had her boobs done so she would look like human Barbie. Vasily, if he had known how much I loved Barbies, would probably have paid whatever it cost to make me look like human Barbie, too. I still remember the first time I heard a boob job referred to as "plastic surgery." I smiled because my brain made a big jump to the dolls I had loved when I was a little girl.

A few days after I sold the dolls, when I was beside my mother's desk at the brandy factory—just visiting for some reason before dance class—Vasily would compliment me on my new jeans. My mother got seriously pissed: at him and at me. The jeans were tight, which was why I liked them.

I don't know, maybe this was the beginning of my end. It was the first time that Vasily took notice of me as, well, a hot chick. But I really was only twelve.

Maybe I just should have given away all those Barbies to the girls in the classes behind me at school. Maybe everything would have been different.

But maybe not. Maybe I was just destined for badness.

You'll see.

. . .

This is how insane things were for me and how quickly my life changed: one afternoon I was walking like I did most days each week from my school to the dance studio. I had a little canvas dance bag with my ballet slippers and toe shoes inside it over my shoulder. The next afternoon I was on an airplane for the first time in my life. I was going to Moscow. Now my ballet slippers and toe shoes were in a handsome black suitcase that Vasily gave me. He called it a "rollie" because it had wheels, and we both laughed.

I stood for a long time at the big windows by a gate at the Yerevan airport and looked at Ararat, thinking how maybe when I next saw the mountain I would be on my way to becoming a ballerina at the opera house. Maybe I would *be* a ballerina at the opera house. I thought this to myself: someday I will bathe in the footlights like a star.

And maybe it was the word *star*, which is just a sun, but then I thought of Icarus and I had a little shudder of fear. Maybe I was more like Icarus than Velvet Bird, and my wings were just wax. Maybe they would melt in the hot lights and I would fall.

...

Vasily's assistant and I boarded the plane together. His name was Andrei, which is very common Russian name, and he had been with me since picking me up at my home in a black stretch limousine. (He called it a "stretchie." Looking back, how innocent does a world seem where grown men use words like *rollie* and *stretchie*?) We sat in the very back of the car, but in the very front of the airplane. I only saw the face of our stretchie's driver when he took our rollies and put them in the trunk, and when he opened the back doors for us. In the car, I focused on the refrigerator built into the seat, which was no less glamorous to me because it was empty, and the side or the back of Andrei's massive neck as he looked at the streets and casinos and the clubs with the strippers—neon versions of naked women over their entrances—on the way to the Yerevan airport.

Andrei was not a big talker. But he was a big smoker. You can't smoke inside the airport or on an Aeroflot jet, which he understood going in, but he was still not happy about it. He kept taking his Jackpot Golds out of his black suit pocket and fingering the box like it was an actual gold brick. Opening and closing the cardboard lid. He was thirty years old, with a shaved head and no mustache or beard. His shoulders seemed the size of a couch, his neck a pillar at the temple at Garni. He could barely fit into his airplane seat and complained lots. But I loved my seat. I had a window. I tilted the seat back almost like chair in my dentist's office.

I figured I shouldn't ask Andrei too many questions: this was a gift, after all, and you do not look a gift horse in the mouth. (I first heard that expression before going down on an American telecommunications executive in his hotel room in Moscow. He had expected a blonde, which I am not, and he was disappointed. I made sure he got over it. At the time, however, and for many months afterward, I believed the expression was this: you do not look a gift in the mouth because it will make you hoarse. I believed the expression was some old superstition about being grateful for all gifts. Speak bad of them, and maybe you'd lose your voice.) Besides, Andrei worked for a wealthy brandy factory president, so I figured he was important, too. Finally he fell asleep on the plane. I stayed awake all the way to Moscow, listening to the sounds of the engines and enjoying the colas and apple juice that the flight attendants kept bringing me. I read the book and the magazine I had carried with me. I watched other people watching movies on their computers or their tablets. This was the most glamorous thing I had ever done, except dance. (Dancing—real dancing on a real stage, not teasing men in my lingerie—will always be the most glamorous thing I ever did.) I felt like royalty.

Some girls asked me later why I was not suspicious. They wanted to know why I thought Vasily was spending all this money on me: airplane tickets, the chance to study dance in Moscow, a place to stay. One girl said I must have been a mountain-sized dope not to have known that something was up. Maybe. But I just thought Vasily was doing it for my mother. I thought he cared about her because she had been his secretary for so many years—and that meant he cared about me. I thought this was my break, my future.

I believed that. Really I did.

...

What did my dance teacher think? Even though her name was Seta, we always called her Madame as students. I will never know what she thought because she wasn't at the studio when I went to share with her my good news and say good-bye. She had been told by some government official that there was a permit issue with her studio space—which meant that someone wanted a bribe—and she was trying to straighten out the problem with the bureaucrat at his office. Andrei and one more of Vasily's bodyguards brought me there to tell her about my audition. But in Madame's place at the studio was an assistant named Maria, who was kind of a dull knife. Still, she was happy for me. She was teaching one of the classes of little girls. She thought this was all very exciting and—because she always seemed to say the first thing that came into her head—told me how surprised she was that I was getting this opportunity and not Nayiri. She implied that Nayiri was a better dancer. (Nayiri was an excellent dancer, but I was better. As I said, I was the best in the class.) The bodyguards explained that Vasily wanted to do my mother a favor. They did not say, which is what I would have liked them to have said, that Vasily had seen me dance and I had earned this honor. But the truth was that Vasily had never, ever seen me dance, which—in front of Maria—made me uncomfortable. I wanted to say something to defend myself, but there really wasn't anything I could say. I thought I looked nervous that moment in the long wall of studio mirrors. It felt odd to be there in pants instead of my leotard. Still, Maria wished me good luck and said that she would clap for me someday when I was on the stage at the opera house.

But it was disappointing for me that Madame was not there. I remember when I told my grandmother that she was gone my voice had broken—which I hadn't expected when I had opened my mouth.

Later I would figure something out: Madame was not at the studio because Vasily did not want her at the studio. The guy had his grubby hands in everything. Everything! He had made sure that Madame was summoned to the government building when I was supposed to be at the studio to say good-bye. Madame knew way more about ballet and my prospects than Maria: she might have tried to stop me from going, even if it would have meant breaking the news to me that I was no Velvet Bird.

But you never know. How do you dim the light of promise? How do you wake someone from such a beautiful dream? How do you break a teenage girl's heart?

...

Here is how you do all three of those things: you take the teenage girl from the Moscow airport to a carefully selected Moscow hotel where you own or have rented all the rooms on a corridor. Then you rape her so violently that when you're done, the girl just puts the sheet with the bloodstain in the gray plastic trash bag that was in the wastepaper basket, so that later she can secretly throw it away.

That is what Andrei did to me.

Then you take away her luggage and her passport and her cell phone, and you have someone stand guard all night long outside her hotel room door so the teenage girl can't run away.

So none of the girls in the other rooms can run away.

Then the next morning, after the teenage girl has somehow cried herself to sleep in the middle of the night, you return with some other young thug and say to the teenage girl, "You take clothes off and suck dick and then we take you home. We promise. This was all big mistake. You are not ready for this life." The girl resists, but then she sees it as her only hope, and so she does it. Somehow she stifles her desire to throw up. She does just what you tell her to do. She does it on her knees for both men. Then for a third. She does more—far more, things she never imagined people did—because this is what you are demanding and because she sees it as her only way home.

Then when she is done, you show her the video you have made. There she is. There you are. Her face is clear. Recognizable. Your face? No one ever sees your face in the video. How clever. You tell her that you will show the video to the whole world— including the girl's grandmother and the reverent fathers and her dance teacher and her schoolteachers and all of her friends—if she doesn't follow your instructions to the letter and do everything you say.

Then, that night, you bring in a woman to convince the teenage girl to eat a little something—and to explain to her just how fucked she really is.

Chapter Four

When Melissa awoke, she could hear her mother and her grandmother speaking in the apartment kitchen, their voices an underwater-like thrum from which only an occasional word would bubble to the surface. She thought the plan was for her mother to go home to Bronxville on the first train; she'd expected that her mother would be gone by now. Apparently, something had changed. She looked at the antique clock on the nightstand—it was so old that a person had to wind it, and the twin bells on the top were lusterless with age—and saw it was not quite seven-thirty. The curtains were drawn on the window, and so she emerged from beneath the quilt and opened one side: it was the sort of city morning where the clouds hung so low that the fog looked a little grimy. She jumped back into bed and curled her body into an egg, wrapping her arms as tightly as she could around her ankles and bringing her forehead to her knees. She liked to lie like this, her eyes shut tight. After a few moments, when she felt her forehead and the back of her neck starting to burn, she would pretend that she was a mythical bird being born, and slowly—as slowly as possible— stretch out her arms and her legs and her torso. She would blink. She would flutter her eyes like a creature seeing the world for the very first time. She would lie like this in the mornings some days before school, just after waking up, but she would also do it some evenings before finally getting undressed and into her pajamas before bed. It was especially fun to do it at the end of the day when she was wearing her more interesting tights. She would sit up and gaze at the patterns, and feel unexpectedly rewarded: the tights that looked like the night sky or the ceiling of a planetarium were always fascinating to her after she had emerged from her egg or (sometimes in her mind) her cocoon. She was intrigued by what the constellations and zodiac signs looked like after opening her eyes and uncoiling her body. She would compare the universe on her legs to the universe her father had created for her on the ceiling of her bedroom, a world of glow-in-the-dark stars (some shooting) and planets (Jupiter, with its playful, winking eye; a cherry red Mars; Uranus, with its celestial hula hoops).

She also liked to do this when she was wearing the tights with the pretend color comics that looked as if they belonged in a Sunday newspaper. She and her parents had gotten that pair at a museum's gift shop a few blocks south on Fifth Avenue. The images were actually paintings by some famous modern artist. But her very favorite tights to be wearing when she was lying like this were the ones with the covers of old children's books on them. Her father had brought them back to her from a business trip to London. She recognized most of the covers, but some were British editions: she knew all of the stories at least a little bit, but it seemed the English used a different image on the front of a lot of their books. They had a different Alice. A different Harry. A different Otter and Badger and Mole. Some of the covers were upside down, but it didn't matter: she would study the characters and designs and recall the stories. She wished the covers didn't stop abruptly near the tops of her thighs.

She was, of course, wearing her pajamas now. Not any of her tights. They were the pajamas she kept at Grandmother's for visits such as these. Red check flannel bottoms. A Snoopy top.

She decided that she should paint her toenails. One of these days when they were in the city, her mother was going to take her for a pedicure. It would be her first—at least her first real one. She had been painting her toenails for years. Before that, her mother had painted them for her. Today they were pink, but the polish was chipped on a few of her nails. Perhaps when she and her mother went to the salon, they might even get what girls on TV called mani-pedis, where you got your toenails and fingernails painted. Very glamorous.

The assistants at her dance studio, the girls who were juniors and seniors in high school, always had their toenails painted. She noticed when they were climbing in and out of their ballet slippers or jazz shoes.

She tried now to hear what her mother and grandmother were saying, but even when she concentrated she could only pick out an occasional word. Clearly they were speaking softly because they didn't want to wake her. Or, perhaps, because they didn't want her to hear. If she were to guess, she would assume it was more because they didn't want her to hear. Her mother was vague about what had happened last night at their home, but Melissa understood two things with certainty: first, something awful had occurred at Uncle Philip's bachelor party, and people had died. Second, her father had done something very, very wrong. Moreover, the combination of awful and her father's behavior had changed the landscape between her parents, and it was—she was sure—a shift that was dangerous. Dangerous for their marriage in ways that she didn't quite understand, and dangerous for her in ways that she did. It threatened the stability of the life that she knew and took for granted.

What precisely had her father done? She had her suspicions. They were as hazy as her mother's explanations, but she knew the basics of sex. She wasn't a moron. She was in the fourth grade. And last night there had been a naked woman in their house. And the men, she conjectured, had fought over her. But was Mom upset because Dad had looked at this other woman? Or had her father done something more? And did that mean he had had sex with her? Or was it Uncle Philip?

She noticed that a strip of the wallpaper was starting to peel where it met the ceiling a couple of feet from the window. There was an ancient water stain—mildew-brown—a few inches above the top of the bedroom's other window. The room, when you gazed at it from the bed, looked a little tired. This weary ceiling was so different from the one in her bedroom at home.

Once more she stretched, elongating her arms and legs—her fingers and toes. (There was some kid song about fingers and toes that they all used to sing in preschool. Perhaps even in kindergarten. She wished she could retrieve it right now, but it was floating somewhere just beyond her mind's reach.) She guessed she should join her mother and grandmother and have some breakfast. Learn what she could. She might even hover for a minute or two just outside the kitchen, in the entryway to the apartment, and eavesdrop.

As she was on her way there, however—as she was walking silently past the apartment's front door—she heard the bing of the elevator on the other side of the door, and then her father's keys. A second later, there he was, opening the door. For a long moment they just stared at each other, neither saying a word. She saw that he had Cassandra with him in the animal's cat carrier. Then he knelt, put the cat carrier on the floor, and wrapped his arms around her. She detected a trace of an unfamiliar perfume—definitely not her mother's. She didn't think he had ever looked worse.

...

Kristin asked her mother to make Melissa breakfast and then led her husband back to the guest bedroom, where only a few minutes earlier their daughter had been fast asleep. The only chair in the room was a violin-shaped monster that must have been designed by Torquemada—usually it just held clothes when they were visiting, and sometimes Melissa's backpack—but this morning Richard sank into it, as if he were shrinking with shame into the seat. But perhaps, Kristin thought as she watched him, she was reading too much into his body language and projecting onto him what she thought he should feel. Maybe he was just hung over. Maybe he was just tired. She noticed that the stubble on his chin was flecked with white. He had bags under his eyes, and her heart opened a little to him. God. What he had seen. There was no eyewash in the world that could make that go away . . .

"Have you slept?" he asked her, his voice weary.

"Not since you called. I presume you haven't either."

He shook his head. "I almost fell asleep on the train. But not really."

"So, tell me everything," she said. "I don't want to know, but I don't think I have a choice. And maybe it will help you to talk about it."

"Why don't you sit down? You look like . . ."

"I look like what?"

"You look like you're about to interrogate me."

His tone surprised her. He probably hadn't meant to sound hostile, but he had. "Well, you would know what it's like to be interrogated, wouldn't you?" she countered.

"Kris, please."

She sat down on the bed. She rested her hands in her lap, a conscious attempt not to appear adversarial.

"You know how sorry I am," he said. "I know what a disaster this is. All I thought . . . all I thought was that I was giving my idiot younger brother a bachelor party. I'm the best man. It's what you do, right?"

"I know. And he is an idiot."

"And I thought it would be more . . . wholesome . . . having it at home. Our home. I mean, I could have had it at someplace sleazy. But I didn't."

"No," she agreed, "you didn't"—though inside she was wishing now that he had.

"You know? Home delivery wings? A vat of guac? Beer? It just all went crazy. And it went crazy so weirdly fast."

"Of course, that is your brother's modus operandi. If you have a choice between partying like a grown-up and partying like a frat boy on spring break, he will always pick the latter."

"It's so true . . ."

"Why don't you start at the beginning?"

"The beginning of the party? Or when the strippers arrived?"

"Please: stop calling them strippers. They weren't strippers."

"Okay."

She glanced down at her pantyhose and her skirt. It seemed hours ago that she had gotten dressed. In the half darkness, she had put on the skirt and the blouse that she had planned to wear that Saturday anyway. It was a matinee sort of skirt. Broadway pantyhose. Black with little pin dots. She liked it when she spent a day or a night (or a weekend) in Manhattan; she could dress in ways that she never could when she was teaching American history at a suburban high school. Half the time when she went to work, she was dressed as casually as the kids in her class.

No, that wasn't quite right. The girls dressed considerably more provocatively. She recalled one of her first days at the school, another teacher—a history teacher named Amy Doud—had asked Kristin to accompany her on crack patrol. Initially, Kristin had been horrified, presuming this was some sort of drug interdiction. She found the very idea that there might be kids doing crack in a suburb this tony a little chilling. But it wasn't about drugs at all. It was about enforcing the dress code. Kristin had watched as Amy walked softly up behind a pretty, coquettish young thing at her locker, the girl's navy thong riding an inch or two up on her hips and above the top of her immaculate white jeans. There was the upside-down triangle of fabric at the very small of her back, the girl's flesh around it shaped into a pair of perfectly formed meringues below the elastic band and a belt-wide strip of skin above it. Amy had deftly—and with preternatural speed—given the girl a wedgie so sudden and so pronounced that the student had been lifted up onto her toes in her flip-flops and squealed. "Dress code," Amy reminded the girl. "Pull that shirt down and those pants up." Then she had turned to Kristin and shrugged. "The glamorous life of a schoolteacher on crack patrol," she said, smirking ever so slightly. "In truth, I do get a little pleasure from this. I really do. Once upon a time, I guess, I was kind of a mean girl."

Now Richard cleared his throat and began. At first, Kristin found herself occasionally interrupting him with a question or a need for clarification—Was it Eric or this Brandon person who first ran his fingers under the front of the girl's G-string? Did Spencer know he was buying sex and not stripping? Did Philip?—but soon it was a blur. It was a rush of images, her mind unsure which she found more nightmarish: her husband naked in the guest room with a whore or a pair of dead men in their house. Her composure unraveled. Suddenly she was crying, her shoulders caving in as she hunched over into her sobs, and she was vaguely aware that Richard had risen from the chair and wanted to sit beside her on the bed. To put his arms around her. But before he could, she swatted at his hands and stood, her posture erect and her back flush against the closet door.

"Don't touch me," she said, weeping in a way that she hadn't in years. "Please, Richard, don't touch me. Not this second."

"Kris—"

"Just tell me the truth. I don't think I want to know, but I have to. I have to. Did you fuck that girl in the guest room?"

"No. I swear it: I did not."

"But she touched you."

"She tried. I stopped her."

She took a breath, sniffled. "So you expect me to believe that you went upstairs with her and took off all your clothes, but you didn't fuck her? Didn't allow her to . . ." and the words trailed off. She could bring herself to say the word *fuck,* a verb in this case of anger and aggression, but somehow she could not verbalize any other act of sexual intimacy. Her mind thought them: Hand job. Blow job. But she could not say such things. It was, pure and simple, too nightmarish for her to bring those visions to life in this room.

"No," he was saying. "I remembered myself. I love you. I love you and I knew this had crossed a line. So I stopped. I swear to you: I pulled back from that sort of . . . adultery."

"Did you kiss her?" she pressed him, her jaw tightening.

He paused and she looked across the room at him. And she knew. Even through her tears, she knew. She could see it in his eyes. Of course he had.

"For God's sake," she cried. "I can still smell her on you."

. . .

Richard knew she was right, but hoped desperately that she was wrong. His wife probably could smell the girl on him. Had things not ended so badly, he would have showered—two, three, God, maybe four times—before Kristin and Melissa came home on Sunday morning. Obviously. He would have scrubbed from his skin all traces of the sordid debauch. But, of course, that hadn't happened. On his way to his mother-in-law's with Cassandra—a man and his cat, how strangely tame he must have appeared to the train conductor and cabbie—he had deluded himself into believing that he stunk only of the random odors of any party. Alcohol. Nachos. Sweat. Cigarette smoke. The pungent aroma of field grass and blueberries just starting to rot that he associated with marijuana. But his wife was right. The perfume and musk of the girl lingered. He carried it on his clothes like pollen.

Now he met Kristin's eyes for a second as she leaned against the closet door like someone about to be shot, but then he glanced down at his shoes. It wasn't her eyes, as sad as they were, that caused him to look away. It was her face: it was so drained of color, it was as if she had the flu. It was the tears he saw running down her cheeks. It was the fact that she didn't want him to touch her. He noticed that he was still wearing his black wingtips; he couldn't recall the last time he had been wearing his wingtips on a Saturday morning. Probably never.

He had kissed the girl. Of course he had. He had kissed her a couple of times, and he suspected that if the night hadn't ended so disastrously badly, he might never have forgotten their first kiss. She had taken him to the den, away from the party because he was the best man and was going to get something special—something different from the lap dance he had received on the living room couch—and she had sat him down in the easy chair there. She had switched off the light, but the door was open and he could see the side of her face in the light from the hallway. They could still hear the music from the living room. She stepped from her thong so she was naked and climbed into his lap. He was aware—blissfully, if he was honest with himself, blissfully—of the way she was rubbing herself against him, which made the moment seem not merely consensual, but mutual; it was as if she wanted him, too. But he was focused as well on the half smile on her face when he looked up at her, and the way her lids had grown a little heavy with pleasure. Or, perhaps, with feigned pleasure. Still, it sure as hell seemed like she was in the zone with him. And then she locked those dark eyes on his and kept bringing her mouth within a millimeter of his, bobbing her lips beside his and shielding them from the whole world, it seemed, with her hair. She was brushing her cheek against him over and over, as if she were a cat marking him with the side of her face. He could feel her breath on him (peppermint), and it was warm. He never planned to kiss her. He certainly wouldn't have initiated a kiss. After all, he was married. Happily married. He had a beautiful wife. But she seemed as into it as he was when she brought her face down to him again, so wanton and desirous; he could feel her yearning, too. No stripper was this good an actress, he told himself. And so this time when she was teasing him with her half-open mouth, he arched his back and met her. Their lips touched and it was . . . electric. He felt her tongue against his; he felt her fingers on the sides of his face and her breasts against his collarbone.

"You're shaking," she'd whispered into his ear a moment later.

"It's fine," he had whispered back.

They would kiss again before going upstairs, and they would

kiss again on the stairs themselves. Each kiss had left him breathless, the air abruptly gone from his lungs. Had his first kiss with Kristin been like this? Of course it had. It had. It had just been such a long time ago.

But then again, had it really been that . . . hot? Their first kiss had been a few yards from the corner of Fourteenth and Fifth, after he had taken her to dinner for the second time, the kiss just beyond the sight of the doorman for her building. She had not invited him upstairs, both because it was only their second date and because she was one of three young schoolteachers in a two-bedroom sublet. She shared a bedroom with one of the other women. The kiss had been clumsy and brief; neither had been sure when he bent to kiss her on the lips whether their mouths should be open or closed. In the end, the kiss had been a little of both, an awkward hybrid. He remembered walking to the subway a little afraid that she would think he was a bad kisser. They'd never talked about that kiss or laughed about it; he wished, in hindsight, that at some point they had. But then again, maybe not. A few nights later he took her to a Radiohead concert, and they had kissed there. And that kiss had been rock concert hot. They were on their feet amid the noise and the bass, and their kissing grew into the most beautiful, wrenching torment imaginable, and suddenly she was grinding against the thigh of his blue jeans and his hands were under her shirt. Even now whenever either of them pulled some Radiohead vinyl off the shelf, it was a prelude to sex—an aural aphrodisiac, the strawberries of sound.

He took a deep breath and looked up from his shoes at his wife, and he lied. "We kissed once," he said, "sort of. Before I knew what was happening she had kissed me. I pushed her away. It felt wrong and she smelled of cigarettes. It was all too . . . too intimate. I was a little disgusted."

She seemed to think about this, and slowly her body hunched over, her arms now wrapped around her chest—not in defiance, but as if she were ensconced in a straitjacket. She was still crying.

"That's the truth?" she asked.

"That's the truth. Absolutely."

She wiped her eyes, and he went to her. He tried again to wrap an arm around her shoulders, and this time she let him. Her body relaxed into his. He noted that she was wearing some pretty sultry pantyhose, and his mind reeled at the idea that he could even think about having sex with her right now.

...

At precisely eight-thirty that morning, Richard called a lawyer from his mother-in-law's guest bedroom. He was beyond tired, but his hangover was responding to the Advil and the gallons of water he had been drinking; he no longer worried that the excruciating spikes of pain behind his eyes were going to cause him to wilt like a flower in a fast-motion film—to just collapse against a door or a wall with his head in his hands. He rang the fellow who had drawn up Kristin's and his wills and set up their trust, relieved that he had the attorney's home number on his cell phone and that the guy actually picked up. He was pretty sure that Bill O'Connell knew next to nothing about criminal law and probably wouldn't end up representing him—if, please, no, he actually needed representation—but he had to begin somewhere. He was glad now that the attorney was male. The last thing he wanted to do was explain to a woman what happened last night. And, as he expected, Bill told Richard that he wasn't his man. But the firm did have a couple of people who could help him, one who was indeed female, and one who was male. Immediately Richard asked for the home phone of the attorney who was male, but Bill surprised him.

"I think you should call Dina. Sam is very, very good, but Dina is a lot smarter than me—and probably, based on what went on in your home last night, a lot smarter than you. She has to be the smartest person I know. And if you ever do need her as a face—in depositions or in court—it would be great to have a woman."

"I'd really prefer a man, Bill."

"Get over it. Sam is terrific—he really is. But in this case, you'll be a lot better off with Dina."

He swallowed hard. He thought of his wife and his daughter. He had to be smart about this. He took down Dina's number.

"One more thing," Bill said.

"Sure."

"Don't talk to reporters. If you get a call and don't recognize or can't see the number, don't pick up."

"Reporters," he murmured, repeating the single word to himself. He recalled what the detective had said in his living room. "Fuck."

"Yup. Be smart about that, too. Don't say anything. Eventually they will find you. It's their job. When you don't take their calls, they might come to your house. They might come to the building where you work. So postpone the inevitable. By the time they corner you, you can just send them to Dina."

He thought again of Kristin and Melissa, this time imagining what they were going to read about him: his looming public mortification. He wanted to crawl into the bed on which he was sitting and pull the covers over his head. He really did need to sleep. Almost desperately. But he couldn't close his eyes. Not yet, anyway. As soon as he said good-bye to Bill, he called Dina. He must have sounded so pitiable, so pathetically in need, that she agreed to meet him in ninety minutes in her office in midtown. He would have used that time to nap, but he had to shower and shave; he needed to wash last night from his body.

...

In his mother-in-law's elevator, he realized that he was murmuring to himself. He shook his head and told himself he was doing this only because he was overwrought and he was alone. He was in no danger of becoming a street mumbler.

But he did recall how strangely sensitive he became on airplanes, especially when he was traveling alone on business. Movies seemed sadder, novels more poignant. He recalled watching a comedy—a wistful little bauble about a pair of aging lovers—he had seen a few months earlier with Kristin, and this time having to dab discreetly at the edge of his eyes. Another time, about fifteen minutes after takeoff, he had pulled a werewolf novel from his bag and started to read. When the werewolf was killed, he had put the book down and found himself . . . unmoored. Wow, he remembered thinking, you're losing it over a fictional dead werewolf? Seriously? He considered whether he was emotionally stunted.

But maybe it was merely his lack of control on an airplane—every passenger's lack of control on an airplane. A subconscious fear of flying. The reality that flights are often about beginnings and endings.

Then again, perhaps it was just the loneliness—the being alone.

Outside his mother-in-law's building he stood for a moment on the curb. This, he decided, was being alone. It dwarfed the loneliness that could besiege a person at thirty-five thousand feet. He was as alone as he'd ever been in his life.

He shook his head. He gathered himself. He hailed a cab.

. . .

Even though it was a Saturday morning and he was interrupting her weekend, Richard was surprised to see that Dina Renzi was wearing blue jeans, a flannel shirt, and pink and black Keds. But her raincoat was Burberry and her attaché was a Bottega—he knew the weave from the women who carried them in his office—with buttery soft cinnamon-colored leather. He guessed that she was his age, her hair a yellow reminiscent of straw. It was a darker blond than that of the girl who had danced at the party, fucked his younger brother, and then epoxied herself to the back of one of the men who had brought her, stabbing him over and over with a kitchen knife. This morning the lawyer had pulled her hair back into a ponytail; he imagined it snaking its way through the half-moon hole in the back of a ball cap when she wasn't at work, just the way Kristin did with her hair whenever they took in a game at Yankee Stadium. It was a fashion statement that Richard found wholesome and sexy at once. She had two rings on the ring finger of her left hand, both with serious rocks in them.

The firm rented the western half of the nineteenth floor of a building on Park, six blocks north of Grand Central. There were a few younger lawyers working in the office that Saturday, too, also in jeans; two were in one of the firm's conference rooms, the magnificent ash table awash in documents and legal pads, and a third was in his windowless, but still nicely appointed, office.

For what Richard guessed was the fourth time in the last ten hours, he told someone what had occurred. Each time he did, he found himself adding some details while omitting others. He would remember a different moment, a different sensation, a different facial expression. With this lawyer, he kept seeing the faces of the two dead men. He recalled the pudgy hands of the thug—and now they were thugs in his mind, not bodyguards or handlers or managers—who had been shot in the front hall. He thought of the thick gold chain around the neck of the one who had bled out on his living room floor, and how it had sunk partway into the crimson runnel carved into his throat. He was reminded of how he and the other men had cowered during the violence. Not a one had tried to save the poor bastard.

When he had finished, he asked her the question that had been gnawing at him all morning long: "Do you think I am in actual legal trouble?"

"No. At least not criminally. And I really don't see any civil exposure. You're positive there are no videos, correct? No photos?"

"Well, pretty positive. All of the guys were told to keep their phones in their pants."

"Pity they didn't keep everything there. What is your wife thinking?"

"She is thinking I am despicable. As, I guess, I am."

"Is she going to leave you?"

"No. I don't believe she will."

"Your marriage will be okay?"

"Yes. I love her. She knows I love her. I believe our marriage will be fine."

"How do you think Franklin McCoy is going to respond? My impression is that you guys are not exactly the wolves of Wall Street."

"We are pretty conservative. And a lot of our clients are as conservative as we are. I'm a managing director. I work in mergers and acquisitions."

"So, what will your bosses think?"

"Of me? Of the party?"

"Either. I was thinking of the party and of the publicity that's coming. The deaths of two people in your living room and your front hall; the Dionysian tone of the whole affair."

"Obviously, they won't be happy."

"I assume your clients won't be either."

"No."

"But no one's going to fire you?"

"I don't think so." He thought of the company's CFO. He thought of his direct boss, a guy a few years his senior named Peter Fitzgerald. Peter was the head of mergers and acquisitions, a job Richard knew that he was in line for someday. The fellow was a great-grandson of one of the firm's two co-founders, Alistair Franklin. He was the sort of boyish, ageless preppie who, despite being somewhere in his mid-forties, looked like a groomsman at a Brick Church wedding—and the most priggish one at that. He was, it seemed to Richard, tragically humorless—and likely to be the firm's CFO eventually. Richard believed that he and Fitzgerald had an amicable relationship, though not an especially close one. They were, alas, never going to be friends.

"Well," Dina said, "that's another issue you should be aware of: being fired."

"Without cause," he added.

"Or with."

He tried to look stoic. "I see."

"I suppose you have a contract with the bank."

"I do."

"Send it to me."

"I will."

Dina was just starting to elaborate on the employment land mines that were now in the ground before him when his cell phone rang. He pulled it from his suit pocket and saw a number he didn't recognize. He let it ring and the call went to voice mail. When the screen showed that he had a message, he pushed "speaker" and put the phone down on Dina's desk.

"Mr. Chapman, hi. Cynthia Prescott here. I'm with the *New York Post*. You probably know why I'm calling and I am sorry to bother you." She left her number and asked him to call her back.

"How the hell did she get my cell phone number?" he asked Dina.

"Maybe from someone at the party. Maybe not. There are lots of sites now where you can look up a cell number."

"Really?"

She nodded.

"Can you call her back for me?" he asked. "Bill told me it would be best if you spoke to the reporters."

"I will. But I see no reason to call her back right now. You haven't been charged with a crime and probably won't be. You said the girls may have looked barely postpubertal, but—"

"I said they looked young, but they were definitely of age."

"I understand. That's where I was going. That was going to be my point."

"Don't I want my side out there?"

She raised an eyebrow and for the first time gazed at him with judgment in her eyes. "And precisely what is your side, Richard?"

He sat there thinking for a moment. He saw the girl Alexandra on the guest room bed, her smile balancing longing and desire without regret. He saw her once more reaching out to him.

He realized that he had absolutely nothing to say.

...

As Richard was leaving Dina's office, he recalled how he had told the detectives last night that he thought the blond girl—the one who was calling herself Sonja—had killed both of the body-guards. Abductors. Whatever. But he really had no idea who had fired the handgun. He hadn't seen it. None of the men had.

Just now he told Dina Renzi the same thing: he thought the blonde had killed both of the Russians, the first with that knife and the second with the pistol she had pulled from beneath the dying thug's blazer.

And this was, more or less, what he had told Kristin had happened—though when he thought back on his conversation with his wife, most of his focus had been on what he had done (or not done) with the girl with the raven-dark hair.

He knew the other men who had been at the party were not so sure. Some, in fact, insisted that it had to have been Alexandra who had shot the dude in the front hallway. Chuck Alcott said so. Eric did, too. They both assumed it was her. After all, they recalled hearing the gunshots no more than a second or two after the blonde had left the living room. Somehow Alexandra must have wrestled the second gun from beneath the other guy's jacket and shot him. There had even been some debate about how close to the chest the gun must have been when it was discharged. Blow-back. That was the word one of the detectives had used. Blowback. How much of the bodyguard's heart or lungs or bone was up the barrel of the gun? Then he'd made a passing remark about the possibility of powder and soot on the shirt. Fabric in the wound. Someone would check, he assured them.

But, the truth was, all of the men from the party really knew nothing. Or, perhaps, next to nothing. Philip's friends agreed that everything had happened so fast—so quickly—that it was hard to be positive about anything. Certainly none of the men had asked the girls for more details when they'd been getting dressed.

And, unfortunately, both guns were gone. And without them and without an actual witness, it was impossible to say who had twice pulled the trigger.

...

Late that morning, a few minutes before Kristin and Melissa were going to leave the apartment for lunch and the matinee, Philip's fiancée called. Kristin was sitting on the living room carpet with Melissa, helping her study for a quiz the child had on Monday about prime and composite numbers. When she saw on her phone that Nicole was on the line, she kissed Melissa on the top of her head and adjourned to the kitchen so she could speak to Nicole in private.

"I'm in shock," Nicole said, her voice quavering and hushed. "There must have been an hour after Philip told me what happened when I couldn't . . . I couldn't stop crying." Nicole was soft-spoken and gentle and kind; she volunteered Tuesday afternoons at BARC—the Brooklyn Animal Resource Coalition—and spent another few hours on Thursday mornings at the assisted living facility where her grandmother was slipping into the confused murk of Alzheimer's, visiting the woman and her friends and helping them paint and play with clay. She was an immensely talented graphic designer, and while her business wasn't large, it was the right size for her; she could work from her home and visit the elderly and the cats that made her happy. She was shy and she was sweet, and neither Richard nor Kristin could understand what in the name of God she saw in Philip. They didn't know Nicole well, but they were confident she was way too good for Richard's younger brother.

"I know," Kristin agreed. "I know . . ." She wanted to be careful about what she said; she believed that Philip had fucked one of the girls (both, for all she knew), because Richard had told her. But she had no idea whether Philip had confessed this to Nicole.

"People were killed," Nicole continued. "I understand those two men might have been criminals. But they're dead now. They're gone. I mean, maybe they had wives or kids. They had moms. They had dads. And they're gone. And those women who killed them?"

"Go on," said Kristin. Nicole's voice had trailed off before she had answered her own question.

"Whatever happened to them before they murdered those men must have been unspeakable. It must have been horrible. Imagine being so angry or so scared that you could kill people like that."

Kristin sat down in one of the kitchen chairs. Ever since Richard had said something about how the girls may have been held in their jobs against their will—how they may have been kidnapped— her feelings toward them had been altered ever so slightly. And even if they hadn't been abducted and coerced into the work, the truth was that no one becomes a prostitute because she wants to. It's always the occupation of last resort. You go there because you need money for food or drugs or (the media's favorite explanation, because it suggested simultaneously that the girls were clean and college was too expensive) tuition. And so she understood Nicole's empathy. But this was still her house that had been soiled. This was her marriage that had been desecrated. In her mind, she saw her husband naked with one of the prostitutes in the guest room. "I agree," she said after a moment. It was just so hard to reconcile Richard with a girl like that.

But then Nicole surprised her by asking rhetorically, "And how could those guys do this to us? How could Richard do it? How could Philip? All the men who were there? I mean, I figured there might be a stripper. I didn't ask. But I figured since it was going to be at your house, it would be harmless. They weren't even going to a strip club. They were going to . . . they were going to West-chester, for God's sake."

"What did Philip tell you?" she asked finally. She simply couldn't resist.

"He wasn't going to tell me anything."

"Probably not."

"He only told me what really happened because it was so clear he was lying."

"And what did he say?"

"He confessed. He confessed that he had sex with one of the girls. He actually thought it would make me feel better when he reassured me that he'd used a condom. Some of the men didn't."

"Have you seen him? Or did you two just talk on the phone?"

"I can't bear to see him. I just can't."

"I understand."

"Tell me, how bad does your house look? How awful?"

"I have no idea. It's a crime scene. I'm not allowed to go home."

"A crime scene? Oh, God, that's terrible."

"Yup."

"Where are you?"

"I'm at my mother's—in the city."

"How mad are you—at Richard?"

"I'm mad. I'm hurt. As you said, I just don't see how he could do this to us. To our family."

"That's how I feel, too," Nicole agreed. Then: "Why do you think they did it? Had sex with those girls?"

"Richard didn't."

"He didn't?"

"No," she said, though she realized instantly both that Philip had told Nicole his brother was equally guilty and that it was possible Richard had lied to her. Maybe he had fucked the girl he had brought to the guest room. But she wanted to believe her husband, because in the shipwreck that was her life this weekend, that was the only debris floating by she could latch onto. "He went upstairs with one, but he . . . he resisted her."

"Resisted her. You make it sound like it was all the girls' fault. It wasn't, you know. I feel bad for them."

"On some level, I do, too. On some level, I even feel a little bad for Richard. It won't be pretty when he goes in to the office on Monday morning." She gazed out the window at the overcast skies. "So, what are you going to do?" she asked Nicole.

"About?"

"About the wedding."

There was a long silence on the other end of the line. "I don't know," she said finally. "I just don't know if I can marry him anymore."

...

While Kristin and Melissa were at the matinee that afternoon, Richard went clothes shopping for the whole family. He had to believe that the police would allow them back into their home by Monday, but that still meant they would need additional clothing. He guessed he could sponge off his suit and press it, but he still needed jeans for tomorrow and shirts for the next two days. He needed a necktie. Kristin said that she and Melissa were fine through Sunday, but they would both need clothing for the start of the week. For school.

Just in case, he bought clothes for Tuesday, too. He spent two hours in Bloomingdale's, shopping as if it were Christmas Eve and he had nothing to place under the tree. He ignored price tags. He bought skirts and dresses and designer jeans and underwear. Then he went around the corner to a special boutique where he bought his daughter two pairs of the strangest tights they had in stock: one pair was nothing but the royalty from a deck of medieval playing cards; the other was covered with doodles of stars and planets and the sorts of spaceships you would see in silent films from the first decades of the twentieth century. He bought them chocolates. He bought his mother-in-law flowers. He bought with the desperate hope that somehow he could buy their forgiveness.

Twice his cell phone buzzed and both times it was Philip. He ignored the calls. He wasn't prepared to talk to his brother and face again what had happened the night before. Twice more there were calls from reporters, neither of which he answered.

The only call he accepted was from a neighbor in Bronxville, a guy he played golf with but who had not been at the party. After all, the people there had been Philip's friends, not his. Perhaps that was why Richard had accepted the call: it was someone who wasn't yet privy to the debacle. He put everything but the flowers down on the sidewalk, and listened. His friend wanted to know why in the name of God there were video trucks from a couple of TV stations parked at the bottom of his driveway and—when he looked closely—a van from the state police. A mobile crime lab. Clearly something was horribly wrong, and he wanted to see what he could do.

"Everyone's okay. At least everyone is in my family," Richard told him. He was about to explain what had happened—offer a *Reader's Digest* condensed version—when he heard his friend's wife yelling something from the next room. It seemed a version of the story was already online: two people were killed at a bachelor party orgy in a swank Manhattan suburb.

"There was no orgy," Richard said simply.

"But somebody was killed."

"Yes. Two people." He was relieved that in the theater across town his wife's cell phone was off. Thank God. She might turn it on again at intermission, which he guessed would be around three-fifteen. And without a doubt there would be calls waiting for her on her voice mail. They would be from worried neighbors, and they would be from reporters. There might be calls from her brother in Boston and from other teachers at the high school. How had this gotten on the web so quickly? How was it already popping up on newspaper websites?

He realized that he would have to warn Kristin not to answer her phone. As he did, he recalled what he had told Dina Renzi: *I believe our marriage will be fine.* Suddenly he wasn't so sure.

Alexandra

I guess my mother had lovers after my father died. She was young. She was human. I remember two different men who took her to the opera a couple of times, and there was another man who she went to a jazz club with on Friday nights when I was nine- and ten-year-old kid. Maybe even when I was eleven. My grandmother would babysit me. But when I asked my mother if this fellow was her boyfriend, she told me, no, he was just a friend.

One night when I was working at the cottage outside of Moscow, I opened the door to the office on the first floor. (I keep calling it a cottage, but it was once some bigwig party official's dacha for sure—which is maybe why Muscovites liked to call it a cottage. Downplay class difference. Americans would probably call it a mansion.) I was looking for Inga, one of the women who helped train us, because I had a question. And she was in the lap of one of the bosses who ran us, a tall dude with a Stalin mustache named Mikhail. She still had her blouse on, but it was unbuttoned, and her skirt was up around her waist. She started to jump off his lap, but he held her there and smiled at me like this was no big deal. I said I'd come back later and backed away. I closed the door. I knew Inga would punish me for not knocking, and she did.

That night I woke up after a dream and stared up at the ceiling of my bedroom. I couldn't remember the dream. But I remembered something else. After school one day I went to the brandy factory so I could show my mother a painting of tulips I had finished in art class. I was maybe seven years old, and so my grandmother brought me. She was talking to someone in the big reception area, and when I saw my mother was not at her desk, I opened the door to Vasily's office. I didn't think to knock. Did I see my mother try to jump off Vasily's lap just the way Inga did—or did I dream that, too? I still don't know. At least that's what I try and tell myself.

But, of course, some days I do know. I do.

...

When I finally had the strength to climb off the bed after I had been raped my first night in Moscow, I went to the bureau with the TV where I had put down my cell phone. That was when I found it was gone. Of course. That was when I looked down and saw that my rollie suitcase was gone, too. At first I was surprised to see that my suitcase had been stolen. Why did they feel the need to take my clothes? Why did they want to take from me my ballet slippers and my toe shoes? Was that really necessary? I guess it was. After all, it was in their nature because they were pricks. A bird has to fly and a lion has to eat gazelle and a Russian mobster has to break what's left of a girl's heart by stealing those things that make her the happiest and feel most like life is worth living after she has been raped.

Over the next few months, I would meet girls who would tell me they got sucked into the life more slowly. Sometimes their pimp was first their boyfriend—at least they thought he was their boyfriend. This was case with those girls who started very young. Eleven, twelve, thirteen years old. Their boyfriends were dudes in their twenties and thirties. They told the girls they loved them, and the girls would do anything for them, even when their boyfriends would beat them. The girls always believed they had done something to deserve the beating.

Other girls thought their boyfriend was their "manager." They were going to be a model, maybe. One girl told me that after a few weeks, her manager said that he needed her to do him and her career a gigantic favor and sleep with some guy who had very big clout. The guy was what her manager called a "game changer," and it would just be that one time. So she did. The next thing she knew, she was down the rabbit hole. All she was doing was sleeping with guys who were "game changers." She never modeled. Not even once.

And so while I did go to Moscow with them when they asked, they did not suck me in slowly. Nope. They made sure I knew right away what I was in for—and what would happen if I did not cooperate.

...

When I discovered that my phone and my rollie had disappeared, I opened the hotel room door. I nearly screamed because there was a tall guy in the hallway watching it—watching my room. He was just sitting there in the plush chair that was near the elevator, looking at different things on his phone. (Knowing what I know now, he was looking at soccer scores or porn, and probably porn.) When he saw me, he just smiled and motioned me back inside with his fingertips like I was little bug in front of his face. He was bald, too, just like Andrei. To this day, I will never understand why Russian mobsters feel the need to shave themselves so they look like cue-ball-head babies. No girl really likes that look. It's big mystery to me.

It would be hours before they would send up Inga, so I went back inside my room and that's when I saw the blood on the sheet. I didn't remember Andrei pulling the bedspread down. Then it dawned on me: I was still bleeding. Not a lot, but a little. It was pooling in my underwear and dribbling down my leg like raindrops on a windowpane. And suddenly I just went crazy like wild animal. I was pounding on the walls with my fists. Then I was slapping the back of the door with the palms of my hands, and I didn't stop even when my skin felt like it was burning. I'm not sure what I expected. Did I think the corridor thug would set me free? Or did I think he would order me to stop? Did I care? The point was, I was trapped. I was a prisoner. In the end, he didn't set me free or yell at me. He just ignored me. I pounded on the walls and the door until I was so tired I just slid to the floor. I looked at the velvet drapes in front of the window. I was on the ninth floor, but maybe there was a fire escape. There wasn't.

I crawled my way to the bed and fell back onto the mattress, where I cried till I was hyperventilating. I was exhausted. It was like evening a few years earlier when I was babysitting an infant on another floor in my apartment building in Yerevan. I just couldn't stop this poor little girl—she was just over a year old—from crying. I held her, I rocked her, I sang to her. I tried to burp her. I changed her diaper—and changed it again. And then she started to hiccup. Not once, not twice. Not for a couple of minutes. For hours. She didn't stop hiccupping and crying till her mother returned. I was convinced she was going to hiccup herself to death. I would have brought her to my mother or my grandmother, but neither was home. And that night in a Moscow hotel room, abducted and humiliated and alone, I was like that.

And I was so tired now. I was so tired.

Eventually I remembered the bloody sheet. I was lying on it. I was lying in my own blood—and then I felt not only violated, I felt ashamed. As angry as I was and as scared as I was, there was still that part of me that wanted to be a good girl. That needed a grown-up's approval. That feared making a bad first impression. I was in a hotel nicer than any hotel I had ever been in before. (In truth, I had never really been to a hotel before. I had been to motels and cabin courts on Lake Sevan, but never anything as luxurious as this.) It seemed to me that I could not allow the maid to see the sheet. I couldn't bear what she would think. I rolled the sheet into the tiniest ball I could and I placed it inside that plastic trash bag. Then I put the plastic trash bag under the bed—at least for now. I told myself that later I would find a way to throw it out.

When I curled up on the bed after that, all I could think of was my mother and my grandmother. I had finally stopped hiccupping, but I was still whimpering. I was crying because my mother was dead and I was crying because my grandmother was far away and I was crying because I had been raped. I was crying because I was terrified. You have no idea what terror is like until you are a teenage girl in bloody panties trapped in a hotel room. It didn't matter that it was an elegant Moscow hotel with a little refrigerator in the room and wineglasses and an ice bucket. It didn't matter that maybe the other rooms on the other floors were filled with oligarchs and tourists.

But what, looking back, seems weirdest to me is this: I remember feeling guilty. I understood this was not my fault: What girl would not want to be ballerina? What girl would not have trusted her dead mother's boss and, with her grandmother's blessing, left with his assistant on an airplane? But all reason was gone with that bloody sheet. All reason was gone when, a few seconds later, I pulled off my panties and put them in the bag with that sheet.

...

The woman said her name was Inga and she was from Latvia, but I had a feeling she was lying. She went on and on about my name, and how I needed a new one. Anahit would not do. Not European enough. Not glamorous enough. Not seductive enough. She wanted me to become—not kidding—Alexandra. In the last twenty-four hours, I had been fucked for the first time and then filmed with some bastard bodyguard's penis deep in my mouth, and now this strange woman is talking to me about why my new name should sound like imperial Russian tsarina. I was in shock. I remember sitting on the bedspread of the bed where the night before I had been raped, and then turning away from this pretend Inga and wrapping my arms around my ribs. I was cold, even though the hotel room thermostat was set high for hotel sex. She kept talking to me in a very sweet, very calm voice—I guess she was the good cop to Andrei's bad cop—about how things would get better, and how this was a glamorous life I had been given, and the sooner I accepted that the better off we'd all be. Her Armenian was very good, but she had an accent I did not recognize. It might have been Polish, but I was just guessing. I had met many tourists in Yerevan, but none from Poland.

"Alexandra is rather like Anahit," she was saying. "That's why I proposed it."

I could have told her that Anahit was the name for a beautiful Armenian goddess not some poor woman who was shot with her family by the Bolsheviks. But I was done speaking that day, because every time I opened mouth, all that came out was either a trapped cat hiss or a sad little cry. She tried to rub my neck and my shoulders through my shirt, but I slapped her hands. It was a reflex.

Finally Inga said that she was going to leave me alone. But she gave me a foil disk with little pills on it and said, "Oh, by the way: if you don't start taking the pill, they will kill your grandmother. It's really simple. And they'll know if you aren't taking the pill, because you'll get pregnant." Then she smiled like kind aunt. When she closed the hotel room door behind her, I heard her say something to the guard, but I couldn't make out the words.

The next day I was a little more communicative. Not much, but a little. And Inga figured out how well I spoke English. She was surprised that no one had told her, and a little miffed. But she was also pleased with the discovery, even though I spoke English better than she did.

Still, it would be a few more days before I would understand something about me that you probably figured out a long time ago: I was a valuable piece of property and they were investing impressive dram in me. I might be just object, but I was fifteen, I spoke English, and I was hot. I had the potential to make them very serious scratch.

Chapter Five

In the dark of the theater, losing herself in a musical about a group of beached whales and the people who try to save them—it vacillated between charming and operatically sad—Kristin was almost able to forget the nightmare that had occurred in her living room (in her whole house, in truth, but at the moment she kept returning to the living room) the night before. There were times during the first act when she sat acutely still, her hands atop the yellow and white Playbill in her lap, her daughter beside her, when she was able to convince herself that all would be well in the end. She felt her body relax into the red velvet cushion of the seat; she immersed herself in the world of the pickup-truck-sized puppets of whales and the plaintive singing of the desperate marine biologists.

But that hope disappeared the moment the lights came up and she switched on her phone at intermission. There were the feverish voice-mail messages. The ineludible texts. The frenzied questions from neighbors and other schoolteachers about the news stories, some of which she decided she would have to scan before returning anyone's calls. There was a message from her brother. She could feel Melissa watching her as she scrolled through the first article, reading the quotes from the police officers and detectives and—dear God—some gregarious friend of her brother-in-law's named Chuck Alcott who apparently was lacking both in reticence and verbal restraint. "I don't know who was more out of control, the two hookers or the guys at the party," he was quoted as saying. He said that at least half the bankers, advertising executives, IT managers, and hoteliers (there was that word again) at the party had had sex with the girls. He said the stabbing of the fellow who had brought the prostitutes was the most horrific thing he would ever see in his life. He added that he had not witnessed the shooting of the second Russian—none of the men had—but it was the other girl who had gotten the gun and pulled the trigger. This Chuck Alcott insisted that he was one of the revelers who had not had sex with the prostitutes.

Her husband, she noted, was described as a wealthy investment banker; their house was called elegant and well appointed; their daughter was not mentioned at all. Thank heavens.

But the part of the story that struck her most was the paragraph about the hookers. Although the headline suggested that the girls had unleashed unspeakable violence in her home, the article—despite the Chuck Alcott quotes—portrayed them as victims. As Richard had said, it may have been their captors they killed, not their bodyguards. The girls may have been sex slaves. They may have been minors. No doubt, the reporter concluded, the pair was trying harder to stay ahead of Russian gangsters than they were the police.

"Is Daddy in more trouble?" Melissa asked her. All around them people were stretching and sharing how moved they were by the first act. Her little girl's eyes were the most remarkable blue, even in the muted light of the theater. Her eyelashes already were lustrous and long. She was a lovely child and Kristin was scared for her. For her future. She thought of the gentlemen's clubs—now there was a ridiculous euphemism—they had passed in Times Square on the way to the theater and decided that, at the moment, she hated men. All of them. They turned girls into whores. Sex slaves. And not just in dark alleyways in Bangkok. Right here. There may have been two in her home.

She wondered what the hell she had been thinking allowing her husband to have a bachelor party at their house. She tried to recall whose idea it was, and couldn't. She just couldn't.

"No," Kristin answered carefully. "He's in the same amount of trouble. There's really nothing new here. It's just . . ."

"It's just what?"

Her brother, both because he was a therapist and because he was older, sometimes felt entitled to chide her for being averse to confrontation. Sometimes when the family was gathered for Thanksgiving or Christmas and she would mention how difficult the school principal was or how badly some parents were behaving, he would encourage her to stand up for herself. He would tell her to draw a line in the sand. Well, this time she had. She thought of her conversations with Richard since that first phone call in the small hours of the morning, and she certainly felt she had asked him the tough questions. She was furious and hurt and she felt betrayed.

"It's just that people are already talking about what happened. I guess I didn't expect that word would spread so fast," she tried to explain to Melissa, and for the first time she saw herself the way other people might see her. She felt ashamed and (somehow) inadequate, which brought back all of the anger she had been feeling earlier that day in the guest bedroom at her mother's. Was she not pretty enough for Richard? Not sexy enough? Not . . . erotic enough? Did her husband need more? Want more? Did he want something—someone—else?

She was, she realized, embarrassed. That was the word. She was . . . embarrassed. How could he be so cavalier with their lives? How could he go and risk ruining all they had built?

Suddenly she wasn't sure she could bear to be around him after what he had done to their marriage. To their family. At least she couldn't bear to be around him right now. Certainly not tonight.

Earlier today she had wanted stability for Melissa. That had been her goal. She wanted this nightmare behind them, and until it was she wanted to minimize the stress on her child. She and Richard had never fought in front of the girl, and she had hoped—expected, in fact—that they never would. But what sort of role model was she for her daughter if she seemed to condone this sort of behavior from her husband? If she didn't, as her brother would have said, stand up for herself?

"The story is on TV?" her daughter was asking.

"Yes, it is."

Melissa seemed to think about this for a second and nodded. Then she looked down at her own copy of the Playbill. Kristin realized that the girl was afraid to look at her.

"But it'll be okay, sweetie," she said, stroking the side of the child's head, running her fingernails gently behind her ear. She could feel own her heart racing and took a breath. She had come to a decision: Richard would have to spend tonight at a hotel. Maybe tomorrow night, too. "It really will," she added.

She didn't try to smile when she spoke; that would have been impossible. She knew the fear she was feeling for the child was unreasonable, but she was unable to reassure herself when she thought about boys and men and the images they had of women in the digital age. Men were predators, and this little girl beside her—her child—was just too beautiful.

. . .

When Richard returned to his mother-in-law's apartment, he presented her with the flowers he had bought, and then together they went to the kitchen to put them in a large vase. The girls weren't back yet from the theater. It was awkward, but Richard took some comfort in his mother-in-law's absolutely remarkable ability to steer clear of unpleasant subjects. She asked him about work. She had him show her the things he had bought for his family, the reasons why he had gone on the shopping spree conveniently forgotten. Or, more precisely, avoided. It was impossible to forget what had occurred last night.

Just as he was starting to put the gifts back in their boxes, Philip phoned yet again. This time Richard took the call, disappearing into the guest bedroom so they could speak in private. He didn't apologize for not picking up earlier, but he began by explaining that he had been meeting with a lawyer and then had gone shopping for Kristin and Melissa. He added that the police had kicked him and his family out of his house.

"Well, thank God you're not home," his younger brother said. "Consider yourself lucky."

"Why?"

"Your place is under siege."

Though he was alone, Richard found himself nodding. He thought of the TV news trucks on the street at the edge of his driveway.

"My building has a doorman and I'm on the fourth floor, so they can't get to me. But I'm also not going out. No fucking way. I will live on Chinese delivery and whatever the hell I have in my refrigerator. Still, I'm going to have to tip Sean big-time come Christmas," Philip said, referring to the fellow who was on duty in the lobby that afternoon. His brother's apartment was just off the East River promenade in Brooklyn Heights.

"How many reporters are downstairs?"

"According to Sean, five. At least it was five the last time he checked. Three men, two women. Some TV, some print."

"How is Nicole?"

"No idea."

"What do you mean, no idea?"

"She's not talking to me. She's holed up in her studio."

"Well, there's your answer. That's how she's doing."

"I wouldn't say she is overreacting exactly, but it would be nice if she saw our side."

"Our side?"

"We could have been killed! My God, two people were murdered in cold blood in your house. How were we supposed to know the strippers were going to go postal? It was awful."

"They weren't strippers."

"Fine. It wasn't our fault that the *entertainment* went postal. It was still awful. And it was supposed to be just a regular old bachelor party. My bachelor party. A guy's got a right to a bachelor party, doesn't he?"

"Philip, it wasn't a bachelor party. It was a . . ."

"It was a what?"

"It was a freaking disaster is what it was."

"But it wasn't my fault. It wasn't your fault."

"Philip, not trying to be judgmental here—"

"Then don't."

"Look, you fucked one of the girls."

"You did, too."

"I didn't."

"Fine, you took her upstairs and did whatever. None of my business. That's not the point. It was my bachelor party. Grooms fuck strippers at their bachelor parties all the time. I've told you the shit that goes down at the hotel. I'm not proud of what I did, but if the girls hadn't lost their minds, none of this would have been a problem. We would have had a good time with some jiggly little things and moved on. We wouldn't have reporters camped out on our doorsteps right now. We wouldn't have spent hours in a fucking police station last night. And my fiancée wouldn't be so royally pissed off that who the hell knows if she's actually going to marry me two weeks from today."

Richard heard his mother-in-law turn on the radio in her bedroom. Classical music. She had turned the volume up high, either because her hearing was suspect or she wanted to give him privacy. He gently pushed the guest bedroom door closed with the toe of his shoe.

"Grooms don't fuck strippers all the time," he told Philip.

"A, they do. The next time you're at a place like Thong, go upstairs with one of the girls to a private room. And B, it's a fine line."

"What is?"

"How much worse is it really to have a naked woman grinding her crotch against yours in a lap dance and—pardon my French— you whipping it out? Obviously, the latter is worse. I get it. But, seriously, how much worse is it really?"

"Listen to yourself. It's a lot worse."

"I'm not so sure," his brother said, his tone petulant and defensive. "It's all just foreplay. A couple Fridays ago when Spencer and I were there—"

"Where? Thong?"

"Yeah. We took a couple of girls upstairs, got a little nasty, and when I got home, I was awesome with Nicole. A beast."

"You made love to your fiancée after going to a strip club?"

"I showered!"

"That wasn't my point."

"And my point is simply that no one was hurt," Philip insisted. But then, when he continued a second later, he had lowered his voice and sounded a little worried. "But this will blow over, right?"

"Are you asking me my opinion or trying to reassure yourself?"

"I mean, as a culture we have the attention span of five-year-olds. Don't you think? Tomorrow we will be on to the next human disaster. And, maybe a disaster we should give a rat's ass about."

"Meaning two dead people in my house isn't a disaster we should give a rat's ass about?"

"You know what I mean: they were hookers who killed some mobster jerks. This isn't, I don't know, a bazillion starving children somewhere in Africa."

Richard looked at his watch. The musical had probably ended half an hour ago. Kristin and Melissa would be back any minute. He tried to will his younger brother to ask him about them, but he knew it wasn't likely. Philip just wasn't hardwired that way.

"Yeah," he said simply, allowing a sliver of sarcasm into his voice. "This isn't a job for the Red Cross. I agree."

"You talk to Mom and Dad?"

He knew he should call them. Should *have* called them. Any second now, one of their friends was going to tell them what they had just seen on TV, utterly thrilled to have something to discuss other than angioplasties or Coumadin or someone's hip replacement surgery. His parents had retired three years ago to Fort Lauderdale, buying a house in one of those developments deep into what had once been the Everglades. There was a golf course that sometimes had alligators among the hazards. Everyone was between the age of sixty and embalmed. "No," he answered. "I haven't."

"Me neither. I think it's almost best to wait for them to call me and then I can say, 'Mom, I didn't want to worry you. It was scary, but I'm okay.' You know, sound brave and stoic."

"That's you, Philip. Brave and stoic."

"So what's next? What did your lawyer say? Spencer's wigging out. He's worried he's looking at some serious legal misery. He's convinced this little clusterfuck is going to bury him in legal fees."

"It very well might. The retainer request I agreed to this morning was impressive."

"And given what you bring home, that says something."

"I guess."

"So what did you learn?"

"Well, those two girls have considerably more to worry about than I do. Or, I guess, than Spencer does. Or you do."

"They killed people. That's kind of obvious."

"They might have been sex slaves."

"Yeah, right."

"I'm serious."

"They were high-class escorts if they were anything," his brother said. "Well paid. Gym memberships. Have a little Pink Wink in their medicine cabinets."

"What in the name of God is Pink Wink?"

"Intimate bleach cream. Are you really that naive?"

"So it would seem. How do you know such things? Nicole?"

"I wish! I know because I'm a hotelier. We're paid to know such things. It's what we do."

"Please. I can't believe your hotelier bosses are going to be happy when they read about this."

"They'll be fine. It is what it is."

"I don't even know what that expression really means. I think it means nothing."

"I'm telling you, they'll be okay. But your bosses? That might be another story, right?"

"Sadly, yes. I think you're right. Franklin McCoy will not be pleased."

"Spencer might get a little grief from management for booking the girls," Philip said. "Well, not for booking the girls—but for booking the girls from someplace sketchy. He didn't use the service we usually use."

"There's such a thing as a service you usually use?"

"I love how innocent you are, my older brother," Philip said, stressing the word *older* in a way that was both loving and conde-scending. "Yes, we do have our go-to girls for this sort of thing."

"Okay, then: Why didn't Spencer use them?"

"He was trying something new. Not completely new. He'd used the service that offers girls like Sonja and whatever-her-name-was—the one you did—once before, and it was awesome. The girls were wild—but wild in a yeah-I'll-do-that sort of way. Not wild in a I'm-going-to-jump-on-your-back-and-cut-your-head-off sort of way. And he wanted something wild for me. For you. For us."

"His heart was in the right place."

"It really was. How was he to know they'd send over two bat-shit crazy strippers? How was he to know you'd wind up with a couple of dead guys in your living room and front hall?"

"I gotta go," Richard said suddenly, surprising even himself. He'd dreaded talking to his younger brother, and the few minutes on the phone had been worse than he had expected. "Kris will be back any second."

"Say hi for me."

"I will," Richard lied. "I will."

. . .

Melissa sat on the plush carpet in her grandmother's living room and matched up her new tights with her new skirts. Her grandmother sat in the yellow easy chair beside the fireplace and read a biography of Amelia Earhart. Cassandra, unused to this new environment, was gazing down at the world a little warily from the top of the back of the couch. Occasionally her grandmother would speak, sharing something about the aviator's life that she had just read or commenting yet again on how unusual or clever the tights were, and Melissa had figured out the pattern: her grandmother spoke the second after they had heard her mother sobbing or her father raising his voice in desperation. Not anger; more like panic. Incredulity. Disbelief. Her parents were down the corridor and behind the closed door of the guest bedroom, but still the sound traveled. Melissa thought of the girls and boys she knew whose parents had gotten divorced. Sometimes the children had moved away; sometimes not. They lived in multiple homes, spending some nights with one parent and some nights with the other. Occasionally they fell behind in their schoolwork. The boys "acted out." (That was the expression her teachers used; her own mother had used it on occasion, too.) The girls grew quiet.

She ate one of the chocolates her father had brought her and looked at the tights with the face cards. Kings and queens and jacks. A harlequin. She thought of fairy tales and wondered why there wasn't a card with a princess. There should have been. It didn't make sense. It was always the princesses that people cared about. She couldn't name a single Disney prince, but instantly she could count on her fingers seven or eight of the princesses. She had met three of them at Disney World a couple of years ago, and now she rolled her eyes when she recalled how she had actually believed at the time that she was meeting Cinderella, Belle, and Snow White.

"This biographer thinks she and her copilot crash-landed on a reef and survived," her grandmother was saying. "They were on this little island for weeks and could have been rescued. Can you imagine?"

She didn't want her parents to get divorced. She wanted only to go home. In her mind she saw a picture from one of her thick books of fairy tales—a book that was so old it had once belonged to her grandmother's mother—of an ominous house in the woods. The second-floor windows were eyes, the French front doors a mouth. In the story, the house was described as brooding. She would have called it hungry.

She told herself she would be brave, if only because she hadn't a choice. But she was scared. She was, she realized, scared for the first time in her life.

A few minutes later her parents emerged from the bedroom. A few minutes after that, her father left for the night. He held her and promised that he would be back in the morning.

Alexandra

So, I became Alexandra. I accepted a life of carrots and sticks. That is not a bad joke; that was just how it was.

For the first year and a half, I lived in the cottage two hours from Moscow by car, but in what direction I couldn't tell you. There were five other girls who had been abducted, three from Volgograd (where Vasily had that second brandy factory) and two from the countryside—from the total middle of nowhere. Those two children made me look like know-it-all college professor. One had never owned a cell phone. One thought babies came from prayer because her male cousins and her uncle had been having sex with her for years and she had never gotten pregnant. So, in her head, a baby arrives when you ask God for one and pray very, very hard. Of course, this had been going on since she was eight. It's hard to get pregnant when you're eight. She was thirteen and was only now getting her period. She was, after a few days, very much like kid sister to me. At fifteen, I was the second oldest. Only Sonja was older—by one year. I would have my sweet-sixteen birthday party in that house. Inga gave me a silver bracelet, which was very pretty, and a dude from Rublyovka with ugly neck scruff pulled my hair while fucking me from behind.

What the six of us had in common was that we were beautiful and our parents were dead or had disappeared. Inga cared for us, as did another mistress or housemother we were told to call Catherine. They were going to teach each of us how to be—Catherine's words—twenty-first-century paramour. That meant learning, basically, to do whatever some guy wants and is willing to pay for. But it also meant learning about makeup and hair and clothes and what to eat (and what not to eat). We ate lots of healthy fruits and vegetables, and we smoked lots of cigarettes. They watched our weight, and soon enough cigarettes were our rewards for staying away from the bird's milk cake or the sugary pastila. We tried on different kinds of sexy underwear and were taught that the panty goes underneath the garter belt, even if that means it's more difficult to go to the bathroom. We played Xbox games. We played Xbox games on a TV set for hours.

The cottage had a minaret and two man-made ponds that we could see from the windows. We never swam in them; they were for show. They went with the gardens. The bathrooms had faucets and bidet handles made of pretend gold. We each had our own bedroom with windows and velvet drapes. This was so we would feel a little pampered when we were not entertaining and so we would have our own space to bring clients when it was time. We ate together in a dining room with a white marble floor and an Oriental carpet with Noah's ark animals. (My favorite creatures were the rug's two giraffes.) We used silver. We all spoke different dialects of Russian, and only Sonja and I spoke Armenian. Only I spoke English. But we figured out how to talk to each other. The girls picked up English pretty quick.

So, that was the carrot: a nice house with nice bedrooms and nice food. Glamorous, yes?

Here was the stick: we couldn't leave the property, we couldn't talk to anyone beyond the gates, and we had to fuck whatever guys they brought to the house. And we were isolated. Totally isolated. We had no computers and no phones. There was not even an old-fashioned telephone in the house with one of those dials you spin that we saw all the time in old movies. It's funny how fast you miss the Internet when it's gone. We had no passports or credit cards or money. We depended on them for all our food and our clothes and our toothbrushes and our makeup and our medicines when we got sick.

And we were locked in our rooms at night—except when we were working. There were men with Makarov pistols in their belts or in shoulder holsters watching us. They had shifts, and they came and went; we were not allowed to become friends with them. Most of the time they spoke to us only when they were yelling at us to return to the terrace when we took our one hour of sunlight outside. Sometimes they'd threaten to lock us away if Inga or Catherine complained about us. Other times they'd make jokes about us to entertain themselves. They called us "little flaps" and "little twats." But usually they just watched us in silence.

And most nights, it seems, we worked: that means we fucked what one of the girls from Volgograd called the "black and whites." (Her name was Crystal and later she would come to America with Sonja and me.) The black and whites were men who almost always wore black suits and white shirts. They never wore neckties. They always had stubble—so much stubble that sometimes Catherine or Inga would talk to them about not abrading our skin. They seemed to be rich, and sometimes they were old enough to be our grandfathers, which does not necessarily mean they were really that old; after all, we were all between thirteen and sixteen years old. The clients were Russian and Georgian and Ukrainian and—and you get the point. Very international, it seemed to us. Many worked in "spirits." Brandy and cognac and vodka. Even, in some cases, beer and wine.

None of them had any interest in us as more than sex toys.

None of them ever paid us; they left the money with Inga or Catherine, or they had paid ahead of time.

And none of them ever complained. We fucked like our lives depended on it—because, we realized, they did.

...

Approval is a funny thing. I needed it from Madame as an aspiring ballerina. I needed it from my schoolteachers as a student poet.

And, eventually, I needed it as a prostitute.

...

I did not view the other five girls as sisters, but we were more than friends. Sonja and I were very close, maybe because we both were Armenian. I looked up to her because she was older. Her family was originally from Gyumri, like mine, and only moved to Volgograd after the earthquake. Much to the annoyance of Inga and Catherine, the two of us were very protective of one another. Sonja also looked after Crystal, since Crystal was also from Volgograd and she was only thirteen.

Sonja was much crazier with the men than I was; she was probably crazier than all of us. I know she did things with them all the time that I only did when I had to. It wasn't that she was getting any pleasure from the business. But she channeled her anger into her work. She was (and I really understood this use of the word *fucking* the first time I heard it) "fucking mad." She was capable of scaring the men—even intimidating them—which meant that once in a while she would get in very serious trouble. The men would complain, though only sometimes would they suggest that she was more girl than they could handle. They would simply say she was difficult. Or disobedient.

That was the worst thing we could be: disobedient.

One time, to punish her for looking Daddy in the eyes—we were never to look Daddy or Mikhail in the eyes—they burned off the hair on one side of her head. I will never forget that smell. Her hair had been regular but beautiful blond.

When it grew back, Inga had her dye it so it was almost white, and then cut it into a bob. Her eyes were sky blue and would grow wide when she was angry inside. Like me, she could dance, and so sometimes the two of us would be ordered to get little parties started. (Mostly that meant stripping to some pop song and then grinding against the men's pants until the men brought us to our rooms.) Sonja and I sometimes talked about what our lives had been like before: hers in Volgograd and mine in Yerevan. She would tell me the little she recalled of her parents, and I would tell her all about my mother and my grandmother.

And with all of us girls there was some competitiveness in our relationships. Even Sonja, crazy as she was, had to have her share of approval—from us and from Inga and Catherine. That's just how it is. You lick the hand that feeds you.

And then, of course, there was Daddy.

Daddy appeared every few days. He was a former Soviet army colonel, probably sixty back then. He had the sort of good looks we saw in older male models in Western magazines. I think of Ralph Lauren ads when I think of him. He wanted us to call him Daddy, and he wanted the six of us to view ourselves as wives, like we were harem people, though there was no single man we were attached to. And he never fucked us. I think he would have viewed that as shoplifting, maybe, or stealing from his own company. And if he really did view himself as a father figure, I think sleeping with us would have complicated whatever excuse he had made up in his head to explain why it was okay to kidnap and imprison us.

So instead he fucked Inga and Catherine. He fucked them whenever he came to the cottage.

He was, we were told, much more powerful than Mikhail or even Vasily. Dudes like Mikhail and Vasily were scared to death of the man we called Daddy.

. . .

One week I was not allowed to use the bathroom. They gave me a tin coffee pot I was supposed to use for everything. I was not allowed to leave my bedroom. I was not allowed my one hour outside each day, because they wanted to be sure I used only the tin coffee pot. Inga checked it to make sure I was filling it up.

What had I done? What was my crime? I was in trouble because a man had said I was not clean there. He was lying. He only said that because *he* was not clean there and I told him we should shower before we fucked.

...

One day Crystal and I were smoking outside the cottage. We were standing in the middle of the big oval in the driveway where cars turned around and watching ducks in one of the ponds. She always looked like little girl who had stolen Mom's cigarettes. She had crazy big eyes and no tits. She was so beautiful at thirteen and fourteen. Out of nowhere she asked me, "You think any of the guys would help us?"

I thought she was talking about the guards, and I motioned with my cigarette at the dude who was watching us from the front steps. "Him? You crazy?"

She shook her head. "Of course not. I hate him. I hate all of them. I meant the black and whites." Her voice was even smaller than usual, because what we were talking about was so dangerous.

"And by *help,* you mean escape?"

"Yes."

"No way. It's too risky for them. Besides, why would any of them want to do that? Anyone who comes here wants us here. We're nothing but pussy to them. We're nothing but pussy to anyone."

She took a long puff. "What if I made one fall in love with me?"

"You're dreaming. These guys? Never happen."

"But what if? He could take me with him. We could go and get help."

"How would he take you with him? Put you in his briefcase?"

"Well, maybe I could ask him to tell someone about us. Tell someone we're here."

"Yeah, the police guys care lots about girls like us. I'm sure every week one of us is fucking a police guy."

She nodded because I was right and she knew it. "They're just so evil," she said after a moment, and we both went quiet because the truth was so sad. When she finally spoke again her voice was totally flat. Sometimes we all sounded totally flat. Like zombie people. "So there's no one to help us," she said.

I stepped on my cigarette and put my arm around her. "At least we have beds and food and cigarettes—and each other. We even have the Bachelor on TV!" I told her, trying to cheer her up with a silly joke. But now she was in one of the moods that we all got in once in a while, and the only way out was to flatline. It's why some girls like us do drugs. Sometimes it's the only way through.

...

How different were all of us? Another afternoon a girl named Elena and I were sitting on the terrace under a beautiful warm sky. The sun was always like drug after so many hours indoors.

"This is kind of a weird fairy tale," she said. We were wearing the miniskirts they made us wear like uniform. They only let us wear underwear when we were working. Other times, such as during the day, they always made us wear short skirts and no panties. We were sitting on the stones, and they were warm on my bottom. It felt perfect. "We're like those princesses in castles who are waiting to be rescued."

"Don't hold your breath for a prince," I told her. I closed my eyes and turned my face toward the sun. "I don't think a prince would come to a joint like this."

"But I like Inga," she said. "I really do. And I think I like Catherine. I mean, do we really want to be rescued?"

"Yes."

"Maybe you do. But this is, in some ways, a lot better than the life I was leading."

I knew Elena's history. She was the third of the three girls from Volgograd. While she was there, she was living with her stepfather, who worked in the large brandy factory. She had been brought to the cottage two days before me. Her mother was dead, and her father had run off years ago; her stepfather recently had been laid off. Suddenly his boss offers to buy his stepdaughter to help him make ends meet. Only an idiot would think this was a coincidence. They knew what Elena looked like. They knew her value. And, of course, they knew her stepfather. He was despicable. He'd been a very big jerk to her, even before he sold her like cow at the market.

"I can do this," she went on. "And if we do our jobs, they take really good care of us. And everyone has to work, yes? Everyone has to do something."

Two years later when I was working in Moscow—more like courtesan now—I spent two nights as arm candy for a very fat but very nice economist from Saint Petersburg. He would use the expression "Stockholm syndrome." He used it on our second night together, when we were having a little pillow talk. I would often tell men stories. Capture-bonding, he said. I knew just what he meant. I thought of Elena and that day in the sun back at the mansion.

Of course, not all our life would be Stockholm syndrome.

Look what happened when I got older and they brought me to America. Land of the free and the home of the brave? Nope. Not in my case. For girls like me, it was nothing more than the home of the disgusting. Perverts and sad men. There were confusing exceptions, such as guys like Richard Chapman. Guys like that could haunt you. But you get the point. And nothing was free—just like in Russia.

...

Sonja and Crystal had faith in hatred. They were good at it. They believed the world is filled with evil and people are devils, and you can only fight evil and devils with hatred.

Me? I was never good at hatred. I felt it. I knew it. But it did not live inside me the way it did inside them. Maybe things would have turned out better if it did. If I had been better at hatred.

Chapter Six

Before falling asleep at the hotel on Saturday night, Richard flipped through the photos on his iPhone. He wanted to see pictures of Kristin and Melissa. He hoped they might calm him. But among the hundreds of images were some scans of shots from his own childhood, and after looking at a dozen photos of his wife and his daughter, he paused on one of Philip and him. There he was at seventeen and Philip at twelve, the two of them in T-shirts on a beach on Grand Cayman. They were on a family vacation. He couldn't believe how long their hair was. He couldn't believe his seventh-grade brother was wearing a T-shirt that said "How to pick up chicks." Granted, the image was of a stick-figure human picking up baby chickens. But still. What were his parents thinking? Sometimes Richard liked to blame his brother's idiosyncrasies on the friends he had made at college—a bunch of hazing- and party-obsessed frat boys who lived for beer pong and porn—but perhaps it was genetic. Maybe Philip had been born a jerk. But Richard didn't view their father as especially sexist. He was a management consultant. Their mother was a librarian. And despite the fact that their father made scads more money than their mother, Richard viewed their parents' marriage as a partnership. It was rather like his own marriage with Kristin. He earned the lion's share of their joint income, but every decision they made was a joint one.

He remembered taking Philip and two of his frat brother friends to dinner one night between Christmas and New Year's when Philip was a junior in college. Richard had his MBA by then and had been working at Franklin McCoy for six months. He brought Philip and his pals to a steak restaurant in the gentrifying meat packing district, but the place was a throwback: heavyset waiters with walrus mustaches who frowned at you dismissively if you ordered any salad other than the iceberg wedge. When it was time to consider dessert, the three younger guys thanked him and bolted. They said they had fake IDs and planned to go to a strip club. Richard knew they thought less of him—they viewed him as a little less manly—because he didn't go with them. But the reality was that he was dating a schoolteacher with hazel eyes and lustrous amber hair that fell to her shoulders. A young woman with a laugh that he loved, and who liked indie rock as much as he did. He didn't see the point of a strip club. Besides, he was planning to work that night. The fact was, back then he worked every night he wasn't with Kristin.

He put down his phone and gazed out the window at Times Square. His room was on the eighteenth floor. He decided he would give almost anything to go back in time. Two days. That was all he wanted. Even a day and a half. Down there somewhere were strips clubs, which instantly made him think of Alexandra. Of strippers and escorts and sex slaves. He recalled the girl's eyes when she kissed him. It was going to be years, he feared, before he would find a way to forgive himself.

He wondered who among the thousands of people out there right now was going to screw up tonight as badly as he had twenty-four hours ago.

...

The next morning was the first time that Richard and Kristin Chapman had been in the newspapers since their wedding announcement had appeared in the *Times*. Richard read the articles just before sunrise, having slept little the night before. The bed at the Millennium was fine; so were the pillows and the heater's strangely mellifluous white noise. He tossed and turned because he feared the quiet of the room and the emptiness of the bed were harbingers. He vacillated between anger and despair, a ping-pong ball lobbed back and forth in gentle, transparent arcs. One moment he felt victimized; none of this, especially those dead Russians, was his fault. The next? He would see himself naked and erect at the edge of the guest room bed, a hauntingly beautiful young woman reaching out her hands to him. Her mouth. And he would be overwhelmed with regret. Sure, he had drawn back. But he should never have been in that position in the first place.

And yet in the smallest hours of the night he couldn't stop thinking about Alexandra: who she was and how in the name of God she had wound up in that bedroom, too. He tried to imagine her shooting the second Russian later that night, but it was hard. He guessed she had. But she seemed too (and he understood the irony of the word, but that in no way diminished its rightness in his mind) innocent. He knew he would never see her again.

In some ways, he found the *New York Times* article more painful to read than the ones in the tabloids, because the reporter simply laid out the facts as he understood them. At least the *New York Post* had alliteration in their front-page headline: STRIPPERS GO PSYCHO. (The accompanying image was a stock photo of a woman's thighs and seductively bent knees in a garter and stockings.) All of the newspapers ran pictures of the front of his house. The *Post* described it as the smallest house on a street full of mansions, and Richard took umbrage with the statement, even though he knew it was true. He also knew it was ridiculous to care; he had far greater concerns than the importunate needs of his ego. The *Times* had quotes from his lawyer, the police, and their neighbors. The

Post had these, too, but they had also interviewed a schoolteacher Kristin worked with.

He thought of what his father had said to him last night when, finally, he had returned his parents' calls: *This is what happens when you think with your little head instead of your big one, Richard. Jesus, I expect this sort of thing from your brother. Not from you.*

Reflexively he'd snapped back, *You expect people to get stabbed and shot around Philip? Seriously? Is that what you expect from Philip?*

But his mother, who had been on the line, too, calmly observed that his father was only referring to the generally adolescent lack of judgment that sometimes marked Philip's decisions.

Occasionally Richard had gotten up in the night and gazed out the window, as he had hours earlier before going to bed. If he stared long enough, the lights would lull him into a momentary stupor. Then the serrated skyline would strike him like a piranha's open mouth, and he would remember where he was and why he was there.

He sighed. He'd ordered up a pot of coffee, but nothing to eat. He was going to call Kristin in a couple of minutes, when he was sure she was awake, and see if he could come . . . not home . . . but to his mother-in-law's and spend Sunday night there. When he had first gotten dressed, he had been quietly confident that she would acquiesce; he was less sure now that he had read the stories in the papers. At the moment, he wasn't even convinced that she would allow him to join them for breakfast or brunch.

. . .

Kristin tried to peruse the stories without conveying any emotion, but it was difficult: the more she read, the sadder she grew. And, yes, angrier, too. They were toxic, and she could feel her blood pressure rising. Her only comment to her mother—at least over a breakfast of coffee and croissants in the Manhattan apartment kitchen—had been that Dina Renzi sounded very competent. Though, she added after a moment, she hoped the attorney's capabilities would never really matter.

"Why is that, dear?" her mother asked. "I don't understand."

"Because I am hoping Richard won't need her for more than"—and here she held up the section of the *Times*—"this. For public relations."

It surprised her that she found the newspaper coverage far more chilling than the local news the night before, or even her home's brief cameo on CNN. The videos were predictable, and she felt she had seen exactly this sort of footage a hundred times before: the beautiful woman with a winning smile, a perfect nose, and expertly coiffed hair standing with a microphone before a suburban home that, hours earlier, had been the site of a domestic cataclysm. There was the cut to a police detective—in this case a woman her husband had already described for her, Patricia Bryant—who was professional and polite and revealed almost nothing. Without a trace of irony her mother had remarked that the house looked nice, especially the black gum trees lining the slate walkway. She was nodding with approval when she shared how much she liked the trees' purple foliage.

"Is Richard coming back today?" she asked her daughter now.

Kristin was about to rub the bridge of her nose; she stopped herself when she saw the newsprint on her fingertips. "No."

"Will you go to him?"

"Will I go to him? Mother, you make it sound like he's a wounded warrior who needs his selfless wife."

"I didn't mean that at all. I was simply wondering if you were going to meet him someplace to talk." Her mother didn't sound defensive; she sounded reasonable. Kristin realized that she herself sounded far less rational.

"We can talk on the phone," she answered. "And I am sure we will."

"Good."

"I'm not going to do anything drastic. I promise."

"I know you won't."

And perhaps it was her mother's simple equanimity, but suddenly Kristin felt very much a child herself—once more a shamed schoolgirl or rejected girlfriend in need of a little mother's love. "I will just be so embarrassed when I'm back at school tomorrow. When I'm in the teachers' lounge and the classroom," she said, and her voice broke ever so slightly. "How will I face everybody? I feel so . . . so violated. I feel humiliated."

Her mother reached across the small circular kitchen table and tenderly, albeit awkwardly, embraced her. She put her hands on her daughter's shoulders and upper back and ran her fingers gently over her linen blouse. Kristin bowed her head against her mother and asked, "How could he do this to us?" And then, much to her surprise, she was crying, her whole body spasming with her sobs. She was vaguely aware that her mother's gray cashmere sweater was growing wet from her tears and her nose, but she couldn't stop herself and she didn't care.

"There, there," her mother was saying. "There, there."

. . .

Melissa ran her fingers over the waist-high border of the wainscoting that ran along the dining room walls. She was afraid to continue into the kitchen because she could hear her mother crying in there. Again.

Before this weekend, the only other times she could recall her mother crying were when Grandfather had died and then, a year later, when Cassandra's brother—their other cat, Sebastian—passed away. Sebastian had cancer and there was nothing more the veterinarian could do, and so they had put him to sleep. The lumps, and they were everywhere at the end, were horrible. Melissa recalled how she had cried, too. The veterinarian had come to their house, and Sebastian had been in her mother's lap when the vet had put him down. Her father had sat rubbing her mother's shoulders. They'd all been in the living room. Even Cassandra.

She recalled Sebastian's death a little better than her grandfather's, because she had been younger when Grandfather died. Not too long ago she had asked her dad if Mommy had cried more for Sebastian, and he had explained that she had been in shock when her father had died. It had been so sudden. So horribly sudden. But still, he had said, her mother had cried plenty.

Nevertheless, Melissa knew that the crying she was hearing now was much worse than anything she had heard from her mother before. It was louder. It was almost childlike in its inconsolability. Hysterical. Her grandmother was trying to comfort her, but having very little success.

Melissa understood that these sobs were brought on because her mother was hurt. Her father had done this. Daddy. She had seen the TV coverage, but she couldn't imagine her father with any woman but Mommy. In truth, she couldn't even really envision that. But it was clear that this . . . wailing . . . was triggered by whatever her father had done with the women at the party, and not because two people had been killed at their house.

Yet when Melissa tried to re-create in her mind whatever had occurred in Bronxville on Friday night, it was the violence that was most real to her. Two dead people. Strangers murdered with knives and guns, their bodies in the living room and the front hall. She recalled the moments she had seen from scary movies; though those moments were few, they were indelible. Surreptitiously—with babysitters or at her friend Claudia's house—she had seen her share of zombies and vampires and corpses on late-night TV. And though she had been frightened, she had always taken comfort in the idea that this was make-believe. There were no such things as zombies and vampires; the corpses always were actors in Halloween makeup. But whatever had occurred at her home on Friday night? That was very real.

Now she leaned against the wall and listened to her mother blowing her nose. She was telling Grandmother that she had to get her act together for Melissa. She had to figure out what she was going to say to her daughter. A second later the wooden chair slid against the kitchen tile. Her mother was standing up. Quickly Melissa retreated through the dining room and down the corridor to the guest bedroom. She didn't want her mother to know that she had been listening. But the one question she was going to be sure and ask her mother when her mother joined her in the bedroom was this: Just how much danger were they in? That was what she wanted to know. She was pretty sure her mother would answer "none," but Melissa was going to try and read her face when she responded. She also wanted to know when Daddy would be back. She feared she was going to need both of her parents to feel secure—but she had a sick feeling that this just wasn't going to happen.

...

Richard tossed his cell phone down onto the hotel bed and watched it bounce on the mattress. He took comfort in his restraint: his initial thought had been to hurl it as hard as he could—a baseball and he was twelve—against the wall with the framed black-and-white photograph of construction workers high atop a Manhattan skyscraper in (he presumed) the 1920s. He had just gotten a call from a lawyer. A fellow who worked at Franklin McCoy and whom Richard had never met. Said his name was Hugh Kirn. Apparently, Richard's boss—Peter Fitzgerald, great-grandson of Alistair Franklin himself, a keeper of the firm's torch, and utterly humorless—thought it best if Richard took a leave of absence. Seems all the managing directors and the CFO himself felt that way. Paid, Hugh had made clear. Paid. Of course. At least for now. And if this blew over? Then they could revisit what to do next, and whether it made sense for him to return.

"Revisit?" he asked the lawyer. "Do you have any idea how long you want this leave of absence to be?"

"No. Let's wait and see."

"Can I talk to Peter? I mean, tell him what really happened?"

"I told you, I'm calling for him. For the whole management team."

"I understand. But can I call him as a friend? Just talk to him?"

"You shouldn't. Please don't talk to anyone at the firm."

"Look, I can't go home. The police won't let me. So, I was planning on going to the office this afternoon and doing some work. God knows I have plenty to do."

There was a pause at the other end of the line as Hugh gathered himself. Then: "No. You can't go there. You're barred from the office."

"I'm barred? You make this sound punitive!"

"It's in everyone's best interests."

"Look, it should be pretty empty. I would just—"

"No."

"No? You're serious?"

He cleared his throat. "I'm serious."

"Who's going to handle—"

"Whatever it is, it will get done. No one's irreplaceable."

"Do you know who we're targeting this week? Do you have any idea what companies I am negotiating with to—"

"Yes. I know everything. We've already reassigned your work."

It was a short sentence, but it was a body blow. *Reassigned your work.* But once he had absorbed it—his mind reeling with the names of his associates and the people he managed who were going to be taking over his (his!) responsibilities—he only grew madder.

"I've got things there I want!" he said. "In my office! Can I at least go there and get them?"

"Like what?"

"Like what? It doesn't matter like what. My office isn't a crime scene. It's not like there's some sort of investigation into something I may have done at the bank. I . . . I want my things!" He realized he sounded infantile, but the words were spilling out now like coffee beans from the bulk food dispenser at the natural foods market. This was madness.

"If you could name some—"

"I don't have to name a goddamn thing!"

"You're upset. I understand. But—"

"Can't I talk to Peter?"

"I said that would be inappropriate."

"No, you didn't. You just said no."

"Richard—"

"Don't *Richard* me in that tone! We don't know each other that well. Wait: we don't know each other at all!"

"We can ship you whatever personal items you want. Family photos. Plaques. Paperweights. We will be happy to ship that sort of thing to your home."

"Plaques. Paperweights."

"Of course."

"This is degrading."

"So was your party on Friday night."

"Hugh?"

"Yes?"

"Be a human. Let me retrieve my stuff. I won't take any files. I won't take any papers. I promise."

"I shouldn't. I really shouldn't. But since you asked like a human, fine. I will meet you at the office. Is four-thirty okay?"

"Where do you live?"

"It doesn't matter where I live."

"For God's sake, I wasn't threatening you. I was asking to see how much of an inconvenience coming into the office will be for you."

"I live on Long Island."

"Then four-thirty is fine. You're doing me a favor, so I won't be a jerk and say that's too late in the afternoon. Can I ask you something?"

"Sure."

"You're going to have security with you, aren't you?"

"Absolutely."

"Fine. See you at four-thirty."

"And Richard?"

"Yes?"

"Since you're coming in, why don't you bring your keys and
ID card? You can turn them in this afternoon. It will save us all a
little trouble in the next few days."

When he recalled the conversation, he thought he had shown
admirable self-control not wrecking his cell phone by heaving it
against the hotel room wall.

...

In the end, Kristin decided that brunch would be best. Sara-
beth's. A few blocks from her mother's. After that, Richard would
have to return to his exile at the Millennium. They met at eleven-
thirty, Kristin and Melissa rendezvousing with Richard near
the restaurant's awning on the northeast corner of Madison and
Ninety-second Street. There were two tables available, one rather
light and cheery near the window, and one in the back corner. The
sun was out for the first time in days, and it was clear the hostess wanted to seat them at the front, where they could bask in its
warmth. Richard surprised her, asking for a table in the rear of the
restaurant. He allowed himself a brief moment of self-pity: this is
my future. A life in the shadows. Hiding. Shamed. But it passed
when he realized that he really did have his wife and his daughter
with him. He rallied, especially when he glanced down and saw
that Melissa was wearing the new skirt and tights he had picked
out for her yesterday.

"They look great on you!" he said, hoping after he had gushed
that his pathetic need for approval and forgiveness wouldn't lessen
him in her eyes. But, of course, he did need her forgiveness. And
she would, he feared, forever think less of him anyway.

"Thanks. They're pretty funky," she said, and he tried not
to read anything into how simply normal her voice sounded. He
kissed her on the forehead and then Kristin on the cheek. She
didn't turn away. He tried not to read too much into that, either,

but it gave him a small measure of hope amid the hopelessness that might otherwise swamp him.

"You must be hungry," he said as they glanced at the menus. "I know I'm famished."

"I had a croissant a few hours ago," his wife murmured. She didn't look up from what she was reading.

"And I had cereal," Melissa added.

"Well, all I've had is coffee, so I'm starving. I will be the goop who licks fingers and knives and both of your plates." He peeked over the top of his menu and took inordinate satisfaction from his daughter's small smile.

"How's the hotel?" she asked.

He shrugged. "Fine. It's a hotel. I wasn't all that far from the theater where you saw the puppet whales."

"I like hotels. You should have ordered room service. I love room service."

"I should have, right?"

"Yup."

"How's Cassandra?"

The girl rolled her eyes and folded her arms across her chest: "Weirded out."

"Is she eating?"

"Uh-huh. But she jumps from one piece of furniture to the next. It's like the carpets are quicksand or something."

"Where did she sleep?"

"I don't know."

"But not with you or Grandma?"

"Nope. Grandma thinks she might have slept on the high shelf in the coat closet."

"The one in the front hall?"

"Yup."

"Well, with any luck she can go home soon. We all can." He turned toward Kristin, but her eyes were still riveted to the menu. Abruptly she looked up and for a brief second he thought she was looking at him, and he felt almost giddy with relief. But he followed her gaze and understood it was only that the waitress had returned and was standing behind him. Over his shoulder. She was about to ask if they would like coffee or tea. Her hair was as black as her dress, and her eyes were the reassuring brown of freshly tilled soil. Her voice was chipper. She was, he guessed, in her early twenties. After she had taken their order—he and Kristin both ordered cappuccinos, while Melissa was having hot chocolate—he turned back toward his wife. Now she was staring at him; he couldn't decide if she was disgusted or merely bemused. He raised his eyebrows, waiting.

"I used to think I understood men," she said. "I don't. Or maybe I just overestimated all of you."

He nodded. He parsed the code: she thought he had been checking out the waitress and was irritated. "Wasn't thinking what you thought I was thinking," he told her, hoping he sounded playful and not defensive since Melissa was present.

"What were you thinking?"

"I was thinking about coffee versus cappuccino," he said. He wanted to tell her that he was no more aware of his surroundings—including the people—than anyone else. Yes, he thought the waitress was pretty, but he took no more notice of her than he would have if the person taking their order had been male. He registered what she looked like; that was it. He swiveled his body in his seat and focused on their daughter: "Tell me more about the musical," he said. "Tell me all about the whales." It was probably going to be impossible to make this brunch . . . normal . . . but he was, he decided, sure as hell going to try.

. . .

As they walked as a family the few blocks back to her mother's, Kristin finally broached the question that she had shied away from at brunch because Richard was trying so hard to make the meal pleasant for Melissa. She was grateful for his efforts; she wished she had had it in her to do the same. "Will you talk to that detective today?" she asked.

"Patricia?"

"Yes. You call her Patricia?"

"I'm not sure I have ever called her anything. If I phone her—which I assume is where this conversation is going—I expect I will call her Detective Bryant."

She noticed a family strolling toward them: a family of three with a son who was probably nine or ten. They looked so happy, Kristin thought. The parents were smiling at something their son had said. She tried not to be jealous, but she pined for that sort of casual joy. She missed the experience of communicating with her husband without sarcasm, anger, or wariness—or (worse, perhaps) depending upon Melissa as a semaphore. How was it possible they had had that only two days ago?

"If you'd like," Richard was saying, "I will call her. And, yes, I'll ask her when we can go home."

She considered correcting his use of the plural pronoun, but that would only be bitchy. They could discuss when he should return home later. By phone. When their daughter wasn't walking beside them. "That would be great," she said. "Thank you."

"Of course. There is one more thing."

She almost stopped walking. Instead she succumbed to superstition and took a long, careful step so that her foot did not land on a sidewalk crack. "Okay."

"Well, it's good news. I can seriously help whatever cleanup team we bring to the house—whether that's tomorrow or Tuesday or, I guess, even Wednesday. The bank wants me to take a little leave of absence. But I'm fine. It's all good and it makes sense."

"How long is a *little*?" she asked. The news didn't knock the wind from her the way it might have before the bachelor party. Before two men had been killed in her house. Before her husband had taken an escort upstairs, stripped, and . . .

She pushed the thought away.

She knew this was devastating to him and he was putting a brave spin on this for her. Like most men, he was what he did. He was an investment banker. He worked hard. He liked his job. He probably liked (And what was the right noun? How could she have been married to him for so many years and not know?) *banking* more than she did teaching—and she enjoyed teaching a very great deal. At least she did most of the time. She turned toward him and tried to see the hurt and the fear (because surely this scared him) behind the facade. And she did see it in the way his lips quivered ever so slightly when he tried to smile, and she could see it in the way that he blinked.

"I don't know," he said. "But we'll figure it out. Not long. I mean that: not very long. And the good news? I'm getting paid. And I like the idea of getting to go home before the two of you and working with the cleanup crew. I'd love to make sure that the house is in tip-top shape so that when you walked in the door you'd never even know what happened."

She thought of what he had told her about the couch. And the painting. She thought of the bodies in the living room and the front hall. He was, she understood, kidding himself. They'd always know what happened. Always. Still, she reached for his hand as they walked. It was a reflex. They walked the last block to her mother's in silence, but holding hands. When they arrived, she nodded at the doorman.

"Are you going to be okay?" she asked Richard.

"Of course! Don't worry, we'll be fine. Remember, I'm still getting paid."

"It's not money I'm worried about. It's you."

"Well, I'm fine, too. I mean it."

She rather doubted he was, but she wasn't going to press him. She simply reminded him to call her once he had spoken to the detective—or whoever at the police station could tell him anything. She watched him kneel and hug Melissa. She accepted another kiss from him on her cheek and his hands on the waist of her jacket. Then she waved good-bye and led their daughter back upstairs to the apartment. She was, she realized, unmoored by his touch. But she was also unprepared to have him beside her in bed.

...

As Kristin was falling asleep that night in her mother's guest bedroom, her daughter beside her, she replayed in her head her conversation with her brother. They had spoken by phone that evening after dinner.

"You should be glad he told you that he went upstairs with the girl," he said. "I think a lot of men would have lied. They would never have told their wives anything." She was relieved that her brother hadn't donned his therapist superhero cowl and asked her how she was feeling.

"But did I really need to know?"

"You said you asked him. He didn't lie."

"Or maybe he did. Maybe he did have sex with her."

"Okay, then. As you just asked yourself: Did you really need to know? Maybe he was sparing you. He was drunk, it was meaningless. So he dialed down what really happened. He told a white lie."

"That's not a white lie."

"Look, I know this sounds awful, but sometimes if you screw up the way some people do in a marriage, it's best to keep whatever you did to yourself. Especially if it's a onetime thing. Does your partner really need to know? Not always."

"And if it wasn't a onetime thing? Who knows what he does when he's traveling? And he travels a lot."

"I like Richard."

"So you trust him."

Even over the phone she heard her brother exhale. "People always surprise me. They really do."

"That doesn't reassure me."

"Whatever he is—whoever he is—he's definitely not his younger brother."

"That's a low bar."

"Your marriage has always struck me as pretty damn solid," her brother said, trying to be more definitive.

And, the truth was, she had always thought it was. They'd been married fourteen years, and it still had its moments of wild electricity. Yes, it was different now that they were forty and lived in the suburbs; it was calmer because they had a daughter who was nine. They were ensconced in their careers. But they'd rented a tiny beach house in Montauk that summer, and those Friday nights when he would arrive for the weekend, joining her and Melissa, had been seriously perfect: the late dinners on that splinter-fest the three of them called a picnic table. The way she and Richard would ravish each other after nearly a week apart, once Melissa had fallen asleep. The margaritas on Saturday afternoons. They'd had her friends out with them two weekends, and the grown-ups had actually danced to the vinyl on the portable turntable that she had brought to the house to surprise him. They had danced like they were back at some grungy rock-and-roll venue near Saint Mark's and once again were in their twenties.

But now she found herself questioning those days in between, when she and Melissa had lived with their cat at the beach. What really had he been doing back in Bronxville? What really had he been doing in the city? She grew angry at herself for doubting him now, because he didn't deserve that. But she couldn't help it. By the time she finally fell asleep, she found herself wondering if her brother was correct and they all would have been better off if Richard had told her nothing—nothing at all.

Alexandra

My first days when I was a prisoner in Moscow, before I was brought to the cottage, Inga would sit beside me on the hotel bed. She would either use her laptop computer or my cell phone, and she would send e-mails or texts to my grandmother and pretend they were from me. At first, she would need to ask me questions: she would want to know the names of my friends at school or the girls in dance class. I was supposed to give her names of people I wanted my grandmother to say hi to, such as Nayiri. Or the name of a favorite teacher, maybe. I was supposed to come up with ballet stories my grandmother could tell Madame.

I considered making up names as a distress signal. Maybe my grandmother would understand this was big mayday and I was in trouble. But what if my grandmother asked me who these people were? Inga would know I was lying, and I was scared of the new ways they would find to punish me.

One time, Inga asked me to pick two things I wanted Grandmother to give to Vasily to mail to me. I picked my hoodie sweatshirt with the logo of the Armenian soccer team and a pair of black pajamas with white silhouettes of dogs with floppy ears. I never got them. What a surprise. Vasily probably just threw the clothes in the trashcan in his office. No, come to think of it, he probably gave them to some other girl whose mother or father was dying so he could worm his way into her family's heart, too—and then kidnap her and make one more human sex toy.

Other times, still pretending she was me, Inga would tell my grandmother how busy I was and how hard I was working. She would write that I loved the dance teachers here. She would say I was making new friends.

At some point, Inga must have suspected that I was thinking of ways to send secret, coded SOS. Maybe I hesitated. Maybe I sounded guilty. She sighed and looked at me with her big eyes like I was huge disappointment to her. Then she told me that if I did not try harder to help, my grandmother would lose her job at the hospital. Vasily would see to that. She said that if I tried to hint about what was really going on, my grandmother might even have a horrible accident on her way to work. Even nurses wind up with broken bones, she told me. And she reminded me (as she did often) of the first video they had made of me naked with the men, and how easy it would be to share that video (or any of the others they had forced me to make) with my whole world in Yerevan.

My grandmother would write back that she missed me, but was so happy for me and so excited for my future. One evening when Inga read me one of those e-mails, I wept so much that Inga rubbed my shoulders and my back, and told me that in the end we would all find happiness. To this day, I have no idea if she believed that for even a second.

...

Prisoners count the blocks in their cells or the rivets on their tin toilets. They count the squares in the metal bars of their door or in the front of the cell window—if there is a window.

I watched television those first days in Moscow. I curled up in a ball on the bed and counted the paisley teardrops on the wallpaper. I counted the stripes on the upholstery on the loveseat. I counted the birds that would sit like bookends on the edge of the roof of the building across the street. I considered breaking the window and screaming for help; I considered breaking the window and jumping to my death.

I thought of all the fairy-tale princesses locked away in towers in dark forests. Why did Rapunzel not kill herself?

Even though I had that TV and a radio, I would sit by the window for hours and stare out at the world that was now kept from me.

By then they had taken my clothes. They had removed the white terrycloth bathrobes from the closet to make sure that I was always naked. (At first, I would try and turn the bed sheets into pretend togas. When they figured out what I was doing, they threatened to take away my blankets and sheets if they ever walked in and the bed was not made.)

The only people I saw were Inga, my guards, and the men who would come fuck me.

...

Before we left for the cottage, I tried to escape from the hotel. Where I would have gone if I had made it is a mystery since I had no money, no credit card, no phone, and no passport. I had no clothes. At that point, I had not even been allowed outside my hotel room. I think I just hoped I would make it to the lobby and then to the street. I would find a police guy who wasn't corrupt. (Even that was going to be long shot.) But I want you to know that I tried.

Months later, I would try to escape the cottage, too. Obviously, that was also a failure.

But first there was the hotel disaster.

One of the dudes who watched the hallway got his tip, which basically was me: call it part of my on-the-job training. Inga would coach me as the guard climbed on top of me. Or I climbed on top of him. This time the guard was called Rad. (Who knows what his real name was? Radomir maybe.) He was drug-addict thin and I guess in his early twenties. He always reeked of cheap cologne. I could smell him in the hallway even through the shut hotel room door. I would watch him through the peephole and breathe through my mouth so I wouldn't have to inhale orange and musk. Rad hoped to be a black and white dude someday, but I didn't see it then and I don't see it now. He was not smart enough. And he was too nice. I mean that.

He had forgotten a rubber, and even though I had been on the pill for seven days, Inga said she would go downstairs and get him one. You can't take chances with new merchandise, right?

"No funny business, you two," she said, smiling like a perky schoolteacher, and meaning simply, "Don't fuck." Then she left the room and he sat back on the bed on his knees, his dick a thin flagpole in his lap, and I leaned up on my elbows. I heard in my head the word *downstairs,* which meant that Inga might be gone a few minutes. And Rad was in the bedroom with me. So, there was no one in the hallway. All I had to do was get past Rad, sneak to the stairwell, race down to the lobby, and then run into the street. Sneak, race, run. I am not a violent girl, but I had just spent a week trapped in hotel room as a sex slave student. This was my big chance: I was ready to attack Rad.

There were identical brass lamps on the tables on both sides of the bed. It seemed to me that I could conk Rad on the head with one. I could grab his clothes—at least his shirt—off the cushy chair in the corner. And I could be off. So now it was a five-step plan: Conk. Grab. Sneak. Race. Run.

I acted like I was stretching my right arm. I purred. I tried to smile at Rad like happy little slut. (I was not yet a "courtesan": I was just a fifteen-year-old kid trying to look like she enjoyed getting banged by strangers with scratchy scruff on their faces.) Then I grabbed the lamp by its stand, using both my hands because I discovered it was too heavy and wide to lift with one hand, and I pulled it as hard as I could. What happened next happened quick: first, the lamp's cord did not pull easily from the wall, so Rad had an extra second to see what was coming and get his hands in front of his face. Second, the lamp had a shade which acted like automobile airbag when I tried to smack him on the skull the first time. When I tried to hit him a second time, he grabbed my arms and suddenly we were wrestling, and for a thin guy he was very strong. Or, at least, he was stronger than me—which is probably no big deal. He kicked the lamp off the bed with his bare foot and pinned me down, kneeling on my stomach and pressing my arms back into the mattress.

"Are you crazy?" he asked me.

And I was yelling at him to let me go, begging and crying that I had to get away, but he just shook his head and laughed. So I spat at him. It was the first time that I had ever spat on a person. I think growing up I had figured I would go through life without ever spitting on a person. I guess not.

It was right about then that Inga returned. She had not had to go downstairs to a drugstore for condoms, after all. She found one in her purse while she was waiting for the elevator.

She looked as mad as I would see her for a long time, her eyes wide like insane person.

Rad tried to take the bullet for me. That's what I mean about how he might have been just too nice for this line of work. Here I had just spat on him and tried to hit him on the head with a lamp, and still he wanted to protect me. He said he had gotten overanxious and I was trying to stop him so I didn't get pregnant. But Inga believed this like she believed in Santa Claus or communism.

I thought they would beat me.

But beating is just not good for the product. Makes it less attractive. Less valuable. They try not to beat a girl if they can help it. (Sometimes, at first, I made it so they couldn't help it.) Usually they drug you or hold you underwater or take away your food.

That night would be the first time they drugged me.

...

I should have kicked Rad in the crotch. I know that now. I did not know that then.

...

There was a new girl on the hotel room floor. I would discover that the next night, when I woke from my drug sleep and heard her banging on walls. At first I thought the banging was a dream. I had had a whole ballet of very strange dreams: exotic flowers (always cut), tropical fish (always plump), and men in black suits (always in need of a shave). But then I knew. I knew exactly what the pounding was. I had pounded just like that myself.

Chapter Seven

Kristin wasn't wild about this reverse commute to Bronxville on Monday morning, but it was clear that Melissa rather enjoyed it. The girl didn't like having to get up so early—the two of them awoke at Grandmother's apartment at five-thirty so that they could catch a six-forty-five train—but once they were seated and the conductor had scanned their tickets, Melissa admitted that there was something glamorous about the experience.

"Well, we'll get to do it again tomorrow," Kristin had told her. Twenty minutes later, they were walking from the station to the school—a long, magisterial, Gothic edifice that looked like it should be anchoring an Ivy League college. All of Bronxville's children went there, whether they were seven or seventeen. It had been built in the early 1920s, and now sixteen hundred students were crammed into it between their arrival for kindergarten and their departure for colleges with (Kristin sometimes joked) nationally ranked lacrosse and soccer teams. Every school day Melissa would go to the elementary school wing, and Kristin would dive into the hormonal, seemingly primeval ooze that marked the high school section. The same architect, Harry Leslie Walker, designed three of the four buildings at the corner of Pondfield and Midland: the school, the library, and the church. When she and Richard were first showing her mother the home they were buying and what would become their neighborhood, her mother had stood at this corner and said, her tone somewhere between judgmental and bemused, "It's pretty: Disneyland for WASPs." But it *was* pretty, and the school was supposed to be very good, Kristin remembered thinking defensively. A year later, she would be teaching there. A year and a half after that, Melissa would be enrolled in the kindergarten.

Richard had managed to reach Patricia Bryant on Sunday afternoon, and the detective believed that the crime lab would be finished sometime on Monday. But to be safe, she had suggested that Richard not schedule the cleaning crew until Tuesday. That meant, he had told Kristin, that they should plan to spend Monday night at her mother's and move back home on Tuesday—after school. After, he hoped, the cleaning crew had left. He had said he would spend Monday night at the hotel, but he hoped that she would allow him to move back home on Tuesday. She had been evasive on the phone, though she knew that in the end she would say yes. After all, he would have been at the house all Tuesday anyway, supervising whatever it was these cleaners were doing. (For reasons she couldn't fathom, she saw the crew working in white hazmat suits, as if they were cleaning up a nuclear plant meltdown.) But she agreed that he should spend Monday evening at the Millennium: one last night of penance.

"Mommy?"

Kristin looked down at her daughter. They were waiting for the traffic light to change so they could cross the street. "Yes, sweetie?"

"Nothing happened in my room, right?"

The child was not looking at her. She seemed to be gazing at a squirrel that was about to shimmy up one of the trees in the small copse by the French bistro. Still, even without being able to see the girl's face, Kristin understood the unease that festered beneath the question. What precisely was Melissa imagining might have occurred there?

"No," she answered, forcing a firmness into her voice that she did not feel in her heart, but determined to provide the reassurance the child craved. "Absolutely nothing happened in your room."

And if she was mistaken? She didn't want to go there. It was already proving too painful and too difficult to move forward.

...

That day the police arrested five men in two separate raids, one in Brooklyn and one in Manhattan, all of whom were linked in some fashion with the escort service that Spencer Doherty used. They were all Russian, though some were now American citizens. Three were charged with, among other felonies, the recruitment, provision, and obtaining of people for the purposes of commercial sex acts. Two were charged with kidnapping. All five were charged with procurement of prostitution. There was the likelihood that some of them would be charged with laundering money as well.

In addition, five young women, two from Georgia and three from Russia, were rescued. None of them, the news reports said, would be charged with prostitution, though that was the sole reason why they had been brought to the United States. The fact that they were not arrested—the fact that the U.S. Attorney's Office was viewing them as victims, not criminals—was deemed a monumental victory by a variety of human and women's rights advocates. All five of them were illegal aliens. All of them could have been teenagers, though their actual ages were not yet known.

None of the men and none of the women, according to the papers or the broadcast news, had ever met the still missing Alexandra or Sonja.

And despite a bail figure that the men's attorneys argued was obscene—after all, none of them had murdered anyone, and the girls were healthy, well cared for, and, the lawyers insisted, rather happy—the three men who were not charged with kidnapping were back on the street by nightfall.

. . .

Kristin's first class that day was her section of AP American History, a dozen and a half juniors who this morning were far less interested in antebellum discord than they were in . . . her. She was asking them questions and trying to fuel a dialogue about the Compromise of 1850, but she could tell from their faces that most of them were focusing only on what may (or may not) have occurred in their history teacher's house. Dead Russians. Whores. An orgy. The boys looked a little awed while the girls looked a little sad. Sad for her. She was, she sensed, an object of pity in their eyes—that is, when she could meet their eyes. All of the students, the boys as well as the girls, looked down at their notes or at some mystical object just over her shoulder whenever she tried to engage them.

"How did the South benefit from the compromise?" she asked, sitting down on the edge of her desk. When no one spoke, she decided to ask Caroline directly. Caroline was one of her go-to kids whenever the conversation stalled. She had eyes that were always amused—sometimes sardonically so—a mane of lush auburn hair, and a statuesque figure that allowed her to wear jeans that looked epoxied to her legs. She was on the student council. She was an editor on the student newspaper. She was, Kristin suspected, a bit of a mean girl, and if she didn't peak in high school (which was always a possibility with these kids), she was going places.

Instead of answering, however, Caroline said—speaking slowly, haltingly, her tone uncharacteristically awkward—"Mrs. Chapman? Maybe it's none of our business, but there's kind of what my dad called at dinner last night an elephant in the room. We're worried. We're . . ."

"Go ahead, Caroline." She thought she could see where this was going and wasn't happy about the direction, but she wasn't sure how to derail the digression. She saw a few of the boys were staring down at their desks as if someone had replaced their AP textbooks with the *Sports Illustrated* swimsuit edition. But not all. Reed was watching her. So was Kazuo. So was Frank. And most of the girls were studying her, each of their faces a different point along the continuum between discomfort and dread.

"Well, my parents said it was better to ask you about all this stuff than not ask you. I mean, if it's upsetting you, it's upsetting us. And it might affect how we do on the AP tests."

Kristin nodded. She got it. The girl's parents were worried that the cataclysm in their daughter's history teacher's personal life was going to affect their darling's AP score—and, thus, where she might wind up in college. Trying to keep her tone measured, she asked Caroline, "Do I look upset?"

The girl waited a second. Then: "Kinda."

Kinda. The word had been spoken barely above a whisper, and yet it seemed to echo in the classroom with Matterhorn grandeur. *Kinda.* Kristin didn't believe she looked upset; she was despairing inside—she was shamed inside, she was smoldering inside, she was confused inside—but she thought she was keeping it together as far as the world was concerned. As far as a bunch of ostensibly self-absorbed adolescents could tell. She found herself starting to tremble at the very notion that Caroline's parents saw in the death of two men and her husband's emotional—if not actual—infidelity only the possibility that their precious child's AP score might fall from a five to a four.

"Well, Caroline," she began, trying (and failing) to maintain eye contact with the sixteen-year-old, "if you don't want to answer my question about the Compromise of 1850, how about taking a stab at this one: How do I look *kinda* upset? Any specifics?"

The girl and her best friend, Ayelet, exchanged glances. They were on the verge of rolling their eyes. "One specific?" she continued.

Caroline sighed, a magisterial teenage exhalation of exasperation. "Um, this," she said, and Kristin saw some of the boys—even Reed, usually so diligent, so quiet—struggling to suppress smiles.

"This?"

"I guess. I mean, I was just asking if you were upset, and you're kind of . . . interrogating me."

"I'm not interrogating you."

"Okay. Fine. You're not."

Kristin wanted to cry. How many times in the past forty-eight hours had she looked at herself in mirrors at her mother's and seen her eyes so red, so puffy that she thought she had looked vampiric? Three? Four? More? It seemed that she had always been crying or on the verge of crying. And when she wasn't, usually it was because she had been seething. But she thought she was keeping it together now. She had avoided the teachers' lounge before school this morning precisely so she would not have to discuss this nightmare with any of her peers and risk breaking down.

Okay. Fine. You're not. She heard the words again in her mind and understood that she had to wipe at her eyes. It wasn't merely that she could feel them growing moist; it was also a feverish, OCD-like compulsion. But if she did, there was the danger that she would be opening the dam and she would be reduced to sobs in front of her class. She took a breath and sat on her hands.

"Caroline," she began, unsure what she was going to say. "Yes. This was an awful couple of days. It seriously . . . sucked." She paused, surprised at her candor and her choice of words. She wasn't trying to talk down to her class; rather, she wondered if she had instinctively reached out to them. "I'm sorry. But the last forty-eight or fifty or whatever hours? The worst of my life. Yup, worse than the death of my father—who I loved a lot. You just never expect to be awakened to the news that there are two dead men in your house. Criminals, yes. People you've never met, sure. But still: a double murder. In your home. And you've probably heard the rest of the story: my brother-in-law's bachelor party got a little . . . crazy. I guess you all know that."

She wondered if she sounded a little crazy herself, but it no longer mattered. She released her hands from beneath her hips and wiped at her eyes. At her cheeks. Because now the tears had been set free, a glacier melting in May, the channels at the edge of her nose brimming with sadness.

"And you know what, Caroline? Your dad was right. That craziness is an elephant in the room. I'm glad you brought it up." She forced a smile. "I am kind of a mess. But you know what else? My family will get past this and I will get past this. I'll make sure you all kill it when AP testing time comes. I'll be fine and you'll be fine. I mean that."

Caroline nodded. Ayelet stood up, and for a second Kristin feared the girl was going to embrace her. She was afraid that was the extent of her collapse: she needed comfort from the teen girls in her class. In her care. The students had never seen anything like this, and she wondered if she was going to have to rewrite the books on adolescent psychiatry and child development: these kids were empathetic. They were actually worried about her.

Fortunately, however, the girl simply handed her a tissue.

"Thank you," she said.

"Welcome."

She blew her nose. Then, as Ayelet was sitting down, she had a thought. "One more thing before we get back to the Compromise of 1850. I know a lot of you have younger brothers and sisters, some in the elementary school. So, I have a favor: when you talk about Mrs. Chapman's meltdown—which I know was epic—please do what you can to make sure the story doesn't get back to my daughter. Melissa is in the fourth grade. Kazuo, your sister and my daughter obviously are great friends. They're in the same class. Same after-school dance class, too. So, I would be seriously grateful if all of you could be—and here is an SAT word to keep in mind—circumspect. Judicious."

Kazuo grinned. "No prob, Mrs. Chapman. These days? She's all about the clothes and inappropriate TV."

"Melissa, too," she agreed, and once again she dried her cheeks with her fingers. She felt her wedding and engagement rings against the skin there, and found herself—much to her surprise—smiling back at the boy.

...

Richard watched the afternoon sunlight pour through the wide restaurant window and brighten the soupspoon beside his napkin. Most of the lunch crowd was gone now, and the hostess was helping a waiter straighten the white tablecloths and tidy the menus. When Richard looked up from the spoon, his brother was talking—it seemed as if his brother was always talking—moving his hands a bit like he was a lunatic given a conductor's baton and an orchestra. The gestures were too big for a table this small. And he seemed to be speaking mostly to Spencer Doherty, who was leaning back rather comfortably in the third of the four chairs. The fourth chair, the one opposite the window, was empty except for the blazer that Spencer had draped over it. He was wearing gray suspenders with silhouettes of people tangoing on them.

"I mean, I know we're lucky to be alive," Philip was saying to Spencer, "and I'm not blaming you. It's not your fault, buddy, it's really not. But how the hell did it all go so wrong so fast? One minute those girls are like this dream come true—"

"Wet dream," Spencer said, pretending to correct him.

"Wet dream. Agreed. But the next? A nightmare. I mean, how much legal trouble are you in?"

"Me? A lot. My lawyer is going to stress that I thought I was just hiring dancers. The problem is that I used this service before, and the girls—different girls, but still smoking hot imports—were pretty much down for whatever. So, it will depend on how much the police feel like digging and how much the feds feel like prosecuting me. It's early, but it looks like the deal will be something like this: no criminal charges in exchange for my testimony against the escort service."

"You would testify against the Russians? Are you nuts?"

"I probably don't have a choice. If I don't, I'm looking at charges that may even include sexual assault on a minor—if they can prove either of the girls was underage."

Richard felt himself cringe reflexively at the word *underage*. He almost said something, but his brother beat him to it. "How would they prove that? And . . . *either*? Does that mean you fucked them both? You dog, you! Wow!"

"I only fucked the blonde. But I had the other one naked on my lap, and it's not like I was sitting on my hands. That could be a problem if it turns out she's a kid. Besides, that's only part of the nightmare."

"Only part? God. Can't wait to hear the rest, man."

"My legal fees are going to be . . . costly. You would not believe what I had to plunk down. Scary big. And I may be looking at some very costly civil crap."

"Civil crap?"

"My lawyer has already gotten . . . overtures . . . from Chuck's lawyers. And Brandon's."

"Are you kidding me? What the fuck is that about?"

"It's all just preliminary right now. But he's hearing words like 'emotional distress.' 'Mental anguish.' All, of course, caused by my 'reckless' conduct."

"Those pricks! Those gutless bastards! Look, I'll call them right now and—"

"Don't. It's Brandon's wife. And I don't know what the deal is with Chuck. It may be nothing at all. This all may go nowhere. But your calling them won't make it better and could make it worse."

"Bottom line, you're not looking at jail time, right?" Philip said, both hands silencing an imaginary percussion section.

"God, no. Can you imagine? Holy fuck, that would be crazy awful. Still, even my legal fees are going to be astronomical. I wonder . . ."

"Go on," Philip encouraged him.

"Do you think your friends at the party would kick in some dough to cover my lawyer?"

"Yeah, I don't see that happening. Didn't everyone already give you a few hundred bucks each for the girls?"

"Most of the guys did. Not all. But this isn't about that. We're not talking a few hundred bucks each. My legal bills are going to be batshit crazy."

"We're all dealing with fallout," Philip told him. "I have a fiancée that is still royally pissed. I mean, I have a sick feeling any minute now she is going to call off the wedding."

"Are you serious?" Richard asked. He had been so appalled at the conversation around him—it was like dining with sexist (and sexually voracious) seventh graders—that he hadn't spoken in a few minutes, and the sound of his voice surprised him.

"I am. And you have to really fuck up to get someone like Nicole so pissed off at you that she calls off a wedding."

"I am really sorry, Philip."

His brother rolled his eyes and put out his hands palms up, the universal sign for *what-the-fuck*. Then Philip turned to Spencer and continued. "Meanwhile, my brother here? Leave of absence from work. Not kidding. His company is making him take a leave of absence. How messed up is that? And I think he's going to have to burn his fucking house down and rebuild it. He'll have to salt the dirt and the ashes. I mean, you saw the living room. You saw the front hall. You saw—"

"Spencer?" Richard asked, interrupting his brother and turning toward his brother's friend.

Spencer swallowed the last of the beer in his mug and waited.

"You're younger than me," Richard began.

"Oh, but I aged in the last two days, man. I have aged a lot."

"Do you guys just naturally bring hookers to bachelor parties? These days, is that a thing? Is that just . . . done?"

"These were party girls. Not hookers."

"You just said you were paying for girls who were down for whatever."

"Well, yes. But it's a fine line. An escort—a real high-class chick—can cost a lot more than what I was paying. Given what I'd forked over and what I'd told them, I kind of assumed they were going to fuck Philip and fuck you. I did. I mean, I would never admit that in a deposition or a courtroom. But even that was just an assumption. It's not like there was a legal expectation. It's not like I was paying a housekeeper and we laid out precisely what she was supposed to clean—or not clean. And I had no idea that the blonde would let me fuck her. That was just a happy little treat. And, man, it was a treat. Wow . . ."

Philip clapped those hands of his. "I know, I know, I know. It was like fucking a porn star—but real!"

"Spencer said he had sex with the blonde," Richard pressed his brother. "And obviously I saw you with her. We all did. But what about Alexandra? Did you have sex with her, too?"

"God, she has a name," Philip said, his grin a little mordant. "Nope, I only fucked the blonde. Why, my older brother? Do you have a proprietary interest in this Alexandra?"

"No. Of course not."

"I was just giving you shit. But seriously, what do you think her real name is? I guess we'll find out when they arrest her."

"Or when they find her corpse," Spencer added. "Which would, I must admit, decrease dramatically that whole underage issue thing they're holding over my head."

Philip sat back in his chair and dropped his hands into his lap. "You know, I kind of prefer just viewing them as the blonde and the one with the black hair. It makes this all easier."

Philip continued to talk, but Richard stopped listening. He was exasperated and had to shut them out.

Still, a part of him was relieved that neither Philip nor Spencer had been with Alexandra. She wasn't his daughter—after the party, he could never view her as a daughter—but he had felt a fatherly pang spring from his chest when he had imagined her with his brother or a creep like Spencer. And the idea of her . . . dead? Or hiding? Or hurt? It left him woozy. He recalled that moment when she had taken his arm on the stairs in his home, and there in the restaurant he looked down at the spot near his elbow. She was just a kid. It just wasn't fair.

He felt a wave of sadness nearly smother him and wondered where she was now.

...

Richard was walking two blocks north of the restaurant on his way back to the Millennium when suddenly someone was calling his name and jogging through the afternoon crowds on the sidewalk to catch up to him. It was Spencer.

"Unless I have managed to get very lost or I have early-onset dementia, your hotel's the other way," he said to his brother's friend when Spencer was beside him.

"I told Philip I had a dentist appointment. Can I walk with you?" He was a little breathless. He dabbed at the sweat on his temples with his handkerchief.

"Sure. But does that mean you really don't have a dentist appointment?"

"Yeah, I lied. I need to talk to you."

Richard couldn't pinpoint precisely what Spencer would need to discuss with him that he didn't want Philip to hear, but he knew it had something to do with the bachelor party. It had to.

"Okay," he said, but he was wary.

"I'm sorry about your leave of absence. That sucks."

"Yeah. It does."

"But it's paid. Right?"

"It is."

"Good."

They were passing a luggage store. Briefly Richard fantasized taking Kristin and Melissa and disappearing somewhere. Someplace you could reach only by airplane.

"And obviously you do pretty well as an investment banker. That's some house you have. And Bronxville? Not a cheap place to live."

He couldn't see specifically where this was going, but the wariness he had felt from the beginning ratcheted up a notch. "I do fine," he said evenly.

"I mean, Philip and I don't make anywhere near the scratch you do. We do what we do because we love it. It's not about the money."

"It's true. You're all saints at the Cravat. A person either teaches Native American kids to read on a reservation in New Mexico or goes to work at a boutique hotel in Chelsea."

He chuckled. "I hear ya. I just meant we chose not to be, you know, investment bankers."

"You have no idea how hard I work," Richard told him. He could have said more. He restrained himself from alluding to what a fuck-up Philip had been in high school and college.

"Oh, I do. You guys work crazy hard."

"Thank you."

"But you're paid for it. I mean, you have assets."

He stopped walking and turned to Spencer. All around them people were passing, sometimes buffered from the world by their earbuds and sometimes in conversations of their own. Reflexively he put his hands on his hips. "Are you about to ask me for money for your own little legal defense fund, Spencer? Is this a follow-up to your feelers at lunch?"

Spencer nodded and then looked boyishly down at his shoes. But Richard could see through the movement. It was an act. Feigned sheepishness. Spencer, like his brother, had no shame. None at all. "Yeah," he said, finally. "You nailed it. I do need a little help."

"No. I'm already paying a hefty retainer myself. But even if I weren't, the answer would still be no."

"Is that it?"

"It is."

"Well, it's not. I mean, I'm pretty scared. Scared enough that I'm having to make compromises with, you know, who I am. What I stand for," the fellow said, looking up at him now.

"You stand for nothing, Spencer."

"I'm honestly not the jerk you think I am. I want your marriage to make it through this mess. I really do. Philip says your wife is kind of hot. And you have a kid. A daughter."

"I think we're done here," Richard said, turning and starting to walk away. But as he half expected, Spencer stayed with him.

"We can be done here," said Spencer, "but it's not in your best interests if we are."

"No?"

"Nope. I'm thinking of your wife. I'm thinking of your career—at that bank of yours."

"Why does that sound like a veiled and utterly misguided threat?"

"Whoa! Where did that come from?"

"Spencer, there's no polite way for me to say this: you are seriously creeping me out. I'm not giving you any money. Let it go."

"I have pictures. Even a little video."

He stopped walking. He knew what Spencer was suggesting, but he couldn't believe it. Instantly he felt sick. "Of what?" he asked.

"Well, some of you."

"Do you mean from the party?"

"Uh-huh."

"You wouldn't have dared. We were all terrified of those Russian strongmen. There's no way you took your phone out."

"I did. Upstairs."

"You went upstairs? You went upstairs in my house?"

"Yup. And there you were. There you . . . both . . . were."

"What kind of pervert are you?"

"I think I would have been way more perverted if I hadn't filmed that little thing you brought upstairs. I mean, I would have preferred you weren't in the shots with her. I know you. And I prefer girl-on-girl porn, to be honest. But that's probably more than you need to know about my personal predilections."

"I should take your phone and break it."

"Which would be dramatic and awesome, but I have already

downloaded the images and video clip to my computer. Also, you would be making my job super easy. I'd make sure the assault got in the papers. Maybe I'd sue you."

"You're despicable."

"I'm not. I'm really not. I'm just scared I have nowhere near the war chest I need to get through this."

"I think you're bluffing. I think you're such a weasel that you wouldn't have risked pissing off the bouncers and taking one single photograph."

"Try me." Spencer reached into his pants pocket and offered Richard his phone.

For a long couple of seconds Richard stared at it. On there, if this moron was telling the truth, was the moment that he regretted most in the world, and a noxious mix of guilt and disgust compelled him to steer clear. And yet he had to know whether this was a ruse for quick cash. "We're on a street in the middle of Manhattan. Not here," he said finally.

"Oh, here's fine," Spencer countered, and already he was holding the phone so Richard couldn't help but see that his brother's loser friend was telling the truth. There she was, Alexandra, naked on the bed, and there he was naked before her; there she was reaching out for him. Abruptly Spencer paused the video and closed the phone window.

"I have about ten seconds on either side. Plenty of her. Plenty of you. She was about to go down on you when my own girl sort of, you know, distracted me and we moved on."

"That didn't happen. She didn't—"

"Yeah, I believe that," Spencer said sarcastically. "Looked good and filthy to me."

Richard felt himself chewing on the insides of his cheeks and stopped himself. The fact was, Spencer was right. It looked incriminating. Certainly it would appear that way to Kristin. He'd already lied to her about the kiss. This video? It would destroy the little credibility he had left.

"How much do you want?" he asked.

"I have a feeling you take home some mighty righteous bucks. I was thinking twenty-five thousand to start."

"To start?"

"Not a lot of money to a guy like you. But it is to a guy like me. And I don't know where this is going."

"What makes you think I won't go to the police? I met a lot of them on Friday and Saturday."

"Because the last thing you want is more publicity. It can't be good at home—or at work. You don't want your wife to see what I have. Or your boss. Besides . . ."

"Besides what?"

"Five words: sexual assault on a minor. They're dangling that one over me. Well, I have video evidence of you with the girl. The police would have way more on you than they have on me."

"She wasn't a minor!"

"I sure hope not. But we just don't know, do we?"

He feared if he didn't leave Spencer now, he might punch him—which, perhaps, was just what Spencer wanted. "Let me think about it."

"I think that's best."

"What's your number?"

"Oh, just call me at the Cravat. I have nothing to hide." Then, much to Richard's absolute disbelief, he extended his hand, expecting Richard to shake it.

Alexandra

I was fifteen years old when I was abducted.

I turned sixteen at the cottage.

When I was seventeen, they brought me back to Moscow and started having me work with Western men: men from the United States and England and France. They brought Sonja and Crystal, too. These men were more refined than the black and whites. I thought they were more interesting. More educated. More perverse. Most nights, things took longer.

My skin wasn't scratched by their stubble.

I was almost eighteen when my grandmother stopped trying to visit. When she stopped asking for photos of me at the dance studio. When she stopped asking questions about my progress and when I might return to Yerevan for a visit. She died on January 6, the day we celebrate Christmas in Armenia, when she was killed by a hit-and-run driver. She was crossing the street just outside her apartment. There was a witness, but the car—the long black sedan of an oligarch—was moving so quickly that he never got the license plate. She was dead even before an ambulance got there. Inga pretended to be so sad when she told me the news, but she wasn't a good actress. I have a feeling that my grandmother had started giving Vasily hard time, asking too many questions about where I was and what really was going on. He got sick of her.

They didn't let me go home to Yerevan for the funeral.

I was nineteen when I reached what they told me was the summit: New York City. They promised us all there would be special freedoms when we got there because, by then, there was no going back. Besides, what was there for me to go back to? My mother and grandmother were dead. I had spent nearly four years on my back.

They told us we were going to get Internet access without a chaperone. Shopping without an escort. Maybe even a phone. That was how much they said they trusted us.

And, of course, there was the deal: freedom in two or three years.

Chapter Eight

On Tuesday, the cops left and the cleaners came. Richard recoiled when he saw the carnage inside his house and recalled the ugliness behind it, and he thought of his wife and his daughter less than a mile away at the school. He watched the cleaners, two young men and a third his age in navy blue jumpsuits that made them look like a cross between the prisoners who picked up garbage along the highway and technicians at a microchip processing plant, as they scrubbed and disinfected. As they blotted and dabbed. As they mopped. He put on a pair of black sweatpants and a Giants T-shirt and threw bottles into recycling tubs. He loaded the dishwasher with plates and glasses and silverware. He ran the dishwasher twice, and still there were plates and glasses in the sink and along the kitchen counters. The men at the party must have grabbed a new glass every time they poured themselves another drink. Someone had been drinking Scotch from the two-handled Peter Cottontail cup Melissa had used as a toddler.

He fed Cassandra and then, when she looked up at him plaintively with her *Oliver!* "More, please" cat eyes, he fed her again. Fortunately, the cat was one of those felines who found people amusing. Once she was full, she seemed rather happy to be home.

She watched the cleaners work from different perches: atop the breakfront, on the stairs, half under the living room pouf. What must the animal have thought on Friday night when the Russians were killed and the blood had drained from their bodies like wine from an overturned bottle? Had she licked some off the tile? Had she wondered why these two strange people never awoke? Had she found the spent shell casings and rolled them around the floor with her paw, as if they were little metallic cat toys?

At one point, when he stood in the doorway to the mahogany-paneled room that had once been a library—his private chancel of movies and music—the cat sniffed the air, her nose twitching with fascination. He smelled it, too. Sex. He glanced at the leather couch and saw the splotches. In his mind, he saw the police investigators swabbing the stains with Q-tips, and then dropping the Q-tips in sealed plastic bags. He saw them using powders to extract fingerprints. Dactylogram. The scientific word for a fingerprint. One night Kristin had astounded him and a friend when they'd been dating by building the word on a Scrabble board from the modest four-letter *gram*.

He realized that there was absolutely no way the cleaners would be done by three-thirty or four in the afternoon, when Kristin and Melissa got home. No. Way. It was possible they wouldn't finish until after most of Bronxville had put their dinner plates in their dishwashers.

He carried the wannabe Bierstadt out to his car, folding down the backseats so he could lay it flat in the rear of the Audi. The blood on the canvas seemed pretty dry, but he was still careful not to touch it because he wasn't wearing gloves. He remembered that he wanted to phone the detective to get the name of her cousin at NYU—the woman who taught art history there. When he went back inside, for a long moment he hovered in the hallway and watched one of the men cleaning; he lost himself in the way the middle-aged fellow dabbed cold water and ammonia onto the wide swaths of blood that had splattered the wallpaper. The guy was working with the concentration of an artist, and Richard imagined that he was trying to resurrect a Renaissance fresco somewhere in Tuscany. And, alas, he was going to fail. It was hopeless.

"Maybe if we'd been able to start on Saturday," he said to Richard, his shoulders sagging a little apologetically. "But the blood has really set in."

"I kind of figured," he said.

"Do you have an extra roll of this paper floating around someplace? A roll the contractors didn't need when they papered the hallway the first time?"

He shook his head. Then he added, "I actually did the wallpaper myself in a couple of rooms in this house. I'm . . . I'm weirdly good at hanging paper. It's one of the few home improvement projects I don't screw up. But this wallpaper was here when we moved in."

"Well, maybe it was time for a change."

"Yeah. Maybe."

Meanwhile, one of the younger guys was using a basting brush to coat the bloodstains on the living room couch with a paste made of water and cornstarch. The fellow had thick yellow hair that fell to his shoulders and a model-perfect Roman beak for a nose. He looked like he should be surfing, not cleaning crime scenes.

"Will that really work?" Richard asked, aware of the way hope—wholly unearned—had leached into his voice.

"Probably not. It's kind of a part of the fabric now. And there's a ton here."

"Of blood."

"Yeah. Blood. Sorry."

"Not your fault."

"Too bad it's not slipcovers."

"I agree."

"Because then you could just trash them and get new ones."

"Yup."

"I mean, I can keep working. It's, like, my job, man."

"But . . ."

"I'd just get a new couch."

"I probably will," Richard agreed.

"I'd say give it to Goodwill, but I think it's too bloody for them."

He nodded. He made a mental note to find some rubbish removal service to take the sofa off his hands. But still the young guy continued to work. They all did.

Eventually, Richard wandered upstairs, eyeballing the bedrooms to make sure that the party hadn't spread there. He was pretty sure it hadn't, but he couldn't be sure. After all, that prick Spencer had been on the second floor. He was under the impression that the police had spent very little time in the bedrooms, because all of the guests had insisted at the station that they'd remained downstairs.

Richard, of course, had told the police—*Confessed?* It had sure felt like a confession—that he'd been in the guest room with one of the girls, and so he presumed that the investigators had at least taken a quick peek in that room. But it really didn't matter what they might find there. Obviously his fingerprints were there. This was his home. He lived here. His fingerprints—and the girl's— were all over the house.

Still, he saw nothing untoward in his and Kristin's bedroom or in Melissa's bedroom. The bedspreads were still army-inspection flat. Well, his and his wife's was. Melissa was nine and usually made her bed pretty quickly before school. But it looked about the way it always did, and there were no glasses or beer bottles in the rooms. There were no ashtrays and no plates that any of the men might have used as ashtrays.

Plates. As ashtrays.

He hated his brother's friends. He hated Spencer in particular. He hadn't heard from him since yesterday, but Richard knew if he didn't call him soon, he would. He hadn't told anyone yet about the threat except for his lawyer, and that conversation hadn't been as helpful or as reassuring as Richard would have liked.

"You said that you and the girl didn't have intercourse. Is that true?" Dina Renzi had asked him.

"Absolutely."

"And no oral sex?"

"Correct."

"So there's nothing criminal on the video?"

"Well, certainly not sexual assault on a minor—if she even is a minor, which I doubt."

"Uh-huh."

"I'm telling you, she had to be eighteen."

"Look, if you're sure that's the case, then maybe you should pay this jerk off. We don't go to the police. Twenty-five G? Kind of a small price for the peace of mind. It would certainly help ensure marital harmony. And it would be one less reason for the press to write about you. Eventually, this story will go away, Richard—unless we keep feeding it with tasty little morsels like blackmail."

"But what if he asks for more?"

"You say he's a friend of your brother's. As despicable as your brother sounds, I have to believe that he and his pals could shame him into letting this go."

"After I've given him twenty-five thousand dollars . . ."

"I think the important things we have to accomplish here are to get you back to work and preserve your marriage. Then, just in case, we need to be prepared if those people claiming 'emotional distress' decide to come after you, too."

"Might they?"

"I told you, I think it's unlikely. It would be groundless. You didn't bring the girls into your home or call the escort service. You said you didn't even know for sure there would be a stripper."

"Quite true."

"Okay then. Maybe you should just view the twenty-five grand as a fine for your indiscretions and move on."

It seemed that his initial reaction on the street—the video would devastate Kristin—was the correct one. Dina was female. It was pure fantasy to think that he could diffuse the threat by telling Spencer that Kristin already knew about Alexandra and he should fund his war chest elsewhere. Something about the way Dina had caved so quickly—*help ensure marital harmony*—made clear that the images on Spencer's phone might be a last straw in ways that he couldn't fathom as a male.

And, of course, there was always the reaction of Franklin McCoy to consider. If it got into the tabloids that a managing director was being blackmailed, he'd surely be finished.

Now he went to the guest room, where he had brought Alexandra, and breathed in the smell of the room. Unlike the TV and music room downstairs, the cat would have noticed nothing new here. It smelled fine—which meant it smelled not at all. He stared at the spot on the bedspread where Alexandra had sat. Where they had sat together. He wondered where her father was. Her mother. He tried to imagine how a nice kid like Alexandra wound up in a foreign country, sitting naked in a strange man's house. He took a deep breath, wondering how long it would be before his memories of this nightmare turned to steam.

...

Much later, he would wander the first floor of his house, noctivagant as his cat. Then he would sit alone at the kitchen table, unable to sleep. Unwelcome in his own bed. He sat there drinking herbal tea, even though he hated herbal tea. He hated all tea. But he still hoped he might somehow get some sleep. Besides, drinking this tea was rather like wearing a hair shirt. He was punishing himself.

Upstairs, Melissa was sleeping in the master bedroom with Kristin. It was Kristin who had insisted. It was Kristin who had somehow kept it together when she surveyed the living room and the kitchen and the front hallway—when she, too, had watched in fascination as the cleaning crew had tried to wash away the stigmas of madness and degradation—and it was Kristin who had then brought Melissa up to her bedroom, the child still carrying her school backpack over her shoulder.

And that meant it was Kristin who had been with Melissa that afternoon when their daughter had found—there it was, right atop the plastic Tucker Tote filled with Barbie dolls, but somehow he had managed to miss it—what the child had mistaken at first for a jellyfish. A sick jellyfish. A dead jellyfish. Something she might have found washed ashore at the beach that summer.

It seemed that Spencer had taken Sonja to his daughter's bedroom. That's where he'd gone on the second floor. And when he was done with her—on his way back downstairs, perhaps just before pulling his iPhone from his pants pocket and peering through the camera lens into the guest room—he'd tossed his used condom onto a child's plastic carton of Barbies.

Alexandra

How I changed. How much I changed. I could see I was the same girl in the mirror, even if now I looked like courtesan instead of regular girl going to dance class. But inside I was different. So different. It wasn't just that I knew things about people. I knew things about me.

...

I said I was a better dancer than my friend Nayiri back in Yerevan, which probably makes you think I am a very ambitious person. Maybe once. And maybe Nayiri and I were competitive. But we were also friends. I would say we were as close as sisters, but I was an only child so I don't know. Once I read an Armenian translation of *Little Women,* and those girls were very different from Nayiri and her two sisters. Nayiri and her sisters seemed to fight like wolves day after day. Nayiri was always angry with one or the other. They stole each other's clothes and bangles, they argued over chores. So, I have no idea what having a sister is really like. But Nayiri and me? We never fought. We had played together as little girls, and then we danced together as we grew up. I would watch her in the studio mirror and she would watch me, so there was a little tension. She perfected her adagios before I did, but I got my toe shoes first. I could pirouette the length of the stage before she could, but she mastered her tours en l'air like boy: full rotations. Maybe she has mastered two rotations by now. It's possible. It's been a long time.

For a while, Inga made up lies I could e-mail Nayiri, too. But I think Nayiri could see we were growing apart. My pretend life must have seemed too glamorous to her. We stopped e-mailing when I was still at the cottage.

Sometimes I lost track of how I had wound up where I was. Who I was. I would hate myself when, sometimes, the sex would feel good. I would hate myself when, other times, the men were lower than pigs. I would hate myself for being too weak to kill myself. Why, I would wonder, had I not thrown myself out that ninth-floor window those first days in Moscow? I would think of my ancestors who had chosen to die rather than be dishonored. In 1915, after their men had been slaughtered by the Turkish gendarmes and the Kurdish killing parties and they had seen their children die of starvation or terrible diseases, many Armenian women would throw themselves into the Euphrates River to drown. Or they would throw themselves off the mountains on the way to desert killing fields like Der-el-Zor. It was, they knew, better than being raped. Better than being nothing but harem girl or the wife of one of the men who had murdered your husband and your father and your brothers and your children.

But I hadn't killed myself in Moscow, and I didn't later at the cottage. I would try and make myself feel better by telling myself I still could.

Anyway, the girls at the cottage were nothing like Nayiri. I probably wouldn't have been friends with any of them except maybe Sonja and Crystal if we'd been classmates in Yerevan or had lived in the same building. But when you are in the same boat, you make the best of the situation. Just like Nayiri and her two sisters, we fought over clothes—even though Inga picked them out specially for each of us—and we snapped about who was better with the black and whites. We even climbed over each other like kittens to get attention and those sometimes smiles from Inga and Catherine.

This is what I mean about capture-bonding. I know it seems strange that we wanted the approval of people who kept us prisoner. But if you are a person who needs no one's approval, you are probably crazy and live alone on an island or the top of a mountain somewhere. We all need to be appreciated, even if it's just because we are taught to spread our legs and smile for a man like this was something we wanted.

And I'll bet there is no one who needs approval more than teen girl.

...

Most of time, I did feel safe—at least when it came to the black and whites who came to the cottage, and then to the Europeans and Americans who came to Moscow. The two times I was beaten by clients, those men were beaten far worse by my captors. One of the men, they told me, was going to walk with a limp for the rest of his life. The other lost a big handful of teeth.

I was far more scared of our guards and our bosses. Of Inga and Catherine. They were geniuses when it came to torture. They knew just what to give and just what to take, and their moods could change like the sky in December. They knew how to keep us on edge—and, if we ever were disobedient, the things they could do that would hurt us the most.

...

In Moscow, I met two girls from Syria. Refugees of civil war there. Tell me, who's worse? Someone who sells young girl or someone who buys one?

...

We did not perform for webcams when we were in Moscow. Inga said there was some discussion among the men about what they called the "risks and rewards," because Daddy thought it was worth exploring. On the one hand, they thought it might be a way to make more money during the day, when most of the time we were killing time in our hotel rooms, smoking and watching TV. She said it was like McDonald's. They started opening for breakfast years and years ago. They already had the griddles, so it was crazy not to use them to cook eggs instead of hamburgers. Inga said Daddy talked about the time difference between Moscow and Los Angeles. When it is eleven a.m. in Moscow, which is downtime for girls like us, it is eleven p.m. in Los Angeles, which is perfect time for men to sit before their computers with their pants off.

But there were problems.

First of all, it would allow us girls more access to computers. Second, it would allow us to meet customers our bosses didn't know. Third, it would mean an online money trail. The computers could be traced.

So, Daddy and the men who ran us thought we might find a way to cry out for help. And then it might be possible for the police guys to find us.

Make no mistake: We were not escorts. We were not prostitutes. We were just slaves.

...

But still they would use this word around us: freedom.

They would dangle it before us like rattle before baby. Like piece of yarn before kitten.

It had been so long, I couldn't imagine. And none of us had been taught to be grown-ups, so freedom was like strange fantasy. We didn't pay bills or have checking accounts. We didn't have credit cards. We didn't know how to do anything but fuck and please people: the people who paid for us and the people who (and Inga and Catherine hated this word, and told us we would feel better about ourselves if we didn't use it) pimped us.

If we ever were actually free, what were we supposed to do? Suddenly wake up and be bank tellers? Nurses?

They said if I gave them two or three years in New York City without any problems—no attempts to escape, all my men happy—I would be allowed to keep a few of my regulars and the apartment they would find for me, assuming I could pay the rent. I would be what they called an entrepreneur, my own boss. It was my body, they said, and we would reach a point where I could do with it whatever I wanted. I would be twenty-one or twenty-two years old and I would be on my own.

We all would.

Anyway, that was the plan. Freedom. Or, at least, a life a little bit more like free girl than slave.

...

Inga and Yulian were with us 24/7 our first week in New York City. We called Yulian the White Russian, but only behind his back. He had thick hair the color of snow, and the shoulders and chest of a man who, when he was young, I bet could have benched close to three hundred pounds. I guess he was fifty. He always seemed a little bored when he fucked me, as if it was beneath him to relieve his urges on one of the slaves. He had been a young politician when the Soviet Union collapsed. The rumor was that he was married, but we never knew for sure. He may also have been one of Daddy's cousins, but that may also have been just a rumor. The men kept their lives private. He carried an antique Korovin semiautomatic pistol that he said was a gift from his godfather. Inga told me one time that Yulian's godfather had been KGB: Soviet secret police. One beautiful sunny day at the cottage, we were forced to watch him shoot birds.

The plan was for Inga to leave us after a week or two in America. Given our value, she was going to spend a little time to make sure our transition was like butter, but her world was Moscow. Not Manhattan. And she did go home after ten or eleven days with us. But Yulian and Konstantin stayed. They were business guys making things happen.

I remember the six of us had flown to the U.S. in two groups—two different airplanes. I was with Crystal and Konstantin. But the planes landed within half an hour, and so all of us were met at the JFK airport by two of the men who were going to help run us, Pavel and Kirill. Each was behind the wheel of an identical black Escalade.

Three weeks later, both of those dudes would be dead.

...

They told me that here in America, I was going to have to start watching the news on TV. Not just *The Bachelor.* I was going to have to start reading the newspaper. I had not been reading much English in Moscow, but I figured I would get it back quickly.

They said I had to do this because here I would finally be a real Western courtesan. And that meant I had to be able to make conversation. Arm candy in New York City must be smarter than arm candy in Moscow.

They said when I was "trained," I would start telling the johns I was an exchange student. I went to a university in Moscow and I was on a "study abroad" program at NYU.

They said an escort who looked like me would be making one thousand dollars an hour by the spring. (They never told me how much I would get to keep.) I could tell Inga was less sure about how much Sonja and Crystal would be worth. They did not speak English as well as me. And they were unpredictable. Sonja had that temper. And sometimes Crystal would slip and say those things that made them know how badly she wanted out.

I never told anyone I went to NYU. I never got the chance.

...

Sonja and Crystal and I each had a tiny bedroom on the third floor of a town house in New York City. We were in Manhattan. Most people think Russian criminals live in this place called Brighton Beach. Or maybe they think the criminals are out in Queens or Long Island. I guess there are some there. Maybe the dudes who run drugs wind up out in Brooklyn. I know there is a lot of muscle there. For instance, the drivers who met us at the airport lived near Coney Island. And maybe that's where Sonja and Crystal and I would have ended up if we had gotten addicted to drugs the way some girls did, which meant working a much cheaper track. But that wasn't us. That wasn't why they had brought us to America.

The town house was in a neighborhood called the East Village, a block and a half from the Tompkins Square Park. It was just off the Avenue C. In my little time there, I really was mistaken a lot for a rich kid from NYU. I am not kidding. When I was outside on the street with one of the men who had brought us to America—dudes like Yulian and Konstantin—people would think the guy was my father. When I was outside with Inga, they would think she was my mother. I always thought it interesting that the students and the shoppers and the police guys we would see on the sidewalks weren't scared of them. But, of course, only I knew the firepower they carried with them in their belts or their shoulder holsters or—in Inga's case—a black purse.

...

On one of our first days in New York City, Sonja and I were sitting on the floor of her little room playing solitaire and Crystal was lying on the bed. It was raining outside. Sonja's room still smelled of the man she'd had the night before, so we had opened the little window. Suddenly Crystal got up and went to look outside at the street.

"I hate it here," she said. It sounded like she was crying, so I stood up and went to her. I rubbed her shoulder through her T-shirt.

"You hate New York City, Crystal dear?" I asked. "Or America? Or is it your room?"

She was just letting the tears run down her beautiful cheeks. She wasn't wearing any makeup because it was only eleven-thirty in the morning. I pulled her against me.

"This room. My room. Your room," she said. Her voice had that zombie tone I have told you about. No emotion. "New York City. Moscow. America. I hate it all."

Sonja slapped a couple of cards down on the carpet. "Get used to it," she said. It was not like Sonja to be short with Crystal, but the sky was so gray outside and we were all getting used to this new world.

Crystal didn't turn to Sonja. She just shook her head in slow motion. "No," she murmured, "I can't."

We heard someone on the stairs, and it sounded like Yulian. So quick like bunny I took a tissue from the box we always had to keep by our beds and wiped her cheeks. "You're just homesick, baby Crystal," I whispered. "We'll talk later."

And we did. Sonja and I both talked to her. Sonja even offered to ask Inga about the two of them switching rooms, since Sonja's room had that window that looked out on the street and Crystal's just looked out at smelly alleyway. But we couldn't cheer her up.

...

If you had met Crystal, you'd see why Sonja and I always wanted to look out for her. She was thirteen when they took her. And she was even smaller than the rest of us. Not even four feet and eight inches tall when she started and not even five feet when they killed her. She was the one they sold to the men who wanted the girls that looked like children. Who were shy. She was the one they dressed like she might still be going to school. She had to wear blue jeans or pink corduroy overalls. While they bought us black and red lingerie for work, they bought her white underpants with Disney princesses and Tinkerbell on the front. On the crotch.

...

Sonja had blue eyes that always looked a little possessed—even a little demonic—and hair they bleached so white that at first it felt like straw and some even fell out. That was crazy scary two weeks for her. This was my Sonja. It was Sonja and me against the world some days, and it was Sonja and Crystal and me they wanted in America. That's how much they liked us—and how good we were at what we did.

And, yes, it was Sonja who, one night in a beautiful house near New York City, went berserk like Xbox demon. We had talked about getting away. We had even fantasized how, but that was usually just to cheer up Crystal. I never thought we would actually do it.

But then that night Sonja and I learned they had killed Crystal, and that was last straw for my Sonja. Me? I just went a little numb. But some part deep inside Sonja just said no more. No fucking more.

Besides, she knew things I didn't. She knew what Crystal had done. And she had overheard Pavel and Kirill that night at the party.

So while her timing might seem insane, it made sense. It made sense especially if you were Sonja. Yes, she went bitchcakes with that knife when there were witnesses—all those men at the party for the bachelor. But she went crazy in a place where it would be harder for Pavel to defend himself. (Kirill, too.) If she didn't succeed, would Pavel and Kirill actually kill us with all of those witnesses? Wouldn't they at least wonder if some of the men would defend us?

Besides, she believed that Pavel and Kirill were going to murder her and maybe me, too, after the party. She'd heard them talking that night. She couldn't wait until later. There might not even be a later.

And so we were off. In some ways, we were the most naive girls in the whole world about everything except sex and makeup and clothing and the *New York Post*. (Once we got to Manhattan, I read them the *New York Post* like it was the Bible and we were nuns. We studied Page Six. We looked for stories about pop stars and reality people and, of course, *The Bachelor.* They had told us to read a newspaper and we sure did.) But it had been a long time since we were free—in some ways, never.

Never.

And maybe we weren't really free, even then. After all, we were terrified. We were afraid of practically everyone. The Russians. The police guys. This was not like that day long, long ago when I was still in Yerevan and I was packing for Moscow. When I thought I was about to become a ballerina. This was not about the future at all. This was just about trying to find ways to be invisible. To stay alive. To not be killed like our poor baby Crystal.

Part Two

Chapter Nine

The conversation Tuesday night was infuriating and brief. Richard texted Philip for Spencer Doherty's cell and then went outside in the dark to call the son of a bitch. He stood in his driveway, occasionally staring up at the light in the master bedroom from which he was exiled.

"You fucked the girl in my daughter's bedroom! You left your goddamn rubber there! What the fuck were you thinking!" he said the moment Spencer answered his phone.

"Not your girl," said Spencer. "I fucked the blonde. So chill, okay?"

"My girl? I don't have a girl! I have a daughter, and—"

"Look, I was drunk. I don't know what I did with the condom. If I dropped it someplace stupid, I'm sorry. Blame it on the tequila."

"You're an ass, you know that?"

"Are you finished?"

"Am I finished?"

"Are you finished getting medieval on my ass about something that really doesn't matter? I kind of assumed you were calling to tell me how I was getting my twenty-five grand. Whether you were going to drop off a check at the hotel or make me meet you someplace for it."

"How can you look at yourself in the mirror?"

"Think about it another day. Maybe two. But screaming at me and insulting me only makes me less . . . patient. And it makes me focus on how much I'm really going to need. So, that twenty-five grand? It just became thirty."

"Already you're asking for more? How did I know you'd do that? Is it because you're such a pathetic, sexist loser?"

"Just words, buddy. Just words. So, here are the only ones you should be thinking about: I will ruin you. I really will. I'm in survival mode. So make no mistake: I . . . will . . . ruin . . . you. Sleep on 'em, okay?"

And then Richard heard him hang up.

. . .

The next morning, Wednesday, Richard sank deep into the leather couch in the TV room and tried to make sense of the unexpected numbness that came with aloneness. The way it had stunned him into a somnambulant torpor. Outside on the street a TV news van had parked for about fifteen minutes, filmed the house, and moved on. They probably had him peering from behind the curtains. He wondered when they'd go away once and for all.

He flipped the channels aimlessly among the talk shows, soap operas, and reruns of ancient sitcoms that seemed to dominate daytime TV, uninterested in a digital buffet even hundreds of channels long, and tried to imagine what Kristin and Melissa were doing or thinking that moment at the school. He was having far more success entering the mind of his wife: yesterday she had looked at the bloodstains and detritus and told him that their house had been scarred. She had seen the used condom and said their marriage had been violated. Last night he had slept downstairs on a futon on the living room floor—there was no way he was going to sleep on the living room couch, now a prop from a splatter film—because it was clear that his wife couldn't abide him beside her after all. She couldn't abide him on the same floor.

Or, more accurately, last night he had tried to sleep. Mostly he had dozed fitfully on the futon, wondering if he would have been better off at a hotel. Kristin said that before she had walked in the front door, she had convinced herself that the party wasn't as bad as her visions. Now? Now she knew it was worse. The condom in her daughter's bedroom had destroyed the fragile equilibrium she had recovered. She was, she had said, her voice muted by despair, unsure now whether they could even stay in the house. In the neighborhood. She dreaded having to return to her classroom.

"But you've been back two days. The worst is over," he had said, believing his argument was eminently reasonable. "It's not like your students will know about the condom."

"But I will," she had countered. "Besides . . ."

"Go on."

"They all know how sordid last Friday night was. Everyone does."

He nodded. She was, he feared, in fact underestimating how sordid everyone presumed the party was. And how squalid. He knew what was in the newspapers and on the web. He knew the sorts of photos and video that existed on Spencer's cell phone. But he sure as hell wasn't going to correct her.

His daughter's frame of mind was less clear to him, in part because she wasn't asking him questions about what specifically had occurred—which, when he was honest with himself, he was actually rather thankful for—and in part because he wasn't sure how much she understood about sex. She hadn't known that it was a used condom when she had started to reach for it, curious. Thank God, Kristin had been with her. He wasn't there, but in his mind he saw Kristin diving like a cornerback to grab a loose football off the ground. She had scooped it up before their daughter could touch it. It was a testimony to the reflexive courage of a mother— the maternal selflessness—that Kristin had grabbed the damn thing with bare hands as if it were a mere pretzel that had fallen to the floor, rather than the preternaturally disgusting biohazard that it was.

Still, he knew his daughter was scared. He suspected that she was afraid for her parents' marriage, and he had a sense she was unnerved that he wasn't going in to work. It was like he was in time-out—which he guessed he was.

About two hours ago, he had phoned Hugh Kirn, that doctrinaire pedant of a lawyer at Franklin McCoy, but either Kirn was truly on another call—as his secretary had said—or he was avoiding him. Still, the lawyer hadn't yet called him back. And so half an hour ago he had phoned Dina Renzi. She'd said she would give Kirn a ring and check in. She would remind Kirn once more how unlikely it was that Richard would be subjected to criminal charges, and how already the public spectacle was dissipating: the stories in the tabloids and on the web were all about Monday's arrests, and filled more with legalese than prurience. Even a tale as juicy as this one—investment bankers and hookers, dead Russian mobsters in a refined Westchester suburb, a manhunt for a pair of female killers—had a pretty short shelf life in the digital age. And as for Spencer's increased demand? She had said two things, neither of which made him feel any better. Pay it. And remember these weren't naked pictures of Jennifer Lawrence someone had hacked from her iCloud account. He wasn't Brad Pitt. They really weren't worth a whole hell of a lot.

He reminded her of all he still could lose, and she had reminded him that this is what happens when you take naked girls upstairs to the guest room.

And now he was waiting for Dina or Kirn to call him back.

Absentmindedly he fingered the Band-Aid on his neck; for the first time in years, he had cut himself shaving, and it was a doozy. Thank God you couldn't kill yourself with a Gillette Fusion razor.

He scrolled through the contacts on his iPhone. He wasn't sure what he expected to find, but he was hoping there was a name there he could talk to. Just call and say hello. He had noticed that none of his golf buddies had phoned him since that one call on Saturday afternoon, and that was well before the scope of the violence and bacchanal were clear. Of course, those guys might be more accurately described as golf acquaintances: a group of men, all five to ten years older than he was, whom he saw on occasional Saturdays. They talked about work and they talked about their families, but he was pretty sure he had never spent any time with any of them away from the country club. Away from the golf course. Their wives recognized each other when their paths crossed at supermarkets and restaurants, but Kristin had never taught any of their children.

He was also acutely aware that none of the people he thought were his friends at Franklin McCoy had checked in. He guessed he was glad the women he worked with hadn't called. He was embarrassed, and he wasn't sure what he would have said—what someday soon he would have to say—to Anna Gleason. Or to Sue Miles. Would they be sickened or merely surprised? He couldn't decide. And the men? He had almost invited two of his male work pals to the party, so he would have some friends of his own there: David Pace and Will Dundon. He always enjoyed having lunch with one or both of them, and they were clearly a pair who wouldn't have minded a stripper and a little harmless drinking. But in the end, he hadn't. And he hadn't, he knew, for the same reason he hadn't invited the men with whom he played golf or the fellow he went to college with who lived in Scarsdale or the male halves of any of the couples with whom he and Kristin socialized. (Lord, the male halves of those couples didn't dare call him: they were all friends through their wives.) He hadn't invited any of his friends because he had understood on some core level that this whole bachelor party thing was kind of juvenile. Kind of disturbing. Kind of gross. He hadn't even told anyone ahead of time that he was hosting it.

He guessed that was why his friends hadn't called him first. But Dundon and Pace from Franklin McCoy? He feared there was another reason, one that transcended awkwardness: self-preservation.

At the moment, he was in exile. He was a pariah at the bank, and he was going to be given a very wide berth.

He wondered what would happen if he called his idiot younger brother and told him what Spencer was doing. *So, Philip, your good friend Spencer is trying to blackmail me.* His brother might be able to shame Spencer into letting go or at least stopping at thirty. But probably not. Spencer was a loose cannon. For all Richard knew, Spencer might go ballistic if the Chapman brothers ganged up against him: he might launch the video. He might become the wolf in a trap that chews off its own leg: upload the video and watch it go viral faster than the flu. He might be throwing away its blackmail potential, but he'd be ruining a certain Franklin McCoy managing director.

Besides, Richard knew he wasn't emotionally prepared to tell Philip that the video existed. He was ashamed. He was Philip's older brother, and older brothers never went to their younger brothers for help—at least not in the Chapman family. He held himself to a higher standard than Philip, and the video compromised that moral authority. He understood on some level that eventually he might have to tell his younger sibling. But he wasn't there yet.

Now he tossed his iPhone onto one of the leather couch cushions beside him and watched it slide over the stains where strangers had been fucking last week. The bottom line? All of those names in his iPhone were worthless. He had absolutely no one on his side but Dina Renzi, and she was only there because he was paying her.

. . .

It was Claudia's family's turn that Wednesday to drive the three girls to dance—Melissa and Claudia and Emiko—and because dance didn't begin until four-thirty, there was always time for ice-cream between school and studio. The ice-cream parlor was around the corner from the dance studio in Scarsdale. The three girls had ballet for an hour and then jazz for an hour. It was, Melissa had heard Claudia's mom observe any number of times, a pretty serious workout, even for kids who were nine. But Melissa looked forward to it immensely: she and Emiko (and even Claudia, once in a while) practiced daily what they learned each Wednesday afternoon. This deep into the autumn, it would be dark when the girls emerged from the studio.

Today Claudia's mother, Jesse, was driving, but equally often it was Claudia's dad. The two of them both worked from home a lot. Her dad was a computer engineer and her mom was a copywriter. Now the three girls were sitting in a booth and eating different variations on the ice-cream sundae, while Jesse sipped her coffee, read news stories and texts off her smartphone, and occasionally chimed in on the girls' conversation. Claudia was sitting beside her mother on one side of the booth, while Melissa and Emiko sat across from them on the other.

Abruptly Jesse put her phone down on the thick wooden table-top and leaned across the table toward Melissa. Melissa thought that Jesse was—very much like her own mom—very pretty. But unlike her mom, Jesse dressed more like a teenager. Or at least, Melissa guessed, like a much younger woman. Her mom said it was because while Jesse worked at home most days, when she had meetings she had to look more stylish and hip than a schoolteacher. Melissa could tell that she must have come straight to the school from a meeting to pick up the girls, because she was decked out in black and gray animal print leggings and a black jacket that looked sort of like a man's, except it was cut like an hourglass. Her leather boots had stitching the same color gray as her leggings.

"So, Melissa," she asked, "how are you?" She had emphasized the verb to stress that she genuinely wanted to know—that she was sincerely interested. Melissa understood that this was no mere social formality, where she was only supposed to nod and say fine. She paused the spoon with her chocolate ice cream in midair and thought for a moment. Claudia and Emiko were watching her. Jesse was watching her. She knew that everyone was talking about her father behind her back, but only Claudia—who, Melissa's mom said, was one of those brilliant math kids who were born without filters—had wanted to talk to her face-to-face about the dead men and the prostitutes in her house. Claudia had wanted to know if she was afraid of the dead men's ghosts (Melissa had not been afraid until Claudia had suggested that the spirits might have chosen to remain in the house), and whether her parents were going to get a divorce because of the prostitutes (she was indeed stressing about that, and the fears only became more pronounced when her mom had told her dad that he had to sleep downstairs in the living room—not even upstairs in the guest room).

But even if Jesse had asked the question with the hope that Melissa would respond with a deep and honest answer, the girl wasn't prepared to go there. At least not yet. Melissa shrugged and said, "Fine." Then she put her ice cream into her mouth.

Jesse shook her head and reached across the booth, gently resting her fingers atop Melissa's hand that wasn't holding the spoon. "I get it," the mother said. "This stuff is really confusing and scary. It's hard to talk about."

"I'd be scared of the ghosts," Claudia piped in. "I told her, Mom."

"Claudia, I specifically asked you not to talk with Melissa about this weird thing you have about ghosts," Jesse said, exasperated.

Claudia shrugged and stirred what was left of her sundae into soup. "Anyway, that's what would make me not fine."

"There is no such thing as ghosts," Jesse said pointedly, staring deep into Melissa's eyes. "I've told Claudia that. And now I'm telling you that."

Melissa looked away. She stared down at the woman's hand atop hers. Jesse's nail polish was a shade of red that reminded her of the maple leaves on the trees in their yard a week ago. Now most of those leaves were on the lawn. If her dad hadn't still been in the city on Sunday—or maybe if they had all been allowed to go home—he probably would have raked them up that day.

"Claudia, dear, I'm not judging here," Jesse was saying now to her own daughter. "But if you want the ice cream to be soup, why don't you just order a shake?"

"Because a shake is a shake and soup's soup."

Melissa focused on Jesse's nails. They were perfect. She wanted nails just like that, she decided. She wanted to wear leggings just like Jesse's.

"How is your house?" the woman asked her, the tone nothing like the playfulness that marked her question to her own daughter about why she insisted on liquefying her ice cream.

Melissa thought about this. She thought about the bloodstains. She thought about the rubber on the blue plastic Tucker Tote lid. Before she could respond to Jesse, however, Emiko was saying something, and so Melissa turned her attention to her other friend.

"My grandmother always saw ghosts," Emiko was explaining. "My grandfather never did, but my grandmother was always seeing them. She saw her aunts. She saw this friend of hers from elementary school who had died super young. She used to talk to them."

Jesse lifted that beautiful hand of hers off of Melissa's, and sat back against the bench on her side of the booth. She folded her arms across her chest. Then: "Melissa, are you scared of ghosts?" Again, there was that elongation of a single syllable—in this case, *you*. A sheep, it seemed to Melissa, when stretched so far. A homonym. *Baaaaaaaa*. She tried to remember how to spell the word for a female sheep, but she couldn't.

"Melissa?" Jesse asked when she didn't answer right away.

She put her spoon into the dish and pondered the . . . undead. She really hadn't been scared until Claudia had put the idea into her head the other day that her house might now be haunted. Certainly last night she had been relieved that she was allowed to share her parents' bed with her mom, even though it was because a man and a prostitute had had sex in her own bedroom, and because now her mom didn't want her own husband in bed with her. Dad had been—and here was a word he had taught her, trying to make light of the situation—*exiled* to the living room. She guessed she would have been scared if she had had to sleep alone in her own bedroom. And now the idea that Emiko—far and away the sanest of her friends—seemed to believe in ghosts, only gave more credence to Claudia's suggestion that she and her mom and dad were now sharing the home with a couple of dead men. Moreover, they were dead men who did bad things when they were alive. Which meant they might not be especially playful ghosts. Not Casper. They might be the kind who killed you in the night. When it was dark. They might be the kind of ghosts who quite literally scared you to death.

"I am a little scared of them," she answered finally.

"A little?"

"A little scared of ghosts."

"I would be," Claudia agreed.

"Claudia? Seriously? Come on," Jesse said. "I just told you, there is no such thing as ghosts. Emiko, that doesn't mean your grandmother was mistaken or crazy. It just means that she was from a . . . a different generation."

Melissa had wanted to speak with her mom yesterday about Claudia's idea that their house might now be haunted, but there had never been a chance. They had found the rubber and her parents had fought, and then her mom had retreated, sobbing, to the bedroom. It had been awful. And it hadn't been the bloodstains or the ruined painting or the gross stains on the furniture that had caused her mom to break down. It had been the rubber.

Her dad had told her mom that he hadn't had sex with the prostitute, and Melissa wanted to believe him. She couldn't imagine her dad telling a lie like that. But it was getting harder and harder for her not to be angry with him: the house was a mess, people were doing gross things in her bedroom, and he had made her mom cry. That was the worst part. He had made her mom cry a lot. And now they might have to move, and her parents might even get a divorce. Those were the things that really upset her; those were the things that really frightened her; and those were the things, she realized, that now had her furious with her dad.

"You haven't seen the bloodstains," Melissa said to Jesse. She wished that Claudia hadn't stirred her Cherry Garcia into goop.

Or, maybe, that her friend had ordered a flavor that was less . . . red.

"There are bloodstains?" Jesse asked, and then answered the question herself. "Good Lord, of course there are. Holy crap. Of course there are. Is it bad?"

Melissa nodded. And then, unsure what she was going to say when she opened her mouth, she admitted, "It's kind of a disaster. The house." It made her ashamed to admit this, but she couldn't stop herself. She just couldn't. She liked Jesse so much, and there was something so hip and charismatic in her animal print leggings and black jacket and perfect red nails—something that made her so different from all the other moms. There was something about her that just made you want to talk to her and accept this great gift of friendship. Of comfort. Of . . . coolness.

Suddenly Melissa was sharing everything that she had been keeping inside her: Her fears that her family was going to have to move. The reality that her parents might get a divorce. The fact that she had almost picked up this wet, messy thing called a rubber that a man had put on his penis.

"It was in your room?" Jesse asked, her eyes widening.

"Uh-huh."

"Wait, what?" Claudia was asking. "A rubber what? What was made of rubber? I don't understand."

But Emiko knew. Melissa could tell. The girl was looking into her empty sundae bowl as if the bottom of the dish was a smartphone with a video. She was embarrassed.

"But the worst part?" Melissa said as she wiped at her eyes.

"Go on," Jesse said. "The worst part?"

"No, wait," Claudia said, grabbing her mother's elbow. "What was made of rubber? Tell me!"

"Later, Claudia, okay? I'll explain to you what a rubber is later."

"I was just asking."

Jesse must have regretted bringing any of this up, Melissa decided; she herself was blinking back tears, Claudia wanted to know all about rubbers, and Emiko was clearly uncomfortable. But Melissa was tired of trying hard to be brave for her mom and to be patient with her dad. Her mom and dad were talking to each other—or, more accurately, arguing with each other. But still. Still. Who was she supposed to talk to? Who?

And so now she took a deep breath and said the first and most honest thing she was feeling: "The worst part? I am so mad at my dad that I almost hope my mom does make him go back to that hotel to live."

Jesse seemed to think about this for a moment. Then, once more, she reached across the table. This time she placed both of her hands atop Melissa's.

...

Richard told himself he was overreacting. Yes, he was furious with Spencer. Annoyed by the news vans, with their George Jetson–like satellite dishes, and the way they appeared out of nowhere like elephants, lumbering briefly into view and then disappearing back into the wild. Alarmed by the portrayal of the Russian mob in the tabloids, and the dawning realization that they might be seriously pissed at him, too, since a couple of their own had died at his house. In his living room and front hall. Did this mean he was at risk—or, more importantly, that his wife and daughter might be at risk? He couldn't say. But he felt vulnerable. Exposed. He was, he realized, on the radar of people with whom he would otherwise never have crossed paths.

Everything, it seemed, was unraveling. He imagined Spencer Doherty's anger if, in the end, he refused to pony up the thirty grand. If a month from now he balked at an additional five. Or ten. Or twenty.

He also wondered if this was all about having too much time on his hands to think.

Still, he could not believe how—and this was indeed the adjective he heard in his head—fucking difficult it was to get a handgun in New York. A week ago, this discovery would have thrilled him. Would have made all the sense in the world. But now? As he gazed up into the midafternoon autumn sunshine, unexpectedly warm this late in the year, he was furious. He needed to do something—anything—and the old guy with a beer belly the size of a Mini Cooper on the other side of the counter had told him that a pistol permit would take a couple of months. He had droned on about county and state and federal regulations.

"Do I look like a guy who holds up convenience stores?" Richard had asked, knowing the question was wholly unreasonable. But he couldn't stop himself. "I just want to be able to look out for my wife and my daughter," he'd added, hoping that the tone of his voice hadn't sounded as disagreeably entitled in reality as it had in his head.

But there was going to be no negotiating here. The laws were the laws. The background check was mandatory. And so he had taken the application with him and left. But character references? Fingerprints? Waiting to hear back from the FBI? This was ridiculous. He was . . . a banker. An investment banker. He was in mergers and acquisitons at Franklin McCoy. He had always been—with, admittedly, one recent, egregious exception—a good husband and father.

The dealer had pinched the bulbous wattle beneath his chin and suggested he get a rifle instead. The fellow had said it was less likely there might be an accident with a rifle, but he could still use it to protect his family. All he needed for that was a hunting license from Fish and Wildlife. Not hard, especially now. After all, it was deer season. He—the store owner—would smooth out the paperwork.

"The paperwork?" Richard had asked.

"You either need proof of a prior hunting license or proof you've taken a hunter education course. I can't get you the license. That would be illegal. Besides, you get those in White Plains. But

I have a friend who teaches hunter education. I can smooth out the education course paperwork—if you pay up front and promise to take the course."

"Wouldn't that be illegal, too?"

The dealer yawned. "Less so. Kind of a gray area. And there are some things I can get around and some things I can't."

"Like background checks."

"Yes. Playing fast and loose with an education course for a hunting rifle—especially for a guy like you? That's one thing. But an illegal permit? Whole other kettle of fish."

Richard sighed, frustrated. He had imagined bringing a pistol with him when he went to tell Spencer to go fuck himself. Just let his jacket fall open so that spineless weasel could see it. Or, in his mind, he'd imagined himself taking a pot shot at the satellite dish atop one of the news vans idling at the end of his driveway. He didn't believe he would ever actually do such a thing, but the fantasy alone fired him up. But mainly he'd had his heart set on a pistol so that he could keep it inside the top drawer of his nightstand, just in case the Russians were as crazy as the newspapers (and, yes, that detective) suggested they were.

And so he had left the store in a huff.

He glanced now at the garage and body shop across the street. This was not one of Yonkers's tonier neighborhoods. In addition to the gun store, there was a tattoo parlor and a pawnshop. A bar with a couple of Harleys outside. He'd been a little nervous when he had parked his Audi out here. But it was fine. Untouched. No one seemed to care.

For a long moment he watched the wide glass window beside the garage bay. Inside, he saw a couple of guys chatting around the desk, and one was wearing a ball cap. Red, he thought, but he couldn't be sure from this distance. On the wall behind the desk was a deer head. A buck with a pretty sizable rack of antlers.

He took a deep breath and gathered himself. Maybe he didn't need a handgun. Maybe he just needed a gun. The dealer was probably right; a rifle would do just fine—at least right now. A hunting rifle. Maybe he could get a handgun . . . later. People knew people, right?

Besides, if a rifle could bring down a buck the size of the one whose head was in that auto body shop office across the street, it sure as hell would stop some lunatic Russian behemoth in his tracks. He recalled how much easier the dealer had said the process was. It was briefer. Less invasive.

And so Richard almost went back inside. Almost. But he paused at the entrance and then turned around and climbed into his car. He thought of the corpse he had seen in his front hall. Shot once in the chest and once in the head. He thought of the splotches and streams of blood he had seen that awful night. He thought of all the blood still left on the wallpaper, the couch, and the painting in the back of this very car. No, he wasn't a gun guy. He wasn't a gun guy at all.

. . .

Kerri-Ann Jennings had not actually fucked the quarterback of the Bronxville High School football team four years ago. The few times she had even embraced him had been the sort of social squeezes that usually accompany an air kiss by the cheek and had occurred in close proximity to one or both of his parents. After football games. At his house for dinner with his whole family. When his uncle was diagnosed with brain cancer. But she liked the boy a lot, and the two had been friends. Good friends. The boy was smart and was applying early decision to Brown. Still, the rumor persisted at the school that the two were fuck buddies. It was the sort of urban legend that made the single, statuesque French teacher wildly popular. The truth was that Kerri-Ann was also friends with the quarterback's mother and father. She was looking forward to teaching the quarterback's younger sister next year. She knew about the rumors and happily kept them alive by saying things to her class in French that were unquestionably inappropriate, but not so ribald that she was ever likely to get disciplined.

Every year or two, it seemed, there were stories about her just like this. But most of the students loved her. The boys fantasized about her in the shower. The girls vacillated between jealousy and awe. The teacher used her tortoiseshell sunglasses and headband as props when she spoke—some days her wild mane of red hair, too—and with dominatrix-like confidence wielded absolute control over her classroom. She relished who she was. She was probably Kristin's closest friend at the school.

"I mean, it's not like Richard had an affair," Kerri-Ann was saying to Kristin now. They were sitting in the back corner of the coffee shop just off Pondfield Road after school, speaking softly so no one could hear them. Kristin hoped Melissa was having a good time at the ice-cream parlor before dance. In a perfect world, the combination of her friends and Jesse and ice cream and ballet would take her mind off the nightmare at home. "It's not like he confessed he had a lover he was meeting lunchtimes at his brother's hotel."

"I used to like that hotel. I sort of hate it now. It's creepy."

"I've met Philip. I think he's creepy."

"He is, I know. Sometimes Richard and I try to delude our-selves into believing that he's just immature."

"You're being kind. He might be in his early thirties—"

"Actually, he's thirty-five."

"Thirty-five? Incredible. I have boys in my classes—you have boys in your classes—who are more mature. The guy's thirty-five years old and no doubt subscribes to *Maxim*. But he's not unique. How creepy are men? I once heard a comedian do an entire set on guys masturbating in cars. He asked how many women in the audience had seen guys doing that, and I swear three-quarters of the women in the club raised their hands."

"God . . ."

"It's hard to believe that he and Richard are brothers. They are just so different."

"I thought so. I like to think so. But I just can't get over the idea that Richard went upstairs with some escort and stripped.

And that's just what he told me. How do I know he didn't have sex with her? How do I know he's not having lunchtime quickies at Philip's hotel? I just feel so violated and betrayed and . . . like I'm not enough."

Kerri-Ann smiled at someone behind Kristin's shoulder and waggled her immaculately plucked sickle-moon eyebrows. And so Kristin turned around. There she saw two handsome boys who she recognized were seniors. The students waved at Kerri-Ann; the taller of the pair raised one eyebrow back at the French teacher and grinned in a fashion that he probably hoped was seductive. In reality, it looked only mischievous.

"You're plenty," Kerri-Ann was saying when Kristin turned back to her. "Have you ever been to a strip club?"

"Why? So I could compare myself to some slinky twenty-two-year-old and see I'm plenty?"

She shook her head. "They're kind of depressing."

"How many have you been to? This is a side of you I didn't know existed."

"I guess I've been three times in my life. Once with some girl-friends from college because we were curious and twice with guys who thought it would be kind of hot."

"And it wasn't?"

She shook her head. "Not for me. You have guys paying women—no, guys paying girls—to show them their junk. That's kind of demeaning for everyone involved, don't you think? And, of course, the girls are so not into the guys and the guys sense it. How could they not? Plus there's this weird undercurrent of self-loathing: the guys know they're losers for paying, and the girls know they're slutty—and not in a good way—for peeling. I don't buy any of that female empowerment bullshit."

"Slutty . . . in a good way?"

"Oh, I've given boyfriends amazing lap dances. In my home. Or his. But it's because we're into each other. It's because it's fun."

"You know, I expected there to be a stripper at the bachelor party. I really didn't care. I didn't mind. I kind of figured every guy there would have seen a naked woman. Richard was doing his brother a solid and hosting a party. It wasn't supposed to be a big deal."

"What's really the source of your pain?" Kerri-Ann asked. "Is it the hurt or the humiliation? I mean, they're two different things."

"I don't want to intellectualize this. It all makes me sad inside. Besides, it's all linked."

"If Richard were in the newspapers because of some illegal insider trading thing, would you feel this much hurt? Or would you just feel humiliation?"

"That's an impossible question to answer. And, just so we're clear, I feel terrible for him, too. I know he brought this upon himself, but I also know he's devastated—and a little scared. Who knows what this could do to his career? So, that's a part of the mix, too."

Kerri-Ann tore off a small piece of the scone she was nibbling. "What if the girls hadn't murdered the guys who had brought them—those Russians? What if there had been no news story, but somehow you found out that the men had been fucking the talent? Would you still feel so much humiliation?"

"Again, I'll never know. But that talent? They may have been prisoners. They may have been minors. Sometimes I think I'm so angry at Richard because it's hard to get pissed off at some poor girl who's doing all this because there are guys with guns making her."

"I'm not a marriage counselor," Kerri-Ann said. "Don't even play one on TV. But this is the sort of stuff I'd try to understand. I mean, if I were you."

"I can't compartmentalize it. It's still too soon."

"Are you thinking of leaving him?"

She steadied her gaze at her friend. "No."

"But the thought crossed your mind, I can tell."

The thought had crossed her mind, but she had not really expected ever to verbalize it. She knew this was among Melissa's biggest worries: her parents were going to get a divorce. But the thing was, she loved Richard. Good Lord, she was furious with him—but she also felt bad for him. Sure, she was embarrassed, but so was he. He was actually disgraced.

"How could it not?" she told Kerri-Ann. "I'm really pissed at him." Her eye caught the chalkboard specials on the wall behind a cappuccino machine, and she was struck by the way someone's penmanship had made all of the lowercase *i*'s look phallic. "Of course, I wouldn't be surprised if Philip's fiancée breaks off the engagement. Cancels the wedding."

"Isn't it soon?"

"It's supposed to be a week from Saturday."

"But right now it's still on."

"Yes. But if I were Nicole—that's his fiancée—I'd break it off."

"Yeah," Kerri-Ann said. "I would, too."

"And yet if you were me, you wouldn't leave Richard?"

"You two have a life together. You've got a daughter. But this Nicole? She still has time to get out."

"That suggests the only reason I'm not getting out is inertia and Melissa."

"I didn't mean that. I meant you know Richard. Whatever happened, it was a mistake."

"We think."

"And it only happened because it was a batshit crazy bachelor party and he was drunk."

"Again, we think."

"Yes. I guess," Kerri-Ann admitted. "You think . . ."

Kristin took a sip of her coffee, cold now, and then sighed. When she looked back at Kerri-Ann, the other teacher was already smiling and waving at yet another group of boys.

. . .

Nicole considered all of the ways she could inform Philip that she was breaking off the wedding. They ranged from going to his apartment in Brooklyn Heights and telling him face-to-face, to sending him a text. A text would manage to be both cowardly and cruel, and it would invariably prove epic: it would, knowing Philip, almost certainly go viral. And why shouldn't it? She imagined the words on the screen of her phone:

After what you did on Friday, I just can't marry you. I'm sorry.

Or it could be a long text that crossed some *t*'s and dotted some *i*'s.

After what you did on Friday, I just can't marry you. I'm sorry. I don't trust you and I don't see a future where I can trust you. I've called the caterer and the church and the people who were bringing the tents to my parents' house. I'll send you a check for what you paid toward the deposit. I'll give you back the ring. I don't want it. Please don't call me. I'll call you when I'm ready.

But even a text that long still conveyed only a tiny fraction of what she wanted to say—which suggested the need for an e-mail. Besides, he would call her, even if she asked him not to. Of course, he would call her after an e-mail, as well. He would call her if she mailed him a handwritten letter, enclosing the ring in the envelope. Philip was nothing if not persistent. It was, perhaps, why she had first fallen in love with him. He was funny; he was playful; he was—at least at the beginning—attentive.

All of which suggested she would have to see him in person, because he was going to have to try for the last word. But she feared that if she went to his apartment, that last word might lead to her backing down. Alone in his living room or bedroom, he would convince her to change her mind. And she did not want to change her mind. It wasn't only that she didn't trust him; she no longer believed that she loved him.

So instead she wrote him a text that said she wanted to have breakfast with him Thursday morning at a place on Montague Street they both liked, and tweaked it over and over on her phone. If she did see him on Thursday morning, it would be the first time in a week—since before he had had sex with that prostitute.

Can you have breakfast with me tomorrow at 7:30 at Evergreen?
We need to talk. Please don't call me. But text me if you can and
I will be there.

After reading her final draft a third time, she pressed "send." She realized that she felt horrible for the girls who had been brought to the party and she felt terrible for the families of the dead men; but, yes, she also felt something very close to despair about the way she had fallen out of love with Philip. She couldn't build a life together with him that began on the bodies of two dead men and the fact he had fucked a prostitute. She just . . . couldn't.

She took the engagement ring he had given her off her finger, but then put it back on. She decided that she wanted to take it off in front of him in the restaurant. The ring was a symbol: maybe— just maybe—it would hurt him as much as he had hurt her if she removed the ring from her finger before his very eyes.

. . .

Melissa was not exactly scared of the Internet, but she knew that there was a world beyond the sites she visited often—sites for school, sites for music and movies, sites about Brownie badges and fashion and hair—that was not meant for a nine-year-old girl. In some cases, it was just a keystroke away. One letter off. An acci- dental dash.

Not quite a year ago, one morning when her dad was upstairs getting dressed and her mom was packing her lunch for school, she had been using the computer in the family room to visit the Girl Scouts website because she had a question about a Brownie badge. She had typed in one of the words incorrectly and wound up on a site so disturbing that she had yelled for her parents reflexively. Even before they had dropped what they were doing and rushed into the family room, she had closed the screen. What she had seen (or, now, what she thought she had seen), was monstrous and gro- tesque. She felt . . . ashamed. Her parents had found the site in the computer's history and deleted it, and told her that she had done nothing wrong. They said she had done exactly the right thing telling them about it. Then they had lectured her (yet again) about the need to be careful on the Internet, and reiterated the house rules, which they admitted she had indeed been obeying when she had inadvertently strayed onto that site.

Now, while her mom was making dinner and her dad was out, she decided to move beyond the site with the funky tights for girls. She took a deep breath and typed in her father's name in the search bar. Her mom had said he would be home for dinner, and Melissa honestly wasn't sure how she felt about that. Her anger toward him had been smoldering for a couple of days. She was irritated with him for making Mom sad—for causing such tension in the house—and she was embarrassed by the attention she was receiving. Even her dance teacher had given her a huge, wholly unexpected hug that afternoon. Moreover, was it possible that her father had done the sorts of gross things at the party that she had seen on the website she had accidentally stumbled upon almost a year ago now?

She read stories about her father on four different sites before she had had enough. She had never heard the expression "sex slave" before, but she had an idea what it meant. She looked up the word *orgy* and was appalled. Again, there were pictures. But she scrutinized as well the sections of the news stories that focused on the dead Russians, because the reporters always quoted detectives who stressed that there were many more men like that pair out there—and that their Russians friends were probably furious and dangerous.

"Sweetheart?"

At the sound of her mother's voice she instantly minimized the screen.

"What?"

"What are you doing?"

"I was trying to find something for school."

"About?"

"Turtles," she lied.

"Okay. Would you like mashed potatoes or baked potatoes?"

"Mashed."

Her mother nodded and retreated. Before the bachelor party, Melissa knew, her mother would have asked her why in the world she was looking up turtles. She would have come to the computer and sat down beside her to see what she had found. She would have asked why her teacher—a woman her mother called by her first name because, of course, they were peers on the faculty—was having them study turtles. Was it a unit on reptiles? Was someone bringing a turtle to school? Were they going to get turtles for the classroom? Now, however, her mother was so distracted that she didn't ask a single question. Not a one.

After Melissa clicked again on the story about the violence in her home, she deleted it. She deleted all the sites she had visited from the computer's history. Then she googled turtles. For the life of her, she had no idea why the first thing she had thought of was a turtle.

. . .

Richard's day ended where it began: on a futon on the floor. Another news van trolling the neighborhood and pausing at the end of his driveway.

He stared up at the ceiling at the dim light from the moon and listened to Cassandra snore ever so slightly in her sleep. He took comfort that at least the cat had not deserted him. Usually she slept upstairs. Tonight she was downstairs with him. His mind, as it had all day, ping-ponged between the unfairness of Franklin McCoy still refusing to allow him to return to work, the sword that Spencer Doherty was dangling over his head, and the hurt he had inflicted upon his family. He was angry at the world, but he was also awash in self-loathing. And somewhere in the maelstrom behind his eyes that was keeping him awake was that poor girl he had brought upstairs in this very house. Sometimes he was haunted by her eyes as she sat on the guest bedroom bed. Sometimes he heard her voice in his head. He thought of her sadness when she spoke about Yerevan. He thought of her playfulness when she described a sculpture of a cat.

Manhunt. Now she was the object of a manhunt. Everyone wanted to find her. The Russians probably wanted to kill her. He was, he realized, terrified for her. It made him loathe her parents, whoever they were and wherever they were.

He sat up on the futon, his head in his hands. He thought of his wife and daughter, upstairs in the master bedroom. He hoped he hadn't made a mistake not coming home with a gun.

Alexandra

Sonja was sobbing when we ran from the party for the bachelor. We were both crazed, we were both all adrenaline. We climbed into Pavel's car, because she said that was how we were going to get away, and she got into the driver's seat. She slammed shut the big Escalade door and right away banged into the side of one of the other cars in the driveway when she was backing out. She didn't know how to drive. Neither of us did. She didn't even know how to turn on the windshield wipers at first, and it was pouring rain. But she had planned this thing in her mind and didn't plan to drive very far. We were just going to the train station, she said, which we had seen when we were driving around Bronxville before the party. We had gotten there so early, Pavel had gone to the village to find a liquor store for his vodka. Sonja figured even she could drive the mile or two to the train station.

"What the fuck were you thinking!" I asked. "Why did you do that?"

"Because they killed Crystal, why else?"

"I know, I get it! But why? Why now?"

"Because I think they were going to kill me tonight—on the way back to the city. They probably would have killed you, too."

"What the fuck? Why?"

"We'll get on the first train that goes to the Grand Central," she said instead of answering my question, and she screeched to a halt in front of a red light by a beautiful brick library and a beautiful stone church. I bumped into the dashboard. I hadn't put on a seat belt. "We'll disappear on the subways. New York City is so big, maybe they'll never find us," she said, and then she banged her fists twice on the steering wheel.

We had ridden the subways before, but I had no idea where we could go. And while Sonja had started thinking about what she wanted to do the minute they told us that Crystal was dead, I was a little nervous about her *maybe. Maybe they'll never find us?* Seriously, that was her plan?

We had a lot of cash, because Pavel and Kirill always carried big rolls of money in their pockets. But I guessed we had also made another four thousand dollars in tips. Richard had given me nearly a thousand when we were upstairs. I almost didn't take it because he hadn't let me finish him, but in the end I did. I knew if I didn't, Pavel would have thought I was hiding money from him. He never would have believed that some dude had just decided not to finish. And after they'd killed Crystal, there was no way I was going to risk getting him mad at me. Besides, I had held up my end of deal. I had earned the money. Still, I had felt a little guilty when we were upstairs in the bedroom and he gave me all that cash. But now in the car, when Sonja and I were running who knew where, I was very glad I had it. I was very glad I had all those extra fifty- and one-hundred-dollar bills.

"Where are we going on the subway?" I asked her when we got to the train station maybe two minutes later.

She didn't answer. "You have the money?" she asked me instead.

"I do."

"And the gun?"

"Yes." I knew she had one, too. They were both Makarovs. She had eight rounds in hers—full magazine. I had six left in mine.

When we were on the platform, she pointed at a train schedule under glass. "See?" she said. "See? There will be train in seven minutes."

"Seven minutes," I repeated.

"That will fucking teach them," she said, and she wiped some of the mascara off her cheek. I knew it was running because she was crying, but we had also gotten soaked when we had raced to the car and then a second time when we had climbed the steps to the train platform. Her eyes were red and her makeup was a mess. I was relieved the platform had a roof. "God, I'm glad they're dead. I am so fucking glad they're dead," she said.

"Tell me: Where are we going?" I was going a little crazy myself not knowing.

She looked at me, but her face was blank behind all that messy makeup. Still, I could tell she had heard me. It was just that she was so lost in her own thoughts that she couldn't answer me that second. And the seven minutes until that train came felt like forever. I kept looking for police cars or one of the cars that we'd seen in Richard's driveway—but I thought a police car was more likely. Those guys from the party were too scared to follow us. They weren't coming. God, one of them was crying when I was getting into my jacket. Another begged me not to shoot him when I put on my skirt. At one point Sonja and I heard a siren when we were waiting on the platform, but to this day I don't know if it was an ambulance or police car. I don't even know if it was going to the party for the bachelor. In the end, no one came after us that night. No one tried to find us. No one came to stop us. In my mind, I saw the men from the party back at the house, and they were staring at Pavel's and Kirill's bodies, and wondering what they were going to do. I saw Richard. Poor sad, sweet Richard.

When Sonja and I had our seats on the train, we made a list of what we had. We had just under eight thousand dollars in cash, which we knew would not last as long as you might think, and we had the credit cards in Pavel's and Kirill's wallets, which we did not believe we could ever use because that would tell people where we were, and we had the two guns and the fourteen bullets inside them. We had that big kitchen knife, but Sonja said she had only brought it because it was evidence. She said she would throw it into a garbage can in the city. (And later she did.)

She turned to me. "Fuck. I left something at the house."

"We left lots of somethings at the house."

"No. Something important. A phone number. I hid it inside a condom wrapper."

"Whose number?"

She put her finger on my lips to shush me. "It will be fine. I can remember enough of the numbers. Trust me. It'll be fine."

She closed her eyes and tried to look calm. We were the only people in that train car. We knew that later the conductor would tell the police about us, but there was no one else who saw two pretty girls whose makeup was a meltdown disaster.

...

Sonja, it would turn out, was full of surprises. When we got off the train in New York City, we took the shuttle to the Times Square. There she bought us blue and red knit caps for a New York football team to cover our hair, and sunglasses at a late-night souvenir shop. She bought knapsacks for this football team, handing me one.

Then we went to a twenty-four-hour store and bought two cell phones that were called "prepaid." She said they were "burners." We hadn't had cell phones since we had been abducted, but sometimes we'd used Catherine's or Inga's or even one of the men's. So we knew how much they had changed. But I was still impressed that Sonja knew that "burners" were the kind we wanted, because no one would know who we were or where we were. There was no contract, she said. We would use them and throw them away. Then we would buy more. She didn't let me come into the store with her, because she didn't want the man behind the counter to remember seeing two women together. She wore the knit cap but not the sunglasses, since sunglasses after midnight would look suspicious.

"We're going to get hotel rooms—but in two different hotels," she said. "People will be looking for us together." She said the knapsacks were so it would look like we were tourists when we checked in, not courtesans hiding from our bosses or police guys.

"We look like schoolgirls," I said. "Not tourists."

She thought about this for a second and then said, "We do. Sort of. We look like we're runaway stripper girls, maybe. That's good. If we don't like the hotels, maybe there's a place we can find for runaway girls."

She was right about how we looked. Schoolgirls don't wear black thigh boots and miniskirts. We hadn't put our stockings and garter belts back on when we left. She was wearing a thong, but neither one of us was wearing a shirt or a blouse under our leather jackets.

"Let's just get off the street," I said. "Any hotel is good hotel." I knew they wouldn't be nice places because we weren't going to use Pavel's and Kirill's credit cards. We needed the sort of hotel that would take our cash and wouldn't care who we were. "Okay? I'm really scared."

"I know, Alexandra dear," she said. "I am, too."

"But tell me what you know. I have to know."

"About Crystal . . ."

"Yes. About Crystal. Why did they kill her? Why were they going to kill us?"

She looked at one of the huge, blinking video billboards, alive even at this hour of the night. They were crazy hypnotic. Then she turned back to me. "Crystal had dude five days ago who turned out to be police guy."

"Oh, fuck."

"I know."

"But he didn't arrest her?"

She shook her head. "She had him again two days ago. He didn't want sex. He wanted her to help him trap Yulian. Inga. You know, all bosses."

"They're too smart. Never happen."

"He promised her she'd be okay. We'd be okay."

"He was lying. We'd go to jail for sure, too."

"She believed him."

"She was crazy then. Crazier than you even."

"I know. But think of how unhappy she was. Think of how much she wanted out. How she dreamed of being rescued."

I nodded. I remembered.

"And Yulian had hunch about Crystal. He had Pavel follow police guy second time he came to the town house—after he left. When Pavel told Yulian he had guessed right and dude was police guy, that was it for Crystal."

"Oh, God."

"And Crystal had told me all about this! Asked me for my advice. I told her to tell police guy nothing, but she was into him. Believed him. So into him, she offered to wear a wire. Only reason she didn't was because he wouldn't let her. Said that was way too dangerous and she was way too young."

A part of me thought this was almost funny: Crystal was old enough to fuck American johns but too young to wear a wire. But obviously nothing was really funny to me that night.

"So Yulian—"

"He beat Crystal until she confessed," she said. "And then . . . well, you know what they did after that."

"And you?"

"Police guy never came to me. I hadn't been asked. But Crystal had told me too much, and Pavel had a feeling I hadn't snitched on her. I said I didn't know anything, but he didn't believe me. He said I could no longer be trusted." She reached out to me and held my arms in her hands. "Look, I don't know for sure they were going to kill you. But I overheard what they were saying about me tonight. It was when they were in kitchen. And if they killed me, how could they not kill you? How?"

This was almost too much news to absorb, and I am smart enough girl that I can absorb a lot. When she felt me shivering the tiniest bit, she rubbed my arms like it was January in Moscow. Then she even gave me a small smile and said, "These blocks have strip clubs." She let go of me and pointed first at one near where we had bought the knit hats, and then down a street where she said there was another. "And there was also one by the Empire State Building, yes?"

"Yes, uh-huh."

"Don't worry, Alexandra, we'll make some quick money at those places before we leave."

"Leave for where?" I asked.

She tucked a lock of her platinum hair under her cap so you couldn't see a single strand. Then she adjusted my cap so you couldn't see any of my hair either.

"Well, we can't go home," she said. "Not to Volgograd and not to Yerevan."

"Too much Vasily," I agreed. Besides, she had no one left in Volgograd and I had no one left in Yerevan. All we had waiting for us in those places was shame.

"That's right."

"So?"

"So, we are going to Los Angeles. Land of the Bachelor. Land of the Kardashians. We are going to disappear into the most glamorous place on earth."

Chapter Ten

All of the men at Philip Chapman's bachelor party had described the two girls to the police, but they had agreed there were no photographs. Not a single one. Spencer Doherty swore that he hadn't taken any pictures. (Did he protest too much? Days later Richard would wonder.)

It wasn't simply that the men had found Pavel and Kirill utterly terrifying—though they did; as drunk as the men were, they were confident that the Russians with their shaved heads really would (worst case) break their fingers or (best case) break their phones if they tried capturing even a single image of either girl or five or ten seconds of video. No, the men kept their phones in their blazers or pants because none wanted to risk banishment from the party; none wanted to risk missing a moment of the girls' performances; none wanted to jeopardize their chance to be taken by the talent to one of the other rooms in Philip's brother-in-law's house. (After reveler Martin Scofield returned to the living room and the blonde had retreated to the bathroom to—yet again—clean up, he told the men in detail how she had finished him off. She was insane, he'd said, she was ravenous; he'd never felt anything like it. After that?

The men viewed the suburban living room—the whole house, really—as their own private seraglio. Each fully expected that he, too, would experience a moment of ineffable carnality with one of the girls, an episode that in memory would outlast the innumerable, inexorable indignities of old age, and offer a fodder for tumescence infinitely more powerful than even the bluest of pills.) And so the police sketch artists did what they could, creating one girl with platinum hair and one whose mane was jet black. They did what they could to bring the girls' eyes to life, and capture the fullness of their lips. They tried to add the demure pitch to the nose of the girl who may (or may not) have been named Alexandra, and the slight upturn to the nose of the one who may (or may not) have been called Sonja. But the pictures were, in the end, relatively blunt objects; certainly they failed to convey the way each of the girls moved, a winsome fluidity that was lissome and licentious at once.

"Did they have any birthmarks or moles? Any tattoos?"

No, the men agreed—and this was one of the only things about which they were all in complete agreement—they did not. Their skin was flawless. Unsullied by either imperfection or ink.

. . .

Thursday morning when Richard woke up, he found a text from Spencer waiting for him on his phone.

So, how are you doing, buddy? Want to talk? I'm thinking of you and your family and your future at that bank of yours.

There was not a word in it that would look incriminating in a court of law, or appear even mildly threatening. But Richard understood perfectly well the subtext beneath the text.

. . .

It was degrading. Kristin knew what she was doing was degrading. But her nerves were frayed and her equilibrium was in shambles. Her self-esteem was in shambles. She knew this was a bad idea—no, this was a terrible idea—but she was incapable of stopping herself. She emerged from the master bathroom shower Thursday morning, toweled herself off, and then stood stark naked before the full-length mirror in the adjacent bedroom. Her and Richard's bedroom. She studied her body with pitiless, hardhearted eyes, finding only the ways it had been diminished by age, methodically ratcheting up the self-hatred. She was forty, and while she knew that forty was not old, it also was not twenty. She believed she was still pretty . . . but was she now only pretty for forty? (She heard the cultural ageism in that question, and chastised herself. But she also knew that she couldn't transcend aesthetic preconceptions any more than her breasts could transcend gravity.) She stared for a long moment at her nipples, objectifying and then loathing them. She had a hint of rib, but did she need a hint more? She examined the crease of her lips, the slope of her nose. She ran her fingers over her cheekbones. She cringed when she saw that she needed a bikini wax—and cringed that she even got them in the first place. It wasn't the pain. It was the whole idea that she was raising her daughter in a world where pubic hair was a problem.

She needed to spend more time at the gym. She needed a different lipstick. She needed . . .

She needed, she told herself, to get dressed. And so she did, but the damage to her psyche had been done.

She had read articles over the years about a man's supposed biologic craving for young women: it was all about primeval procreation, in theory, the need to plant seed in fertile soil. Maybe. But the idea of Richard desiring a woman perhaps less than half his age—half *their* age—was at once appalling and infuriating. She thought of a line from Nabokov: "Because you took advantage of my disadvantage." *Lolita.* In this case, however, Kristin felt that she was at the disadvantage—not the young thing. The truth was, she feared, all men were Humbert Humbert. Maybe they weren't pedophiles lusting after twelve-year-olds, but didn't Lolita look old for her age? Older, anyway? Sure, there were MILFs in porn, but Kristin had a feeling that considerably more men wanted their porn stars to be students at Duke University than moms from the bleachers at a middle-school soccer game. She—a forty-year-old female history teacher—may not yet have morphed into Shelley Winters, but it was getting harder and harder to compete with the real-life Lolitas of the world.

Yet men's tastes in pornography weren't really the issue, were they? It was one thing for a middle-aged man to access his inner ninth grader and lust after a porn star on his tablet or TV screen; it was quite another to bring a prostitute (or, far sadder, a sex slave) upstairs in this very house. Some lines were more blurred than others—at the word *blurred,* her mind conjured an appalling music video from a few years back—but the line between lusting after a porn star and fucking an escort was clear. Berlin Wall clear.

When she was dressed, she sat on the bed to put on her shoes. She had grabbed a pair of modest heels today from her closet. She wondered if this was how the girl had sat before her husband last Friday night on another bed in another room just down the hall. She saw the girl vividly in her mind. Her insouciance. Her mouth, half open with carefully feigned desire. Her youth. She closed her eyes, wishing her imagination were impervious to pain.

...

Nicole stirred the berries and granola in her yogurt parfait. She was nauseous, sick with loss and despair, but she felt that she had to order something. Across the booth (thank God he had gotten a booth, she had thought when she first arrived, and thank God he had arrived before her), Philip was wolfing his western omelet as if he hadn't eaten in days. She feared he had missed all the signals she had offered since she had gotten to the restaurant. He had stood and embraced her, apologizing with uncharacteristic zeal, and she had not lifted her arms to hug him back. He had tried to peer into her eyes in a way he almost never did—with an earnestness that suggested he was not simply hearing whatever she had to say, he was listening—and she had looked down at the toes of her boots. He had offered to take her jacket and hold it for her while she had slid into her side of the booth, and she had replied that she would be more comfortable keeping it on. She glanced down at the engagement ring since she knew this was the last time she was ever going to see it.

"It was a nightmare," Philip was saying now. "You can't imagine how awful it was to see that crazy bitch stabbing the Russian dude. I will never be able to scrub that image from my eyes. Never. We thought she was going to try and kill one of us next."

She wasn't completely surprised that he was trying to elicit her sympathy. And, the truth was, she knew that it must have been terrifying.

"And then we heard the gunshots, and that's when we thought we were all going to get killed. I mean, Chuck Alcott fell to the floor, just sobbing—sobbing!—like a baby. And I know I ducked."

"You ducked."

He sipped his coffee and nodded as he swallowed. "Maybe more than ducked. You know, it was a reflex. I knelt behind the couch."

She assumed that *knelt* was a euphemism. *Knelt* suggested a gradual descent and some premeditation. She was pretty sure that even *duck* was a euphemism: it was likely that he had thrown himself to the floor as if someone had tossed a hand grenade into the room.

"I mean, guns and knives at what was supposed to be a harmless bachelor party?" he added. "That's nuts!"

She agreed that it must have been horrifying for him to have witnessed the murder of the two bodyguards, but there was never anything harmless about this bachelor party. And so she told him precisely that.

"Look, I know it got a little out of control," he said. "We all drank too much. But you know how sorry I am, right? I wouldn't have told you if I wasn't sorry and knew I could assure you that I would never, ever do something like that again."

"You only told me because you got caught," she countered.

He held his fork as if it were a pointer and glanced at the tines. There was a bit of yellow egg there. "But I know we can get past this. I know I can."

She wanted to say, *Well, that's big of you.* But she still hoped she could remain above sarcasm. She wanted only candor in this final breakfast. "I can't," she said instead.

"And what does that mean?"

"It means . . . it means a lot of things. It's not just about trust, and how that's gone. I kept hoping you'd grow up or expecting you'd grow up or believing you'd grow up. And that's crazy on my part. Because you won't. I used to love that little boy in you. But now that little boy is just a horny teenager who wants his women to be skanky girls gone wild. Beautiful things with eating disorders."

"Not you. You know how much I respect you."

"And yet you stare at other women on the street. You really think I don't notice?"

"I'm a guy. It's how I'm hardwired. If it bothers you, I'll stop. I usually only do it when some woman is dressed, I don't know, provocatively."

"If it bothers me? Really? It never crossed your mind that I might not want you ogling some other girl's ass?"

"I'm not perfect, I know that. I'm not my brother, I'm not—"

"I'm not sure that your brother is much better."

"You would be in the minority thinking that."

She dropped her spoon onto the white plate with the parfait glass, embarrassed by how much noise it made. "Damn it, Philip, this is not about your sibling issues!"

"I'm sorry."

She could feel people in the restaurant watching them. She could sense Philip's fear that she was about to make a scene. She hadn't wanted to make a scene; she certainly hadn't planned that she would. But at this point? It didn't matter. What mattered was that if anything good had come from that appalling debauch at his brother's, it was this: she had (and the ghoulish irony of the expression was not lost on her) dodged a bullet.

"How dare you say, 'I can get past it,' as if that means you're such a big person or you're better than me? How dare you! It really doesn't matter if you can get past it. I can't," she said, and she was crying, her voice a little lost in her sniffles, but she didn't care. She didn't care at all. She stood and lifted her purse over her shoulder and held out her left hand. Then, with her right, she pulled the engagement ring off her finger and—as he was standing, reaching out to her, imploring her to stop, to think, to not throw away all that they had—she tossed it onto the table. It bounced onto the floor, and Philip fell to his hands and knees—dove, as a matter of fact—after it. As far as she knew, he never followed her out the door or tried to catch her, because she never looked back.

...

Later that morning, Richard reassured his younger brother that Nicole might change her mind in a few weeks or a few months. But he didn't believe it. He only said she might because he felt he had to say something, and he couldn't quite read the tone of his brother's voice on the phone. But the wedding clearly was off. That part of the conversation was brief and, it seemed, almost rote. It was as if Philip had grown accustomed to the news, bad as it was, and in hours had jumped four stages to acceptance. In truth, Richard wasn't surprised that Nicole was leaving him before they could even get to the altar; Kristin, he surmised, would have done exactly the same thing. Any woman with even a teaspoon of self-respect would. Nevertheless, he felt bad for his brother. It seemed the collateral damage from Friday night was only getting worse for everyone.

"Are you weirded out that all those Russian dudes made bail?" Philip asked him suddenly.

"They didn't all make bail," he answered carefully.

"Okay, most. I find it amazing that one was the guy who Spencer used to talk to on the telephone when he was lining up the girls."

"You do hang with an impressive crowd," he said. He still hadn't decided whether to tell Philip what his despicable friend was doing and enlist his help. He guessed this was because he suspected, in the end, he was going to pay the guy off. Maybe after he had written the check or transferred the money he would rat Spencer out. Inform Philip that his friend was a dirtbag. But he kept coming back to the reality that there was no guarantee Spencer wouldn't keep coming back for more, which was one of the reasons why he hadn't called his portfolio manager and moved around some money already.

"The guy was just a voice on the line," Philip was saying. "They never met."

"Next time, Philip? Tell him to just use Craigslist, okay?"

"Yeah, that's a deal," his brother agreed, though Richard would have preferred that Philip had said there wouldn't be a next time. Then: "Spencer is fucking terrified. He just can't believe those guys are back on the street."

"He probably should be terrified."

"He even got me a little wigged out. But, like, what would the Russians want with us, right?"

"I guess."

"You guess?"

"I guess."

"You're supposed to do better than that, my older brother. You're supposed to reassure me."

"Am I?"

"It's part of the Older Brother Contract."

"Good to know."

"And I gather his legal quicksand is just getting worse."

At this, Richard felt himself perking up. "Oh?"

"Brandon Fisher's lawyer called his lawyer again yesterday afternoon. Brandon's wife checked herself into some clinic."

"Oh, please."

"I know. But between the Russians and the lawyers, Spencer is not a happy camper."

"Well, I'm not either."

"Would you do me a favor?"

He braced himself. "What?"

"Mom and Dad are kind of bummed about the wedding. They really like Nicole. I'm sure they'll call you later today or tonight."

"And?"

"Tell them I really am okay. Reassure them."

"Yeah, no problem. I can do that." He took a little pride, unseemly as it was, in the reality that as far as he had fallen, he remained—at least in the eyes of his brother and their parents—on a higher moral ground than Philip. This was, of course, a low bar. But still . . .

"What's next?" Philip asked.

"For me? I don't know. See what the Rorschach on the living room walls and the couch makes me think of this morning."

"The couch is still there?"

"A rubbish company is picking it up, but they can't come until Saturday."

"Have they seen it?"

"No."

"Well, won't they be surprised when they do. Me? I'd just drag it outside and burn it."

"The couch is the least of my problems," he said, and his brother murmured something not wholly intelligible in assent.

After hanging up, Richard saw a news van driving slowly past the house. He fantasized giving the camera crew the finger if they pulled into his driveway. He sighed: it was almost Halloween. He wondered if they'd get any trick-or-treaters this year, or whether he was such a pariah that no self-respecting parents would allow their children anywhere near the Chapman front door.

Alexandra

Somehow I slept. I did. I slept in a ball with the sheet over my head, but I really did fall into a deep sleep in the hotel room.

It was only when I woke up the next morning that every siren on the street scared me. I was two blocks from Sonja, and that didn't help. The room was on the third floor and looked out on an air shaft. No fire escape. What worried me? Not fire. I worried because I had nowhere to run if they came for me.

They. The Russians. Police guys. Anybody.

I had made up my mind I would use Kirill's pistol if the Russians came, but I would surrender if it was police or soldiers at the door. (I don't know why I expected soldiers, but I did.) I would go to the jail Inga and Yulian had told me about on the Rikers Island, as awful as they had made it sound. But I would shoot the Russians, because this time they were not just going to make me pee in a coffee pot. They were not just going to burn off Sonja's or my hair. They were going to kill me.

I thought Sonja and I needed to run much farther away. If we were going to Los Angeles, we should go to Los Angeles. We really had not run far away at all. I looked at a subway map and could see the block right where the town house was where we had been living the day before. I counted the blocks. We were only forty-five streets north and ten avenues west.

But Sonja thought this was fine, at least for now. We needed to lay low—not travel right away when everyone was keeping an eye out for us. And they would never look for us right under their noses. Besides, she said, we were not going to be here long.

Still, by daylight this plan seemed crazy. Even if we got to Los Angeles, I was not sure why we would be safe. I lit a cigarette even though I wasn't supposed to smoke in the hotel room and opened the window to blow out the smoke. Oligarchs like Vasily, I knew, had tentacles like giant squids.

...

I wondered if I would have been brave enough to help the police guy if he had come to me. I couldn't decide. But I did know this: Crystal may have been into him, but she was taking a chance for all of us. She was thinking of Sonja and me and all the girls they were bringing to America. I knew that in my heart. If she had gotten free, we all would have gotten free. I thought about that as I smoked, and I went from very, very scared to very, very sad.

...

Sonja and I were going to meet at nine o'clock on Saturday morning at a pizza parlor we had seen the night before. That was our plan. I woke up earlier than that. When I put out my cigarette, I made a list. It made me think a little less about how sad and scared I was—maybe because it made me think I was in control of something. I added up how much money we had and how much we were spending. There were the two hotel rooms and food and the clothes we were going to have to buy. If we really were going to Los Angeles, we would need to be making a lot more money every night than we were spending, because we would need a lot more money than we had. Whoever was going to steal us our passports or make us fake ones was going to want a lot of money. The plane tickets would cost nothing compared to a couple of fake or stolen passports.

I told Sonja this as we ate our pizza for breakfast. We were standing at a counter that faced a wall, but there was a mirror so we could see who was coming into the place. I was so hungry. I hadn't eaten since before we had left for the party the day before. We were still wearing our knit caps with the sports team logos on them. And even though we were inside, we were wearing our sunglasses.

"I don't know how strip clubs here work, but it can't be any crazier than it was in Moscow, yes?" she said.

"What do you know about Moscow strip clubs?" I asked. "You never worked in one."

She held the last of the crust like it was chicken bone, and looked at it. "You take your clothes off and men give you money. You take the right ones to special rooms and finish them off. You give some of the money to the club managers. How complicated is it?"

"We're wearing hats and sunglasses because we don't want people to find us," I reminded her. "Because we don't want to be recognized. And your plan is to stand in front of a roomful of men completely naked? Why don't we just go back to the town house and say, 'We're here! Come kill us!' Why don't we just go up to one of those police guys outside and tell them who we are?"

"No one knows what we look like."

"The men at the party do!" I told her, and I thought of the faces I could remember. I thought of the bachelor's brother. Richard. I thought of the bedroom upstairs where we went.

"They're not looking for us, I promise you. Those little dicks? They are scaredy-cats. Besides, why would they want to find us? They don't. They are terrified of us. So, my opinion? We have three nights."

"Three nights?"

"I think we have three days and three nights before it becomes too dangerous. We each take two clubs. We work a day shift in one and a night shift in the other. We make as much money from tips as we can and then we count what we have. On Tuesday I meet with the dude who will get us the passports—"

"You know someone who can do that? Here?"

She nodded. "He was at the town house last Tuesday. He was with Crystal and me."

I knew who she meant. Fellow was Georgian from Tbilisi and now lived in Queens. Clearly had black market connections. Tall and blond, with perfectly trimmed blond beard. Was acquaintance of Russians, but not a friend. "The guy—"

"Don't ask me questions. I don't want you to know too much if this blows up in my face."

"No. You have to tell me."

"Fine. It was his phone number I left at the party. I hid it in condom wrapper. But then like dope I brought that one upstairs. The paper is in the bed or by the bed. I forgot to get it. But I think I remember enough of the telephone number. It might take a few dials, but I'll find him," she said. She rinsed her mouth with the soda in the paper cup. Then she continued, "On Tuesday night, we're on airplanes to California. Different planes, but we will meet at the Los Angeles Airport. Maybe I will have Kim Kardashian pick us up." She was smiling when she said Kim's name. How she could joke amazed me.

"So, Tuesday night," she repeated when I said nothing.

I thought about this. It was Saturday morning. Saturday night was a big night for these clubs. Even I understood that. "Maybe we could start tonight somewhere."

"Maybe? Of course we can! We have to! We have to start this afternoon!"

I wasn't so sure. Would the girls who already had spots at these clubs let us in? I wouldn't want to share Saturday men and Saturday tips with some new person who just showed up out of nowhere.

But it turned out the girls didn't matter. Only the managers did. And when we took our clothes off for them, they wanted us. By two o'clock that afternoon, we were both working and we were both making money. She was at a club on the Tenth Avenue and I was at the one by the Empire State Building. Then we switched. We worked until four in the morning on Sunday, when the clubs closed and there were no men left to pleasure.

...

I think the managers were surprised at how much money we turned over to them at the end of our shifts, and that was even after tipping out the bouncer, the bartender, and the DJ. One club wanted 40 percent of our take and one wanted 50. One had a bouncer who was okay with whatever we did with a man in the champagne room, as long as he got his take. The other club, which I guess had gotten busted by the police, did not want us doing anything to make the men finish except grind hard against them when we were in their laps—when they still had their pants on.

Still.

Still. We were both amazed at how much money we could make—and how fast we could make it.

...

On Sunday, when we were walking in the middle of all the crowds, I asked Sonja how she could have fucked one of the men at the party for the bachelor in the bedroom that belonged to the little girl. She shrugged her shoulders.

"It was where the guy brought me," she said.

"Which guy?"

"The one with the suspenders. Spencer. The one who hired us."

"You know you didn't just leave condom wrapper and phone number there. You also left the used rubber."

"Maybe he did. I didn't. Rubber's man's problem when we're done."

"Not cool for that girl," I told her.

"If you were so worried about the girl, did you pick it up?"

"No."

"Then don't judge me, okay? Not cool for that girl," she mumbled, and I did not know if she repeated what I had said to mock me or because my leaving it there wasn't cool either.

...

I tried not to draw attention to myself when I was not on the stage or in the men's laps. I did not talk much to the other girls, except for the woman who—like Inga or Catherine—was supposed to teach us the rules of the clubs and what kind of makeup we were supposed to wear. She also had us buy the clothes from her that we were supposed to take off, but that was just a thick G-string, a bra, and a baby doll. (The shoes were the most expensive part, and it angered Sonja that each club made us purchase shoes from them. I told the woman at the second club that I had high heels already, but it didn't matter. I still had to buy from them.) Neither club had much of a stage or a pole. One had mirrors that showed us off in nice way when we danced. The rooms were dim, but one club had sexy red lighting. (Both had lighting in bathrooms that was crazy bright. Sonja said this was so there would be no funny business in there. Men also could not bring booze into bathroom. Why? Because they might give it to girls who are old enough to dance naked and pleasure the men, but not old enough to drink the booze legally.)

Mostly we were just supposed to go from man to man, pull off our tops, and give them their lap dances. The room was like some of the parties we had in Moscow: a lot of men in suit pants and shirts, and a lot of mostly naked girls. No big deal. I had my come-on line: *I'm the one you've been looking for tonight,* I'd purr. *I know because I've been looking for you.* A lap dance was supposed to last a song or part of a song at both clubs, and I was supposed to get twenty. I was getting forty and fifty. When I would take the men to the champagne room for something extra, that extra was three hundred if I used my hand and five hundred if I used my mouth.

...

Some of the other dancers were moms and some were college students and some had other jobs. Some had boyfriends, but I did not meet any who had a husband. Some danced to pay for their drugs. And some were just there because they were pretty and didn't know what else to do. Some had been doing this for four or five years, and some were just doing it until something better came along. Only some, I could tell, were totally fine with taking the men to the champagne rooms and finishing them off. Some did not approve of me because I did.

But they could judge me. I didn't care. One girl would buy extra panties, rub them between her legs, spray a little perfume on them, and sell them to dudes for fifty or even one hundred dollars. Another girl used to let some guy rub her foot with one hand and himself with the other. She thought she was better than me. That was fine.

At one of the clubs I became friendly with a girl named Zooey, but only because she kept reaching out to me to be nice. Most girls were not that friendly. No allegiance. They would say things behind each other's backs like "She's such a child." Or "She's such a whore." Or "She's such a bitch." I was telling everyone that I was Polish girl named Kasia, and so the manager had me dancing as Kesha—which was also the name of a singer, of course. Zooey was from Cleveland and two years older than me. She was very tiny and had the most beautiful dark eyes and the most perfect dark skin.

She pulled me aside after I came back from one of the champagne rooms.

"You know how to make sure they're not cops, right?" she asked me. My heart sank a little because for a second I feared she knew who I was. I must have been silent too long, because she said, "You know, undercover cops?"

I shook my head. "How?"

"Have them touch your boobs before you touch them. Maybe even have them finger you before you touch them."

"Why?"

"A cop can't arrest you for prostitution if he engages."

"And then it's okay?"

She laughed a little bit. "It's never okay. But at least you're not going to get busted."

...

I almost didn't go back to work on Sunday afternoon. I saw the newspapers on Sunday morning. I turned on the TV set in my hotel room and saw what the reporters were saying. There were no pictures of Sonja and me, but there was—everywhere!—the word *manhunt*. Two TV anchor ladies argued about how "dangerous" we were. One said we weren't dangerous at all. We had "merely" killed the creeps who were holding us hostage. The other said maybe that was the case, but we were still very violent. I thought I was going to be sick.

I told Sonja it would be crazy to go back out to the clubs on Sunday afternoon, but she said there was no reason to believe anyone would think either of us were the girls from the party. She reminded me that everyone was thinking "pair." She reminded me that no one knew what we looked like. She reminded me that it was so crazy what we were doing, who would guess for even a second we were the girls from the party.

And she was right. Once again we danced and did what we had been taught to do. We made men happy and we made more money.

When we were done with our second shifts early on Monday morning, I asked Sonja, "And when we get to Los Angeles, what? Really, what?" We were near the entrance to the subway on the Broadway, where we had agreed we would meet. It was four-fifteen in the morning. It was still busy. Four-fifteen in the morning, and there were people out like it was the middle of the day in some places. There were all those yellow cabs and cars and trucks delivering bread.

"What do you mean?"

"You know what I'm asking," I told her. "Who will help us there?"

"Kim," she said.

"I'm serious."

"Honestly? I don't know. I just know we can't stay here."

...

It was amazing how many men wanted to take me to dinner. It was amazing how many men told me they wanted to take me to hotel room after my shift ended. It was amazing how much money they said they wanted to spend—if I left the club for a few hours.

But, in the end, I knew I would make more if I stayed. Men always pay more at places like that when they're hungry.

...

On Monday, late in the morning when I was waking up, I saw on the hotel TV that the Russians had been arrested. I saw they had also arrested some of the girls.

I was so excited that I watched the TV standing up, clicking between the news stations to see the story over and over. I wished that Sonja had been with me. I felt a little, tiny glimmer of hope and wanted to hold her hands and jump around the room. I am not kidding: that was how I felt.

But as I watched the story a third and a fourth time, I realized that I did not recognize any of the names. It didn't seem like Yulian or Konstantin was in the group the police guys had arrested. And they didn't reveal the names of the girls. (Not that I would have known them. No one had introduced Sonja or Crystal or me to any of the other courtesans.)

And then I wanted to ask Sonja what she thought it meant that Yulian and Konstantin were not in jail. I wanted to know if she knew any of the names who were. But we were really trying not to use our cell phones—just in case. And so I sat on the bed and smoked and waited to go to work and smoked some more. I did not care that I was stinking up the room and they might kick me out or try and make me pay big penalty fine.

...

When we left the clubs after our Monday-night shifts, we figured we were done, and we went to our hotels to get some sleep. We wouldn't go back to the clubs ever. It was all about how much money we could make in three days and nights from lap dances and tips—and we had made lots. Sonja said she had reached the passport guy on the ninth or tenth dial and was going to meet with him Tuesday at lunchtime. I said I would join her, but she said I couldn't. She promised me she would call my phone between two and three in the afternoon and hang up. That was the signal that I should go downstairs from my hotel room and meet her at the pizza parlor.

...

I woke up around nine in the morning on Tuesday and could not fall back to sleep, even though I had only been in bed a few hours. I went outside and walked around the Times Square. I was just about to light a cigarette when I saw two men looking at me, and I was sure they were Russian. I was standing in front of a beautiful Broadway theater. Maybe this was crazy paranoia, but I still wrapped my hand around the Makarov I had tucked into my skirt and hidden behind my jacket. And then, when I saw a yellow taxicab with its white light on near me, I waved to the man and jumped inside. I told him to go to Thirteenth Street. I just made that up. I had no reason to go to that street. When we got there, I told him to go to the Second Avenue. When we got to the Second Avenue, I told him to go to the Central Park. I kept looking out the back window like I was in one of the movies we used to watch back in Russia, but I never saw a car following me.

"What did you do?" the man asked me when we got to the Second Avenue. He was from India.

"Nothing."

He didn't believe me, and he asked me to pay him for the trip so far. He didn't make me get out, but he wanted to be sure I had money. So I paid him and he started his meter all over again, and he drove to the First Avenue and turned his taxi so it was going north.

I finally got out near the Hudson River. Then I walked back to my hotel, past one of the two clubs where I had been stripping over the weekend.

I decided Sonja and I couldn't get out of New York City fast enough, but I really wasn't sure why Los Angeles would be better. I had a feeling I was going to be looking over my shoulder for the rest of my life.

And I remember wishing I spoke French. If I did, I thought, maybe we could go to Paris. Sure there were Russians in Paris. But maybe not ones who wanted to kill me.

...

In my hotel room, I waited. I would have been so happy to watch an episode of *The Bachelor* on the TV, but there wasn't one on.

So I just kept pressing the channels on the remote control, smoking more cigarettes, and thinking of how I wished Sonja had not knifed Pavel. How I wished Crystal had not talked to police guy. How I wished we had not come to America. I looked out at the bricks of the air shaft and the dirt on the walls, and I wondered if my mother in heaven could see what had happened to me. I wondered if my grandmother could. I wondered what Nayiri was doing. And I thought of Richard Chapman. I guessed he was back at his beautiful office in a sunny skyscraper somewhere, surrounded by other big-deal executives like him, and their secretaries and super fast computers—not like me, all alone in a room and very scared, with only stupid TV for company.

...

And then two o'clock in the afternoon came. And then three o'clock. I waited there all afternoon for my phone to ring that one time and then stop. It never did.

I kept flicking the safety on the gun off and on, off and on.

Finally at five o'clock I called Sonja's number, let it ring once, and then hung up. But she didn't ring back. Not at five or six or seven. Never.

And while I didn't know what had happened to her, I knew in my heart I was never going to see my Sonja again. I prayed she was alive, but I was not confident. I was not confident at all. I had been in bad trouble before. I had been in bad trouble plenty of times. But this? I had never before felt so cornered and so scared for my life. They were coming for me—they had to be—and I had no idea how or where I could run.

Chapter Eleven

As lunchtime neared Thursday, Melissa walked between Emiko and Claudia back toward the brick school building after gym. Their class had just played soccer . . . yet again. Neither Melissa nor Emiko was a fan of the sport, but they certainly preferred the soccer unit to flag football. Claudia said she didn't enjoy it either, but she brought the same feral energy to soccer that she brought to skiing and dancing and Xbox games. Still, even Claudia agreed that she would be happier in a few weeks when they were inside doing gymnastics.

Abruptly Claudia said, "I think we all know what it means."

Melissa turned to her. Her friend had dirt all over her hands and arms and her chin. Claudia ran hard and kicked hard, and the girl had taken a couple of tumbles that morning. Melissa didn't have to ask Claudia what she meant by *it*. Neither did Emiko. They all knew because they had all been thinking about it ever since Melissa had asked them that morning what they thought the term *sex slave* meant.

"I mean, we know about the slaves and we know what sex is," Claudia went on.

"There were slaves who were men. Does that mean that a sex slave can be a man?" Emiko asked.

"I guess. But I bet they're mostly girls. I mean, it's an expression. Sex slave. Someone who is ordered to have sex."

"But who owns them?" Melissa asked. "Slaves had owners." They were entering the gymnasium now and crossing the basketball court, and Melissa lowered her voice because it seemed to echo inside here.

"Maybe your uncle?"

"My uncle did not own them. I've seen his apartment. It's small. Where would he even keep a sex slave? Where would he keep two?"

Emiko corrected them both: "It was the men who were killed. They were the ones who owned them. That would make sense, right? The sex slaves killed their masters."

Melissa could tell that Claudia was about to add something. But then the three girls saw the gym teacher watching them, and they all went silent. Melissa looked down at her sneakers. She thought about her father wanting a sex slave, and grew disgusted.

...

Dina Renzi found Hugh Kirn almost childishly petulant, but decided that any man with eyes that blue—they were cobalt—was probably used to being a jerk and still getting his way. Getting whatever he wanted. Now he sat across from her in one of Franklin McCoy's smaller conference rooms, though it still had a panoramic view of the East River and Brooklyn.

"Did you know that the only vegetarian option at Harry's is a four-egg omelet?" she told him soon after arriving at the investment bank, not so much small talk as an attempt to build commonality. The restaurant wasn't far from the bank's offices on Water Street, and she had had lunch there two weeks ago. She thought a joke about Harry's might loosen him up. "Four eggs.

Does anyone—especially someone who isn't going to order the steak sandwich—really want a four-egg omelet?"

"It's a steakhouse," he said, not looking up from the manila folder in front of him that he had just opened. His hair was the color of cinnamon, and his eyeglasses were wire rims, rectangular and severe. Inside the folder, in addition to Richard Chapman's personnel file, she could see tear sheets from some of the recent newspaper stories about the debacle in her client's home.

"It's an angioplasty waiting to happen," she said.

"So, Richard Chapman," he began, clearly disdaining any interest in irrelevant conversation. "Frankly, I think the man should be seriously grateful. He's still getting a paycheck from us."

"I disagree. This leave is punitive and there's no cause. He violated no company policy. He hasn't been charged with a crime—and won't be."

"If it were punitive, it would be a disciplinary leave of absence without pay. This is merely an administrative leave."

"Forced."

"It is mandatory, yes. And I would say there is cause. His presence here—and with our clients—is a public relations problem. We really don't want to be associated with him right now. Would you? We feel the need to make a statement as a company—to distance ourselves from behavior we don't condone."

"He's a victim, too."

"Yeah, right."

"He allowed his brother's friends to have a bachelor party for his brother at his house. That's what he did—and that's all he did."

"And two people were murdered."

"Precisely! Two people were murdered. Your employee was doing his brother a favor and wound up a witness to a horrible crime. But he did absolutely nothing wrong."

"We both know that's not true. He had prostitutes and mobsters in his home. The media has suggested it was an orgy."

She noticed a couple of pigeons on the window ledge, one with a boxer's broad chest. "The media is sensationalizing the sex," she answered carefully, because she knew that pig Spencer Doherty had some sort of video. "It was a bachelor party. I am going to go way out on a limb and guess that every male managing director at Franklin McCoy has been to a bachelor party. We all know what goes on at them."

"I promise you, I have never been to a bachelor party where the men were engaging in intercourse with prostitutes."

"And no one has accused Richard Chapman of doing that."

"The investigation is ongoing."

"It's a murder investigation. No one is going to charge your employee with having sex with a prostitute," she assured him.

"I hope not—for his sake and this company's."

"When can he come back?"

"I can't answer that."

"Every day you bar him from the office you are defaming his character."

"Oh, that's bullshit. We haven't said or written anything about him that's public."

"Are you sure? Are you that confident that there isn't a single e-mail between anyone at Franklin McCoy and any of your M and A clients that would make you . . . uncomfortable in that regard?"

He tilted back his chair and folded his arms. "Are you really going to play that card?"

"Look, the entire idea that you have put him on leave is, arguably, defamatory."

"So, he's going to sue us? Really? And then expect us to take him back with open arms?"

"No one wants to sue you. For reasons that I can't fathom, he actually likes all of you. He misses you," she said, hoping sarcasm hadn't leached into her voice. She reached into her Bottega and held up her own copy of his personnel file. "And he is, from what I understand, rather good at what he does. There's only love and more love in his performance reviews. It's just one big happy bromance."

"Having him here doesn't look good."

"Get over it. I promise you, your clients already have. You're an investment bank. God, if the world can get over Eliot Spitzer and Hugh Grant, it can get over Richard Chapman."

He rolled those magnificent blue eyes up at the tiles on the ceiling. He wasn't even trying to hide his vexation. "Tell me: What do you know? Do you have any sense of what's coming in the newspapers tomorrow? Or what will be online tonight?"

"The Middle East. Nude reality TV shows. Black boxes from aviation disasters. Taylor Swift. The usual."

"But nothing about our employee."

"Nothing about one of your managing directors—at least as far as I know."

"At least as far as you know," he repeated.

"That's right."

"Let's talk more on Monday."

"Let's talk more tomorrow."

"You really are working those billable hours, aren't you?"

"I'm looking out for Richard Chapman. The billable hours are just a bonus," she said, careful to smile in a manner that wasn't in the slightest way disingenuous. She made a mental note that when she filled in her client on her meeting with Kirn, she would see if he had paid off Spencer Doherty.

...

Alone in his house, his wife and his daughter both down the hill at the Bronxville School, Richard made sure that there were no vultures—his new pet name for the news vans—and went outside. He popped the trunk to his Audi and stared at the wannabe Bierstadt, which was still streaked with the blood from a dead Russian pimp. He really did have to deal with it. Here he had nothing but time on his hands, and still he hadn't called that detective's cousin at NYU. Wasn't there some expression about finding a busy person if you wanted to get something done? Maybe if he could just get the blood off the painting . . .

Maybe . . . nothing.

He recalled how he had tossed and turned on the futon last night and wished he had bought that hunting rifle. Or at least started the process. It would do him no good with Spencer—you couldn't just lean back in a bar and reveal it like your hidden carry—but it might have given him some peace of mind when he thought of the Russians. He knew intellectually there was no reason to be scared for his family. They wanted the girls, not him. At least that's what he was reminding himself now, in the clear light of day. It was in the small hours of the morning when all horrors seemed plausible. Even likely. Hadn't his brother told him that Spencer was terrified?

Well, maybe Spencer should be terrified. There was a guy at Franklin McCoy from Texas who once said about a bastard CEO whose company they were trying to sell, "Some people just need killin'." He said it with a twang that only appeared when he wanted to make a point. Well, in the Russians' eyes, Spencer probably just needed killin'—and to them it wasn't a joke.

Of course, Kristin would have been absolutely furious if he had brought home a rifle. She would have been convinced that he had, once and for all, lost his mind. And, perhaps, he had. Last night, he had stared up at the ceiling, awash in the superstitious fear that by failing to buy a weapon, he was inviting disaster: his family would be killed while a rifle lay dormant in its box in a gun store in Yonkers. If only . . .

If only . . .

Well, fuck the *if onlys*.

Fuck this goddamn painting.

Fuck Spencer Doherty.

Fuck the news vans and the Russians and the bastards he thought were his friends at Franklin McCoy.

He held the painting by two opposite sides of the frame as if it were a serving platter and marched to the bottom of his driveway. He stood before the antique wrought-iron post with his mailbox, raised the painting over his head, and then smashed it as hard as he could against the black metal finial, impaling it. Skewering it.

The tip pierced the canvas, and the mailbox widened the gash. Then, the painting dangling on the post, he grabbed loose strips of it with his hands and shredded them, pulling them apart as if he were ripping the tenderloin from chicken breasts. He cursed it. He swore under his breath. And when he lifted the painting back off the post, the slivers dangled like entrails. For a moment he held it in his hands, unsure why he wasn't wholly satisfied. But then he got it. Then he understood. He slammed the frame down onto the asphalt, splintering the wood on two sides and unhinging the corners.

Fuck you, he hissed at it. *Fuck you.* Now he was satisfied. He had to admit when he was throwing away the frame and the canvas, he really did feel a little better. No. He felt a lot better. He almost wished there had been a vulture present to capture his madness on video for the world.

He glanced at his watch and thought about what he would be doing if he were not killing time on this appalling leave of absence by destroying a painting. He counted back the hours to the bachelor party, numbering the intervals of twenty-four in his mind. How many hours ago had the guests started to arrive? How many hours ago had the two Russians been killed? He thought once again of that poor girl on the bed with her feet not touching the floor. She was still on the run somewhere. At least that's what the newspapers said. She was either on the run or she was dead. No, not dead, he thought. Please, not dead. Her death, he feared, might really push him over the edge. Would make his little catharsis with the painting just now seem like a round of golf.

He realized that he had to get out of the house. He saw that the car trunk was still open and slammed it shut. He combed his hair in the driveway, and climbed into the Audi. Then he drove down the hill to the school. There he waited in the parking lot, soaking up the cool autumn air and the bright midday sun, waiting for those two consecutive periods when he knew that Kristin was on break. The hours when she usually did errands or grabbed a bite to eat. He thought he would surprise her and take her to lunch.

. . .

Philip Chapman stood beside Spencer Doherty with his back against one of the black marble obelisks behind which statuesque young women—dressed always in black sheath dresses, spike heels, and a shade of lipstick so red the company christened it Provocateur—would check guests in and out of the Cravat, and lost what it was that his friend was telling him. He had been surveying a part of his little empire, but now he was watching a young woman in a white skirt and matching blazer nuzzle a man a generation older as they crossed the lobby and disappeared inside an elevator. The guy was handsome, and the suit was a perfectly tailored charcoal gray pinstripe from Brooks Brothers. It was so clear that the pair was about to have a lunch-hour quickie in their hotel room. He imagined they worked together at some investment bank like his brother's, but one based in Chicago or L.A., and they were in town for a series of meetings with clients. He fantasized about the woman's lingerie beneath that skirt and blazer. He told himself that it was okay to think like this, now that Nicole had dumped him. Broken off the engagement. But he also suspected that he would have been envisioning the woman's panties and bra—a demi thing, he decided—even if he was still getting married a week from Saturday.

"Anyway," Spencer was saying, "that's what my lawyer thinks will be the deal."

"Sounds okay to me," he murmured, as the elevator doors soundlessly slid shut. "And you feel good about that?"

"You didn't hear a single word I said, did you?"

"I heard a few."

Spencer looked at his watch. "God. You're incredible."

"Okay, I'm listening. I promise."

"They were threatening me with sexual assault on a minor. They were threatening me with managing a sex tourism business. Even that's a Class D felony. Do you have any idea how many years in prison I was looking at if I were convicted of sexual assault on a minor? Do you realize how completely fucking ruined my whole life would have been?"

"You wouldn't have been convicted. You just used a stripper service that had benefits."

"But I knew they had benefits. And I did have sex with that blonde."

"You weren't alone."

"Anyway, if you care, I told them everything—and I mean everything—and I've agreed to testify. So instead I'm not even looking at a Class A misdemeanor: promoting prostitution. My lawyer, at first, thought that was the goal. Get this shitstorm down to a misdemeanor. But by testifying, I'm getting off scot-free."

"And that nasty business with Chuck and Brandon?"

"Really, Philip, I might have been talking to the fucking wall."

"I'm sorry."

Spencer sighed, exasperated. "Brandon's wife is still claiming to be out for the count, which my lawyer says is all part of the negotiations. But the settlement—assuming we reach one—won't be pretty. And Chuck's lawyer has gone off radar. Not responding to e-mails or phone calls."

"Which may mean Chuck has come to his senses, right?"

"Hah! That, too, is part of the negotiations. Any way you look at it, no matter how or when or if we settle, I am financially fucked. My legal fees alone are going to be a world of pain."

"That whole night now is nothing but pain. None of us have gotten off easy."

"But some of us are in far deeper shit than others. So, tell me . . ."

Philip looked at Spencer and raised his eyebrows expectedly. It was unlike Spencer to stop in mid-sentence. "Go on."

"So, tell me . . . you hear from your brother?"

"Often. Why?" Philip noted how his friend wouldn't meet his eyes, and thought this was odd: it was as if Spencer was actually experiencing a little guilt over the tsunami he had unleashed.

"Just curious."

"God, are you getting a heart?" He clapped him good-naturedly on the shoulder. "Are you getting a moral compass? I'm proud of you, Spencer! You're feeling bad about this natural disaster, aren't you?"

"He's your brother. He's smart. I was just wondering what he was saying."

"Mostly he's saying he's pissed at Franklin McCoy. Mostly he's saying his house is a mess."

"Interesting."

"He'll be okay. He is smart, you're right. And he's loaded. His wife is pretty. He's everything I'm not."

Spencer nodded, but he didn't disagree with him. Philip rather hoped—expected, in fact—that he would. And so they both were quiet for a moment. Finally Spencer said, "Can I ask you something?"

"Of course."

"Do you ever think about those Russian dudes? I can't get that moment when they were killed out of my head. The poor bastards. I've had nightmares about getting attacked just like that. I keep thinking of the knife in that one guy's neck."

"Well, that's cheery."

"A few times, I've woken up with the sweats. I know it's unreasonable . . . actually, I don't know that at all . . . I *tell myself* it's unreasonable, but I really do worry sometimes that those Russian guys are going to come after me for ratting them out."

"I know you do."

"I mean, if you were them, wouldn't you want a guy like me dead?"

"You didn't rat them out. You told the police the name of the service you used."

"And that might be all it takes to get a person killed, right? Some of those dudes are already back on the street. They paid their bail and they're out. And now I've agreed to testify. That can't be good."

"Remember, *those dudes* didn't kill anyone. I'm serious. The killers here were those two girls. And I don't think those girls have got anything against us," he said, and he recalled the way the blond one had ravenously clawed at him, the muscles in her beautiful neck growing taut as she arched back her head. Afterward, he'd imagined he would somehow find the right words to ask Nicole to grab him just like that. To roll her head back like that. Alas, he could now take that little bit of wordsmithing off his to-do list.

"I guess. But don't you wish you could somehow delete the images of those poor bastards bleeding out from your brain?"

"Honestly? I don't think about that so much."

"Are you serious?"

He shrugged. "Look: obviously I'm never going to forget it. Obviously I was a second away from wetting my pants when it was going on. But mostly I think about how amazing those girls were before they went banshee."

"Well, I've learned my lesson. I have so learned my lesson."

"I have, too," Philip said, but in one of those moments of rare and uncharacteristic self-awareness, he thought of that woman in white upstairs now in the hotel room, naked atop the older guy, and he realized he hadn't. He knew in his heart he'd learned nothing at all.

. . .

"I'm really not hungry," Kristin said, dropping the menu back on her placemat at the restaurant. It was a single sheet of paper, calligraphed and copied that day because the menu changed daily at the little bistro near the school—though rarely did anyone from the school eat there, at least during the school day. Today the restaurant was filled with ladies of a certain generation who lunched. And that generation was her mother's. Other than a table with an elderly gentleman in a bowtie surrounded by three women, Richard was the only male in the small dining room.

"Really? You have to eat," Richard said.

"I did. I had some soup during my first break. If I'd known you were coming, I wouldn't have . . . but I did. Sorry."

"Have some coffee. Please. So I'm not eating alone."

"Of course."

"I just thought a surprise lunch would be nice."

"It is," she said, and she reached across the table and took his hands. "This is really sweet of you. I appreciate it. And it is nice. It really is."

"I have to admit, I was a little afraid you wouldn't want to be seen in public with me. I was afraid it might be too embarrassing."

"Oh, I'm fine. Or I'm getting fine. I don't know. I think I'm actually more worried about your embarrassment at the moment."

He turned toward the table with the four older customers. They were indeed glancing surreptitiously at him. He gave them a small wave, and instantly they all looked down at their entrées. "Well, I earned it," he said to Kristin.

"I know. But a lot of men get away with a lot worse."

"Thank you."

"You're welcome."

"But you're still not hungry."

She shook her head. The truth was, however, that she was famished. She had lied about the soup. And she had eaten nothing for breakfast. She was haunted by dual images: the sight she had seen when she had studied herself in the mirror and the fantasy she had created in her mind of the prostitute who had led her husband upstairs. Quickly she drank the entire glass of water before her, hoping she could trick her brain's hunger center.

"I thought this afternoon I might research wallpaper designs for the front hallway," he said.

"Are you kidding?" She couldn't imagine him taking the time to find wallpaper designs. But then again, just yesterday he had come home from a furniture store with iPhone photos of possible couches to replace the one they were getting rid of on Saturday, as well as a stack of catalogs from the showroom. She was shocked, a little awed, by his initiative.

"Yeah, why not? Maybe find some paper with that great CBGB's bathroom feel," he said.

She smiled. The bathrooms there had always been appalling. But she and Richard had danced at the club and listened to music at the club and—one memorable evening—made out at the club. "Retro graffiti? Spray paint chic?"

"Absolutely. Did you have a chance to look at the catalogs I brought home? Think about what sort of new couch you'd like?"

She had carried the catalogs upstairs, but after reading with Melissa and then grading papers, she had turned out the light and gone to sleep—though first she had stared for a moment at Richard's side of the bed. At her daughter, asleep there instead of her husband. "I didn't. Sorry," she answered. She felt a little sheepish.

"It's okay. No need to apologize." He looked once more at his menu. Then: "Remember that old joke about men and quiche?"

"I do. Are you thinking of ordering the quiche?"

"I am."

"I never thought a man was less of a man because he liked quiche."

He smiled. "Thank you."

She sat back, wondering how this had all become so awkward. They had been married for nearly a decade and a half. They had been in love even longer. How was it they were struggling to make conversation? How was it their relationship had become an uncomfortable first date? She hated this. She loathed this. It was pathetic and . . . awful. Hadn't they once been at least a little feral? A little less tamed? What the hell had happened to their nights at places like CBGB's? What the hell had happened to the ease with which they would go to dinner and a movie and make love while Melissa was at a friend's house for the night? She watched him look around for the waiter and made a decision. It was a snap decision, but at the moment she wanted nothing more than to find their way back to where they had been—to who they had been. To who they once were.

"Don't order," she commanded him.

He looked confused.

"We've got almost an hour," she told him. "We're going to go home and go upstairs. And there you are going to fuck me silly."

...

The next morning, Friday, Melissa was finding it easier not to be mad at her father. A little, anyway. After all, her mother seemed now to have forgiven him. Last night her parents had slept in their bedroom together for the first time since before her uncle's bachelor party. She had even seen her mom kiss her dad on the cheek when she had come into the kitchen for breakfast, as her dad was making her lunch for school. (She tried to recall if her father had ever made her lunch before. She had to restrain herself from making suggestions; she had to trust that Mom had told him what she liked.)

But she still found herself unsettled by what he may have done at that party and a little adrift in his presence. The expression *sex slave* kept coming back to her. Moreover, her father still wasn't allowed to go back to work: he was still being punished by his bosses. Their house was still awash in unsettling vestiges from the party last Friday night, such as that awful couch.

And her uncle's wedding was off. She was no longer going to get to be a flower girl, and she had been looking forward to that; she had been looking forward to that a lot. She loved the dress, and she had no idea now if she would ever have the chance to show it off. It was red velvet; it had a white collar and pearl buttons. When else would she have the opportunity to wear it? She'd probably outgrow it before she was asked again to be a flower girl.

When the phone on the kitchen wall rang, both of her parents turned toward it as if it were the smoke alarm. Then she noticed that they both looked at each other. Her father answered it; her mother leaned against a counter, holding her coffee mug with both hands. Melissa finished chewing the bite of toast in her mouth and swallowed. She planned to listen carefully. But then her father took the phone with him and wandered through the dining room and into the living room, and she couldn't hear a word of what he was saying.

"Who is it?" she asked her mother.

"I don't know, sweetie."

"You look worried."

"No."

She didn't believe that—her mother *was* worried—but Melissa could only sit against the back of her kitchen chair and wait. Both she and her mother waited.

A minute or two later, her father returned. "I'm . . . I'm going into the city today, after all," he said.

"Really? Was that someone from Franklin McCoy?" her mother asked. "Was it that lawyer you despise?"

"Nope."

"Dina Renzi?"

He had gotten dressed that morning in blue jeans and a black hoodie. Now Melissa watched him put both hands in the kangaroo pocket. At first, she thought he looked a little bewildered. But then she understood that this wasn't confusion at all: he was stunned. "Not her, either."

"Don't keep us in suspense," her mother said. "Who was it?"

"It was the police."

"That detective? Detective Bryant?"

"A different one. A man. He was in the city. He . . ."

"Go on."

Her father looked at her. "Melissa, your mom and I are going to talk about this in the other room. It's nothing you need to worry about, I promise. So, why don't you finish your breakfast and then I'll finish making your lunch."

She motioned at her plate and the cereal bowl, empty except for the last of the milk and a few floating Cheerios. "I'm done," she said. She noticed the little pieces of toast left like bits of bark on her plate, and added, "I don't eat the crusts."

"Sweetie—"

"No!" she cut her father off, that disgusting expression—*sex slaves*—bubbling to the top of her mind, incapable of being repressed. She was about to say more, but the words caught in her throat. She blinked, but her eyes already were welling up. Her parents were stunned at the way she had silenced them with that one definitive syllable.

"Okay, Melissa," her father said gingerly. "What?"

"I want to know what the police want. I'm tired of learning everything about that party online or at school."

And that was when the room seemed to really go mad. Her father wanted to know what she was doing reading about the party on the computer, and her mother was asking her what people were saying at school. They were talking at the same time, over each other, their words running together like the great buzz at the Broadway theater before the show started last week, a burble from which all meaning had to be extracted from the single words that would rise up from an otherwise incomprehensible thrum. It made her angry. It made her furious. She didn't know why she was the one who had to answer questions. None of this awfulness was her fault. She'd done nothing wrong. She just wanted things to be the way they were.

Suddenly both of her parents were kneeling on the kitchen floor beside her, rubbing her arms and her back, because those tears had become sobs. She tried to stop, shaking her head and rubbing her face with her napkin, but she was a mess. She just couldn't help it, and now all those questions were forgotten as her father kept saying, "It's okay, it's okay," and her mother kept murmuring, "Shhhhhh. Shhhhhh."

But it wasn't okay, it just wasn't. That was horribly clear, because now her mother was asking her father again, "What did the police want? Why are you going into the city?"

Melissa felt her father looking at her again. And this time he answered her mother, all the while continuing to rub her back. "I'm going to the morgue. They want me to identify the body of a person who was . . . who passed away. They think it's the body of one of the girls who was at the party."

Her mother sat back on the floor as if she were a toddler. "No," she said.

"Do you mean you have to go look at a dead body?" Melissa asked her father, sniffling, her voice now a desperate little pant in her head.

Her father nodded. "Yes. One of the girls."

For a long second, Melissa focused on the way he had said the word *girls*. At the way a moment earlier he had said *girls at the party*. She repeated the expression in her mind. *Girls at the party*. But they weren't girls. They were sex slaves. And now, it seemed, one of them was dead.

Part Three

Alexandra

I had lots of American cash, but no idea how far it would go or how useful paper money really was. It wasn't just that I only knew how much some things cost in New York City. Things like manicures and spray tans and makeup at stores like Sephora. It was that even I understood you couldn't just buy an airline ticket with dollar bills. They think you're a terrorist and are going to hijack or blow up the airplane if you try. You need a credit card, which I didn't have yet. I remembered what Sonja had told me when we were buying our train tickets when we left Bronxville: you could buy bus tickets and train tickets for short trips with cash, but you couldn't rent cars or fly anywhere on airplanes without what she called "plastic." Besides, even if I did have a credit card, wouldn't the police guys find me? Of course they would. And then I would be in that dungeon of a place called the Rikers Island because they thought I was a murderer.

I knew I needed to find someone who could make me a pretend person passport and pretend person credit cards—someone like the Georgian from Tbilisi. But I wasn't sure where to begin, so that was as far as I got that afternoon with a plan. Still, I took every dollar I had and I left the hotel. I took the gun, which I loaded and tucked inside my leather jacket. And I took the clothing I had bought, which obviously was not very much. It all fit inside the backpack Sonja and I had gotten in the Times Square. It was seven o'clock at night.

I threw my phone into a garbage can on the street. If Sonja hadn't called me by now, she never would. The only people who had my number were whoever had Sonja's phone. And I was afraid that somehow they would use our calls—use my number—to track me down.

The main thing was, right that second I had to find a new neighborhood. I had no clue how much Sonja had told them before they killed her or beat her up or put her on a plane and sent her back to Moscow—or someplace worse. I figured I had to stay far away from the two clubs where I had stripped for the men or either of our hotels or anyplace near the Broadway. I knew I had to stay away from the East Village. So that evening I started walking north on the Tenth Avenue, not sure where I was going, when I saw a newspaper in a rack on a newsstand with the headline that some of the Russians had been let out of jail. They had "made bail." I stared at the headline for a few seconds. It made me a little nauseous. But then I kept walking.

...

Maybe if they hadn't made bail, I would have gone to police guys and tried to explain what happened. But they did make bail.

And this meant Americans were probably as corrupt as Russians.

Maybe if I knew or could somehow find police guy who had talked to Crystal, I would have gone to him. But that was at least as crazy impossible as finding someone who could get me pretend person passport.

Besides, the police would only see me now as Kirill's murderer. They would only see me as whore who shot pimp.

And that would mean American prison for sure.

...

The neighborhoods in New York City change as fast as they do anywhere. Yerevan. Moscow. One minute you're on a block where girls like me sit on men's laps in clubs, wearing nothing but G-strings and high-heel shoes, and the next minute there are luxury apartment buildings or beautiful brick town houses that look like they belong in another century. There are mothers walking their little girls home from early evening ballet class. (When I saw those girls with their dance bags, I crossed the street. It was like whatever I had could be contagious. Just breathing on them would turn them into courtesans.) I saw a father in a business suit and raincoat holding his daughter's hand walking in my direction. She was maybe six years old and she was holding a Barbie doll in a red ball gown. I thought of Richard and his little girl. Based on the pictures of her I saw in his house, she was older than this child. But maybe not by much. She still had her Barbies. I had seen the plastic box of them in her bedroom. I saw the rubber the suspender dude had left there after fucking Sonja.

It seemed to me that Richard was a good father. A good husband. A good provider. At least that was the feeling I got. (And girls like me have to learn to trust our feelings about a person. We have to figure out who the dude is from a first impression. It can help us make our money, and it might help us save our lives.) He was not an oligarch, but he had a nice house. If that plastic tub was all Barbies, then his little girl might have had as many Barbies as me when I'd been a kid back in Yerevan. And I bet Richard had actually paid for those Barbies. That was different from my father. He left me all those Barbies before he died, and he had never paid a single ruble—not one single dram—for any of them. (It's a long story.)

Anyway, when I thought of Richard, I thought of how he was so worried I was cold that night when I was sitting on the bed. How he wouldn't fuck me because he was married. How he had bought his daughter so many Barbies. He was a man—and here was a word I did not normally think of when I thought of men—that a person could trust. It had been a long time since I had thought of a man that way. Mostly men were just animals who had needs. Even the TV Bachelor. Even all of the TV Bachelors. I wanted romance, I wanted a man to kneel and give me a rose, but girls like me do not meet men like that. We just don't. It's movie fantasy that we do, even when we are pretty.

And I was never gaga for any guy. I was never in love. I had regulars at the cottage and in Moscow, but I was never going to be so stupid as to think they could love me. Maybe if Richard had fucked me like all the others, I wouldn't have continued to think about him. Maybe if my father hadn't died when I was so young, I would have looked at Richard the way I looked at most of the johns. (People say girls like me have daddy issues. Maybe. But it's not a universal thing. Not all sex slaves are orphans. Not all whores wish their fathers—living or dead—had paid them even teeny tiny teaspoonful of attention.) But, for whatever the reason, I found myself wondering if Richard could help me. Would help me. Not healthy. Not normal. Not smart. I let the idea go.

When this father I saw on the Tenth Avenue and his little girl with the ball gown Barbie passed me, he was listening carefully to something she was saying. She was talking about a kitten. I guess it was their kitten. The girl's hair was as dark as mine, willowy and long. A fairy tale girl. Her peacoat was red. I wondered if maybe she was Armenian. I had not met any Armenians in America, but before Inga had returned to Moscow, she'd told me there were lots here. Most were descendants of the survivors of the Genocide. There had even been two Armenian churches I had walked right past those first days: Saint Illuminator's on Twenty-seventh Street and the Saint Vartan Cathedral on the Second Avenue. Saint Vartan looked just like the Armenian churches I had seen growing up. It had a round dome, but otherwise it was all vertical lines. It was beautiful. I had stood outside there on the street with Inga and Sonja and Pavel and Crystal, looking up at it. It would have fit in perfectly in Yerevan.

"Want to go in?" Inga had asked Sonja and me, but Pavel said we didn't have time. Besides, I would have been too ashamed. I was who I was. Whores don't belong inside churches like that.

At some point—I don't know when—the Tenth Avenue became the Amsterdam Avenue. And still I kept walking. It had been dark since I left, but the side streets seemed even darker now. I stayed on the avenue. I considered trying to find a subway entrance, but I didn't know where I would go. I wondered what would happen if I just rode the subways all night long.

I would probably fall asleep and be robbed, that's what would happen. Or a police guy or subway driver would figure out who I was.

So I kept walking, sometimes stopping to get juice from a little store or—one time—a slice of pizza. But mostly I just smoked and walked, smoked and walked. I might have walked until I collapsed, but at 103rd Street I saw something: a youth hostel. It was a handsome brick building that looked like it should have been a government office. They had beds for less than fifty dollars a night. I would not have a room of my own, but that almost made me feel safer.

It certainly made me feel less alone.

I decided I would stop there and sleep, at least for the night.

Chapter Twelve

Richard wished he had thought to ask the color of the girl's hair. The dead girl's hair. The one in the morgue. He was driving now to Brooklyn, using his Garmin to guide him to King's County Hospital, heading south on the Major Deegan. He was being led, he saw, to the FDR Drive and then the Brooklyn Bridge, which made him wonder if he should detour into the Heights and insist that his younger brother join him on this cataclysmically awful errand. Make him experience a little more of the lash and woe. Feel a little bit more of the pain. But he wasn't going to do that. His younger brother could drive him crazy—find new ways to infuriate him—but birth order was always going to rule. His younger brother was always going to be that: younger. Which meant there was no reason to subject him to this. Besides, he really didn't want Philip with him if the girl on the slab was Alexandra. He honestly wasn't sure what he would do if it were—but he knew that his brother would find his grief incomprehensible. Philip would have guessed mistakenly that his anguish stemmed from a crush. A lingering infatuation. But the despair wouldn't have been lodged in that section of his soul; it would instead be taking up room in the part of his heart that he reserved for children. For his daughter.

The girl was young and beautiful and did what she did because she hadn't a choice. She deserved so much better than the ontological hole through which she had fallen.

As he drove, he considered praying silently that the corpse would be the chemical blonde, but he feared there was something a little despicable about praying for one of the two girls to be alive at the expense of the other. Also, he didn't really pray. He was a Christmas and Easter Christian only. It seemed disingenuous to start praying now, especially about something like this. But he knew what he wanted; he knew what he hoped. That was, alas, undeniable.

He was grateful for yesterday and tried to focus on that. Never in his life had he been so relieved as when his head had hit the pillow beside Kristin yesterday afternoon during lunch. He had her back. It might take years to fully regain her trust, but no longer did he fear for the future of his marriage. Now if he could make the right choices, do the right things, he might be able to win back his daughter. Melissa, he could tell, was somewhere between embarrassed by him and mad at him. As she should be. There was a bridge he had yet to rebuild, he thought with a pang. But how was he to replace the fallen span? How do you explain what he did, what he had desired, to a nine-year-old girl? To *his* nine-year-old girl? Clearly, it was going to take time to regain her trust, too. But maybe eventually she would figure out how to forgive him—and the simple joy that is normalcy might return.

A yellow cab honked as it passed him on the right, the driver giving him the finger for being distracted and driving too slowly, but when Richard glanced down at the speedometer he saw that he was motoring along at fifty-five. Not awful. Not geriatric. Still, he tried to focus more on the crowded, tortuous highway. But it was difficult. He kept seeing the faces of people he loathed: Spencer. Hugh Kirn. A couple of Russians who called themselves Pavel and Kirill, though none of the detectives he had met believed for one second that those were their real names.

But the person whose face infuriated him the most was Spencer.

And so he made a decision. He was not going to pay the bastard a penny. Paying a bribe only suggested that he had something to hide—and, the fact was, he didn't. He was already a public spectacle. He was going to tell Kristin that there was a video and it might be painful for her to see it—that is, if she chose to watch it. But she already knew the tawdry outlines; the video was mere lineament. He would devote his life to making amends for that one moment, if he had to.

The same went for his daughter. Someday he would tell her about the video, too. He didn't know how, but he would.

And as for those bastards at Franklin McCoy, well, they could go fuck themselves. They were self-righteous and smug, and they were far from the only game in town. They weren't even the only game on Water Street. He knew how good he was at what he did. And if he did leave, he had a feeling that Dina Renzi would make sure that his exit package was substantial.

The traffic slowed, and abruptly he came up behind the cabbie who had given him the finger a few minutes ago. Briefly he considered slamming his car into the back of the bastard's taxi. He knew he wouldn't really do such a thing; his life was enough of a mess as it was. And while he would readily admit that he had issues, road rage wasn't among them. But the idea of rear-ending the cabbie had indeed crossed his mind. How dare that moron give him the finger? How dare he? Was he on his way to the Brooklyn morgue? Nope. Was he on a forced leave of absence from a job he really liked and desperately missed? Nope. Did he have a couch in his living room that looked like a prop from *The Walking Dead*? Nope.

He braked and inched forward along with the rest of the traffic. He turned on the radio, steering clear of News Radio 88 and 1010 Wins. The last thing he wanted was a reminder of what a disaster the rest of the world was. He found a station with sports talk, and tried to lose himself in the debate about how to rebuild the Giants' offensive line. But he failed. Try as he might to think of anything else, his mind would always roam back to the mess he had made of his life and, saddest of all, to the corpse at the hospital where he was headed. And so he finally allowed himself a small prayer. He succumbed. He prayed that the girl with the coal-colored hair was alive.

...

"It was called Mountain Day when I was at Smith," Kristin was explaining to Melissa and Melissa's friend Claudia as the three of them stood with the very last of the commuters on the platform of the Bronxville train station. Kristin was doing something now that she wished she had done four days ago, back on Monday morning: she was taking a personal day. She was taking a personal day with her daughter and one of her daughter's friends. Something about Richard having to drive to Brooklyn to ID a body had pushed her over the edge and given her the idea. She and her daughter simply weren't going to go to school today. That's all there was to it. And they were going to bring Claudia with them when they played hooky. As Kristin had anticipated, Jesse was all in: she didn't mind her daughter joining them for a day off in the slightest.

"One weekday in the autumn, we'd all wake up and hear bells," Kristin went on. "The bells in College Hall and the quadrangle and the chapel would all ring like it was, I don't know, 1918 and the end of a war, and that meant that all classes were canceled. We—the students and faculty—had the day off and we could do whatever we wanted. The college has been doing it for forever. And this, girls, is our own personal Mountain Day."

"Why did they ring bells at the end of a war?" Claudia asked her.

"To let people know it was all over," she answered.

"Why not just tell them on TV?"

"There was no TV in 1918."

"But there were newspapers," Claudia argued. "I think a newspaper would be a better way to tell people a war is over than ringing a bell. I mean, when the students at Smith College heard the bells, did they think it was the end of the war or they just had no school?"

"Claudia, don't take everything literally," Melissa said to her friend, rolling her eyes.

"What does that mean?"

"It means," Melissa began, but then the thought stalled. She didn't know quite what it meant. What she meant. She just knew that Claudia took everything . . . literally. It drove Melissa crazy sometimes. It drove everyone crazy sometimes.

"You're right, Claudia—about the bells and the newspapers," Kristin told her. "People knew the war was over because of the newspapers. And the newspapers had informed them that the bells would ring when there was an armistice. When there was peace. I just meant that we heard a lot of bells on Mountain Day at Smith."

The three of them stared for a long moment in silence at the train tracks. It was chilly this morning, and the temperature wasn't supposed to climb above forty-five degrees that day. When Kristin exhaled, she saw her breath. But it was sunny and the sky was cerulean. Her plan was to take the girls to the Museum of Natural History and then the Museum of Modern Art. She was going to see if her own mother would like to join the three of them for lunch, though she guessed this was a long shot: her mother's social calendar filled up far in advance. Given how much the two girls enjoyed clothes shopping, she assumed they might also wander into some of the stores on Fifth Avenue or Rockefeller Center. They might visit Capezio for new leotards and dance tights.

She wished the girls were still in third grade. A year ago, she could have taken them to the American Girl store, and they would have been in heaven for hours. Now Melissa hardly ever played with her American Girl dolls. Kristin wasn't sure she had picked up any of them since school had started in September. Soon they would be as much a memory as her plush pals from Sesame Street— Zoe and Abby and Elmo—or her Barbies.

She shuddered ever so slightly when her mind roamed to the Barbies, because that meant she saw once more the used condom on her daughter's Tucker Tote. She wondered which of the two prostitutes had been in Melissa's bedroom. Was it the one who later would bring her husband to the guest room? Or was it the one who would steal one of her kitchen knives and—according to the media, not her husband—nearly decapitate a Russian with a sequoia for a neck? (Richard had been more circumspect: he had said only that the girl had stabbed the fellow in the throat.) She had never liked emotional chaos, but she was feeling this morning that her composure—so frail since the bachelor party—was under siege. Hence the need for this Mountain Day. When she thought of the dead body in the morgue, she felt bad that she had any preference at all when she contemplated whether it was the one who had been with Richard or the one who had rained hellfire down on her bodyguard. Her captor. Whatever. But—and she could admit this only to herself—she did have a preference. Of course, she did. The truth was, she did not wish that either girl was dead. Had been murdered. But the inalterable (and unutterable) fact was this: Richard was now on his way to ID one of them, and somewhere deep inside her she hoped that the victim was the girl before whom her husband had stood naked. The girl who had led her husband upstairs, where the two of them . . .

Where the two of them either did nothing or something. Probably she'd never know for sure.

"Train's coming," Claudia was saying. "There's a movie about a lady who throws herself under a train when it's coming."

"It was a book first," Melissa corrected her.

"Doesn't matter. Is that the worst way to kill yourself or what? What a total mess! You're like . . . you're like hamburger meat."

"You should see our couch," said Melissa, and she shook her head.

"Wait, what? Your couch?"

Wait, what. The train began to slow, and Kristin heard those two syllables echoing in her head. Melissa looked up at her, clearly wondering if it was okay to tell her friend about the couch. She shrugged. It was fine. The doors opened, and she herded the children into the car, the last of the commuters—the women as well as the men—making way for her and the two girls. She half listened as Melissa told her friend about the blood on the sofa, and then the blood on the walls and how there was a blank spot where once there had been a famous painting.

"It wasn't that famous," she corrected her daughter.

"No?"

"Nope."

Wait, what? The words continued to reverberate inside her. A Ramones song? No. Something else. Someone else. It didn't matter. This morning it simply felt like the story of her life—at least her recent history.

...

"Yes, that's her," Richard murmured, his voice wan. "She said her name was Sonja." The pathologist was a muscular guy perhaps five or six years his junior, with hipster eyeglasses—thick black frames that made him look like he should be an *Apollo 11* engineer—unruly black hair, and a nose that clearly had been broken at least once. Maybe twice. He had introduced himself as Harry Something. Richard had already lost the fellow's last name, but he thought it might have been Greek. He'd pulled the sheet down only as far as the bottom of the girl's chin.

Beside him was a New York detective, a fellow who reminded Richard a little bit of his father: they had the same dark bags under their eyes and the same ring of short white hair running along the back of their heads from ear to ear. Richard's father had retired a couple of years ago; he guessed this detective would soon. He was wearing a tweed jacket and a white oxford shirt without a necktie. He looked more like an English professor than a cop.

"You're absolutely sure?" the detective asked him.

"I am."

"I mean, given the decomposition—"

"It's her. I'm sure." He was relieved it wasn't Alexandra, and that made him feel both a little guilty and a little unclean. The sensations were related in a way he couldn't quite parse here among the morgue's cold lines and antiseptic counters. Its balneal tiles and polished chrome. Its Proustian-like aroma of biology lab. Harry, the pathologist, had warned him that the odor from the cadaver would dwarf that smell, but still the stench from the body had caught him off guard. He'd nearly gagged. The girl, now a mephitic shell, reeked of decay and dirty water, and he'd taken a step back—away—so the principal smell was the combination of disinfectant and bleach that had greeted him the moment he'd walked in the door. The stench of formaldehyde. But he had recovered. Breathing only through his mouth, he leaned in again. He had, to use an expression his brother sometimes used—and always in the context of endeavors that in point of fact demanded neither heroism nor spine, such as downing a shot of particularly wretched tequila or agreeing to bowl one more game at some trendy bowling alley in the small hours of the morning in Soho—manned up. The corpse had been found in the water beside an old dock in what had once been the Brooklyn Navy Yard. It was bobbing like a buoy against one of the pilings, trying to wend its way to the shore.

"Now that you have her—her body—will you be able to figure out who she really is?" he asked the detective.

"Maybe. But not likely. Not from this," he said, waving his hand over the sheet. "Those guys we busted earlier this week? They're the clues to who she really is. Where she's from. They know where their friends got her."

"So . . . *they* . . . did this to her."

"Yes. *They* did. At least that's what common sense would suggest."

"God. So awful. So sad," Richard found himself murmuring. He looked around the windowless room, at the half-open refrigerated locker from which the body had been removed so he could ID it. In an adjacent room—a room with brilliant white walls, bright surgical lighting, and a sloping autopsy table with drains for the fluids that flowed from the cadavers as their mysteries were plumbed with scissors and bone saws and jugular tubes—he heard a radio. He heard a song. Frank Sinatra singing "My Way." He'd watched his father-in-law dance with Kristin to that song at their wedding. It wasn't Sinatra himself, of course, but the live band had done a beautiful cover. He hoped someday he would dance to that song at Melissa's wedding. He tried to imagine her at twenty-five, but couldn't. He just couldn't.

"So, those guys in jail," he asked the detective, "are they talking?"

The detective shook his head. "A few are already back on the street. And they all have very good lawyers."

"But they will? Eventually?"

"Talk? Hard to say."

"Are they all this violent?"

"Some are. Some are just businessmen. But these dudes—the ones who most likely did this? I would say they're not real big advocates for the sanctity of human life. Why?"

"Just asking."

"Tell me. Go ahead."

"Well, this all began in my house. The people who did this—they know that. They know where I live. And seeing what they did to this girl scares me. It makes me worry about my family. I have a wife. I have a nine-year-old daughter."

The detective seemed to ponder this. Then he raised his brows, and when he did his eyes went a little exophthalmic. "My gut tells me they don't have a whole lot of interest in you or your family. I mean, they might. As you said, some of them have anger management issues. And maybe if they thought you were protecting one of their girls they'd come for you. Maybe if they thought you were a witness to something. But it's not like you're hiding one of their girls in your guest room. It's not like one's hanging around your sunroom."

"No. I don't even have a sunroom."

"There you go."

Harry started to pull the sheet back over the corpse, but Richard stopped him. "Everything okay?" the pathologist asked.

"Yeah. It is. I just thought I should see her face a few seconds more. Pay my respects, I guess." He tried to craft a similar face in his head for her father. Someone who would have wanted to walk her down an aisle and dance with her at her wedding.

"Okay."

Her eyes were open, more blue than he had remembered. Cornflower blue. Her hair was the same almost alabaster blond. The skin, from so much time in the water, was inhumanly white and looked almost gelatinous. Blubbery, he thought. Blubbery.

"Would you pull the sheet down?" he asked.

"Really?" The pathologist sounded dubious.

"Just to her collarbone. I want . . . I want to see."

"No, you don't." This was the detective. Richard looked up at him. He was shaking his head ever so slightly.

"I feel an obligation."

"An obligation?"

"Yeah. I know. It's crazy. But somewhere she has family. Or, I guess, had family."

The pathologist glanced at the detective, and the detective shrugged. So Harry pulled the sheet down almost to the woman's breasts, and Richard's first thought—perhaps because they had told him how she'd been killed, perhaps because he knew, more or less, what was coming—was wonder that the head had remained attached to the body. He saw only the spinal cord and a single rope of muscle between her collarbone and her jaw. It was like a Halloween skeleton.

"Those are posterior neck muscles," the pathologist was saying, pointing with two fingers. "They severed the carotid artery and the jugular vein, which is all it would have taken to kill her. But then they cut all the way through the larynx. And then some. There would have been more tissue left, but it washed away."

"So they killed her the way she killed one of them?"

"Apparently," the detective said. "But later this morning we'll do an autopsy and confirm that's the cause of death. It probably was. No evidence of bullet wounds. But these guys will check. Do a toxicology report. The usual."

Harry pulled the sheet back over the girl and leaned against a Formica counter.

"What happens to her body after that?" Richard asked.

This time it was the detective who looked at Harry. The pathologist arched his eyebrows and coughed once into his elbow. "Autumn allergies," he said, apologizing. "No idea why they get to me even in here." Then: "We'll keep her on ice for a bit. Just in case."

"In case you actually find a family member?"

"That's right."

"But we won't," the detective added. "Hart Island. That's where we bury the anonymous. It's in the Bronx. A couple of inmates from Rikers will handle it."

"Any news on the other girl?" Richard asked.

"The other girl from your party?"

"Wasn't my party," he said, correcting the detective. He hoped he hadn't sounded as defensive in reality as he had in his head.

"Sorry. The party at your house," the detective agreed. "We haven't found her yet. With any luck, her body will wash up, too."

From the moment Richard had confirmed that the girl on the slab was Sonja, he had failed to consider that Alexandra might be dead, too. In his relief, the notion had been vanquished from his mind. When he had asked about Alexandra just now, he had meant, *Any news on her whereabouts? Any leads where she might be hiding?* And so the possibility—so likely in the detective's opinion—that her body was decomposing in the East River hit Richard like a slap. Of course. Of course, it was in the East River. They'd most certainly killed her, too. For the second time since he had walked into the morgue, he thought he might be sick. The world went fuzzy. He gulped a little burbling acid back down his throat.

"You need some water?"

It was Harry. Richard blinked and breathed. He saw the pathologist's hand on his arm, but he had to look there to feel it.

He focused on the room and tried to gather himself. He was clammy now and he felt like shit. But at least he wasn't going to vomit. "Sure," he said. "I'll have a glass. Thank you."

"You got pretty pale there," said the detective. "You okay?"

The record shows—

"Yeah. I'm . . . I'm fine," he said. From somewhere far away the radio had returned.

I took the blows—

Harry handed him a paper cup, and he took a small sip.

And did it my way.

His eyes lingered on the pathologist's elbow, where the fellow had covered his cough, and he thought once more of that moment on the stairs in his home when Alexandra had held on to his elbow. He saw there her demure and lovely fingers. He saw her eyes. He saw her dancing in a wedding dress, but with whom he couldn't say. How—and why—she had morphed from inamorata to daughter, he couldn't say. But he was relieved. Maybe it made him less . . . hateful. He heard horns. A violin.

But with the revelation came a disturbing feeling that he wasn't, in the end, ever going to dance at his own daughter's wedding. It wasn't as visually concrete as a premonition (which he didn't believe in, in any case), and he tried to take comfort in that. He reminded himself that there were no clichés about men's intuition. But it wouldn't go away, even when he tried to drown it in his relief that he had regained his wife, and that Alexandra—living or dead—would live on in his memory as a child and not a whore.

Yes, it was my way.

Alexandra

I stayed in the youth hostel two nights.

I stayed in the waiting area of an emergency room at a big hospital on the third.

And, then, on Friday morning, I took the train back to Bronxville.

...

I went to the hospital emergency room on Thursday to hide. That's all. No one had hurt me. I hadn't had some terrible accident. Once a cabdriver almost ran over me, but that was my fault because I was walking across a street in sleepwalker daze. He didn't end up hitting me, and so I didn't die like my grandmother. He swore at me to pay attention.

And so I did. I paid lots more attention. And when I did, it felt like they were getting close. They: the police guys. Yulian's dudes. His cue-ball-head babies who actually were killers. Even in the hostel it felt like the walls were closing in on me. I had stayed two nights in this lower bunk, curled up in little ball beneath a sheet that smelled of soap, dozing, but with one eye open when I was awake. I slept with my knit football team cap on. I slept with the Makarov beside me.

And finally, it seemed to me, I needed to move on.

Some girls at the hostel had wanted to be my friends. Girls from the Netherlands and England and Texas. They were young and pretty, some of them, and would have made good prostitutes. But they were there to see the city and America as tourists. They wanted to see the museums and then dance. They wanted to see the Times Square and then dance. If they pleasured men—and I do not know if they did—it was because they were also getting pleasure themselves.

Two of the girls worried about me because I was dozing with that cap on. I had told them I was cold and maybe I was getting a cold. They wanted to share with me their NyQuil. To make them happy and so they would leave me alone, I drank some. I think that is when I slept the deepest—and that scared me. But I know I was in deep sleep because I had such dreams. I dreamed of my grandmother, maybe because I had almost died like her. I dreamed of a man who I thought was my father, who was telling me stories of a town called Chunkush, where so many of my ancestors had been slaughtered in 1915, and of a crevasse in the ground that seemed to fall to the center of the earth. But still the Turks and the Kurds had filled it with bodies. That's how many Armenians they killed there. Ten thousand, at least. And I dreamed of a house in Bronxville and a man named Richard. The two of us were sitting on the edge of a bed, and he was feeding me a Middle Eastern sugar cookie called a *maamoul*.

...

What I figured out about hospital was this. It was super easy to hide there in the emergency room. At least it might be for a day or two. How I found out was total accident.

I left the hostel on Thursday morning with my knapsack and my money and my cigarettes. It was so early the sun was rising, and it was yellowish-red like welding.

I hid my pistol again underneath my jacket and I walked east across the Central Park. I wasn't sure where I was going. But I needed to go somewhere. Do something. Keep moving. I did not know what my destination would be. I did not know anything except I should not risk staying at the hostel any longer. People asked too many questions. Eventually someone would figure out who I was. Eventually the wrong kind of person would find me—and kill me.

As I was leaving the park on the Fifth Avenue, I felt funny. I felt the hairs on the back of my neck standing at attention. I felt like I was being followed. I opened my bag and took out my compact like I was a girl in one of the movies we used to watch in our hotel room in Moscow, and used the mirror in the lid to look behind me. I saw a police guy by trees on the sidewalk on one side of the street, and I saw a black Escalade outside apartment building on the other. The Escalade had its engine running. Both could be nothing. Coincidence. But either could be something. When I walked down Ninety-sixth Street, the police guy stayed where he was, but the Escalade pulled out and turned left. Maybe he was following me. Maybe not. I walked to the end of the long block and turned left onto the Madison Avenue and started walking north, which actually was crazy dumb. I should have turned right, so the one-way street would work in my favor. The car couldn't have followed me.

But it didn't matter, because the light was red, and so the driver had to stop and wait. I walked a little faster. I was almost, but not really, running. And when I crossed Ninety-eighth Street and the traffic was again moving north, I saw hospital. It was called Mount Sinai. And in I went. I walked fast like I had a place to go. I knew how to walk around hospital from all those weeks years ago when my mother was dying in one, and from all the times when I visited my grandmother there.

But this hospital was not just bigger than the one in Yerevan. It was total madhouse—and, for me that day, this was a good thing. A very good thing. The emergency room was like a maze.

There were rows of little cubicles with curtains, long corridors with too little light, and nooks with chairs where people—some sick, some families—could wait. There were always workers pushing machines with cuffs and wires and screens. There were always doctors and nurses looking at clipboards and tablets.

Sure, there were plenty of police guys in the crowds. But they weren't interested in me. No one was interested in me. I took a chair in a dark corner—it was all dark corners—and spent hours watching the drunks and the old people and even some guy who had been stabbed in the arm. I watched all these beautiful and handsome young nurses and doctors in their scrubs walking from the counters to the cubicles. I watched the families come and go. An old man died in one of those cubicles. Sometimes the patients would be treated and go home, and sometimes they would be wheeled on gurneys to hospital rooms upstairs.

I don't think I ever fell asleep because the chairs were not that comfortable. But I closed my eyes. I got potato chips and sodas from the vending machines.

Sometimes I would go back outside, make sure there was no Escalade, and smoke.

Sometimes I wished I still had my phone. What if I had made a mistake throwing it away? What if Sonja had been trying to find me? But I knew in my heart I had done the right thing—the safe thing. She was gone.

And so I was lonely.

I was so lonely, I considered finding a man. I wouldn't be courtesan. I would just be friendly. But obviously that would be insane. I needed to stay hidden until I could get help.

By Friday morning, I probably looked like shit. It had been almost twenty-four hours since I had left the hostel, and I hadn't showered or slept. My leather jacket probably looked okay, but my skirt must have looked dirty. I was standing on the corner smoking a cigarette, and a police guy came up to me. He was young, maybe twenty-five or twenty-six, and he was a little heavy. He had boyish eyes.

"Young lady, you okay?" he asked me.

I held my cigarette down by my waist so he wouldn't have to breathe the smoke. My heart was beating like crazy because I was afraid he might know who I was. I considered dropping the cigarette and squashing it with the toe of my boot, and reaching into my jacket for the pistol. But I wasn't going to shoot this dude. That gun was only for Yulian or the cue-ball-head babies.

"Yes," I lied. "I'm okay." I motioned back toward hospital. "My mom is in there. She has lung cancer. It was a long night."

"Jeez, I'm sorry," he said.

"Thank you."

"Okay. You just looked . . ."

I smiled—my best polite girl smile. "I know. I think I'm going to check in on her one more time. Then I go home and shower."

He smiled back at me and then walked on.

I couldn't hide forever. I had known this for three days. But talking even for thirty seconds with the police guy made this clear. I needed help. I needed to do something. I needed to do something now.

That's when it hit me. What I really needed was a miracle, and maybe the miracle was still behind or beside or in little girl's bed in Bronxville—Sonja's condom wrapper with a tiny piece of paper with a phone number on it. It might be my best chance. Yes, it was possible it was the Georgian who had turned Sonja over to Yulian. I am not big dope, I thought to that. But why would he? He didn't work for Yulian. And she had business deal for him. So, maybe she never even got to the Georgian. Maybe Yulian got to my Sonja first. And maybe Richard, the only john ever who didn't fuck me or use me or hit me or want something from me that he just couldn't have, would help me find that tiny piece of paper. Who knows? Maybe he would even help me find the Georgian.

It was a risk, but I had to do something, yes?

And so I decided I would go back to Bronxville. To the house where it all began.

Chapter Thirteen

Before leaving the hospital in Brooklyn, Richard had sent Spencer a text. He wrote that he had something for him and to meet him at Rapier, a restaurant a few blocks west of the Cravat. He suggested eleven-thirty. Spencer had texted back a smiley face. Richard assumed that meant he would be there.

And now it was eleven-forty-five, and there was no sign of the guy. Richard had taken a seat at the end of the bar—a redoubtable slab of burnished mahogany—that gave him a view of the entrance. He had ordered a beer, largely because of where he had just been and not because of what he was about to do. He couldn't recall the last time he had started drinking before noon. Just when he was about to text the fool once again, he saw him outside on the sidewalk, taking a last drag on his cigarette and then flicking the still-smoking butt to the ground. Then he was pushing his way through the glass doors and eyeing the tables. It took him a full ten seconds before he spotted Richard at the bar and smiled his way past the hostess.

"The bar, eh," he said, taking the stool beside Richard. "Sometimes I like to eat at the bar, too. Feels kind of manly."

"We're not eating," Richard said simply, hoping to take Spencer's unendurable self-satisfaction down a peg.

"A liquid lunch? That's fortifying, too." He got the bartender's attention with the singular ease of a drunk and ordered a vodka tonic. "Good to see you, Richard. Though you're looking pretty informal for an M and A stud. Black hoodie and jeans? This is . . . what? Your *Breaking Bad* chic? Or is this your hausfrau costume while you wait for Franklin McCoy to take you back?"

"Casual Friday."

"I approve. And, I must say, I'm very glad you're going to be a friend and have my back on this one. Just when things seemed to be getting worse, it seems you've come to your senses and are going to make everything at least a wee bit better."

"Oh, I think we both hit rock bottom this week. I don't think things could possibly get any worse for either of us."

He rolled his eyes. "Oh, they could. They really could. Just wait till you see me testifying someday. But it beats jail. And, thanks to you, I will have paid my legal bills—at least some portion of them."

"They're that bad?"

"So bad. And I am expecting it will take beaucoup bucks to dial down Chuck 'Shithead' Alcott and ensure that the frail Mrs. Fisher makes a full recovery."

"Nuisance suits."

The bartender brought Spencer his drink, and Spencer tapped it against Richard's bottle before taking a generous swallow. "I know."

"But," Richard added, "that party really might have ruined the Fishers' marriage. Or scarred Chuck Alcott in some way. That's one more thing we have to live with."

"Well, I didn't put a gun to Brandon's head and say go fuck the talent or else. And Chuck could have left whenever he wanted."

"Maybe he didn't want to be a killjoy. Maybe he didn't want to pass judgment on Philip at his bachelor party."

"That's why you took one of the girls upstairs and fucked her in the guest room?"

"I didn't fuck her, Spencer," he said, lowering his voice and hoping that Spencer would follow his lead.

"Your loss, in that case."

"I was drunk."

"We all were."

Richard considered adding that he only viewed being drunk as an explanation—not a defense. But there wasn't any point. So instead he let the thread go and said, "Anyway, given all the money pressures you're feeling—"

"I wish that was it. I am constantly looking over my shoulder and expecting to see some skinhead bruiser amped up on steroids. I look on the street and see black SUVs everywhere."

"Can't help you there."

"My lawyer says I am worried for naught."

"There you go."

"But still . . ."

"But still. So, it seems to me, my thirty thousand dollars will barely make a dent into what you may need."

"Happy to make it thirty-five."

"How do I know you won't?"

He smiled cryptically and took another sip of his drink. "You don't."

"In the old days, I would pay you—you know, get down in the muck with you, really sink to your level of leech and—"

"Flattery will get you everywhere. If you want, I can simply send you my legal bills and whatever part of Mrs. Fisher's 'treatment' I'm saddled with. Let you handle it."

"I would sink to your level and hand you a check for thirty thousand dollars," he went on. "And you, in turn, would hand me the negatives and the prints. But now? I have no guarantees. You could be storing the digital files anywhere. For all I know, they're already in the cloud with all your other filth."

"Okay, you brought me a check today for thirty. I will, of course, take that off your hands. And someday soon, I may ask you for more. But if that day comes, I will give you my assurance that

I have deleted the files everywhere and you have nothing at all to worry about. You will have my word as a scholar—and, I guess, a bit of a rake."

Richard swallowed the last of his beer. "No, you're not a rake."

"Well, I can try. Gives me something to aspire to."

"You're just a grotesque little parasite. And kind of a loser," he told him, standing. "And I've decided, Spencer, I'm not paying you a penny. Send the pictures to my wife. Share the video with my office. Do it right this second, for all I care."

Spencer turned to face him, and for the first time Richard felt he had the creep's full attention. "You will regret that," he said slowly.

"Nope. I won't."

"Sleep on it. I can wait until tomorrow."

"Oh, I feel okay about this decision. As a matter of fact, I feel pretty damn good about it. One more thing."

Spencer glared at him, a slow seethe starting to fester. He waited.

"The tab? It's yours." Then he turned away and left the restaurant, grinding the remnants of Spencer's cigarette into the sidewalk as he exited Rapier's glass door.

...

As Richard was heading north on the FDR Drive, his cell phone rang, and he saw on the dashboard screen that it was Dina Renzi. He was still agitated (though, yes, also rather pleased with himself) after standing up to Spencer Doherty. In addition, he knew, he was still rattled from the morgue. Now that he could only wait to see if or when Spencer dropped the hammer, his head was awash with the vaporous images of the dead. There was one bleeding out on his living room couch. Another in his front hallway. There was one who had been pretty nearly decapitated. And so he waited for the phone to stop ringing, and soon enough he heard the ping that told him he had a message in his voice mail. Only then did he press "listen" and wait for Dina's voice to fill his car speakers. He didn't believe there had been enough time for Spencer to send a video or photos to Franklin McCoy and for someone to watch it, digest it, and fashion a diatribe to launch upon his lawyer. But you never know. Maybe it was possible.

Nevertheless, he was pleasantly surprised when he heard Dina's voice sounding uncharacteristically chipper.

"Hi, Richard. I hope you're out and about and doing something fun. Call me back. I might have good news. I don't want to get your hopes up and over the moon, but it sounds like your friends at Franklin McCoy—and I am using *friends* with at least a small scoop of irony—want to meet next week. Hugh and I have gone back and forth since our meeting the other day. And the vibe I'm getting now is that they want to figure out a way to save face and maybe green-light your return to work. It's not a done deal, but I think we are, as we like to say, moving in a good direction. You may be back helping big sharks eat little sharks—That is what you do, right?—before you know it. So, call me back. Bye."

He thought how he might be back in his office in a week or two, and how much he craved that. He considered briefly whether he had made a mistake ignoring his lawyer's advice and telling Spencer to go fuck himself, but he reminded himself that this decision was about trying to do the right thing. He would not allow himself to regret standing up to the cloacal ooze that purported to be his idiot younger brother's best friend.

He breathed in deeply through his mouth and tried to keep his attention squarely on the bumper and taillights of the shoddy-looking locksmith van directly ahead of him. He tried to be happy. But it was difficult when he surveyed his world this afternoon. He kept recalling the dead girl in the morgue, which made him think of Alexandra, who most likely was dead now, too.

No, happiness wasn't possible. He should lower that bar. Accept something less. And again the word *normalcy* came to him, as it had on this very road earlier in the day. He yearned for it. But he couldn't imagine what it would take for his life to return to . . . normal.

...

You won't always think rubber when you think Barbie.

It was something her older brother had said to Kristin earlier this week, the Tuesday evening when she and Melissa had finally returned home to Bronxville and they'd found the used condom atop the box of Barbies. She'd phoned her brother because she wasn't yet prepared to share this latest, lurid indignity with any of her female friends, but she had to tell someone. And her brother had listened, walked her in off the ledge, and told her before they hung up for the night that associations changed over time. Invariably they were diluted by experience. Someday, and it might take a year and it might take a decade, when she thought of her daughter's Barbies, she would think once more of the hours she had spent sharing the dolls with Melissa on the living room floor and making up stories. She would think tenderly of the games they would play. The worlds they'd create. She'd think of the clothes and the cars and the furniture. She'd think of the shoes.

Now, as she stood with Melissa and Claudia before a long, wide wall of the dolls in the FAO Schwarz on Fifth, she decided her brother was wrong. At least he might be wrong. Who could say what she would think about as she neared fifty? When she was a grandmother at, perhaps, sixty?

She and the girls had wandered here not because they had any interest these days in Barbies, but simply because they were exploring the entire store. They'd strolled here after the second museum. Something frivolous after all that self-improvement. They'd gone first to the Apple Store next door, descending beneath the colossal glass cube, but the world below was like a subway car at rush hour. No technological marvel was worth the effort it would take to press through the human crush. And while the toy store was less crowded, Kristin guessed that the fourth graders beside her had already outgrown 90 percent of the inventory.

She sighed, half listening as the girls made fun of some of the Collectible Barbies. At the moment, it was the *Twilight* Barbies that were giving them the giggles. The *Divergent* Barbies. Carlisle. Edward. Tris.

Whatever happened to naming all the men Ken? Whatever happened to Skipper?

Near the Barbies was a wall of Monster High dolls, a group even more anorexic than the Barbies. The Monster High kids had emaciated stick-figure bodies and balloon-like, goth white heads that were dramatically out of proportion with their arms and legs. They had fashion model eyelashes and pouty red lips, miniskirts and high heels. Names at once ghoulish and suggestive. Honey Swamp. Draculaura. Catty Noir.

Beside them was a line called Fairy Tale High. The classics get slutty. The Little Mermaid in fishnets. Cinderella in leggings and a croptop. Alice in Wonderland in a blue-and-white-striped micro-dress that barely covered her ass.

"Emiko has those leggings," her daughter was saying, as she pointed at Cinderella.

"I love them," said Claudia. "I want a pair. They're so hot."

An expression came to her: *You're a doll.* Translation? You've done me a solid. Thank you.

She's a doll. Translation? She's pretty. She's compliant.

A doll. Synonyms? A babe. A chick. A sweetie.

Hours ago—museums ago—Richard had texted her that it was the girl he thought was named Sonja who he'd identified on the mortuary slab. The chemical blonde. She had not asked what next. What now. She had not asked whether this meant that the girl who had led him upstairs was still alive, or whether she was dead, too, and her body had simply not yet turned up. But it would. She had simply asked if he was okay. He'd texted he was.

Okay. She had no idea what that word meant in the context of a morgue.

"I like her dress," Melissa was saying. She was pointing at Alice in Wonderland. Slut Alice in Wonderland.

"I like that outfit," said Claudia, motioning at the vest that barely hid Belle's breasts. Slut Belle's breasts.

In all fairness, Kristin knew that once upon a time her Barbies had been pretty slutty. She had often undressed her Barbies and Kens, and allowed the dolls to go to town on each other. Spreading the girls' legs as wide as she could. She'd been doing this while playing in the semidarkness underneath a robin's-egg-blue blanket that she had draped across her parents' dining room table.

Good Lord, it had only been two or three years ago that she and Richard had been laughing as the two of them polished off a bottle of wine at all the ways they had encouraged their daughter's Barbies to perform unspeakable acts, while Melissa's head was turned or she was searching for a particular Barbie gown in that Tucker Tote. It was how they kept their sanity, they had confessed to each other—yes, they both did it—as they sat on the floor with their girl and played with her dolls for hours.

All that had been changed by the condom. All that had been subsumed by the condom.

Here was the inescapable reality: ten years from now if she did not instantly make the synaptic leap to *rubber* when she thought Barbie, it would only be due to Alzheimer's. Early-onset Alzheimer's. Or, maybe, a traumatic brain injury. She looked around at the walls of the toy store, which were pink. She noted that the paisley swirls on the floor were pink. The lighting was a little pink. Sure, it was possible that a decade from now she might also think *pink* when she thought Barbie. She very likely might think *plastic*.

But first and forever? She was always going to think *rubber*.

She looked at her watch. They should probably continue on their way to Grand Central. They had to catch a train home.

...

Richard knew this was neither a vision nor a dream, and his first reaction was flight. He should continue right past his driveway. Instead of braking, he should hit the gas pedal and drive up the thin street off Pondfield Road. Drive around the block. Just take a moment and try and figure out what the hell the girl was thinking.

But he didn't. His brother might do that, but he wouldn't. Instead he glided up his gently sloping driveway and came to a stop just before the garage doors.

The girl was sitting on the front stoop of his house, her chin resting on the knuckles of one hand, a cigarette dangling from the other. She was wearing a knit cap with the Giants' logo—his team, a sign or a coincidence he couldn't have said—and sunglasses, but he knew instantly it was her. He could see enough of her face. Her lips. Her posture. He recognized the leather jacket.

But he would have known it was her regardless of what she was wearing. It wouldn't have taken a sixth sense. It took only a glimpse.

She didn't move when he shut off the car engine and pulled the key from the ignition, but he could tell that she was watching him. He was watching her. She was wearing a miniskirt and boots, and he had one of those thoughts that was comically inappropriate in his mind, and caused his lips to quiver upward ever so slightly: *What would the neighbors think? Hot girl in a miniskirt and boots, smoking a cigarette on my steps?*

Well, never mind what they thought. They couldn't possibly think less of him. He couldn't possibly think less of himself.

Mostly, he realized, he was smiling because Alexandra was alive. That detective was wrong, all wrong. Thank God. (Had he murmured those two splendid words aloud in his seat? He thought he had.) Her decomposing body wasn't about to wash ashore somewhere in Brooklyn or on Staten Island, or bump for hours against the stanchion of a Navy Yard dock before someone called 911 or fished it from the water. Nope. She had wound up . . . here. In Westchester. And she was, quite clearly, breathing. Not decapitated. Not drowned. He was so relieved that he was shivering ever so slightly when he climbed from the car. She didn't stand until he had crossed the driveway and marched all the way up the slate walkway and front steps. When she finally did rise, she held her cigarette away from the two of them and bowed her head against his chest. He felt the wool cap against his neck and the earpiece to her sunglasses against his collarbone. He felt her whole body lean into him.

"I bet you did not expect to find courtesan back here," she murmured.

Awkwardly he rubbed her shoulder blades. He felt simultaneously that it was morally wrong to touch her, and morally imperative that he did.

"No," he agreed, "I didn't. I . . ."

She waited.

"I was afraid something had happened to you."

"You thought I might be dead."

"As a matter of fact, yes."

He felt the rise and fall of her chest as she breathed. "Nope. Still here."

"I'm very glad. I was afraid for you." He wondered if she knew her partner was dead. Sonja. He considered telling her where he had been earlier that day, but then thought better of that idea. In time. Maybe.

"I couldn't think of anyplace else to go," she murmured.

"Well, I might have started with the police," he said, a suggestion born more of paternalism, he hoped, than self-preservation.

Abruptly she pushed him away with her free hand and took a step back. "No. I am not going to jail."

He wished he could see her eyes behind the sunglasses. Was this an admission that she had shot the Russian in the front hallway?

"They showed me the Rikers Island. They told me about prisons in America," she went on, her voice a little louder now, a little more frantic. "I know what goes on there. I know what really goes on there."

"Whoa," he told her, putting his hands up, palms open. He wasn't sure who *they* were, but presumed it was whoever had brought her to America and then, most likely, butchered her friend. "Let's go inside. Let's talk, okay? I want to know who you are. Who you really are. I want to know what you need—what I can do."

"You won't call police guys?"

He shook his head. "I can't promise that I never will. But I won't right this minute."

"Look . . ."

"Go on."

"I've come because Sonja might have left something here by accident. Something important. I need it."

"I'm sure it's long gone. The police were here for a couple of days. Anything Sonja left is in a police evidence locker somewhere. I mean it. They scoured the downstairs."

"It was upstairs."

He thought about this. He recalled what his wife had found in their daughter's bedroom. "They were less thorough there," he admitted. "What is it?"

"A phone number. It was hidden in"—and she seemed to grow almost shy when she continued—"a condom wrapper. Sonja went upstairs with a man."

"I know." He gazed for a long moment at the street and the houses around them "Okay, let's go inside. We'll look. We'll talk there."

"You worry about people next door?" she asked.

"Alexandra—and it is, Alexandra, right?"

She gave him a strange half nod that he couldn't quite decipher.

"Well, Alexandra, the people next door are the least of my problems—and, I would wager, the least of yours."

. . .

But the condom wrapper and the slip of paper weren't there. They weren't anywhere in the bedding, and they weren't behind the mattress. Together Richard and Alexandra actually moved the bed, and they searched amid the clothing and books and video game discs that had wound up over time beneath the box spring. And Richard was relieved. He knew if he found the number he was going to give it to the police; he certainly wasn't going to allow this girl to try and make a run for it with an illegal passport and fake credit cards.

It was only when he was making the bed once more, pressing the sheets under the mattress, that he understood what had happened: Kristin had thrown the bedding away Tuesday night. She hadn't wanted to wash the sheets or the pillowcase; in her opinion, there was no water in the world hot enough to cleanse them for their little girl after a strange man and an escort had had sex in that bed. And the garbage had been picked up yesterday morning. If the number had ever been in this bedroom, it was long gone.

"I'm sorry," he said, a white lie that he hoped would help console her.

She was leaning against Melissa's bookcase. "It was my only hope," she said, her voice flat. "That was it."

"No, you'll be okay," he said. "You will." He suggested they go downstairs and have a cup of coffee while he figured out what to do next.

...

They sat at the kitchen table and drank coffee. It was barely two-thirty in the afternoon; he doubted that Kristin and Melissa would be back for at least another couple of hours, which diminished any sense of urgency he might otherwise have been feeling. He could text Kristin to see what they were up to—make sure they were still somewhere in midtown Manhattan—but somehow that felt incriminating. Later, he thought to himself, a text like that could only come back to haunt him. He assumed by the time Kristin returned that either he would have brought the girl to the police station or the two of them would be sitting right here. He certainly wasn't going to hide the fact that Alexandra had shown up at their house. He wouldn't; he couldn't. Still, that conversation was not going to be pretty.

She had taken off her sunglasses and knit cap, and brushed her hair with a white plastic brush she had pulled from her backpack.

Now she looked more like the girl who had sat naked upon one of the beds upstairs, and less like the runaway waif who had been waiting for him outside on the stoop.

"What if my wife had come home first? What if my wife had been here when you knocked on the door?" he asked, hoping he hadn't sounded judgmental or angry. He was honestly curious as to what she was thinking.

"I would have said hi. I would have asked to look upstairs in bedroom for piece of paper."

"I'm serious."

"Me, too. I would have said hi. I would have asked her for help—just like I asked you."

"But why in the world would you think she might help you?"

"Did you tell her we had sex?"

"No—because we didn't. But I told her I went upstairs with you and we almost did."

"Wow. Did not see you doing that."

"We're married."

"Look, I am in very big trouble and you are very nice man. It seemed to me that you must have very nice wife."

"I do have a very nice wife. But she's human. She's not a saint. Hell, maybe she is a saint; she isn't divorcing me. But she was really mad at me. I'm not an adulterer. I don't have affairs. And yet, you are . . . well, Alexandra, you're beautiful. You're beautiful," he repeated. "And you were there on that bed and, that moment, mine. I mean . . . tell me something."

"Okay."

"How old are you?"

"Nineteen."

"You swear that's the truth?"

"Yes."

"God. That is still so ridiculously young."

"There are girls like me who are younger."

"That only makes this all the sadder. And at nineteen? You're not that other woman. I mean, my wife would never view you as a romantic rival. But I was upstairs with you. I was undressed. We were undressed. That should never, ever have happened. And so my wife is—was—justifiably pissed off at me. To be honest with you, Alexandra, I'm not sure she would have helped you."

"I know that expression, 'other woman.' I am mere courtesan. Plaything."

He sighed. *Courtesan* and *plaything* were both euphemisms, though each word conjured for him a very different image. The first summoned Versailles. The second? A motorized toy car for a child. But he knew what she meant. He knew exactly what she meant.

"Where is she now?" asked Alexandra.

"She's in the city with my daughter."

Abruptly Cassandra appeared out of nowhere and leapt onto the kitchen table, nearing sliding into Alexandra's cup and saucer. The cat looked at the girl and then at him. He lifted her into his lap, but she was more interested in sniffing the girl's backpack and boots and jumped back onto the kitchen floor.

"So, if your wife comes home and finds me here?" she asked.

"I would wager, at least at first, that she would be a tad angry."

"Then I should leave." It was a statement, not a question.

"No. You can't leave. Not after what I just saw. Where I just was."

"You were at work? You get to dress like boys' soccer coach at work?" She was smiling ever so slightly.

"No. I wasn't at work. I wish I had been at work, but no such luck," he said. He sipped his coffee and gathered himself. He had to tell her about her friend. She had to know. "I was just in Brooklyn," he continued. "I was at King's County Hospital. I was at the morgue. I was asked to identify a dead body."

"Sonja," she said, that smile instantly evaporating and her voice growing wistful and sad. She reached into her jacket pocket for a cigarette. He considered stopping her, but then didn't. Let her smoke. If a cigarette was going to help her hear this, fine. He had no plan, he realized, no plan at all. He was fumbling in the dark, trying on the fly to figure out what the hell was the right thing to do.

"Yes. Sonja. I'm sorry. I'm very, very sorry. I guess you two were friends." He watched her light the cigarette with a cheap Bic lighter, and he found himself focused on her fingers and the polish on her thumb. He stood up and found her an ashtray in a cabinet filled with place settings and serving dishes they never used.

"We were friends," she said. "But I knew it. I knew she was killed."

"How?"

The tip of her cigarette glowed like a planetarium constellation when she inhaled. "She didn't call me when she was supposed to. Our signal."

"Do you know who killed her?"

"I do. Guys who worked for dude named Yulian. Bunch of cue-ball-head babies."

"How did they not kill you?"

"I wasn't with her." She took another long drag on the cigarette. "Maybe it's good thing we didn't find that number. I would have used it—gone to the Georgian—and maybe gotten myself killed like Sonja."

A thought came to him and he sat up a little straighter. How in the name of God had he not realized this the moment he saw her on his front stoop? He recalled what the cop had said to him that morning in the morgue: *Maybe if they thought you were a witness to something. But it's not like you're hiding one of their girls in your guest room. It's not like one's hanging around your sunroom.*

"Yes. Obviously they're after you now," he said.

"Obviously."

"Could they be on their way here? To my house?"

"I don't think I was followed. Maybe they were following me in New York City. But I was at your front door a long time and no one killed me."

"But they might look for you here."

She shrugged. "I had to go somewhere." Then she rose to her feet, saying, "I'll go. I'm sorry."

Quickly he put his hand on her shoulder and stopped her. "No, don't. Please . . . don't. You came here for help. I'll help you." Nevertheless, he knew that no good could come from her being here. A collage of faces flickered behind his eyes: There was his wife and there was his daughter. There were the girl's bodyguards, now dead, but there were plenty more just like them. And there were the detectives he had met in the past week, the women and men who had explained to him that his house was a crime scene or showed him the secrets that only a morgue could share. But Alexandra was far more child than whore. She was nineteen. He couldn't possibly send her outside into the chill October air, where all that awaited her were men like Spencer Doherty and, eventually, death. He thought of the hunting rifle he'd chosen not to buy. The bullets he'd seen in the box. But then he recalled Sonja's corpse and realized that he could have purchased an assault rifle—he could have bought a bazooka—and he still wouldn't have had a chance against the kind of men who brought Alexandra to America.

"You won't call police guys?" she asked.

"I haven't yet," he said, and she sat back down. And so he did, too. "But if I'm going to help you, I need to know a couple of things."

"Like what?"

"Like your real name. I'm going to go way out on a limb and guess that it's not Alexandra. Outside just now, you said . . ."

"No, it's not Alexandra."

"Okay, then. What is it?"

"Anahit."

He repeated it. "That's pretty."

"Armenian. Means goddess."

"Were you both—you and Sonja—Armenian?"

"Yes. But Sonja grew up in Volgograd. I grew up in Yerevan.

She had blue eyes, remember? Very rare for Armenian girl. It's because her grandmother was part Russian."

"How long have you been here? In America?"

"A month."

"So you'd only been in the United States three weeks when you were brought to my brother's party."

She nodded, and for a moment they both were silent as they recalled how it was exactly a week ago that their worlds had collided—and exploded.

"Why did Sonja kill your bodyguards? Why last Friday night?"

She raised a single eyebrow. "Just guards. Not bodyguards."

"I'm sorry. Is that why she killed them? Because they were your . . . your captors?"

"She was afraid they were going to kill us on way back into New York City. There was a third girl you never met. Crystal. They had already killed her because she was talking to police guy." She put her cigarette down in the ashtray, and he stared at the circular smudge of her lipstick on the filter.

"A detective," he repeated, trying to focus. "She was talking to a detective? Who was he working for? A Manhattan D.A.? Or the U.S. Attorney's Office?"

She looked at him, confused, and replied, "For police guys. He was working for police guys."

"Got it," he said. There was no point now in explaining the fine points and particulars of a criminal investigation in America. "So, the police know about you?"

"I don't know what they know. I just know they arrested some dudes this week and then let most of them back out. A girl like me has no power. I can't trust them."

He shook his head. He would correct her. He would tell her that she needn't fear the police, she needn't worry about going to jail. She was going to be fine. Perhaps he would introduce her to Dina Renzi. The firm would surely pro bono their services on her behalf. Besides, she wasn't a criminal. Not really. She was a victim, for God's sake! All this fear she had about jail? She was never going to jail. He began crafting in his head how he would explain to her what the witness protection program was—if she even needed such a thing, which he thought was unlikely—and how she'd be fine. She'd be just fine.

"Look," he began, "the police are already investigating the people who brought you to America. That's clear. They know you were doing what you were doing against your will. But let's also be clear about this: it was Sonja who killed the two men at the party. Right?" The question was out there before he could frame it properly. He believed in his heart this girl was incapable of that kind of violence, but after all she had been through, one never knew. But, just in case, he had meant to lead her more, to make sure that she didn't tell him something he shouldn't know—something not even Dina Renzi would want to know.

Instead of answering him, however, she reached into her leather jacket and pulled out a handgun. Instantly he grew alert. Not scared, not at all. But watchful. He was surprised, and understood on some level that he shouldn't have been. Of course she had a gun. Of course.

"That's what you think?" she asked.

Instead of answering, he stared at the weapon. Here he had tried and failed to come home with a handgun just the other day, and now there was one in his kitchen. Just a few feet away. In the slight hands of this nineteen-year-old girl. It was, it seemed to him, strangely and surprisingly beautiful. Russian, he surmised, though he couldn't have said why. It actually looked a bit like the kind of pistol James Bond used to carry—the old James Bond. The Sean Connery Bond. She dropped it onto the table, rattling her cup and saucer.

"What makes you think I didn't kill Kirill?" she continued when he was silent. "What makes you think I didn't kill that big, mean cue-ball-head baby?"

"Because I don't," he answered finally. He sat back in his chair and folded his arms across his chest. "Because . . . Anahit . . . you didn't. Okay?"

Using a single finger, she spun the pistol in a circle on the table-top, pushing the gun by its grip. "Six bullets left in magazine. Six. You don't know me. You don't know anything about me."

"Then tell me something," he said. "Tell me one thing. Tell me one thing I should know."

Alexandra

I told him lots.

I told him about my mother and my grandmother and the sculptures on the streets in Yerevan. I told him about Vasily. I told him about the cottage and Moscow and coming to America. I told him that like his little girl, I once had whole trunk full of American Barbie dolls.

"But how?" he asked. "Where in the world did you get them? How did you get them?"

I only had three cigarettes left in the pack, but I smoked another one as I told him. I told him the story just as it had been told to me.

...

On Wednesday, December 7, 1988, my father and grandfather—my father's father—were stealing two boxes of wristwatches for a Communist Party official. Very big-deal guy. The official was going to give them away at fancy gathering at his fancy dacha on Lake Sevan. And the wristwatches were with other stuff in these two crates.

My father and grandfather were smooth operators. You had

to be in the Soviet Union in 1988. But they were also strong and smart and kind. My father, my mother said, was among the bravest freedom fighters in Nagorno-Karabakh. He was a hero. I wish I had gotten to spend more than eighteen months with him, but I didn't, and I don't remember a single thing because I was just a baby and then just a toddler. I told Richard how my father had died in hydroelectric plant accident.

The crates had come to Armenian city you've never heard of called Gyumri. They had come to the airport from East Berlin. That's how long ago this was. And Gyumri was still called Leninakin. The watches were supposed to go to a jewelry store at the Alexandrapol Hotel. It was the sort of store that has velvet ropes and plush carpeting and glass cases with lights inside them to make the diamonds glitter like a disco ball. But that party official had other ideas. My father and my grandfather worked at the airport, and so it was easy for them to "redirect" the crates into my grandfather's sand-colored Lada. They put one crate in the backseat of the car and one in the trunk. It barely fit, not because the crate was so big but because the trunk was so small. One time, I was dancing at a party for group of Moscow gangsters—it was scary, because Moscow gangsters are so insane they make cue-ball-head babies look like kindergarten teachers—and someone made a joke about putting a body in the trunk. Then someone else said that it would have to be very little body. It sure couldn't be anyone in the room, they laughed, not even me or Sonja, who was with me that night. It's true. You can't even fit a teenage exotic dancer who is really just sex toy into the trunk of a Lada.

My grandfather and father were supposed to drive the wristwatches to Lake Sevan, but my grandfather had forgotten the directions to the dacha. They were on the dresser at his and my grandmother's apartment. And so the two of them went there. Six stories and thirty apartments, lots of concrete and many thousands of cinder blocks. And none of it built to withstand an earthquake, especially the sort of 6.8 magnitude earthquake that would destroy the city. They say the Soviet Union building codes were the same in Gyumri, where there was always big chance of an earthquake, as they were in Kiev, where there really wasn't big chance at all.

Of course, Kiev had other problems in 1988. The city's not that far from Chernobyl, and 1988 isn't that far from 1986. As Americans like to say, do math.

My grandfather ran up the stairs to my grandparents' apartment on the fifth floor while my father waited in the car, smoking a black-market cigarette. My grandfather probably went two steps at a time, skipping every other stair. He was very vigorous. My grandmother used to put her hands on his cheeks and kiss him, calling him her Cossack.

It was while my grandfather was upstairs that my father heard the rumble. It was very low. But he knew what it meant.

Within seconds, that rumble became a roar. As my father was snuffing out his cigarette, the road rippled up like giant sea swell, the asphalt growing cracks like big black spider veins. Then some of those veins swelled into canyons wide enough to swallow whole cars. But not my grandfather's Lada. Instead, my grandfather's Lada was suddenly facing uphill. The telephone and electrical wires were snapping, and the transformers on top of the poles became like the sparklers children play with on big holidays. Then one by one they exploded.

My father climbed from the car, planning to run up the stairs and rescue his parents. Crazy, yes? But he was their son. Then, before his very eyes—which soon would be filled with so much dust that he would only be able to see out of his left one for hours—the building pancaked. It just collapsed in a funnel of smoke and soot that fluttered down upon him like volcanic ash. He was twenty-three years old. Most of the buildings on that street pancaked like that; most of the people were flattened. The whole street was rubble.

They say every single family in the city of Gyumri lost at least one person in the earthquake. Every single family.

Young mothers were running like it was an Olympic race to the schools because there were rumors that the schools had crumpled like aluminum foil. They had. And here is saddest part. If the earthquake had come even five minutes later, lots of those children would still be alive, because the school bells would have rung by then and dismissed the kids for recess and lunch. They would have been outside playing or walking home, instead of trapped inside as the buildings collapsed.

My father dug through the mountain of bricks and timber and glass where his parents had lived, even though he was half blind. The wiring was all like Medusa head. Everyone on the street dug like crazy people. Everyone in the city dug into the night. People dug until their fingers were broken and the skin on both sides of their hands was gone. But humans couldn't lift the rubble from five- and six-story buildings. There were too few backhoes and bulldozers for so much damage, and it was nearly impossible for vehicles to drive down the roads because great chunks of the pavement had been thrown into the air like playing cards, and buildings had melted into the streets.

My father had awful choice when the darkness came. Did he stay with his mother and father, who were beneath the rubble, unsure if they were dead or alive, or did he leave them and go search for his wife? He said it was agony. He told himself he would dig for half hour more and then go find her. He would see what was left of their apartment. (It would still be standing, but most of the windows would be broken and there would be no heat or electricity or water for months. And this was in December. My parents took in lots of their neighbors, and they all huddled together for warmth. Some of the old people compared it to Leningrad in 1942. For many years other survivors would live in tin houses called *domiks*. The government built them that winter. They were only supposed to be in them maybe one year. When I was twelve I went to Gyumri with my mother, and there were still whole neighborhoods of *domiks*. It was so depressing my mother just wept.)

Finally my father gave up. There were some people buried alive beneath the rubble, but not my grandparents. They were just buried. But you could hear other victims begging for help. Pleading.

Sometimes, he said, you just heard moaning. Seven hours of digging and my father had helped drag eleven corpses from the rubble, but he had found no one who was still breathing. They would need backhoes to pull the rest of the dead from that pile.

He struggled back to the Lada through the flashlights and bonfires and the headlights from the ambulances and fire trucks at the end of block. The Lada was fine, but he couldn't drive it anywhere. The streets were cratered like the moon. The road was choked with the bricks from collapsed buildings. So, my father did the only logical thing: he took those two big boxes of wristwatches, balancing them like circus clown, and walked home through the disaster area that hours ago had been a city. His plan was to sell the watches for food on black market, which was going to be gigantic after the earthquake. This is what I mean about my father being operator. He was very resourceful. A dependable provider. A good husband.

All around my father that night walked zombies. Heroes, too. But mostly zombies. He saw two teenage boys carrying an old woman who had lost a leg. One of the boys was shirtless because he had turned it into a tourniquet and wrapped it around the woman's thigh. The shirt was now the color of pomegranate wine. He saw a green and white bus on its side, the dead passengers half in and half out of the broken windows. He saw whole rows of cadavers, some mangled. People were calling out names, sobbing, wailing. It was biblical. It was like end-of-world time.

My mother was not home when he got to the apartment. She was out looking for him. Kooky comedy of errors, right? Wrong. It was all just horrible, all just errors. There was no comedy. So he left the boxes in the living room and went back outside to find her. All night long he walked. All night long, my mother walked, too. It wasn't just the wreckage that made it so awful. Everywhere there were bodies. Bodies on ruined curbs, bodies on trucks, bodies in big holes in the ground. Arms in trees. Legs, somehow barefoot, in store windows, the broken glass shards like Christmas icicle displays. They both saw heads with no torsos or arms or legs, the eyes open and the lips seeming to mouth the word "How?" They both saw the worst thing in the world you can see: bodies of children.

It would not be till the sun was rising that my mother and father would both be in their apartment at the same time. They were, like everyone in the city, in shock. My father told her they would be okay. They would use his boxes of watches for food. They would survive.

But the thing was, there weren't watches in those two crates. There were Barbies. My mother said when he opened the boxes, he tilted his head and raised his eyebrows into a pyramid—she would imitate him and it always made me smile as a girl—like he was a confused university student. Then he got it. He sat back against the wall and lit a cigarette. He was still on the floor with the boxes. My mother curled up next to him. The apartment was freezing, and her breath matched his smoke. "Someday," he said finally, "we will have lots of daughters and they will have some very, very nice dolls."

If he hadn't died so young, I think I would have had sisters. With all those Barbies, it should have been my parents' destiny to have lots of girls.

But, of course, my father did die young. And so all those Barbies were mine. I didn't have to share them with anyone. I didn't *get* to share them with anyone. They were still in their pink boxes over a decade later, when I was growing from chubby toddler to skinny little girl with stick-figure legs, and my mother started giving them to me. She gave them to me one a month, always on the first day, for nearly five years. I have no idea where she hid two boxes, each big enough to hold twenty-eight American Barbie dolls, when I was a girl. Our apartment wasn't so large.

But my mother did. See what I mean? She was amazing lady.

...

Of course, my mother would die when she was young, too. Not as young as my dad, but young. She was forty-five years old. I was, as I told you, fifteen.

"And it was right after your mother died," Richard said to me, "that Vasily kidnapped you?" He sounded so sad.

"Few weeks, yes."

It was that moment that we both heard the car doors slamming outside his house. We'd never heard the car pull into his driveway. It was maybe four-thirty in the afternoon. We looked toward the hallway and then down at the kitchen table, and at the Makarov that was still right beside the ashtray with my big mess of cigarette butts and ashes.

Chapter Fourteen

Alexandra grabbed the Makarov, swiping it off the tabletop with the speed of a feral cat—claws extended—snatching a barn mouse from the hay. It hadn't crossed Richard's mind to reach for it, not when she'd first dropped it on the kitchen table and not when they heard the car door in his driveway. Together they stood, but he motioned for her to wait where she was.

"It's just my family," he told her.

"How do you know?"

"It couldn't be anyone else," he said, hoping this would reassure her (though the realization did not give him particular comfort). But he was already anticipating how he would introduce Alexandra to Kristin and Melissa, aware that whatever he said would have to be perfect. He would have one, brief chance to explain to his wife that this young woman was perhaps the person she was likely to hate most in the world, but for better or worse the role of paladin had fallen to him—and now he had to help her. They had to help her. Together they had to convince Alexandra that the police were not going to put her in chains in some Bedlam-like dungeon. The reality was it was time. It was time to call the police. And it was

time to call the police because they were the girl's only chance—
regardless of whether she'd killed the second Russian.

He took a breath and opened the front door, and there indeed
were his wife and his daughter, the two of them about to ascend
the steps. He went outside onto the stoop and shut the door behind
him.

"Hey, Dad," said Melissa.

"Hey, sweetie," he said back. He could see in his wife's eyes
that already she was on full alert because he had closed the front
door.

"What's going on?" Kristin asked him.

"She's here. The girl from the party. She needs our help."

His wife started to shake her head, and Richard honestly wasn't
sure whether she meant they could not—they would not—help
her, or she was simply incredulous. He reached out for her arm, and
he took it as a good sign that she didn't slap his hand away.

"I am . . . dumbstruck," she said simply.

"The girl from the party?" Melissa repeated. "The sex slave?"

"She's just a girl, Kris," he said, not precisely ignoring his
daughter, but knowing that he had to address his wife's issues first.
"Whatever happened, it's my fault. It was always and only my fault.
But—"

"Why haven't you called the police?"

"She has a gun," he answered, and with that short statement
instantly all that he wanted to say—all those possibly perfect
words—were gone, wafting away from him like dandelion seeds
on a spring breeze.

Kristin pushed him away and took Melissa by the hand. "Are
you crazy?" she said to him. She started dragging Melissa back to
the car. "A gun in our house? We're leaving right now. I'll call the
police when we're out of here. Come on, Melissa."

"Please don't. Don't go. Don't call the police."

"I'm not endangering our child. We're going!"

"She's no danger to us."

"She has a gun!"

"She's a danger to herself. That's all. That's my fear. I'm afraid she's going to get herself killed."

"Richard, you've lost your mind," she said, and it seemed as if she might have been about to say more. But she stopped. She stopped because behind him the door was opening, and there she was. Alexandra. Richard saw Kristin putting their daughter behind her, protecting her, as if she expected Alexandra to start shooting.

"I go," Alexandra said, and she was pulling her knit cap over her ears. "I go."

"No. You should stay. You have to stay. But tell me now, tell me once and for all: Did you shoot"—and he paused, unsure whether he was pronouncing the thug's name correctly—"Kirill? Did you?"

He knew that Alexandra had heard him; she had to have heard him. But she didn't answer, because she and Kristin were staring at each other. Or, to be precise, Kristin was staring at Alexandra. And Alexandra? She was looking both at his wife and his daughter, her gaze flat, her expression impenetrable. Melissa was peering around her mother's ribs, as if Kristin were a tree and this were only a game of hide-and-seek.

"Tell me!"

She didn't entirely return to him. Her focus was still elsewhere, though she was turning her head ever so slightly. Somehow, something in addition to his wife and his daughter had stolen her attention.

"He shot himself," she said finally.

"What?"

"He was about to shoot Sonja. Was going to kill her for killing Pavel for sure. Was going to kill her right in front of everyone in your very nice living room. But it doesn't matter. I go."

"Give me your gun," he said. "Give me your gun and go back inside. My wife and my daughter will come inside, too." He turned toward his wife and met Kristin's eyes; for a moment he couldn't read them. But then she nodded ever so slightly.

"I promise you," he told the girl, "you'll be safe. Someone was talking to Crystal. That means someone knows what those men were doing to you. Demanding of you. Someone is investigating them. You're not the criminal here."

"They won't believe I didn't shoot Kirill."

"Let's go inside. You can tell me exactly how it happened. But give me the pistol first."

He felt his wife and his daughter watching him. He had his wife back; he never again wanted to lose her. But he knew just how fragile that new bond was. How delicate. At the same time, he wanted his daughter to view him with neither disdain nor disgust. Maybe she understood he was a little clumsy, but let that be his gravest fault in her eyes. Wouldn't any father sign up for that rep? Pure and simple, he wanted everything to be the way it had been seven days ago. God, seven days. One week. How had all he had taken for granted evaporated in the roaring, animal heat from one bachelor party? But he knew the answer to that. He needed only to glance at this Armenian girl to remember. But now he wanted only to make amends, to make things right. To caulk the hollow in the heart of his family. To make sure this poor girl whose soul had been battered almost since birth was safe. (And after viewing that body on the slab this morning, never again would he question the actuality—arguably, even the tangibility—of the soul, because without it he had seen that we are all just decomposing flesh.)

"Are we good?" he asked Alexandra, and he extended his hand to her, palm open.

"We're fine," she answered, her gaze oddly far away. "But it doesn't matter. They still have last laugh."

He followed her eyes. They were no longer on his wife and his daughter. She was looking beyond them, beyond the car and the driveway, down to the corner where their little street met Pond-field Road. There, at the very intersection where almost every day of his life he or his wife made a left- or a right-hand turn in their vehicles, and where—just once—his Audi had rolled backward and driverless, a ghost car, was a black Escalade. It was just like the one that had brought this Alexandra into his life. It was emerging from the driveway beside the now empty house where their neighbors, the Habeggers, had once lived. Where, apparently, it had been parked. Waiting. Watching. It hadn't been there when Richard had returned home; he would have noticed it. It must have arrived in the last hour or two. But none of that mattered, none of that mattered at all, because now it was moving inexorably toward him, toward them, rolling almost in slow motion past the realtor's blue and white "For Sale" sign on the Habeggers' front lawn.

"Run!" He barked the word at Kristin and Melissa, and he pointed toward the trees on the side of their home, denuded and autumnal now, and the houses behind theirs. For a second they didn't move, not understanding what he saw or why he was yelling. But then, either because he yelled once more to *Go! Go now!* or because Kristin had spotted the car and understood that this was connected to the girl and the dead who were now forever a part of their family's life story—dead men (two), a dead girl (one)—she pulled her child by the hand like she was but a small dog on a leash and started to run.

And then, almost at the same instant when once more he was wishing he had brought home a rifle, words crossed his mind the way that subtitles flash across the bottom of a foreign film: *God. This is how it ends. This is how I am going to die.*

But then the girl opened the glass storm door and used both her hands to push him so hard back inside the house—through the doorway and into the front hall—that he fell into the colonial side table and then onto the floor. A ceramic bowl with an autumn-scented potpourri fell beside him and broke, the spices and scraps of evergreen and faux pumpkin scattering onto the floor like confetti. She pulled shut the wooden front door so she was outside alone on the steps. He was just starting to push himself back to his feet to get her, to drag her inside, too, when the world seemed to explode and he heard the gunshot and the door above him was splintered.

Alexandra

Richard yelled like crazy person for his wife and his little girl to run. Maybe because he didn't deserve to die—none of them deserved to die, this wasn't his fault, this wasn't their fault—I pushed him hard as I could back inside the house and slammed the door. I shouldn't have come. Big selfish decision on my part.

I saw his wife and daughter turning to go, racing around the side of the house, and I could see on the poor girl's face such confusion and such terror. I had heard her call me a sex slave through the front door. I guess because I was watching them, I never saw the gun—I took my eyes off the Escalade for just long enough. So I only heard the shot.

It's so strange what you remember and what you don't.

The girl from the party? The sex slave?

...

Kirill wore a shoulder holster. Pavel used the kind that straps onto a belt loop. Think American cowboy or police guy. It meant that he kept his shirt untucked sometimes when he wasn't wearing his black blazer so you couldn't see the gun, but he liked that look.

Thought he looked cool. Different tastes, that's all. But it meant the two guys drew guns in different ways, even though they were both right-handed, because Pavel kept his gun on his right side and Kirill kept his on his left. Kirill liked to cross-draw. His right arm had to cross his chest to pull Makarov from beside his left ribs. From almost under his armpit.

The night of the party I had been in the doorway between the living room and the hall when Sonja jumped on Pavel's back with the knife. I was stunned. Totally stunned. I knew she was avenging Crystal, but nothing else. Not yet. She hadn't told me anything. And there was Kirill, coming back from bathroom on the first floor of the nice house. He looked up from his zipper when he heard the big commotion in the living room. There was the thump from the little table that got turned over when one of the men at the party jumped away from Sonja with her knife and Pavel, there were the yelps from some of the men who were screaming things like *What the fuck?* and *No!,* and there was the sound of Pavel gagging as he swung his arms around, trying to get Sonja off him, before he finally fell over the back of the couch. All this chaos and noise? Happened almost at once. Within seconds. Kirill couldn't see what it was, but his first thought was to reach for his gun before going in. Which was when I threw myself at him. I don't know what I thought I was going to do. He was big guy. They were all big guys. It was just reflex. I landed on him right when he was pulling his gun from his shoulder holster. I landed on him right when he must have been using his thumb to flick off the safety.

And when I landed on him, by mistake he squeezed the trigger.

So he shot himself. Point-blank. The gun was maybe an inch from his chest. Maybe right against it. We both fell onto the floor, me on top of him, the Makarov between us, and for a second I thought I was the one who was shot: I felt so much blood on my belly and my tits and my neck. I had felt the back of his knuckles slam so hard into my ribs that I thought it must have been the bullet. The blast was almost in my ears, so my head was ringing and I was crazy deaf. But then I pushed up onto my knees and saw that all of that blood was his. I saw the way his white shirt was turning black and the way he was spitting it up—choking, just like Pavel.

And then Sonja was there, naked as me. At first her lips were moving, but I couldn't hear what she was saying. She took my hand and lifted me up, still talking, me still not hearing. Kirill's gun was in his fingers, so she bent over and took it from him. She fired a shot into the bastard's bald head, and then she handed me the pistol. I guess she was already planning that she would take Pavel's.

"We have to get dressed," she said. This time, maybe because she shouted, I heard her. I heard the words like I was underwater. But I understood.

I used a towel from that bathroom to wipe some of the blood off my chest and my stomach. And Sonja? She turned around and spat on Kirill's body.

...

If it had been the other way around, if Kirill had liked belt holsters and Pavel had liked shoulder holsters, it would have been me who would have been shot in the front hallway that night. Think of how a guy draws his gun. Kirill would have been pulling his gun from his right hip, not pulling it across his body. He would have fired it smack into my thigh or my hips or my belly.

Before we went back into the living room with the cue-ball-head baby's Makarov, Sonja took that little bathroom towel from me and dabbed at some of Kirill's blood I had missed on my ribs.

...

The police guy. If only . . .
If only Crystal hadn't talked to him. Or . . .
If only Crystal hadn't been caught. Or . . .
If only she hadn't told Sonja. Or . . .
If only Sonja hadn't killed Pavel. Or . . .

If only she had gotten to the Georgian before they got to her. Or . . .

If only I had found the police guy who met Crystal. Or . . .

Or think of it all in whole different way.

If only my dad didn't die in such horrible accident. Or . . .

If only my mom didn't get such horrible cancer. Or . . .

If only I didn't have such stupid dreams about being ballerina . . .

I don't know.

I will never know how much is my fault and how much is theirs. No one does, right?

Chapter Fifteen

At the sound of the gunshot, Kristin threw her daughter to the damp earth, a sloping patch of yard by the garage that was always in shade because of the house and a copse of nearby evergreens, and fell on top of her. She could smell the autumnal reek of humus beneath the moldering, wet leaves; she could feel her daughter breathing hard through her navy blue peacoat. There she waited for . . .

She didn't know what for. A second shot? The sound of running feet? A car engine? Sirens?

"Shhhhh, don't move, love, don't move," she murmured into her daughter's ear. She decided she would count to ten. Then she would roll over and turn around. If no one was coming, she would lift Melissa from the leaves and dash to the next house. The Sullivans.

And if the bullet had hit Richard? God. Please, no. Please, please no. She wasn't sure she could bear it. But she couldn't risk their daughter's life by going back. How in the name of heaven could she help him anyway? No, she needed to protect Melissa. It was what he would want. He'd told them to run, and that was the only thing to do.

And if it was the girl who'd been shot?

She was . . . tiny. Never had it crossed Kristin's mind that she would look more like a child than a . . . than a prostitute. No. She wasn't a prostitute. She had been kidnapped. Even Melissa had said the words: she was a sex slave.

"Mommy, I can't breathe," Melissa whispered, and for a split second Kristin feared that it was her daughter who had been shot, and in the midst of her convoluted mental gymnastics she had failed to notice. But then Kristin got it: she was trying so desperately to protect her little girl that inadvertently she was smothering her. She raised herself up on one elbow and looked over her shoulder. The Escalade was idling—Had anyone even gotten out of the car?—but there didn't seem to be anyone coming after them. Could whoever was in the vehicle even see them? For all they knew, the two of them were already at the next house. At any house.

She reached into the back pocket of her pants for her phone and dialed 911 with her thumb.

. . .

Richard could see sky through a vertical chasm in the front door—a sky tinged with eggplant as dusk rolled in from the east— and the skin on his hands and his face was awash in pinpricks: the small shards of glass from the storm door that had been blown in through the rift. He felt like a coward, a feeling that was exponentially worse than feeling like a bad husband or even a bad father, and so he pushed himself to his feet. And, in fact, he was peculiarly not scared. Perhaps it was because of what had transpired in this very house a week ago. Maybe it was because of what he had seen at the morgue that very morning. Didn't matter. He brushed the glass off his hands (which only made the skin there hurt more) and stood up. He presumed the girl was dead, but he had to be sure. He had to be sure that Kristin and Melissa had fled. The Russians might kill him, too, but if the last things he did in this world were warning his wife and his daughter to run and seeing if there was a life he could save on his front steps, that was not the worst way to exit. Once he had brought the girl inside—if, by some miracle, she was still alive—then he would call the police.

So he opened what was left of the door, once more thinking to himself, *This is how it ends. This is how I am going to die,* but this time not caring. Not caring at all. So be it.

And there he saw the girl on the ground. Her body was a heap on the stoop—a marionette without strings—her left arm dangling over the side of the concrete, her legs and her hips against the antique milk jug that now housed a dying red zinnia. She was on her side and bleeding—bleeding out?—from a wound somewhere in her abdomen or chest that he couldn't see. But there was a rivulet starting to spread across the coralline plateau, ballooning already into a puddle. It seemed, on second glance, to originate nearer to her stomach. He knelt before her, presuming she was unconscious, and lifted her arm onto the concrete and rolled her onto her back. When he did, she surprised him and opened her eyes.

"If only I didn't have stupid dreams of being ballerina," she murmured, her voice so soft that he wasn't sure he had heard her correctly. Her leather jacket was unzipped and the stain on her blouse—no, this wasn't a blouse, it was a T-shirt from a tourist kiosk or souvenir store in Times Square—reminded him of the moment when Melissa's friend Emiko had spilled fruit punch all over her white dress at one of his daughter's birthday parties three or four years ago. Everything had been pink. Of course. He shook his head involuntarily, shuddering at how the mind could link something as horrific as a bullet wound with a little girl's birthday party. And then, perhaps because Alexandra had seen him shaking his head, she tried to repeat herself, this time abridging what she had said. Fewer words. Fewer syllables. "Stupid to dream of ballerina," she whispered, and ever so slightly she winced.

He shushed her like she was a baby and tried to smile down at her, but his eyes were welling with tears. He reached back with one hand to open the glass storm door.

Which was when he heard the second gunshot, was aware of

something slamming into his head with incalculable force—for the tiniest fraction of a second he thought, *Car accident,* as if he imagined his head was slamming into a windshield—and then . . .

And then nothing.

. . .

The lead EMT, an admitted adrenaline junkie with thick black hair he slicked down with a gel his girlfriend brought home from the salon where she worked and earlobes (ears, actually) forever deformed from the myriad piercings he'd subjected them to when he was younger, knew this very hot teenager would be dead if the bullet had pierced the heart. And if the bullet had penetrated the lung, there'd be bubbles in all that blood. Pneumothorax. One of those classic sucking chest wounds that he had seen before in Yonkers and Mount Vernon, but never here in Bronxville. Untreated, there would be hypoxia and shock and, eventually, death. But treated? Eminently survivable. Pop open an occlusive bandage to seal the wound. Maybe perform a needle decompression, the needle the size of a pen tip, and insert a catheter to allow the air to escape the chest.

But this wound was lower. And no bubbles.

The EMT's name was Charles, and he liked people to call him that, because even though he thought he looked nothing at all like a Charles, in his opinion he looked even less like a Charlie or a Chuck. This call was about as good as it got if you were into EMT rush, and he knew it was going to stay with him a long while if they saved this chick's life—and if the shooters, wherever they were, didn't whack him, too. When he arrived, there were two people down. Cops everywhere, a SWAT team en route. A chase for some Escalade. Some little girl—near catatonic—being walked away from the shitstorm by a couple of moms pulled straight from a TV commercial for laundry detergent. It just didn't get better than this.

When he'd gotten to the teen on the stoop, a woman—the

victim's mom, he'd assumed at first, until a cop had told him otherwise—had already taken off her coat and wrapped it like a blanket around the girl to try and keep her warm. That had been smart and he'd been impressed. She'd been pressing a folded hand towel against the hole in the victim's side, holding it down as hard as she could when he and his partner, Ian, had run up the walkway to the front porch. The towel was a robin's-egg blue, and the monogrammed C was white. He saw that the teenager's blood had seeped through the layers of plush cotton the moment they lifted off the woman's jacket. Her heartbeat and blood pressure were rising, as her body tried to compensate. But a stomach wound in battle? For better or worse—and, in the old days, usually worse—you could live a long time. What he couldn't tell from where the bullet had entered was whether it was in the stomach or the intestines or the liver. Given the blood, he guessed liver. He threw on a nonrebreather mask to get as much oxygen transport as he could from her diminished blood volume.

And then there was this: the spine. Even if this chick lived, for all he knew the bullet had severed the spine, and she'd be left paralyzed.

Still, thank God that woman had kept her warm and sacrificed a good hand towel.

While he had gone for the girl, Ian had beelined for the guy whose body was lying half in and half out of the doorway. It was holding open the storm door, the window blown out, and at first the two EMTs could only see the victim's legs. But Ian had joined Charles almost instantly to help with the girl, because the dude was long dead. Probably killed in a heartbeat. The poor son-of-a-bitch's head was half gone, and so he wasn't their problem: they weren't supposed to bother with or even transport the dead.

So their focus was only on the girl. Stabilize her and get going.

Which they did. Charles decided pretty quickly that she was going to live. Pulse was elevated, skin was clammy. May have lost a freakish amount of blood. But he'd seen a lot worse.

As they were starting across the lawn with her, a couple of cops helping Ian and him carry the stretcher and the IV and the oxygen tank to the ambulance, they passed the woman, and he said, "I think you saved her life. Nicely done."

The woman nodded. She looked about as white as he'd expect a person to look after pressing one of your monogrammed hand towels on a bullet wound that must have been a fucking spigot when she started. When they got to the ambulance and she was no longer in earshot, Ian whispered to him, "Buddy, that was her husband back there. The one with, like, only half a head."

He nodded. The woman, he thought, must have really loved this chick they were bringing to the hospital. Maybe the cop was mistaken when he'd said the victim wasn't her daughter. She had to be. Had. To. Be. To keep this one alive with her husband's corpse right there? That was love, man. That was love.

Alexandra

The first time I woke up, I knew I was in hospital room. I didn't know if it was hospital in jail, but I didn't think so. It seemed nice, and there were no handcuffs on me. There was no police guy around. It was, I guessed, early in the morning. I could see the sky growing light outside the window. I had tubes going into my arms, and I felt an ache in my side. I thought of my mother and my grandmother, and I thought of the hospital in Yerevan. I thought of all the time I had spent in that hospital. Then I fell back into drug sleep. I don't remember a single dream from those days. Not one.

...

It was third or fourth time I woke up that they brought in police guys to ask me questions. I didn't trust them, but I was done fighting. And there was no way I could run. There was no place for me to go. I asked them about Richard, but they wouldn't tell me anything. Kept changing subject.

They told me I was going to live and that Yulian and Konstantin were in jail. They were not sure where the guys they had sent to kill me were, which did not make me feel very safe. But they said they would find them or they had already left the country, and either way I would be okay. Maybe. I was so weary I told them whole story. By then, I might have told them whole story even if Yulian and Konstantin weren't in jail. I told them everything I have told you. One of the police guys looked like a grandfather. So many wrinkles on his face. So many pouches. Other one was woman with nice eyes who told me I could call her Patricia. They both asked me lots of questions. They said they wanted me to tell my story in a courtroom, and that was the best thing I could ever do for Crystal and Sonja and girls like us. So I said I would do that, too.

Older guy said I was not going to jail, that was just crazy talk they used to scare me.

But, still, when I asked him where I would go after hospital, he couldn't tell me. He wasn't sure. He just knew it wouldn't be jail. But Patricia said they were bringing in a therapist for me—lady I could talk to who would have lots more answers.

Finally, after asking and asking and asking again about Richard, they told me. It was Patricia. She held my hand and told me whole story. She said the big reason I was alive was Richard's wife.

And that's when, finally, I wept.

...

All day, it seemed, I was crying. One time, when the tubes were taken out of my left side and my catheter was plucked so all I had left was little drip in my right arm, I pulled the sheet and the blanket over my head and curled into a ball and sucked on the pillow like it was a baby bottle and I was a baby. I cried like I had years ago in a hotel room in Moscow, those body-shaking sobs that take your whole breath away. A nurse tried to help me, but I told her, no, no, please go away. I tried to explain, but I had no air for words other than short ones like *no* and *away*.

Idea crossed my mind I could drown from my tears. Remember that word, *noyade*? Execution by drowning.

But this time, unlike in Moscow, I wasn't crying for me.

I was crying for my mother and my grandmother and baby Crystal and Sonja dear. I was crying for Richard and his wife and his kid. His little kid. A girl like me who once played with Barbies and now had no dad. I was crying because there was just so much violence and just so much death.

...

They brought in that lady therapist for me, and I asked if it was because I was insane girl. Crazy girl. She told me they did not think I was insane. She said it was because of what I had been through. This lady—her name was Eve—told me she was there for me because people are supposed to have sex because they are in love, and that was something I did not know. She was very elegant and spoke with a very proper accent. She was maybe forty years old and said she had once been a courtesan, too.

I decided I was going to like Eve when she gave me a heavy coat and some boots and walked me to the edge of hospital parking lot and handed me a cigarette. I no longer had any tubes in me, not even the one in my right arm, but I was very sore and had to take baby steps. I was happy to have on more than little hospital gown and little hospital slippers. Eve said she did not approve of smoking, but I was getting desperate and cranky, and she wanted me to be able to "focus on my options." It had gotten cold and I could see her breath.

She took me to a corner of the parking lot where there would be no reporters. She said there were reporters and TV guys who wanted to talk to me, but I didn't have to talk to them and probably shouldn't until I had met with some lawyer lady she works with. She said from now on my life should be just that: my life.

...

Options. Such a word. Such an idea. Try having options when you have never had options before. Very difficult.

I figured when I got out I would go to Los Angeles, which was Sonja's plan. Find a Bachelor. Find Kim. I knew I couldn't go home to Yerevan—not with Vasily. Not with so many cue-ball-head babies. But then Eve told me instead I could go to halfway house if I wanted. I told her that I still had all my money. (No one had stolen it, which seemed even bigger miracle than miracle I was alive.) But Eve thought I should live with other girls for a while in a place in Brooklyn. She said halfway house was not called that, when I asked, because it was halfway between two places or because it was half a house. It was a place where I could live with other girls and learn to be normal girl. I could even go back to dancing, if I wanted.

"It's been too many years. You can't just pick up and be Velvet Bird," I mumbled.

"I didn't say you'd be preparing for the New York City Ballet. I only said you could go back to dancing. It might be . . . fun."

When she said I would be living with other girls, I grew suspicious. Maybe this Eve was actually like Inga or Catherine, and she had just been nice to me for a couple of days because she was worming her way into my life like Vasily. I would never forget how it had been dance that had turned me into sex slave in the first place.

"So, I live with other girls like courtesan?" I asked. "I thought you didn't want me to be courtesan. I thought I had options."

But Eve said it would be nothing like that. It was for girls like me who did not want to be sex slaves and whores. The next morning, she brought in a girl for me to meet who lived there right now. Girl was from Kiev. She used to dance, too. Now she was taking lessons at studio again. She said there was a full moon coming, and she was going to be dancing in a little Brooklyn show where they had built a stage by windows in old factory so the ballet would have actual full moon as backdrop.

I asked her more about this halfway house, and she made it

sound okay. Not perfect. But not scary either. And I would have
to go somewhere.

...

And then there was this. When I read about Richard's funeral
in the newspaper and saw the things that people on TV were saying about me, I asked Eve to please tell Richard's wife how I knew
it was all my fault and I was so sorry. So very sorry. I asked her
to please thank the lady so much for saving my life. And Eve said,
"Maybe you should thank her yourself. Would you like that?" It
seems telling her myself was all part of having options.

My hospital room looked out at trees and a thin river, and was
maybe only two miles from Richard's house. I guess it was near
the cemetery, too.

The day after the funeral, Eve made phone calls and got phone
calls back. She said if this worked out, if Richard's wife came to
hospital, it would just be our secret. It was nothing police guys ever
had to know. No way. So, I understood she was breaking some
rule, but so much of my life was breaking rules and she was doing
me big favor, I didn't care. I wanted to do one nice thing and tell
this widow that her husband was good man and she was good lady.

Eve talked on her phone in the hallway outside my hospital
room a couple of times. Then she came back in and said, "She's on
her way here. Right now. She's bringing her daughter."

...

I wanted to put on makeup and lipstick, but I had none and Eve
would not lend me hers. She said it didn't matter how I looked. I
must have been fretting like crazy girl, so Eve said—lying maybe—
that I looked fine.

And then there they were. In my hospital room. A mom and
her little girl. A widow, like my mom. A girl with no dad, like me.

"I'm Kristin," the lady said, her voice wobbly. "And this is Melissa."

The girl looked at me with wide eyes, but said nothing. She stood right beside her mom at the edge of the hospital bed. She was wearing a pink puffer coat. Lots of down in the puffs. Kristin had on the same navy coat she'd been wearing the day we saw each other for the first time, and I got shot and Richard got killed. She was pale and looked very tired. Maybe sickly.

"I'm Alexandra."

Eve looked at me and said, "You can tell them your real name. If you want."

"I'm Anahit."

"Armenian, right?" asked Richard's wife. Her voice was very soft. I had to listen carefully to hear.

I nodded. Then I said, "Thank you. You saved my life."

"You're welcome."

"I bet lots of women would have let me die."

"No. I hope that's not true." Then she said, "I don't know how much my husband told you about us. Melissa here is nine." The girl nodded. She was wearing very colorful stockings on her legs. Looked like raining books. "She wanted to come, too."

"Hi," said the girl, and with one hand she gave me a very small wave. I think she was a little scared of me—of what I was.

"Hi," I said back. "I like your stockings."

"They're tights," said Richard's wife. "Not stockings. They're tights."

"Thank you," said the girl.

"Richard told me a little about you two. He loved you lots. I know that. He loved you so much."

"Why don't you both sit down," suggested Eve, and she pointed at the empty bed and then at this ugly orange chair. "Want me to bring you some coffee or a juice?"

"No, we're just going to be here a minute," Richard's wife said. I was glad she didn't want any coffee or a juice. I didn't want

Eve to leave us alone. But Kristin sat in the chair, and Melissa put her hands on the mattress of the other bed and hopped onto it. She unzipped her coat but didn't take it off. For what felt like very long minute, but probably wasn't all that long really, we sat in silence. I wanted to tell little girl it is overrated thing to be pretty. It is overrated thing to be fetching. It is overrated thing to bathe in the light like a star. But I didn't know where to begin.

"Are you in a lot of pain?" Richard's wife asked me finally.

"No." Then I added, "Not like you."

"It's different."

It was, but I didn't say anything. Biggest difference? I would get better. She wouldn't. Little girl wouldn't. Hopefully, little girl wouldn't become whore like me. I didn't see why she would. She still had her mother. She still had a nice house. But I guess you never know. Maybe they would leave that house. Maybe they *should* leave that house.

Kristin took a big breath and sighed. Then: "After the funeral, Richard's brother, Philip—the bachelor—told me I should steer clear of somebody named Spencer. Just ignore him, no matter what. I have a feeling you know why."

I shook my head. "He hired us. He was guy at party. He—" and I stopped myself. He was the guy who'd been upstairs with Sonja in the little girl's bedroom. But I didn't want to say anything about that in front of Melissa.

"Well, according to my brother-in-law, Spencer has pictures of you and my husband. The kind that might," and here she paused, looking once at her daughter before looking back at me, "make me sad. He told Philip about them before the funeral. He thought my brother-in-law might . . . negotiate . . . with me. But instead Philip went right to the police. My brother-in-law is a jerk, but he loved my husband. Anyway, I thought you should know. Those pictures can't hurt me. Not now. But someday, if Spencer ever does share them, they might hurt you. I felt I should warn you."

"Nothing like that can hurt me either."

"Okay then."

"Okay then," I repeated.

She looked around the room. "I should have brought you some flowers. God. I have nothing but flowers at my house."

"No one's ever brought me flowers. I wouldn't have known what to do with them."

"You'd figure it out. Mostly you just put them in water."

"Thank you."

"The strangest thing is this. When I came here—when Eve called—I thought I was coming to forgive you. I was quite literally going to tell you that," she said. I waited. Eve waited. She was trying to find the right words—the perfect words. I know the feeling. "But that's not correct. Because you don't need my forgiveness. You didn't do anything wrong."

"I did many wrong things," I corrected her.

"Maybe. But you didn't kill my husband."

"I shouldn't have come to your house. I didn't think cue-ball-head babies would be so smart."

She raised her eyebrows into pyramid. Eve explained what I meant. "The traffickers," she said. "This particular group of Russians. Anahit calls them that because they shave their heads."

"I see. But you couldn't have known. And you had to go somewhere."

I shook my head and started to say again how many big mistakes I had made, and to tell her about the piece of paper with the Georgian's phone number. But the words got lost in my mouth because suddenly I was crying again. I put my face in my hands and swatted Eve's fingers when she went to touch me, because I didn't want to be touched and I didn't want to be forgiven, and I wished to God I could stop crying. But I couldn't, I couldn't, and the way I was shaking made my side hurt, which made me cry even harder, I guess. Somewhere, and it seemed so far away, I heard the girl's feet hit the floor as she jumped off the bed, and I heard Eve leading her and her mother from the hospital room. I heard the door shut.

Then I lay there all alone until it was dark. I lay there until I fell into deep sleep, and this time I dreamed. I dreamed of the cottage, but all of us girls were princesses and the only men we saw were our fathers. We all had our mothers, and they fed us bird's milk cake and sugary pastila, and even though we all slept in one big room, every night our mothers would come tuck us in and kiss us good night.

And in the morning? In the morning I woke up. I looked out the window at the moon, setting against a deep blue bedspread of sky. There it was. Full and round and incredibly white. I thought of dancer girl from Kiev. Her show. Down the corridor I heard two nurses laughing. *He got you that? For your birthday? Seriously?* I pulled my arms from beneath the sheet and rolled over. *Don't judge him!* More laughter. *Well, then, don't judge me!*

In my mind, I imagined all the things halfway house could be, but it was just word game. I knew.

And I watched the moon and knew this was not the end. This was not even halfway. People still danced. People still laughed. This was just morning, and I was just nineteen and somehow, despite everyone and everything, I was alive. I sat up in bed and took a sip of the apple juice from the cup on the nightstand. I fluffed my hair. I hoped Eve would come for me soon.

Acknowledgments

As always, thanks are in order. I learned a great deal from all of these readers, but I am especially grateful to each of them for sharing some very specific expertise:

Lauren Bowerman—criminal prosecution and the law. (This is the fourth time that Lauren has appeared in my Acknowledgments. That might be a record.)

Mark Flowers and James Yeaton—re-breathers, sucking chest wounds, and EMT rush. (This is James's second appearance.)

Haig Kaprielian—CODIS, crime scenes, and the morgue.

Noelia Mann—the sex trafficking of underage girls.

Khatchig Mouradian—Armenian history and names. (This is Khatchig's second appearance.)

Steven Sonet—civil law (and how to be civil in a negotiation).

Anna Stevens—strippers.

Marc Tischler—cadavers. (This is Marc's third appearance.)

Ani Tchaghlasian—investment banking.

Jacob Tomsky, author of *Heads in Beds,* who explained to me the difference between a front desk manager and a rooms executive of a hotel.

And Scot Villeneau—the Makarov pistol.

I also want to thank novelist Stephen Kiernan: he didn't read an early draft, but he was a great ear when we would bike and discuss the story.

Among the books I read that I still think about are Rachel Lloyd's *Girls Like Us*; Caitlin Moran's *How to Be a Woman;* and *Desert Nights* by Edik Baghdasaryan and Ara Manoogian. I also want to express my admiration for novelist Vahan Zanoyan. His two novels about an Armenian girl who is abducted into the world of Russian and Middle Eastern sex slavery, *A Place Far Away* and *The Doves of Ohanavank*, are riveting.

I am grateful as well to my early readers: my lovely bride, Victoria Blewer; our astute young daughter, Grace Experience; my gifted editor, Jenny Jackson; and my splendid agent, Jane Gelfman.

Finally, I want to express my appreciation for the Coalition to Abolish Slavery & Trafficking. CAST is one of the many important organizations that work to assist people trafficked for the purpose of forced labor, sexual slavery, and other instances of appalling human rights violations. Their website is www.castla.org. I also want to thank Girls Educational and Mentoring Services—founded by Rachel Lloyd of *Girls Like Us*—for their efforts on behalf of commercially and sexually exploited young women. Learn more about GEMS at www.gems-girls.org.

A NOTE ABOUT THE AUTHOR

Chris Bohjalian is the author of eighteen books, including such *New York Times* bestsellers as *The Light in the Ruins, The Sandcastle Girls, The Double Bind,* and *Skeletons at the Feast.* His novel *Midwives* was a number one *New York Times* bestseller and a selection of Oprah's Book Club. His work has been translated into thirty languages, and three of his books have become movies (*Secrets of Eden, Midwives,* and *Past the Bleachers*). His novels have been chosen as Best Books of the Year by the *Washington Post,* the *St. Louis Post-Dispatch,* the *Hartford Courant,* the *Milwaukee Journal Sentinel, Publishers Weekly, Library Journal, Kirkus Reviews, BookPage,* and *Salon.* He lives in Vermont. Visit him at www.chrisbohjalian.com or on Facebook or Twitter.

A NOTE ABOUT THE TYPE

This book was set in a version of the well-known Mono-
type face Bembo. This letter was cut for the celebrated
Venetian printer Aldus Manutius by Francesco Griffo, and
first used in Pietro Cardinal Bembo's *De Aetna* of 1495. The
companion italic is an adaptation of the chancery script type
designed by the calligrapher and printer Lodovico degli
Arrighi.